Half-Witch

Half-Witch

a novel

John Schoffstall

Big Mouth House
Easthampton, Mass.

Big Mouth House

150 Pleasant Street #306
Easthampton, MA 01027
info@smallbeerpress.com
smallbeerpress.com
weightlessbooks.com

Distributed to the trade by Consortium.

First Big Mouth House Printing
July 2018

Library of Congress Cataloging-in-Publication Data

Names: Schoffstall, John, 1952- author.
Title: Half-witch : a novel / John Schoffstall.
Description: Easthampton, MA : Big Mouth House, [2018] | Summary:
Fourteen-year-old Lizbet and witch girl Strix embark upon a perilous quest
where the fates of Lizbet's father and Heaven are at stake.
Identifiers: LCCN 2017047748 (print) | LCCN 2018007742 (ebook) | ISBN
9781618731418 | ISBN 9781618731401 (alk. paper)
Subjects: | CYAC: Magic--Fiction. | Witches--Fiction. | Heaven--Fiction. |
Fantasy.
Classification: LCC PZ7.1.S33653 (ebook) | LCC PZ7.1.S33653 Hal 2018 (print)
| DDC [Fic]--dc23
LC record available at https://lccn.loc.gov/2017047748

Text set in Minion.

Printed on 50# 30% PCR recycled Natures Natural paper in the USA.

For Jayne
Who held my head above water until we got to land

Chapter 1

My sword's a rose,
My pen's my nose,
My belt's a snake,
My comb's a rake,
My voice a bell,
My heaven, hell,
A crow my king,
My kiss a sting,
My day is night,
My love is spite!
    —A rhyme of Strix

When Lizbet Lenz was eight years old, she and her father, Gerhard, fled their home in Frucy-sur-St. Jacques.

"Why do we have to leave?" Lizbet asked. "Why do they hate us?"

Unforeseen accidents, Gerhard explained sadly. Misfortune. Mistrust.

Clinging to the back of Gerhard's horse, they rode for their lives. An angry mob chased them. Lizbet, riding behind Gerhard and gripping his coat in her fists, risked a glimpse backward. Among the crowd she saw Marguerite and Huguette. Marguerite and Huguette were Lizbet's best friends in the world. She had shared everything with them. She had confided in them all the secrets that she could never, ever tell anyone else. They had all promised to be friends forever.

Marguerite and Huguette ran in the mob beside their brothers and parents, shouting curses at Lizbet and Gerhard.

Burning tears blurred Lizbet's eyes. *I hate friends,* she thought. *I hate them. I'll never have a friend again. I promise.*

After Frucy, Lizbet and Gerhard settled in Souvilliers. Lizbet broke her promise, and made friends with a girl named Rosemonde. But after a few months she and Gerhard had to flee again. Lizbet's heart broke in a different way: this time she was the betrayer, unable to say good-bye to Rosemonde, unable to make good on any of her promises to her.

"Why do we have to go away again?" she cried to Gerhard. "Why?"

Misunderstandings, Gerhard told her, sighing. Unreasonable expectations. Good intentions gone awry.

And so they traveled to Yblitz, where they lived for more than a year. Until one night, when men in clanking armor pounded on the door of their fine house, yelling that they had a warrant for Gerhard's arrest. Gerhard and Lizbet had to slip out through the scullery entrance and make off on a horse that Gerhard said was a "friend's," but Lizbet was pretty sure they were stealing.

Bad luck, Gerhard explained, shaking his head and clucking his tongue. Misadventures. Poor timing.

They fled to Zwandt. From Zwandt to Pforzenhausen. To Zoltwice. To Padz. Lizbet learned her lesson. She stopped having friends. Having friends just meant enduring the pain of losing them, again and again. Her only friends were her dolls, her father, and her God, to whom Lizbet prayed that Gerhard might someday prosper, and that she might live in one town all her life, like a normal girl.

God was always friendly and sounded sympathetic, but He just didn't get what being a "normal girl" meant. He liked to ramble on about about fasting. Or martyrdom. Had Lizbet ever considered becoming an anchoress, He asked?

"A what?"

An anchoress, God explained, was someone who let herself be walled up in a cubbyhole in some church for her entire life, with nothing to do but pray all day long. It was like solitary confinement, except that you hadn't done anything to deserve it.

It was the absolute opposite of being a normal girl.

Each time Lizbet and her father made their home in a new town, it wasn't long before they had to flee again. Each time Gerhard had a new excuse. Every year Lizbet grew more lonely.

The year Lizbet was fourteen years old, they settled in Abalia, in the farthest east of the Holy Roman Empire, beneath the snow-capped peaks of the Montagnes du Monde, the highest mountains in the world. No one knew what lay beyond the Montagnes.

This surely must be the edge of the world, Lizbet thought. *We have to stay here. We have to, because there's nowhere further to go.*

But one day, after they had lived in Abalia for almost a year, disaster struck.

At some point during Lizbet's afternoon classes, it began to rain mice.

The mice may have started falling during the last half of "Realms Despoiled on Account of the Uterine Fury" or the first part of "Economic Geography of the Saracen Kingdoms." While Dame Mother Pallidum's nasal voice enumerated the principal rivers of the Caliphate of Andalusia, Lizbet noticed that Bruno, in the seat just ahead of hers, was staring out the window with unusual intensity. *He'd better pay attention to Pally soon,* Lizbet thought, *or Pally's Rod of Chastening will get busy.*

Brigitte, two seats over and a row ahead, also had her head turned to the window. And Robin in front of her.

The Dame Mother's voice stuttered to a halt. She turned her gaze to the window and stared.

Things were falling past the window, larger than snowflakes, and darker, and it was too warm for snow in April, anyway. One falling object landed on the sill, put its forelegs up against the glass, and wiggled its pink nose.

A mouse.

Another came behind it, and another, and another, until the sill outside the window was piled high with mice, black, white, fawn and dappled, wiggling their tails and their curious noses, tumbling over each other, falling off the sill to the ground. Teacher and class watched in silence.

Lizbet climbed onto her chair and stood on tiptoe to see out the window. She was a thin, pale girl on whom adults always felt they had to urge second helpings at the supper table. Her hair was straight and square cut, her features narrow and precise. In her black school gown and white pinafore, dark hair and pale face, she resembled a handful of ebony and ivory keys fashioned for some celestial piano, but omitted by an absentminded angel.

One by one, every student in the room turned their gaze from the mice to Lizbet, standing alone on her chair. Lizbet ignored them. In her fourteen years, she had lived in a dozen cities in five nations. Lizbet was always the stranger, always the foreigner. Because no one made things easy for her, she had learned boldness beyond her years: she went where she liked, demanded her due, and was not afraid to elbow her way to the front of a crowd. In her secret heart, loneliness tugged at her, and love for her ne'er-do-well father, and piety to God. But in standing up to the world of suspicious strangers into which life had dropped her, Lizbet was a lion in petticoats.

She squinted into the bright light from outside. The school grounds already were covered with a heaving, squirming blanket of millions and millions of mice. She knew what all the other students were thinking. They thought it was her father's fault.

It was always her father's fault.

Never satisfied with the modest rewards of honest labor, Gerhard Lenz spent his lifetime peddling harebrained moneymaking schemes, disastrous alchemy recipes, quack medicines, and other frauds and follies across the breadth of the Holy Roman Empire, from West Francia to Dalmatia to the Hansa to the eastern reaches of the Abalian Pale. Here, in Abalia, Gerhard had declared himself a magician. He had wormed himself into the favor of Abalia's ruler, the Margrave Hengest Wolftrow. As always, he had been unable to make good on his boasts. His career had been one magical mishap after another. None, though, had been half as bad as this.

A blizzard of mice, blanketing the landscape. There would be such an uproar. Once again, Gerhard's endless schemes and deals and plans had led to disaster. Once again, they would have to flee.

Lizbet looked around at the silent classroom of narrowed eyes and disapproving lips. *Why can't things stay the same?* she cried silently to herself. *Why can't I just live in one town for always, like a normal girl?*

"What?" she said, loudly, fiercely, to the accusing eyes and mouths, daring them to challenge her. "What is it? Why are you staring?" They all turned away.

Mice continued to rain from the sky.

When the cathedral bells rang five o'clock and school let out, the streets of Abalia were still lively with mice. Squeaks filled the air and echoed off the buildings, along with the shouts and curses of hundreds of human mouse hunters. Official sorts of men dashed hither and thither: vergers, prebendaries, rectors, prelates, and sextons from the cathedral, marshals-of-the-peace from the Provost's office, pudding-faced inquisitors from the fearful chambers of the Morals Proctor, black-hooded torturers and scrofulous gaolers from the Houses of Correction. All had been pressed into service in the campaign against the mice.

A beadle in great coat and top hat led the schoolchildren home through the dim canyons of Abalia's twisty streets. First the boys, two abreast, in black coats and trousers, stiff white shirts, and floppy black velvet ties. Then the girls, distaff copies of the boys in white pinafores over ankle-length black gowns. Behind the last of the children hobbled an ancient beldame, nose and spine as crooked as a root, whose job it was to cuff any stragglers back into line.

The children's march homeward quickly became a rout. Torrents of mice washed over the children's shoes and tried to run up the boys' trousers and the girls' stockings. Boys and girls shrieked and danced about, brushing the mice off themselves. Sextons ran up and down the street, beating at the mice with their shovels. Soldiers fired off their muskets and blunderbusses. Inquisitors flogged fleeing mice with barbed cat-o'-nine-tails. Prelates stood on doorsteps delivering sermons against the mice.

The humans had help from another source. Abalia's goblins were everywhere, waddling about, grabbing up mice and shoving them into their mouths. They came a little higher than Lizbet's waist, and were as wide across as they were tall. Their round bellies never seemed to fill, but only grew larger until they dragged on the ground and the belly's owner had to support it with one hand as he walked, continuing to drop luckless mice into his mouth with the other.

Lizbet shuddered. Goblins. Horrid piebald skin, hairy, floppy pig ears, mouths as big as buckets.

Goblins were despised by everyone. The night watchmen killed them on sight, because goblins ate anything that moved, cats, dogs, poultry, even snacking on unwatched infants. During the day, they hid in sewers and sour basements, and ventured forth only after dark. But the promise of a cornucopia of mice was apparently enough to make even a craven goblin brave the daylight.

Ever since she was very small, Lizbet had suffered nightmares of falling into a goblin sewer. In her dream, the sewer was a bottomless ocean of stinky, hairy goblins. Her body sank through the goblins as if through water. Deeper and deeper she sank, farther and farther from the surface of the earth. As she plunged downward, the goblins' twisty, clever fingers and flappy lips touched everywhere on her body. When the horror became unbearable, she screamed, and woke up.

The street was pandemonium. Vergers, gaolers, soldiers, and goblins pushed their way through the children in pursuit of mice. The children broke ranks, shrieking and frantically brushing mice off themselves. Lizbet waited until the eyes of the beadle and beldame were elsewhere. Then she hiked up her gown and petticoats and dashed away into a side alley.

She needed to get home. She guessed that her father would already be packing up their possessions and preparing to flee. Although, where could they possibly go?

As she ran out of the alley's top end, she nearly collided with a goblin gang that was rambling up the Boulevard of Slaughtered Saints, eating their way through the mice as they went. Lizbet gasped, and started back.

The biggest goblin snorted. "Lilywackin' lubgubler slumlickin' pootz!" he spat out through fleshy, wet lips.

Lizbet's urgency overpowered her fear. "Oh, stuff it," she snapped. She pushed her way through the goblins and ran up the Boulevard. Derisive laughter and vulgar noises followed her.

Three blocks farther, past the Streets of St. Simon (shot with arrows by Arians) and St. James of Antioch (mangled by Manicheans), up the Street of St. Therese (fricasseed by Frisians). Poor Therese had actually been more boiled than fricasseed, but the alliteration helped Lizbet remember her.

Lizbet's spirits lifted as she neared the neighborhood of Little Diligence, where her father rented a house. All afternoon, since the mice started falling, she had been thinking about their imminent escape. Which clothes, books, and keepsakes could she pack? Which must she leave behind?

These thoughts steadied her mind. By the time Lizbet arrived at her house, she was halfway to putting Abalia behind her. Having a plan, Lizbet thought, helped put you in control of a crisis and ease the fear of an unknown future.

However, as military men say, no plan survives contact with the enemy.

In the falling dusk, Lizbet saw the group of soldiers milling about in front of her house. More mouse hunters? As she approached, the front door opened, and two burly soldiers emerged.

Between them came Lizbet's father in his magician's robes. He stumbled as he walked. Iron shackles clanked at his ankles and wrists.

In an instant, all of Lizbet's plans collapsed. Her heart skipped. "Father!" she yelled.

Gerhard Lenz's head jerked about. His eyes sought her. "Lizbet?" he called.

"Silence!" one of the soldiers barked, and hit Gerhard with his baton. Gerhard grunted in pain.

"Stop it!" Lizbet cried. She tried to push though crowd of gray uniforms, toward her father.

Muscled arms held her back, meaty hands pinned her wrists behind her. She struggled helplessly. "Don't hurt him!" she yelled.

"Who's this girl?" one man asked. He had a face something like a weasel and something like a pickaxe. He wore a captain's insignia.

"That's my father," Lizbet said. "What are you doing to him? Why is he in chains?" She thought she knew, but desperately hoped to hear otherwise.

"Your father's under arrest, by order of the Margrave," the captain said. "He made all these mice, y'see?"

"Please understand, it was an accident," Gerhard Lenz said. His voice trembled. "My spell went wrong. I was, I was trying to make a rain of gold. It's what the Margrave wanted. I don't know why it didn't work. I, I could try to cast a rain of cats. D'you think? That might help."

"Ever occur to you to cast a rain of common sense instead?" the captain said. "The Margrave don't want the town covered in cats neither. Little girl, stand back."

The soldiers holding Lizbet shoved her to the ground. Others pushed her father down the street. His leg shackles nearly tripped him, and he staggered to keep his balance.

"I'll go with him," Lizbet said. She struggled to her feet.

"You can't go with him," the captain said. "He's bound for the Houses of Correction."

The Houses of Correction. Chilly stone cells. Manacles. Rats. Filth. Torture if you didn't tell the magisters what they wanted to hear, flogging or hanging if you did. Lizbet's chest squeezed so tight she couldn't breathe. "I'm still going with him," she insisted.

"Go back in your house and wait for your mother," the captain said. "If she wants your daddy free, let her go beg the Margrave tomorrow."

"I don't have a mother," Lizbet said, forcing herself not to cry. "My father's all I've got. If you're putting him in a dirty cold cell, put me in one too."

The captain stared at her for a moment. He scratched the

stubble on his chin with grubby fingers. "That might be for the best," he said. "Only not the same cell as your daddy's. One at the Orphan Asylum instead."

"What?!" The Orphan Asylum was little better than the Houses of Correction for children.

"Missy, you're an orphan now, looking at this situation after a certain fashion. Certainwise your father can't father to you. How old are you, anyways?"

Lizbet didn't want to say she was only fourteen. She was pretty sure they wouldn't let someone her age live alone.

"I don't need to go to the Orphan's Asylum," she said. "My uncle will take care of me."

"Eh? Uncle?"

"He's arriving home later."

The captain looked doubtful. "That uncle came up awful sudden. Maybe I'll wait for him. What's his name?"

"Um . . . Mr. Bunbury. He's coming home late. Really, really late."

"Uh-huh." The captain sucked in the sides of his cheeks, and chewed on them thoughtfully. The soldiers arresting Lizbet's father had already stamped away down the street. The remainder of the captain's patrol shuffled their feet restlessly, cursed at the mice, or tried to skewer them with their bayonets.

"All right, missy," the captain said at last. "You're on your own for now. But the Magister of Children will get informed of this on the morn, and he'll dispatch a marshal 'round to chat up this convenient uncle of yours." He waggled a bony finger at her. "Make sure Mr. Whad-ya-callum is here to make an account of himself, understand?" He shouted to the rest of his soldiers, "Hustle your haunches, my scruffies, we've other mice to kill tonight."

Inside, the house was dark, chilly, silent. Lizbet threw a shovelful of coal from the scuttle onto the banked embers in the kitchen stove, and worked the bellows on them until they glowed. Last night's supper kettle was still sitting on the stovetop; she removed a stove lid and set the iron kettle over the opening to warm.

From the stove she lit a taper, and from the taper she lit the kerosene lamps in the kitchen, the parlor, and her bedroom. By the time the stove had begun to warm the house, the savor of pork sausages, sauerkraut, and caraway perfumed the air. The house should have felt friendlier.

Instead, it felt empty and eerie, like a portrait painting from which someone had erased the sitter's face.

When the leftover dinner was hot, Lizbet ladled out a bowl and sat down at the kitchen table. She lifted a spoonful to her lips. Then, without eating, she set it back with trembling hand. She pushed the bowl away. She began crying helplessly. Every breath was a sob. Every sob made her chest ache as if it would tear apart.

What was she to do?

Since they had arrived in Abalia, her father's attempts at magic had done nothing but go wrong. The ill-tempered talking goose that insulted passersby until someone shot and roasted it. The clockwork woodpeckers that pulled the nails out of buildings, thinking they were grubs. The love potion that made Johan, the smith's boy, become impassioned with his own left great toe. Even months later, he sometimes kissed it on the sly, when he thought no one was watching.

Not that Gerhard's other ventures had been any more successful. The year before, when they lived in Padz, Gerhard had promised friends that his contacts among the aristocracy would steer juicy sinecures, emoluments, and offices their way. Nothing of the sort happened, and Gerhard and Lizbet had to flee because Gerhard had lavishly borrowed of his friends' silver to work his wiles, and could not pay it back.

Like the time, fourteen years ago, when he promised the daughter of the Comte d'Hille that he was a traveling prince in disguise. The Comte's daughter believed him. The result was Lizbet.

Lizbet loved her father. He was funny and charming and kind and attentive, always willing to listen to her, or read to her, or get her a palomino pony for her tenth birthday, with a wavy mane that hung almost the ground. Even if the pony had to leave two weeks later, when Gerhard had no money to finish paying for it.

She loved her father, but she had no illusions about him.

However, Gerhard had never been in trouble as bad as *this* before. How was she supposed to get him out of jail?

Lizbet cried harder.

The soldier captain had said that her mother should go beg the Margrave in the morning. Margrave Hengest Wolftrow ruled Abalia. He ruled the surrounding boroughs and rural counties, and was Wildgrave over the wilderness beyond, called the Abalian Pale. The Pale stretched from the Falls of the Nur to the high country, the timberline, and the snowy peaks of the Montagnes du Monde. It was said that that in Wolftrow's youth, fresh from conquests of the Bulgars, Tuscans, Catalans, and Berbers, he had ventured across the Montagnes into the lands beyond. He was the only man who had ever done this. Or, at least, the only one who had ever returned.

In Abalia, Hengest Wolftrow's word was absolute and unquestioned. He answered only to the distant and half-legendary Empress Juliana, called the Pixie Queen, who sat on the Throne of Charlemagne.

Wolftrow could free Lizbet's father from prison. If he wanted.

If Gerhard were not released, Lizbet's fate was certain. She would never be allowed to live alone, without an adult. When "Uncle Bunbury" was found to be a fib, Lizbet would be taken to the Orphan Asylum. In the Asylum, the proctors beat you if you so much as smiled. Or so people said. They beat you even if you didn't smile, just on principle. There were rumored to be gangs of older orphans who ran the Asylum from the inside. The younger boys were sent into the streets at night to steal. Even worse things were done with the girls.

Lizbet shook her head. Awful, awful, awful. And most awful of all, once in the Asylum, she would be trapped there. Any chance to free her father would be lost.

She hadn't much time. She would go to the Margrave in the morning and beg for her father's freedom.

Lizbet dried her eyes with her napkin and finished her dinner, thinking about what she would say to the Margrave.

Before climbing into bed that night, she changed into her nightgown and knelt beside the bed to say her prayers.

After she thanked God for her supper, peace in the realm, and the health of the Empress (she did this every night), she prayed for her father, and herself, and for success with the Margrave in the morning. "I need specific advice," she added. She knew God couldn't reply. Not at the moment. "I'll talk to you soon about that, okay?"

She blew out the lamp and crept into bed. She could hear the rustle of mice in the walls. They must be in everyone's house by now. Tormented by restless thoughts and fears, Lizbet tossed and turned for what seemed like hours before falling into an uneasy sleep.

Chapter 2

Lizbet awoke before sunrise. She washed her face in the basin of water by her bedside, shivering from the cold. She dressed in a hurry, wrapped a makeshift breakfast of bread and cheese in a handkerchief for later, and stuck it in the pocket of her pinafore. When she stepped out the front door, the town was still dark, only a little paleness on the eastern horizon promising dawn. Clouds concealed the stars. The raw air cut through her clothes.

Lizbet nervously glanced this way and that. Kidnapping or robbery might befall a solitary child.

Or worse. In Abalia, at the edge of the known world, even the winds were perilous. At age fourteen, Lizbet was almost out of danger, but on windy days younger children risked having their souls blown out of their bodies by the winds that howled down from the Montagnes du Monde. Wise parents kept young ones indoors when it was blustery out, but every year a few were caught by a sudden gust and their souls were blown away. One cannot live without a soul. A child deprived of one became weak and wan, and eventually perished, the boys dying of asthenia, the girls dying of the vapors. With the passing of years, however, souls become ever more tightly bound to the flesh. Adolescents were at little risk, and adults not at all.

At this hour before dawn, the air was cold but still. Lizbet hurried down Abalia's narrow avenues between high stone buildings. Her footsteps echoed forlornly in the empty streets. Now and then a mouse skittered across the cobble-stones or regarded Lizbet with tiny dark eyes from a curb.

She arrived at the Cathedral of St. Dessicata as the bells in the tower began ringing for Lauds. The first cocks were crowing in the distance. Lizbet crept in and found an empty confessional. "Forgive me, Father, for I have sinned," she said to the hooded priest behind the screen.

Confession done, she found a seat in a pew. She waited impatiently through the Benedictus, a few intercessory prayers, and the Lord's Prayer. Only a scattering of worship-ers were present: some old women, a few priests, and a score of boys from the Orphan Asylum, who crowded into two pews near the front, guarded by proctors. They wore the ugly yellow clothing orphans always wore. People said it was so they might be easily caught if they ran away.

At the priest's bidding, Lizbet joined the queue of people waiting to take the Eucharist. When she reached the front, she crossed herself, knelt, and opened her mouth. The host was dry and bland on her tongue. She sneezed, and hurried back to her seat as quickly as she decently could. She had so many questions! She hoped the right Person answered.

Communion was always a gamble: Lizbet never knew whether she would get to speak to God the Father, Christ the Son, or the Holy Spirit.

She liked the Holy Spirit best: a warm, silent presence that secretly healed the wounds of sin and sadness in Lizbet's heart, and filled her with serenity and love and a determina-tion to be a better Lizbet.

Christ the Son was nice enough, but He always over-whelmed Lizbet with well-meaning advice of questionable usefulness, everything from carpentry tips to how to cast out devils, when all Lizbet usually needed was a sympathetic ear.

This morning she found herself connected with God the Father. As it so often happened, he was in a mood to chat her ear off. He rattled on about the poor quality of souls lately, problems with impertinent angels, setbacks in Heaven's war with the armies of Hell, and a hundred other complaints. Lizbet couldn't squeeze a word in. She became fearful that the host would dissolve to nothing, and all communication with Heaven lost, before she got to ask her questions.

Finally, she got an opening. ". . . and the last three sunsets just haven't looked right," God said somewhat querulously. "Too much pink, not enough peach. Or maybe they needed fewer clouds. What do you think, Elizabeth?"

God was the only one who ever called her "Elizabeth."

"Lord, I have to ask you something!"

"Hm? Oh, of course. I'm sorry, here I am, going on and on about nothing. No consideration. What can I help you with, Elizabeth?"

"They put my father in the Houses of Correction."

"Yes, I know. Shocking. Both of you have my sympathy. Did you know that the experience of having to cope with adversity strengthens the soul? It builds character. Read any of the classical authors. They all agree on that."

Lizbet frowned. Sometimes God just missed the point. "That's great," she said, "but right now, I mainly want to get my father out."

"Of course. And that daunting task has my blessings. Good luck, Elizabeth! I'll be cheering you on!" The Divine voice glowed with good will and enthusiasm.

"I need your advice though. What should I do?"

"If you won't think it selfish of me," God said, "might I suggest prayer? Novenas are recommended in times of crisis. Have you heard of the 'storm novena'? 'Pray up a storm,' as they say! Let me explain . . ."

The host was almost gone. Desperate, Lizbet interrupted, "I'll pray as much as you want, but please, please tell me what exactly I should do to get my father out of prison!"

"Hm," God said. "I believe the Margrave could release your father. Have you considered asking him? Politely, of course."

"Yes," Lizbet said impatiently, "I'm going to ask him, but how do I get him to do what I want?"

"Well, if it were me, I'd threaten him with a plague of boils."

"But it isn't you, it's me!"

". . . limits . . . choices . . ." God's voice was growing fainter.

Summoning her courage, Lizbet shouted, "Can you threaten him for me?"

Silence.

Lizbet looked around. Everyone else in the cathedral was staring at her. Had she actually yelled the last part aloud? Her cheeks burned. "Sorry," she said. Staring at the floor, she scuttled down the pew and almost ran up the nave to the door.

She doubted God would really curse the Margrave with boils. That kind of thing happened in Scripture, but all sorts of things happened in Scripture that you never saw actually *happen*.

When she left the cathedral, morning light was beginning to creep over the passes between the peaks of the Montagnes du Monde. A few horse-drawn wagons and goat carts rattled over the cobblestones. The scent of mutton sausage grilling beside a vendor's cart made Lizbet's mouth water and reminded her that she hadn't eaten yet. She unwrapped her bread and cheese and gobbled them greedily as she walked.

Lizbet's next stop was the Margrave's Palace.

The rococo limestone and marble of the Margrave's Palace dominated the center of Abalia. The Chambers of Vengeance, where dour magisters in white powdered wigs and red satin robes bound men over to guillotine, prison, or outlawry, stood to its left. The Houses of Correction stood to its right. Three stories of flint blocks quarried from the Montagnes du Monde, it was as square and gray as a building stone itself. Tiny barred windows hid whatever deeds occurred inside.

The gates to the Palace were guarded by a pink-cheeked youth little older than Lizbet herself, in orange and blue pantaloons and sleeves that puffed out of his silver cuirass. He barred her way with a halberd. "What's your business in the Palace, pretty thing?" he asked. He raised an eyebrow.

Lizbet flushed. She usually left the house only in the company of an adult chaperon. Strangers didn't dare address her as "pretty thing." "I want to see the Margrave," she said.

"But does the Margrave want to see *you?*" the boy asked. His halberd didn't budge.

Lizbet's worries had been all about speaking with the Margrave. She hadn't imagined she might not even be able to get to the Palace door.

"I need to see the Margrave," she insisted. "It's important." She didn't want to admit that her father was imprisoned. Not to this boy.

"So you say," the guard replied. He licked his lips. "But perhaps you are lying. Perhaps you are the witch of the Grove of Frenzy in disguise, come to assassinate the Margrave? Prove to me you're not."

Lizbet couldn't speak. Of course she wasn't a witch! The accusation was so absurd she didn't know how to meet it.

The guard rested the butt of his halberd on the ground, bent close to her, and said, "I've an idea. Witches, not being normal flesh and blood, aren't warm and sensible, like us people. If you're a witch, your flesh is likely cold as the wind. Give us a buss, cute bottom, and if your lips are warm, that's proof you're no witch." He smiled, parted his lips, and bent toward her.

Lizbet stepped back. The guard made a sour expression. "Ah, a witch then. Be off, pretty witch. Until you can prove otherwise."

"You just want to take indecent liberties!" Lizbet exclaimed. "You don't really think I'm a witch!"

"'Indecent liberties'?" The guard spat on the ground. "Fancy words, for a none-too-fancy lass. Girls better than you are being kissed all over this town." His eyes looked her up and down, dwelling too long where they should not. Lizbet threw up her arms to cover her bosom. "You're not nobility," he said. "You're a common girl, like I'm a common lad. You're not too good to kiss me."

Lizbet had never imagined such a situation, or such insolence. Hot anger filled her.

"I'm here to get my father freed," she said, clenching her fists until the knuckles were white. "He's in the Houses of Corrections. His name is Gerhard Lenz. He's a magician. He's the one who cast the rain of mice yesterday."

The guard's eyes narrowed. "You don't say."

"I am his daughter," Lizbet said, meeting his gaze, "and I know his craft. Let me in the Palace this instant, or I will change your fingers and toes to mice, your nose to a vole, your tongue to a rat, and then call down a rain of cats and terriers to eat you!"

The guard's pink cheeks turned splotchy. "Uh . . ."

Lizbet braced her legs, rolled her eyes back in her head, and raised her arms to the sky. She made her voice as low and throaty as she could, and shouted, *"HY . . . ZY . . . HINE—!"*

"All right, all right, stop!" the guard said quickly. He nervously examined his fingers. "Just go in. Forget what I said."

Lizbet needed no second invitation. She brushed past him through the gateway.

Behind its iron fence, the Margrave's Palace was set fifty feet back from the street. A wide flagstone walk led across lawns just turning the luminous green of early spring. Lizbet was halfway to the Palace door when the guard's voice yelled behind her, "You don't have a cute bottom, anyway! It's as big as a haystack!"

Lizbet swiveled. "HY . . . !"

"All right, I'm sorry!"

Lizbet hurried up the walk. Her father hadn't taught her any magic. Her "spell" had been all a bluff. Like Uncle Bunbury. Over the last day Lizbet was piling one lie on top of another.

She was shocked by herself. She worried that the next time she spoke to God, He'd have something to say about it.

Inside, it took a moment for Lizbet's eyes to adjust to the Palace's dim anteroom. Men in military dress or frock coats hurried here and there. Directly in front of her, a balding fellow in uniform presided behind a table. He gestured her over. "State your business with the Palace," he snapped when she approached. He glowered at her through steel-rim spectacles.

"I'm here to see the Margrave," Lizbet said. "It's about—"

"Sit there," the man said. He pointed to a row of benches against the wall, where a dozen anxious-looking commoners huddled together. "Wait your turn. The Margrave will be seeing petitioners and complainants at noon, or after."

Her success with the guard outside had given Lizbet a little courage. Instead of going over to the bench, she said, "I need to see him now. It's about Gerhard Lenz."

The man at the table was unimpressed. "Isn't it always? Mouse damage is the popular complaint this morning. Sit with the others, wait your turn." He motioned to another person who had come in behind her. "Out of the way, little lady."

"I'm Gerhard Lenz's daughter. I'm here to get him out of prison."

The man tilted his head, and his watery blue eyes regarded her over his spectacles. "Huh," he went. "Huh-huh. Huh-huh-huh-huh-huh-huh . . ."

If a blacksmith's bellows could laugh, it might have sounded like that, if the bellows also had tuberculosis. Lizbet endured the peculiar noise for a few seconds, then said, "I'll find my own way." She glimpsed a marble stairway spiraling upward at the rear of the anteroom. She headed for it.

"Hans!" the man with the bellows laugh yelled behind her. "Show this girl to His Lordship's office. Huh-huh. She may regret her eagerness to get there."

Hans was a soldier, clad like the boy outside, but older. He motioned Lizbet up the stairway and ascended behind her.

She paused at the first landing. A labyrinth of bookcases stuffed to bursting with books sprawled out in every direction. Flickering oil lamps in sconces lit the scene dimly. Bent-over men with carts shuffled through the stacks, sorting, rearranging, reshelving.

Lizbet paused, but Hans behind her said, "Keep moving."

The floor above was the same. And the floor above that. Lizbet turned a questioning glance to Hans.

"Keep going," he said. "His Lordship's offices are on the sixth floor. His Lordship is a bibliophile."

"I thought he came from Saxony?" Lizbet said.

"A 'bibliophile' is a man mad with books. His Lordship buys books by the hundred. He has agents in Albion, Barbary, Cathay and the Indies. They send him crates of books from the ends of the earth."

After five flights, the staircase ended at a narrow door bound in iron, to who knows where. Hans passed it by, instead leading Lizbet down a short passage into a large and noisy room full of ink-stained male secretaries bent over high desks, pecking with their quills at paper and parchment. Short fat men in frock coats toddled about, bossing the secretaries. At the office's other end stood a great mahogany door guarded by a munifex with a musket. The munifex swung the door open at Hans's request. Lizbet swallowed hard, and walked in.

Tall windows facing east filled the room with daylight. Lizbet had an impression of high walls of bookshelves that almost seemed to close in overhead, like trees bending over a forest glade. More piles of books were stacked around the room, and on top of a table that stood between her and the windows. The tabletop also held scattered small jars and flasks of many shapes and sizes, made of crystal, china, or brass. Behind the desk, silhouetted by the light from the window, a man. A man broad and tall.

"State your complaint," Margrave Hengest Wolftrow said. "Be quick."

His form like a looming shadow. His voice like the wind through reeds. Hengest wore fur-trimmed dark silks. He rested his hands on the desk in front of him: each hand was larger than both of Lizbet's hands put together. Light from the window behind poured around him, but barely illuminated him.

Lizbet would have expected a man so large to seem as solid as a mountain. But staring at the Margrave's dark form was like like staring into the dim recesses of an empty bookcase in a shuttered room.

She realized that she was trembling. She had bluffed the stripling guard at the gate, but she didn't think she was going to be able to bluff the Margrave.

"I'm Lizbet Lenz," she said. "I'm very pleased to meet you." Oops, should she curtsy? She tried to curtsy, but almost fell. Her heart was going as fast as a sparrow's. Her palms were sweaty, and she tried surreptitiously to rub them on her pinafore. "I'm here to get my father out of the Houses of Correction," she said. "To ask you, I mean. Please, that is. Please, your . . . Lordship. I'd like you to release him. Please."

Hengest regarded her in silence for a moment. "Your father is in the Houses of Corrections on account of his crimes," he said. "Half of Abalia is here to complain to me about this business with the mice."

"But he didn't mean it," Lizbet said quickly. "And I promise he'll never do it again."

Hengest made a dismissive gesture. "How do you propose to set right the mischief your father has done? The town is in an uproar. Work and wages lost. Mice have scattered to infest every man's house and barn. How are these troubles to be repaired?"

Lizbet was silent.

Hengest shook his head. "Your father remains in prison, lest he cause me even more trouble. I deny your request."

That was all? It was over? In moments, Lizbet's chance to free her father had fled. "Please!" she said. "I'll . . . I'll do anything to get him out. Anything you want. Please. Please!"

She realized, despairing, how useless her words were. What could she, a mere girl, offer this great magistrate?

Instead of replying, Hengest reached for one one of the vials on his desk. He tilted it, and a few tiny spheres, like pearls, fell into his palm. He returned all but one to the vial. The remaining sphere he rolled between thumb and index finger for a moment, while staring into space. Then Hengest popped it into his mouth and swallowed.

For the first time, light from the window illuminated his face. His gaze returned to Lizbet. Hengest's stare was intelligent, unsparing, and sad. Hengest's form seemed more solid, less an empty void than simply a man in dark clothing.

"'Anything,'" Hengest finally said. "But what's needed isn't 'anything.' What's needed is magic. Magic brought the mice, magic must dispose of them. Are you a magician, then?"

"No . . ."

"Your father said he was a magician. I believe he misinformed me. There is no good magic this side of the Montagnes du Monde. Over there, it's different. They have all the magic in the world there."

That didn't help Lizbet. The other side of the Montagnes might as well be the other side of the moon. 'She'll marry you over the Montagnes' people said when a man's sweetheart jilted him. 'I'll be rich when I cross the Montagnes,' men said when they lost at dice.

No magic this side of the Montagnes du Monde? "What about the witch?" Lizbet said. "Maybe the witch could—"

Instantly Hengest leaped to his feet. He loomed over her. "Never speak of the witch!" he shouted.

Lizbet almost shrieked. She clapped one hand to her mouth. "I'm sorry!" she said.

Hengest released a breath. "Witches have no magic, anyway," he said. "Not what you would call 'magic.' A paltry lot of fiddlers and tinkers, that's all witches are." Hengest's eyes swept over her, but could not seem to focus. "You have nothing for me," he said. "You can do nothing for me. Your father could do nothing for me."

"But how am I to get my father out of prison?" Lizbet burst out. "You're keeping him in prison! For just a mistake!"

"Greater men than your father have suffered their entire lives for a mistake," Hengest said. He motioned to the munifex by the door. "Take this girl away. We have no more to say to each other."

The doorkeeper at the Houses of Corrections had a bald bullet head. His face was covered with seeping pustules. He let Lizbet in for the few pennies in her pocket. Another gaoler led her through dim stone halls that smelled of urine, down a creaking wooden staircase to the basement, where they found her father in a cell. "Please open the door?" she asked the gaoler.

"How many pennies you got?" the gaoler asked.

"Why, none. I gave them all to the doorkeeper!"

"Bring more next time, girlie," the gaoler said and smirked. He stumped off.

Behind a door of rusted iron bars, Gerhard Lenz sat miserably on the floor. No cot, not even a mattress. Filthy straw on the floor, a leather bucket for a toilet. "Lizbet, sweetheart, is that you?" he mumbled. Their fingers touched through the bars.

Lizbet gasped: Gerhard's right eye was blackened, his lips swollen, and his nose squashed and bloody. He wore only a linsey-woolsey undershirt. "Father!" Lizbet said. "What happened to you? Where are your clothes?"

"Oh, sweetheart, they stole them," Gerhard said. "And they hit me."

"Who? Who did this?"

Gerhard didn't know. Guards? Other prisoners? In the soupy dusk of the Houses of Corrections, who could be certain? Guards were scarcely distinguishable from criminals.

"Father," Lizbet said, "I went to see the Margrave. I asked him to let you go." She bit her lip to hold back the tears. "He wouldn't do it. Father, I don't know what to do next. What can I do to make him let you go?"

"Dear, I don't know . . ." Gerhard's voice, usually cheerful and confident, was distant, thready, and uncertain. It chilled Lizbet. She had never heard him sound like this. "It's so dark in here," Gerhard said. "It makes it hard to think. All I can hear is the cries of men being beaten. What can you do for the Margrave? Whatever you think best, I suppose. I can't think of anything."

"Father!"

Lizbet was frightened. Gerhard always had a plan, a plot, a trick, a card up his sleeve. He had always been able to find just the right thing to spirit them out of trouble. Gerhard Lenz was the fox with endless wiles, the bird who could not be caged.

But now he was caged at last. The effect that even a night of imprisonment had on him was terrible to see. His spirit had been broken, and spirit was all Gerhard had. He hadn't much in the way of character, or depth of intellect, or physical strength. To break his spirit was to break the man.

Lizbet *had* to get him out. She was certain he would die if not released.

Behind Lizbet, a rough voice: "That's enough for you, missy. Time to go." The gaoler placed a big hand on Lizbet's back and gave her a shove down the rubbish-strewn corridor. She stumbled and almost lost her footing.

But there was one more thing she had to ask Gerhard. She swiveled and ducked under the gaoler's arm. "Father!" she yelled into the grate. "The Margrave said he needed magic. He said all the magic in the world is over the Montagnes du Monde. What is he talking about? No one can cross the Montagnes."

"You go when I tell you to go, cheeky little whore!" the gaoler yelled. He grabbed Lizbet's arm and swung her around.

"There's a book," came Gerhard's voice from the darkness of his cell. "It's a book of magic, or something. They stole it from him when he crossed the Montagnes, years ago. He only remembers little bits of it. He's been searching for it ever since."

The gaoler shoved her away from Gerhard's cell. She stumbled down the corridor, toward daylight. She called back, "I'll find a way to get you out, Father! I swear I will!"

The sun brooded low and orange in the western sky by the hour Lizbet arrived home. She had walked miles through the city streets and hadn't eaten since breakfast, and she was ravenous. As she was heating up the last of the sausages and sauerkraut on the stove, there was a knock on the door.

Fears fled through her mind. She sneaked to a window, nudged the curtain back a hair, and peered out.

It was only Drizzle, a neighbor's boy. Drizzle was a couple years younger. He was always cheerful, whether or not the situation called for cheer, poked his nose into everyone else's business, and talked before he thought. She unbolted the door and cracked it open an inch.

"You weren't in school!" Drizzle said, grinning. His voice rang with both shock and envy.

"I know I wasn't in school," she said. "My father—" She thought of softening the truth, of saying Gerhard was 'away,' or something, but then she thought: *Why bother?* "My father's in the Houses of Correction. I've been trying to get him out."

Drizzle cared nothing for her father's ignominy. He was too excited about his own news. "Do you know who was here today? The Magisters of Children! Ursula saw 'em." Ursula was Drizzle's sister. "She's home sick, and she saw 'em. They came to your door. They had all leather on, and chain-mail gloves. Ursula says the gloves are if little children bite 'em. They asked Mother about your uncle. I didn't know you had an uncle, Lizbet!"

"What did your mother tell them?" Lizbet asked.

"I don't know. Lizbet, are you going in the Orphan Asylum? Father says the Asylum breeds highwaymen and strumpets. Are you going to be a strumpet?"

"No!"

"Then are you going to be a highwayman? Are you going to have a big black stallion and a blunderbuss pistol?"

"Listen, Drizzle," Lizbet said, "tell your mother that if the Magisters come back, she should tell them I've gone to live with my uncle Bunbury. Okay?"

"So you're not going be a highwayman?" Drizzle said, disappointment in his voice.

Once she had shooed Drizzle away and locked the door, Lizbet tried to eat. She had to force her food down. Each spoonful traveled in a painful knot from her mouth, down behind her breastbone, to her stomach.

The net was closing in. The Magisters of Children were already on her trail.

Maybe she *should* be a highwayman. Was this how people started as criminals, she wondered? When the world wouldn't let them do anything else?

Lizbet was horrified at what she was thinking. To disobey the people God put over you was a sin, and a crime. Lizbet had always been a pious and obedient child. Now, within a single day, she had told lies time and again, and—for just a moment—she had dreamed of becoming a criminal.

What kind of terrible person was she turning into?

She didn't want to become a terrible person. She didn't want to be anything more than Lizbet, quiet, gentle, *good* Lizbet, fourteen years old, for ever and ever.

She cried herself to sleep that night. She cried until the pillow was damp and she had to turn it over to put her head on a dry spot.

In the morning when she woke, her tears were gone. In their place, dry-eyed resolution to do what she must to free her father and keep herself out of the clutches of the Orphan Asylum.

What would a highwayman do? she wondered.

Chapter 3

Lizbet washed with a washrag and dressed in work clothes, not school clothes: a short dress of tough brown serge, canvas bloomers underneath, knee-high wool socks, and roomy, dumpy, scuffed leather boots that you could walk miles in without hurting your feet. She had looked her best when she went to the Margrave yesterday, and when she talked to God, and it hadn't made a bit of difference with either of them.

She gobbled a breakfast of cheese and stale bread, and left by the house's back door as the cathedral bells were tolling eight o'clock. She didn't know what time the Magisters of Children were coming back, but she guessed they'd show up at the front door, and she didn't want to run into them.

Lizbet went directly to the Cathedral of St. Dessicata. You were supposed to fast before receiving the host. She hadn't fasted. You were supposed to go to confession. But Lizbet had too much to confess, and didn't have time. God would just have to put up with it. The short mid-morning service called Terce was in progress as she entered. She sat through two psalms, clicking the toes of her boots together with impatience and anxiety. When the priest invited the churchgoers to take the sacrament, Lizbet trooped down the aisle with a handful of others.

She trembled at a little at the thought of what she was about to do.

She crossed herself and knelt before the priest, close enough to smell the incense and camphor on his robes. The priest took one host from a gilt and silver pyx presented by an altar boy and placed the host on her tongue. Lizbet rose, turned, and walked back to her seat. As the host began to dissolve, she heard a familiar voice:

"Lizbet!"

It was Christ Jesus.

"How long has it been?" Jesus asked. "So glad I was able to catch up with you! I've been running my tail off banishing devils down in the Hebrew Quarter. They called me for Lilith again. Third time this month. I've been tangling with her for almost two thousand years, and it's not that I don't love her—I love all created beings—but Lady Lil is one tough cupcake."

Compared with His Father, Jesus was an easy touch when it came to sin. He often simply laughed off minor infractions.

"Jesus," Lizbet said, "forgive me, for I am about to sin." She reached her pew and sat down.

"Don't I know it," Jesus said with a sigh. "It's not easy being fallen. Except Mom, who's immaculate and all, but if you're like most of us, it's hard to resist the temptation to kick the cat now and then. Look, here's a tip. If you're about to sin, say the multiplication tables under your breath. Not only does it distract you from sin, but it helps your schoolwork. Ice cold baths are also great. Mostly for impure thoughts, they don't help much with sloth or envy. Also, they're not really safe in winter—"

"I don't need advice," Lizbet said. "I need forgiveness. For a sin I haven't committed yet." She wiggled in the pew, trying to see the priest. Had he finished giving communion?

"Lizbet," Jesus said, "that's not how this works. If you sin, Heaven can forgive you. But stocking up on forgiveness before sinning—take it from me, that's a theological and ethical quagmire. What sin did you have in mind? I can give you some great ideas how to avoid it—"

Oh, well, it was worth a try, Lizbet told herself. She rose from her pew and started back down the aisle, toward the priest. She was almost too late. The last woman to take communion was getting to her feet, the priest had already put the cover back on the pyx—

Lizbet broke into a run. Her pounding footsteps echoed down the nave. People in the pews turned to look. When she halted in front of the priest, he stared at her curiously and said, "Miss?"

With a swift gesture, Lizbet knocked the gilded lid off the pyx, grabbed a fistful of consecrated hosts, and dropped them in her skirt pocket.

The priest gasped. For a moment he just stared at Lizbet. Perhaps he had never seen or imagined such a thing before. Perhaps he doubted his own eyes. Lizbet turned and walked back up the nave.

"Lizbet?" said Jesus. "Lizbet, put them back." The host in her mouth had almost dissolved. Jesus's voice became faint "That's not—"

Lizbet swallowed hard. The host vanished down her throat. Jesus's voice cut off in mid-sentence.

She was halfway to the cathedral door. Behind her, the priest yelled, "Miss! Stop! You can't do that!" Hurrying footsteps.

Lizbet didn't think the priest would be able to run very fast in his vestments. See, it had been smart to wear a short skirt and bloomers. She sprinted for the open door.

Outside, a sunny, chilly April morning. High above, deep-throated bronze church bells tolled the half hour. Lizbet ran across the cobblestone square in front of the cathedral, dodging between passersby, wagons, carts, beggars, and between the stalls and merchants' stands that lined the square's sides. No one paid special attention to a running girl in plain clothing.

She crouched behind a draper's stall. She peeked out with one eye. The priest stood, scowling, at the cathedral entrance. He turned back and forth, his gaze searching the square.

It did not light on her. After a minute, the priest returned inside. Had he given up? Or had he gone for reinforcements? Lizbet didn't know, and didn't wait to find out. She hurried out of the market square, not looking behind.

Lizbet reflected that she had never even heard of anyone stealing the host before. Sins, big and small, were piling higher on Lizbet's head. And there was one more sin to come, worse than all the rest.

She let herself in by the back door. She sneaked through her own house like a thief, stopping to listen before turning every corner. She was fearful that the Magisters of Children were already nosing about. But she found no one.

Lizbet packed a drawstring sack with extra socks and underwear, a bar of brown lye soap and a towel, a jar of quince preserves, the rest of the cheese in the larder, and a hard sausage. She also stowed two prized possessions: a book of verses and a tiny pearl from a fresh-water mussel she'd found in a creek.

Hardest to leave were her dolls. Eight in all. She'd carved wooden sticks for body and limbs, and purchased white china heads that she'd painted herself. She'd sewn their dresses with love and care. Her dolls were the friends she wished she had, the friends she wouldn't let herself have. When she was younger she'd walk them up and down and make up conversations for them. They'd meet and share secrets. They'd talk about their gentleman friends. They'd have a spat and then make up.

Lizbet couldn't take them with her. She hoped, hoped, hoped they'd still be here when she got back.

In Gerhard's study she found a handful of pennies and couple of silver guilders in a pouch. His grimoire, bound in leather and polished brass, was too big to carry. There were only a few spells in it anyway, inscribed in Gerhard's swirly handwriting filled with curlicues and swish-swashes. The spells were nearly useless. How to turn dust motes into gnats. An incantation to make noses bigger. Hengest was right. There was no real magic. All the magic Lizbet had ever heard of was small, silly, and pointless.

At the very back of the grimoire, Gerhard had scribbled one long and complicated spell over and over, with many words crossed out and replaced, as if he had been trying to discover the right words by chance. It was titled "To Conjure Gold." Maybe this was the spell that went wrong and made sky rain mice?

Noise from the front of house. The rattle of the door latch. The creak of the front door opening. Men's muttering voices. Whoever it was must have a key, and hadn't bothered to knock. Lizbet's time had run out. She pictured people rummaging through her father's possessions and was disgusted by the thought of Gerhard's work, silly though it might be, falling into their hands. She tore all the spells out of the grimoire and stuck them in the pocket of her skirt.

Carrying her sack of possessions, Lizbet walked as quickly and quietly as she could toward the rear of the house. She was almost to the kitchen and the rear door when a man's voice yelled, "Little girl! You, there! Halt!"

For an instant, Lizbet stared in terror. A huge man in black robes and leather harness strode down the house's center hall toward her. His robes swung as he walked, and his chain-mail gloves clinked with each step. A marshal of the Magisters of Children.

Lizbet darted across the kitchen, hit the door running, and half-leaped, half-fell down the rear steps, into the alley. The marshal came running after, still yelling for her to stop.

She took off down the alley. Behind came the marshal. Two other men were with him. At the alley's end, Lizbet turned and ran down the Street of St. Therese. She dared a glance behind. The marshals were catching up. Lizbet's sack was heavy. It swung back and forth as she ran, throwing her off balance and slowing her down. Her heart crying out in despair and loss, Lizbet dropped the sack and sprinted away.

Pope Venomous the Third Avenue. Hog Alley. Redcrosse Square. Lizbet was a good runner, with an adolescent's strong wind and limber frame. Unburdened, she gradually outdistanced the panting marshals in their heavy gear. On Redcrosse Square she slipped into a sacramental supply shop. Standing back from the entrance, she pretended to browse through a rack of prayer cards which depicted the Virgin Mary being stabbed through the heart with swords. Lizbet covertly sneaked glimpses though the shop's front window.

Minutes passed. There was no sign of the marshals.

Lizbet was safe for the moment, but she had won a Pyrrhic victory. She had lost all her favorite things. She had lost the food and clothes she thought she might need on her journey.

She didn't cry. Maybe she had used up all the tears she had last night.

She ventured out of the shop. The marshals were not to be seen. As wary as a highwayman with a price on his head, Lizbet headed west.

The city of Abalia clung to a hillside, one of the foothills of the great Montagnes du Monde. To go west in Abalia was to go downhill. Lizbet descended westward, down the Avenue of Famous Virgins. The houses on either side by degrees became more humble, and the passersby on the street more shabby. At last Lizbet arrived at the end of Abalia and stood at the top of the Wall of Virtue.

The Wall of Virtue was a granite cliff face in the mountainside. A single stone staircase traversed it. The Wall of Virtue separated Abalia from its wicked stepchild below, Abalia-Under-the-Hill. No one from Abalia went into Abalia-Under-the-Hill. Although, Lizbet thought as she descended the staircase, the steps seemed awfully well-worn for steps that no one ever used.

At the bottom of the Wall, a street of gray mud continued steeply down the hillside. A foul-smelling open sewer ran down its center, carrying along garbage, dead rats, bones, and worse. Buildings on both sides were timber and peeling stucco rather than stone or brick. Tethered goats bleated and scrawny chickens scratched in dooryards. Lizbet looked behind her: up on the hill, the gray mass of Abalia proper glowed in the early afternoon sun. Above the city rose the spikes of its towers and steeples, like the spore stalks of a vast and dismal gray mold. At the bottom of the hill in front of her, a dark forest spread out. This was Lizbet's goal.

A group of men lounged on the porch of a tavern by the road. As Lizbet passed, their gaze lighted on her. One young man rose from his seat. His coat was unbuttoned, his shirt half out of his pants.

"Hey there, pretty thing!" he called.

Lizbet hurried down the hill. To her dismay, the man hopped over the porch rail and followed after her. So did two others.

"Where you needing to get to, all so hasty, my love?" the man called out from behind her.

Lizbet's foot slipped in the mud. She fell onto the road. Her hands and knees were an inch deep in the mud. She struggled to her feet, but her fall allowed the man to catch up with her. He took her right arm in his, and his left arm went around her back and gripped her waist. "Such a fall, darlin'!" he said. His breath had the rotten-lilies stink of used-up alcohol. "Won't you tarry for a spot of victuals with us? This is a dangerous neighborhood for a tender young body such as yourself. Best you stay with us a while."

"No!" Lizbet said. She dug her feet into the mud and pulled away. One of the other men grabbed her left arm, but she pulled free of him too and plunged down the hill, running, barely keeping her balance on the steep, slippery ground. Her heart pounded with effort and fear.

"Grab her, Carl," one of the other men yelled. "She's no business here. Let's have some fun with her."

Pounding footfalls and heavy breathing behind her. Lizbet ran as fast as she could without falling.

She reached the bottom of the hill. The road and buildings gave out. The forest, dense and dark, loomed ahead. Even though spring growth was just starting to leaf out the trees, their limbs were so tight and tangled she could not see into the shadows. She searched the wall of tangled vines and saplings for an opening.

From behind, a voice broken by panting yelled, "She's going in the damned Grove of Frenzy! I ain't going in there after her."

The voice of the first man, whom the other had called Carl: "Then you're out of luck, she's all mine!"

"And you can have her, and the witch as well."

There! An opening in the green wall of forest, and a path leading in. Lizbet headed for it.

A dozen yards into the forest, she stopped. Darkness engulfed her, as if she had run into an unlighted cellar. The air was so humid and thick it stuck in her throat. When the souls of children were blown out of their bodies by a high wind, sometimes they blew into the woods and haunted the dim glades, lost and confused. The awful fancy came to Lizbet that she might breathe in these lost souls. The air was heavy with scents of vegetal growth and decay.

Heavy footsteps behind. Lizbet forced herself to walk forward again, deeper into the forest. As her eyes adjusted to the dimness, Lizbet could see the pale trace of a path between the mossy rocks and ferns. She hurried on as fast as she dared, frightened she would trip on a vine or stone.

Behind, she could hear Carl's heavy boots, and heard him cursing at the darkness, the rocks, the hanging vines. Still, he came on.

Ahead, the path branched.

Lizbet was at a loss for which direction to take. Tales said a witch lived in this wood, a witch who ate babies, who compounded magical potions of great power and expense, who flew through the air, who was lascivious with devils. A witch of high whimsy and mercurial temperament, who might conjure you up a prince's ransom or metamorphose you into one of her milk cows, as the mood took her. Or so people said. No one actually admitted seeing her, speaking with her, or asking her for a boon. Some swore she was naught but a tale.

The Margrave's rage when Lizbet mentioned the witch had given Lizbet faint hope. All her other choices gone, she had resolved to find the witch and ask her for her help.

That the witch might be hard to find was a complication that had not occurred to Lizbet.

Right or left?

Right was good. Left was bad. If the witch was evil—was there any other kind of witch?—maybe she lived at the end of leftward-branching paths. Lizbet took the left-hand fork.

Within fifty yards, the path branched again. Again, Lizbet turned left, but her hope ebbed a little. Who knew where these paths led, or whether there was a witch at all, anywhere in the wood? To make matters worse, she could hear Carl's footsteps still behind her. She looked down. Her boots were making imprints in the moist earth anyone could follow.

She thought of running off the path, into the forest's dim depths. But she was fearful of becoming even more lost. A path must mean at least that people did come this way. Even if there was no witch, maybe there were woodchoppers who lived in this forest and could help her. She ran on.

Left, left, left, left, left, left. The path branched and branched again. Lizbet took every left fork. The woods became thicker, darker. Sometimes Lizbet thought she saw movement in the tangled depths, or the flash of watching eyes. Vines, dripping with moisture, hung like nooses across the path, and she had to push them aside. Behind, she could hear Carl panting.

Lizbet's legs were weary. Her breath was short. Her head spun with worry and exhaustion. It came to her that there was a problem in just picking the left-hand path: it might simply lead you in a circle.

At that moment, the woods gave out, and Lizbet found herself at the edge of a clearing. Across a patchy lawn, a gaggle of gray geese regarded her skeptically, and honked. A couple of pigs rooting in the turf paused to look up, snort, and paw the ground with their trotters.

Just ahead of her, at the end of a mossy stone walk, stood a house.

It was like no house Lizbet had seen before. It rose three stories, or three and a half, or four, or perhaps four and three-eighths: dormers, gables, roofs of slate, tile, thatch, or tin piled on top of one another, until the eye was confused, and she couldn't tell where the building ended. Emerging from the clutter of rooflines was a forest of tiny towers, spires, smoky chimneys, and even a widow's walk. The house was partly stone, partly brick, and brightly painted wood, and stucco, and wattle and who knew what else. It was as if dozens of other buildings had been chopped up and recombined into one. A score of poles of brightly painted wood or enameled metal leaned into the house's walls and corners like a cathedral's buttresses, as if the whole structure might come tottering down without them. Flags sewn with peculiar devices fluttered from angled flagstaffs.

Behind her, the crunching of Carl's footsteps approached. Whoever lived in this crazy house, Lizbet had to take a chance with them. She ran up the walk, up six stone steps, to a big red door. The doorknocker was brass, shaped like a grotesque face sticking out its tongue, and as big as Lizbet's head. With effort, she lifted it and let it drop. Its clang made her ears ring. "Please let me in!" she yelled. "There's a man after me!"

No response.

She lifted the knocker again and slammed it down against its brass anvil. And again. And again. Its noise echoed off the house, and off the forest all around. "Please!" Lizbet yelled. "Please open the door!"

"There you are! What a din you're making. You've run me a pretty mile this morning, sweetheart! What do you intend to give me in return?"

Carl stood at the edge of the yard, his hands on his hips, breathing hard. He noticed the house, and his gaze rambled over it. "What have we here? What a trash heap of silly rubbish! Looks like it was tinkered together by some drunken simpleton."

"It is not!" Lizbet said.

"Uh?"

"This house is not silly rubbish! It's beautiful. I like it."

For a moment, Carl was struck dumb. Of all the things that Lizbet might have said at that moment—begging Carl to leave her alone, praying to God, or just plain crying in fear and frustration—defending the beauty of some stranger's most peculiar house was probably not what he had expected.

Lizbet said it because she was tired of running. Tired of feeling lost and afraid. Whatever was about to happen—and she feared the worst from Carl's grubby hands and beery mouth—the very least she could do was not to cooperate with it. The least she could do was tell the truth.

And it was the truth. Lizbet was used to Abalia's maze of twisty dark streets, where houses were forbidding cliffs of gray flint jammed together, looming over the street to shut off all light. This ridiculous, lawless house, made of a thousand different things, awkward and gangling and teetering to fall down, was the funniest and best house Lizbet had ever seen.

Carl recovered himself. "You'll like me more, lassie," he said, and strode toward her.

Lizbet had run out of time and choices. Why wouldn't the people here open the door for her?

Then the thought came to her: Why didn't she open the door herself? Maybe it was locked. But maybe it wasn't.

She put both hands on the brass doorknob, turned it, and pushed. The door swung inward so easily she almost lost her balance and fell.

Within stood a woman. The most beautiful woman Lizbet had ever seen.

"Hello, dear," she said. "I'm Mrs. Woodcot. My word, I thought you'd never stop pounding on the door. I actually thought of opening it, just to ask you to quit. No need to come in. Just leave your baby on the doorstep."

Chapter 4

Folk of Abalia were fair-skinned, like most northern folk, but Mrs. Woodcot had a complexion as pale and translucent as icicles. Her lips were narrow and expressive, her eyes gray and lively, her eyebrows as thin and delicately arched as the wings of a hawk. Her bosom emerged from a lacy decolletage as round, white, pretty, and cold as two scoops of vanilla ice cream.

But what was this about a baby? "I don't have any baby," Lizbet said.

"No baby? You've come alone? Oh, that's too bad, love. If you've no baby for me, you must go in the press yourself. That's the rule. But do tell me your name first?"

"My name is Lizbet Lenz," Lizbet said. "That man's after me. Can you help?" She turned and pointed at Carl, who was now just outside, a few steps away. His mouth hung open slightly. He stared through the doorway at the pale and beautiful Mrs. Woodcot.

"So you haven't come alone, after all," Mrs. Woodcot said. "That's lucky for you!" She beckoned to Carl with a crooked finger. She smiled at him. Lizbet caught just a glimpse of that smile. It warmed her through like laudanum. Mrs. Woodcot's smile made you feel that everything in the world was all right, even things that weren't all right at all.

Mrs. Woodcot spoke to Carl. It took a moment for Lizbet to realize that she didn't understand what Mrs. Woodcot was saying. Although she spoke what seemed like normal syllables, with the rhythm and lilt of ordinary speech, Lizbet couldn't get the syllables to fit together properly into words. They were like a song with music but no lyrics.

Mrs. Woodcot did something with her dress and her breasts. Carl embraced her. Lizbet heard them laugh together, a chuckling sound. Carl's hands were inside Mrs. Woodcot's clothing. He was kissing her mouth. Together they crossed the room.

Lizbet had hoped Mrs. Woodcot would slam the door in Carl's face and lock it, and let Lizbet wait in her house until Carl went away. This sudden development of friendly relations worried her.

She had about decided that Mrs. Woodcot was the witch. She tried to remember what they said about witches in stories. It wasn't safe to tell them your real name, they said. Don't eat anything in a witch's house. Never sleep in a witch's house. Never give a witch any article of your clothing, or a strand of hair, or even a nail paring. Never look a witch in the eye, or she will ensorcell you. Lizbet had looked Mrs. Woodcot in the eye. Was Lizbet ensorcelled? What would it feel like if one were ensorcelled?

She noticed the rest of the room's furnishings for the first time: a countertop like a druggist's shop; racks all around the room, filled with bottles and urns (also just like a druggist's); in the back, a staircase leading upward. One item was unlike any druggist's though: a shining circular brass machine, about a yard wide and a yard high, with a hinged brass lid and a capstan on top. Some years before, during a time when her father was briefly prosperous, Lizbet had been taken to an expensive restaurant. It had a duck press. They put a roast duck in it, turned a lever, and essence of duck flowed out the bottom, to be whisked into a delicious sauce by a chef in a white apron and toque who came to your table.

Mrs. Woodcot's device reminded Lizbet of the duck press. Only it was much larger, and it was decorated with brass carvings of a boy and a girl, instead of a duck.

Mrs. Woodcot and Carl approached this device. Mrs. Woodcot broke from Carl's kiss, giggled, and gave him a playful shove. The edge of the press caught the back of his legs. Carl lost his balance, tipped backward, and fell neatly into the device.

"Oopsie-daisy!" Mrs. Woodcot said cheerfully. She clanged the brass lid shut and locked it with a silver hasp.

The capstan had four long brass spokes. Mrs. Woodcot grasped one. "Here," she said to Lizbet, "take the opposite end, dear, and help me turn." Her pale finger beckoned.

It was all too obvious what was about to happen to Carl.

Lizbet shrank back. "No," she said. "No, I can't. I don't want to."

"What?" Mrs. Woodcot released the spoke and put her hands on her hips. "But you lured him here, after all. Therefore, his fate is your responsibility. He's an evil fellow, out to despoil your virtue, have his way with you, lead you down the primrose path of dalliance, and doubtless many other euphemisms as well. It is your moral duty to help administer his just desserts. Come, don't be lazy, child, grab the lever and put your shoulder into it."

"But I didn't lure him here," Lizbet wailed. "He followed me. And I don't think his fate is my responsibility. I was just walking down the road. And anyway, maybe he meant to do something bad, but he never actually did anything." She shook her head. "What you're saying doesn't make any sense."

"Oh, for goodness' sake, it's not supposed to make *sense*," Mrs. Woodcot said with exasperation. "I'm trying to exploit your youthful innocence, deference toward adults, and sexual fears to trick you into doing something you would not do otherwise. Why can't you just play along? Mortals are so tedious. If you won't help me, I must find someone who can. Strix!" she called in her musical voice. "Strix, my darling poppet, come and help your mother!"

A girl stood at the bottom of the stairwell, not a dozen feet away. Lizbet drew her breath. The girl had not been there a second before. She had not come down the stairs, or entered the room. She was just suddenly *there*.

The girl's arms were crossed over her still-boyish chest. She scowled. "You're not my mother," she said.

"I am speaking metaphorically, Strix," Mrs. Woodcot said.

"And don't try to exploit my youthful innocence, because I haven't got any."

"I *know* that. So if you don't grab the lever and help me squish the lustful lout, I will beat you."

"Well, that's more like it," Strix said.

She stared at Lizbet with disdain. She looked about Lizbet's age. The first thing Lizbet noticed about her was her color: while Mrs. Woodcot was whiter than any person Lizbet had ever seen, Strix was browner. Lizbet had heard that in the pagan kingdoms of the uttermost south men were brown because the sun baked them like bread in an oven. But she had never seen one.

Strix was lighter than bread crusts, but darker than tea with milk. She was the brown of autumn leaves swirling in the breeze, the brown of speckled trout, drifting among the shifting shadows of a brook. On one cheek, faint parallel lines swam beneath the surface, as if she had been tattooed. She had large brown eyes which didn't match, a small turned-up nose, and red-auburn hair, curly and wavy, like a bird's nest of rusted wires, half gathered on her head with hairpins, the rest tumbling down her back. Her dress was brown too, a simple shift but covered with layers and layers of gauzy mantles and overdresses, all in shades of brown, tan, taupe, sand, umber, charcoal. All the colors of the rainbow, if rainbows ran from brown to black. She wore high black lace-up boots. There was something unnatural and disturbing about those boots, but Lizbet had no time to figure out what it was.

Strix gripped the capstan lever that Lizbet had refused. She and Mrs. Woodcot bent to their work. With a sound of groaning metal, the capstan moved. The thick, threaded shaft connecting the capstan and the press slowly turned. From within, Carl's muffled voice. "Mrs. Woodcot, darling, I seem to be trapped!"

"Yes, honeybunch," Mrs. Woodcot called. "Don't worry your little head, I'll fix that soon."

"I knew I could count on you," came the voice from the press.

"Speed, Strix, speed," Mrs. Woodcot said, huffing with effort. "If we don't do the job quickly, we'll get nothing from him but *Timor*."

Strix grumbled, but pushed harder. Round and round went the capstan. The threaded shaft sank into the press. Mrs. Woodcot said to Lizbet, "Do you know it works the same with chickens? If you get a chicken drunk before you chop its head off, it will be more tender when you cook it, because it died relaxed. It's also helpful to get seraphim and incubi drunk before entering into negotiations with them. Drink incapacitates them for sexual intimacy though. They're much like chickens that way."

"Darling? It's getting tight in here," came Carl's voice from inside the press.

"Almost finished," Mrs. Woodcot chirped.

"Uh," Carl grunted.

"Do you know any sea chanteys?" Mrs. Woodcot asked brightly. "They'd be just right for this kind of work."

"No," Strix said. "I hate the sea. It's too wet."

"Oh, pooh," Mrs. Woodcot said. "There's nothing more boring than a picky child. Strix, go away and come back when you're forty."

A shining trickle of fluid appeared in a trough at the base of the press. "Lizbet," Mrs. Woodcot called. She pointed to a rack of apothecary jars. "Run like a good girl and get the jar marked *Libido*, if you please. Surely that's not too much for you?"

Lizbet thought about it, and decided that she might as well. Carl's fate was definitely out of her hands. In truth, she wasn't all *that* unhappy that he had come to a sudden end. Was she terrible to feel that way? Probably. She decided that she liked feeling both smug and guilty at the same time. The two contradictory moral sentiments complemented each other, like the sweet-sour tang of lemonade.

The *Libido* jar sloshed a bit when she took it down from the shelf. It was black porcelain, and warm, almost hot to the touch.

"Hurry!" Mrs. Woodcot called. She took the jar from Lizbet, held it under a brass spout at the base of the press, and turned a tiny spigot. A curved stream of seething crimson liquid hissed into the jar. Steam rose from the jar's mouth. Lizbet wondered what it smelled like, and bent to sniff it, but then drew back. Maybe that wasn't a good idea. She had studied enough Latin in school to know that *libido* meant "lust." Lust was still a largely unknown quantity to Lizbet. She thought she might have felt lustful once or twice, but wasn't exactly sure. She felt certain that feeling lustful at this particular moment wouldn't be helpful.

Carl certainly had a lot of *Libido* in him, Lizbet thought. It almost filled the jar.

"Now, hurry and get the jars for *Pax*, and *Misericordia*," Mrs. Woodcot said.

Pax meant "peace" and *misericordia* meant "mercy." *Pax* proved to be tiny opaque azure gems that fell into their apothecary jar with a pleasant clicking sound. There was very little *Pax* in Carl though. He had even less *Misericordia*, a sweet-smelling gray-green dust: no more than a teaspoonful.

As she watched Mrs. Woodcot fill the jars, Lizbet said, "You're the witch, aren't you?"

"Of course, dear," Mrs. Woodcot said.

When Lizbet first opened the door, Mrs. Woodcot had thought she had a baby with her. "People bring you babies?"

Mrs. Woodcot nodded. "Yes."

"I thought you stole babies."

"Is that what they tell you? Mortals are full of lies, dear."

Now that Lizbet thought of it, babies who were "stolen by the witch" tended be from families who were having difficulty feeding the children they already had. And they tended to be girls.

"People are awful," Lizbet said.

Strix gave a contemptuous laugh. "Mortals are good-for-nothing. Including *you*." She stuck out her tongue at Lizbet.

Lizbet clenched her teeth. However horrible Mrs. Woodcot might be as a witch, at least she was courteous. Lizbet was glad she wouldn't ever have to see Strix again.

Next out of the press came bubbling *Felicitas*, and *Amor*, that smelled like roses, both in very small amounts. There was almost half a jar of *Ira* though, hot, black, and sticky like tar. *Spes* came next, a small quantity of glistening white beads, like tiny pearls.

Lizbet had seen the Margrave take a pill just like that. In Latin, *spes* meant "hope."

The last affection to come out of the press was *Timor*, an almost weightless clear liquid with an unpleasant chemical odor that permeated the room. *Timor* meant "fear."

"That's the end, we're done," Mrs. Woodcot announced. "Strix, clean up please." Strix grumbled. Mrs. Woodcot frowned at Lizbet. Her wingy eyebrows tilted like a hawk stooping on its prey. "All done, dear. By the way, why are you still here? Most mortals would have fled in terror when we started to squish the late Mr. Such-a-One."

"Carl."

"Whoever. Run along now. Bring me a baby when you get too many. Boys will make sure you get too many, then they will complain about it.

Boys are hypocrites.
Girls are too.
Mortals are vile.
Toodle-oo!"

She had maneuvered herself behind Lizbet somehow, and her cold, bony hands were gently but irresistibly urging Lizbet toward the door.

"Wait!" Lizbet said.

"Oh, you're so demanding! What now, love? Make it quick, or I may squish you too."

"No," Lizbet said, "you won't."

Mrs. Woodcot let go and put her hands on her hips. "What! How dare you contradict me!"

"You said if I came alone, I had to go in the press myself. You said that was the rule. But I didn't come alone, and you got to squish Carl. So now you can't put me in your press."

Mrs. Woodcot spanked her hands together, as if she were knocking dust from them. "For a mortal, you're annoyingly perceptive. It's true, it's against the rules to squish you. Still, it's time to go. I declare you *personna au gratin.* Good-bye!"

Lizbet stood her ground. "Not until I get what I came for."

"What? I got rid of Carl for you. What else could you possibly want?"

"It's not about Carl. He was an accident. I just sort of picked him up on the way."

"That was careless of you. What is it, then?" Mrs. Woodcot yawned. "Be quick! I'm already bored with you."

"I came to ask your help," Lizbet said.

"That's easy enough," Mrs. Woodcot said. She smiled beautifully. "Refused!"

"You don't even know what I want!"

"And I don't care." Again, her hands propelled Lizbet toward the door. "Get along with you, now."

The next moment Lizbet was standing on the step, and the big red door slammed closed behind her. Immediately she turned and tried to open it. This time, though, it was locked, and resisted her efforts.

Lizbet yelled, as loudly as she could, "I need your help in crossing the Montagnes du Monde!"

The door popped open. Mrs. Woodcot looked out. "What did you say?"

"I said," Lizbet said, "I need your help in crossing the Montagnes du Monde, because I'm trying to find a book of magic that the Margrave lost, so he'll free my father who's in prison, and people say witches fly on brooms, so I was thinking that maybe you could fly me over—"

"That's what I thought you said," Mrs. Woodcot said. The door slammed shut again.

Lizbet assaulted the door with both fists. "Please!" she yelled. "Please, please, PLEASE, PLEASE PLEASEPLEASE-PLEASE!" She lifted with knocker and slammed it down again and again.

No response.

When she was exhausted, Lizbet sank down onto the cold stone step, her back to the locked door, and let her mind go numb.

The pigs in the yard stopped rooting up the grass for a moment and oinked at her. The geese honked. From a shed, two cows batted their lashes at her mournfully.

Chapter 5

When snakes walk,
And horses talk,
Then I shall wed the air!
When fire's cold,
And newborns old,
His scion shall I bear.
　　　—a rhyme of Strix

After some time, Lizbet rose to her feet again. She walked to the edge of the dooryard, and turned for one last look at the house. It really was a remarkable house. And Mrs. Woodcot, for all of her being a witch, was just as strange and funny as her house. Under other circumstances she thought she might have liked to have tea with Mrs. Woodcot, or listen to her stories about being a witch. Mrs. Woodcot was different from anyone Lizbet had ever met.

But she wasn't safe at all.

Lizbet retraced her steps, turning right at every fork, until she came out of the woods and found herself at the bottom of Abalia-Under-the-Hill, and daylight again.

Barely daylight. Even after she emerged from the Grove of Frenzy, its long chilly shadow covered her. Behind her, the sun had almost sunk behind the trees. In the purple-black eastern sky above Abalia and the Montagnes du Monde, the stars had begun to come out. A breeze blew trash around Lizbet's feet: scraps of brown paper, a discarded teabag, a bird's nest of rusty wire.

Lizbet was still determined to cross the Montagnes du Monde. She would walk, if necessary. It didn't seem hopeful she would succeed, but she had nowhere to go, and no one else to ask for help. She wasn't going to let the magisters put her in the Asylum, and if she had even the slightest chance to save her father, she wasn't going to let it slip away.

From the eastern edge of Abalia, dirt roads led up into the mountains, past sheep crofts and cattle pastures, into the fir barrens. She would have to climb higher than that, though, if she hoped to find a way through the mountains.

But first she had to get through the town. It would be night soon. If Abalia was not quite safe for a child during daylight, it was perilous at night. Lizbet had less to fear from the Magisters of Children and their marshals than from common criminals. Most immediately, the road back to the Wall of Virtue led past the tavern where Carl and his friends had been drinking. The friends might still be there. She might detour through the surrounding countryside, but that held the same perils as the city itself, and danger from wild animals to boot.

Lizbet decided she needed advice. She sat on the ground and fished from her skirt pocket one of the hosts she had stolen. She slipped it into her mouth and let it dissolve on her tongue. When she sensed God's presence (He always made her nose stuff up, rather like hay fever), she said, "Hi, Lord."

"Good evening, Elizabeth," God said.

"Lord, I need advice."

"My advice," God replied, "is to obey lawfully constituted authority, and not to consort with witches. But you don't want to hear that, do you?" He sounded peeved.

"I need to know how to get over the Montagnes du Monde," Lizbet said.

"No, you . . . excuse me a minute," God said.

Her nose cleared out. What could God be up to? Bit by bit, the host dissolved. Lizbet fretted.

Finally, the Divine presence returned. Lizbet acknowledged this event with a sneeze. "I'm sorry for the interruption,"

God said. "Satan's armies had a bit of luck—just luck, nothing more—and things were touch and go there for a moment. It's advice, you want? About the Montagnes du Monde?" His voice became stern. "Elizabeth, now see here. You haven't any reason for crossing the Montagnes. The whole idea's cracked. You'll most likely die. I regret that your father's imprisoned, but it's all perfectly lawful. As for you, you can't just go gallivanting around the countryside. The Orphan Asylum is the proper place for you, until you are of age. Now, I want you to go straight to the Chambers of the Magisters and turn yourself in."

"No!" Lizbet protested. "The Asylum is awful! They beat you for no reason! They'll turn me into a highwayman, or a strumpet. My father will die in prison!"

"I am aware of the horrors of the Asylum," God said soothingly. "Two of its recent Chancellors and any number of its inmates are now in Hell, and not enjoying it one bit, I might add. My advice to you is to brace up and make the best of the matter. Suffering is part of My Divine Plan. 'The Problem of Pain,' it's often called. It's a question that the greatest theologians have never satisfactorily addressed: why a loving, omnipotent Deity permits the innocent to suffer. Your time in the Asylum will allow weeks, months, even years of reflection on this important question, with the bonus of personal experience. Elizabeth, this is an unparalleled opportunity for spiritual growth.

"If worse comes to worst, and the Asylum ruffians try to make you a thief or a whore, think of it as a call to martyrdom. Consider St. Lucy, a Christian girl whom the Roman governor Paschius sentenced to be a prostitute in a brothel. When she refused, Paschius had her head struck off. What Christian virgin wouldn't want to be like St. Lucy?"

"I wouldn't!" Lizbet said. "I certainly wouldn't want my head struck off." The conversation wasn't going at all the way she liked. "Can't you just please tell me how to get over the Montagnes du Monde? Lord, I've always been good. Except for lately, that is. I say grace, I pray every night, I go to Mass with my father. I forgive my enemies. I do all that."

"Elizabeth, it pains me to find a good girl like you in this difficult situation. I am sympathetic. Truly, I am."

Lizbet swallowed the remainder of the host. Presently, she was able to breathe through her nose again.

She had stolen the hosts because she knew she was embarking on a difficult and dangerous undertaking. God had always been a friend, willing to lend an ear, or sympathize when she had a bad day. It was true, she had never had to depend on His advice before, but she had never needed much. It was discouraging to find, in her hour of utmost need, that God's advice sounded depressingly like that of any other grown-up.

For all the help God was, He might as well be dead.

Lizbet thought about throwing away the rest of the hosts.

She heaved a sigh and started up the road.

The sun had set. There were no street lamps here in Abalia's slums. Shadows engulfed the road. Lizbet could hear the chittering of rats, and now and then one ran across her path. The sluggish flow of sewage and garbage down the center of the street released a stench that made her gag.

She walked rapidly, trying to keep to the shadows. She scanned the street, and the tumbledown buildings on either side, alert for trouble. Although, if trouble found her, she didn't know what she could do except run.

"Hi!"

Behind her, almost in her ear.

Lizbet suppressed a scream. She swiveled to face the voice's owner.

Strix.

Strix glared at her. "Are you going to say hello?"

"What are you doing here?" Lizbet asked.

"You're so rude! I hate mortals. I hate them with a passion!" Strix said. "Why do I even have to do this?"

"Do what? I don't want you here!"

"Then that's two of us," Strix said. She dug in the dirt with the toe of her boot. "Mrs. Woodcot made me come after you. She said I'm supposed to . . . to take you over the Montagnes du Monde."

"Oh! Well. Good, then! That's good."

Lizbet's thoughts were racing in many directions at once. This development was both wonderful and horrible. She was going to get to fly over the Montagnes du Monde! But she had to go with Strix? That made her want to vomit.

A thought came to her. "Listen," Lizbet said. "I've got an idea. You don't have to come. I'll borrow your broom, fly over the Montagnes, and come back. If you don't want to be with me, you don't have to."

This plan did not get the reception she had hoped. "That is such a *stupid* idea!" Strix yelled. "If I even had a broom I wouldn't trust you with—wait a minute, we've got trouble." She grabbed Lizbet's hand and dragged her into the shadows where an unruly briar hedge spilled into the road. They crouched in the dirt beneath the briar canes. Thorns poked Lizbet through her socks.

"What are you doing? Let go of me!" Lizbet said.

"Shut up."

The touch of Strix's hand didn't feel like flesh, but crackly, slippery and dry, like a pile of leaves, or papers. Lizbet got goosebumps, and she tried to pull her hand away.

Strix squeezed her more tightly. "Don't move," she whispered. "Don't make a sound. I've got us knit into the shadows. See those two men?" She pointed up the street. "They saw you. They're headed over here."

"What do you mean, 'knit into the shadows'?"

"Everything that's dark and whimsical is my nation," Strix said. "I can knit us into the shadows, the way a design is knit into a garment. It's a witch thing." Her face was hidden in the dark, but her voice was smirky. "Mortals can't see us now. Not well, anyway."

In fact, Strix herself was barely visible to Lizbet. She could see Strix's hand grasping her own, but when she tried to trace Strix's wrist and arm up to the rest of her, her eyes lost track. Beside her on the road was a tangled ball of rusty wire—the exact shade of Strix's hair, come to think of it—a pile of dead leaves, some scraps of paper, and a knot of brown twine, but no Strix.

The men approached. One hungry-faced and hollow-cheeked, the other thick-necked and fat-bellied. They were the ones with Carl earlier. They came to within a few feet of Lizbet. Lizbet trembled. The thick-necked one said, "I saw her. That girl. The one that went into the Grove of Frenzy."

"Carl's still not back," the other said.

"Won't be back," Thick-neck said. "Not from that place. Don't know how the girl's back. Maybe she's a witch herself. Maybe she *lured* Carl into the Grove. They do that, you know."

That was the same thing Mrs. Woodcot said. The unfairness of the accusation bit into Lizbet like a tooth. Without thinking, she yelled, "I did *not!*"

Strix's hand, like a pile of leaves and smelling oddly like tea, clamped over Lizbet's mouth. Thick-neck looked straight at her.

For long seconds Lizbet met his eyes, terrified. Then, to her astonishment and relief, his gaze slid away and went searching elsewhere. "Did you hear that?" he said to Hungry-face. "She's here somewheres. Look behind that hedge."

The men stumped off. Lizbet released her breath. They had looked directly at her, but hadn't seen her.

"Boy, was that ever stupid," Strix whispered in her ear.

Strix's hand pulled at her, keeping her in the shadows of hedges and buildings. When they had gone a quarter mile, Strix let go of Lizbet's hand, and there she was again, although her tawny skin and clothing almost blended into the night even when she wasn't "knit into the shadows."

Lizbet had been thinking about what Strix had said just before. "Did you say you didn't have a broom?" she said. "I thought witches flew on brooms."

"Not me," Strix said.

"So you're not a witch?"

"I am too a witch!" Her mismatched brown eyes glared at Lizbet. "Well, almost nearly. I'm still learning."

"I thought you were going to fly me over the Montagnes du Monde," Lizbet said.

"I never said 'fly,'" Strix said.

"Then how are we going to get over?"

Strix shrugged. "I dunno. Walk, I guess."

Lizbet stopped. "I can walk myself. I don't need *you.*"

"You can't even get through this town yourself, without me to hide you from danger," Strix said scornfully. She kept on walking up the road.

That was true, Lizbet admitted to herself. All right. She'd let Strix help her navigate the dangers of nighttime Abalia, but that was it. She'd ditch Strix as soon as they were on the other side of town.

They reached the Wall of Virtue without further incident. Several suspicious-looking characters on the road gave them the eye, but none tried to waylay them. Lizbet's legs ached, and she realized that she was ravenous. She had walked or run for most of the day, and hadn't eaten since breakfast. The day's high emotions and dangerous events had sustained her, but now hunger caught up with her.

She looked about. Lamplight shone from the windows of a grubby pothouse built in the shadow of the Wall. Voices and music drifted from its door. Lizbet worried that there might be danger for an unaccompanied girl in a place like that, but once they had ascended the Wall into Abalia proper, it was doubtful they would find any victualer still open. Honest citizens of Abalia locked themselves into their safe stone houses at sundown.

"Strix," she said, "I'm going in that pothouse. I don't know if it's safe. Can you come with me, and knit us into the shadows if there's trouble?"

Strix looked doubtful. "The place is full of mortals. I can't stand mortals. Why do you want to go in there anyway?"

"I'm hungry," Lizbet said. "I haven't eaten all day." Strix, she decided, was proving less and less help.

"Oh, you don't need to go in there for *that*. Wait a moment." Strix crouched down. A rundown building with empty black windows faced the street here. Strix crept along its wall. She faded from sight.

"What are you doing?" Lizbet said.

"Hush," came Strix's disembodied voice.

Abruptly, she appeared into view again. She straightened up, and ran back to Lizbet. "Here!" she said.

Between index finger and thumb, she held a mouse by the tail. Its legs worked frantically, its sleek gray body twisting back and forth.

Lizbet flinched back. "Ewww! What's that for?"

"You said you were hungry," Strix said.

"It's cruel to make fun of me! I can't eat mice!"

"Why not?"

"People don't eat mice, that's why!"

Strix shook her head. "Mice are very good," she said. And as Lizbet watched, horrified, she tilted her head back, opened her mouth wide, and dropped the mouse in. Smiling, she chewed a few times, then swallowed.

"Ohhhh," Lizbet wailed, "that's disgusting! I'm going to be sick!"

Strix stepped back. "Really?"

"No, I'm exaggerating. It's just something people say. But it's still disgusting to eat mice."

"Don't be stupid," Strix said. "Mice are yummy. And for some reason, there are an unusual number of mice around today." Lizbet composed her features and tried to look innocent. "Such a feast! Anyway, how do you know you don't like them unless you try one?"

"I am *not* going to eat a mouse. I'm going into the pothouse. If anything happens, I'll run out and you can knit me into the shadows."

Inside, a few men and women lounged around a handful of battered tables. A old man with a twisted nose played a leaping, swooping tune on a fiddle, while a woman with a shockingly low neckline and high hemline danced in a way that you could see her white thighs above the tops of her stockings. Lizbet blushed.

The barkeep sold her a loaf of black bread, dried beef, and a couple of hardboiled eggs. Lizbet paid with some of the pennies she had taken from her father's study. No one else seemed to notice her. Apparently an unchaperoned urchin frequenting a pothouse at night wasn't unusual in Abalia-Under-the-Hill.

Outside, she found Strix creeping along the building's foundation, still stalking mice. A pang of pity went through Lizbet. Strix was arrogant and insulting, but—

"Here," she said, holding out one of the hardboiled eggs. "Take this. It's an egg."

Strix's voice was haughty. "I know what an egg is."

"Then you know it's got to be better than mouse," Lizbet said.

After a moment of hesitation, Strix snatched the egg from her hand. "Thanks," she said, as if uttering the word caused her pain. She nipped off the large end of the egg with her teeth as elegantly as a cigar smoker guillotining the end of his cigar with a pocket knife. *She must have teeth like razors,* Lizbet thought. The thought made her shiver. Strix popped the egg out of its shell in one motion and caught it in her mouth. She chewed and swallowed.

Then her mismatched brown eyes opened wide. She made little gagging or coughing sounds. Strix looked as if she had swallowed a live coal.

"Are you okay?" Lizbet said. A terrible thought came to her. "Was the egg gone rotten? Oh, I hope not." She wondered if she should wallop Strix on the back, the way you did to children who swallowed buttons.

Strix glared at her. "There was nothing wrong with the egg," she said.

"Then what's the matter?"

"Nothing's the matter. For *you.*" Strix almost spat out the words.

What an ungrateful brat, Lizbet thought as they walked along. She resolved not to do Strix any more favors.

Chapter 6

They strode quickly but cautiously through nighttime Abalia. Save for Lizbet and Strix and the odd gaggle of night-prowling goblins, the streets were deserted. Strix had never been in the upper city. "I like it," she said. "It's very dreary and depressing. All the buildings look alike."

"I wouldn't think you'd like it," Lizbet said. "It isn't at all like Mrs. Woodcot's house. That doesn't even look like itself. It's like a dozen different houses having a wrestling match."

"I like Mrs. Woodcot's house too."

"How can you like both things? They're completely different."

"I like all sorts of different things. It would be boring to like just one thing."

However, when they went by the cathedral, Strix gave it an evil look.

"You don't go to church, do you?" Lizbet asked.

"Certainly not," Strix said.

"You're not an . . . atheist?" 'Atheist' was about as bad as it was possible to be, in Lizbet's opinion. Worse than being a heretic. Even worse than being a Mussulman or Hindoo or fire-worshiper.

"Nope," Strix said.

"That's a relief," Lizbet said.

"I believe in God," Strix said. "I just don't like him."

"I like him very much," Lizbet said, "although we do have our quarrels now and then. My name means 'Consecrated to God.'"

Strix said, "My name is the name of an ancient demon that flew in the sky at night, and ate the flesh of mortals. It had its feet on top and its head on the bottom, instead of the usual way around. What does 'consecrated' mean?"

"It means my life belongs to God."

"That's awful," Strix said. "What are you planning on doing about it?"

"I'm not planning on doing anything about it!"

Strix shook her head. "If it were me, I'd be fighting to get free. It's awful to have one's life owned by someone else."

"You don't understand—" Lizbet began.

Strix glared at her. "I understand perfectly," she said, with such venom in her voice that Lizbet thought it wisest to drop the subject entirely.

As they climbed eastward through Abalia's rising streets, the buildings gradually became farther apart, and the Avenue of the Famous Virgins decayed from cobblestone, to brick, to gravel, to rutted earth. Before long they had left the city behind and were walking through hilly countryside, the lights of Abalia far below. The dirt road ran between high banks, where the night wind hissed through the grass. Sometimes Lizbet and Strix passed a wooden gate to a farm road. It was full night. The moon shone brightly.

When Lizbet was too tired to walk any farther they stopped at a farm where they found an unsecured barn. The barn was full of cows, and the floor was sodden and stinky with manure. However, the haymow was dry and a suitable place to rest after they had shooed out a few chickens. Lizbet hoped the chickens' annoyed cackles wouldn't wake the farm's owner.

Lizbet snuggled into the hay as best she could. In the distance, wolves howled. Lizbet had intended to tell Strix she didn't need her company as soon as they had left Abalia behind. But listening to the howls in the darkness, and wondering what other dangers might be ahead in the mountains, made her reluctant to send Strix away just yet. This 'knitting into the shadows' business wasn't perfect, but it was better than nothing.

Strix was still up, a dark silhouette in the moonlight, fussing with something in the middle of the haymow floor. "What are you doing?" Lizbet asked. "Aren't you tired? Go to sleep."

"I'm making watch horses."

"'Watch'—huh?"

Strix put something down in a puddle of moonlight on the plank floor. A straw animal, no bigger than one's hand. Lizbet could even make out details of the ears and mane, the powerful muscles of the thighs, the luxuriant tail. It really did look like a little horse. Lizbet was impressed, in spite of herself. She loved dolls, she missed her own already, and to find that Strix had skill in doll-making made Lizbet think a little better of her. A little.

The straw horse whinnied—a tiny, plaintive sound— reared, and trotted across the floor, its head bobbing.

"Eeeeee!" went Lizbet. She flinched away.

Strix's hand was immediately over Lizbet's mouth. "Shut up! You'll give us away!"

"What . . . how . . ."

"To watch over us. To let us know if anyone comes."

"But how . . . ? How does it . . . move?"

Lizbet couldn't see Strix's expression in the darkness, but her voice was proud and snooty. "Witches make things. We break things apart. We make new things out of the pieces. Magic. Don't bother your head about it. It's quite beyond the understanding of mortals."

Biting her tongue against an angry retort, Lizbet burrowed more deeply into the straw. Her anger was no match for her fatigue, however, and she was asleep before she knew it.

Lizbet awoke to the sensation of mice tap-dancing on her face. No, not mice, it was one of Strix's 'watch horses.' Before she could react, she felt Strix's hand, like a pile of leaves, over her mouth, and her other hand grasping Lizbet's own. By now Lizbet knew what that meant. She held as still as she could.

A man's face peered over the edge of the haymow. "Nope, ain't none of those tramps up here," he called down. "Don't know what was making noise last night, then." An inaudible voice from below. The man's face disappeared, and Lizbet heard the rungs of a ladder creaking.

Lizbet and Strix waited until the two men had driven the cows out, and the barn door creaked closed behind them, and then some more time for good measure, before they climbed down from the haymow and snuck out of the barn.

On the road again, for breakfast they ate some of the bread and dried beef Lizbet had bought. The morning was chilly, chillier than Lizbet would have liked, having come without coat or cloak.

"It's colder than you would think for this time in April," Lizbet said, shivering.

"We're already a lot higher into the Montagnes du Monde than Abalia is," Strix said. "It's only going to get colder. We should turn back."

"Of course we won't turn back," Lizbet said. "We've only just started."

"We'll probably freeze to death before long," Strix said cheerfully.

"You sound like you want to quit," Lizbet said.

"Of course I want to quit," Strix said. "I told you before, I'm only here on account of Mrs. Woodcot. If you quit, I can go home."

"Well, I'm not going to quit," Lizbet said. "So you can forget about that."

"Will you quit when you're frozen stiff?"

"I'll walk faster, to keep warm," Lizbet said. Strix just grumbled.

They passed no more farms. As they climbed the road, the fields around them became less sod and more rocky outcrops. The road itself became rockier, steeper, and harder on Lizbet's feet, even in her walking boots. The sunlit peaks of the Montagnes du Monde high above them, though, seemed no closer. Although the snow had already melted where they were walking now, the peaks remained snow covered throughout the year. Lizbet could see plumes of snow, whipped up by fierce winds, swirling off the steep-sided mountaintops.

Frequently they crossed over streams, bubbling and frothing with spring melt-water. It tasted wonderful, icy-cold, laden with faint mineral flavors. "I've never had water like this," Lizbet said to Strix as they paused at one rushing brook. She cupped the water in her palms and let it dribble down her face. "It's like you're drinking the mountains themselves. You're taking them into your body, making them part of you, making their soul part of yours."

"Cows in the upper meadows drink from the same streams," Strix said. "Do you feel your soul becoming more like a cow's?" She squinted at Lizbet. "Maybe you look more like a cow already."

"Why do you have to spoil everything?" Lizbet complained. "Strix, you're so rude."

"Only to mortals," Strix said. "I am perfectly polite to jinn, peri, dakini, tengu, and any other beings who *matter*."

Lizbet said, "People who are polite are polite to everyone. Being polite only to important people isn't really being polite. It's being servile."

"I am not servile! How dare you call me servile?"

"Anyway," Lizbet said, "Mrs. Woodcot is a witch too, and she's not rude."

"Mrs. Woodcot doesn't have to hike miles into the mountains in the company of a prissy mortal mooncalf." Strix looked her up and down. "A *short* prissy mortal mooncalf."

Strix was a half inch taller than Lizbet. Maybe a quarter inch.

Lizbet's Christian charity, normally considerable, now abandoned her. "It's obvious Mrs. Woodcot is not your mother," she said with decision. "She would never have raised a daughter with the manners of a drunken tinker."

Strix laughed, a sharp sound like a bark. "Mortals are so stupid," she said. "Not only did Mrs. Woodcot raise me, she *made* me."

Lizbet hesitated. She had not expected that. "Only God can make people," she said.

"Huh," Strix said. "I thought people were made by lovers, tangling up their limbs in untidy knots and exchanging vile fluids. I don't understand where God comes in." She peered at Lizbet closely. "Are you catching a pestilent fever? Your skin is very red all of a sudden."

Lizbet knew little about the practical details of physical love, but Strix's description was uncomfortably close to what older girls had told her in horrified whispers.

"Anyway," Strix said, "I'm not people. The old fussbudget in the sky has nothing to do with me. Mrs. Woodcot made me out of papers, dead leaves, cinnamon, twine, old teabags, wire and beans and shells and whatever else she had around the house. That's how witches do. I told you last night. We make things."

"I've never heard of such a thing," Lizbet said, staring at her. Paper? Dead leaves? She remembered how odd Strix's hand had felt: it was exactly like holding a hand made of dry leaves tied together.

"Mortals don't know anything about anything," Strix said with satisfaction. "Look here." She pointed to her left cheek, where dark parallel lines swam beneath the tawny surface. "Read this."

"Read?" Lizbet bent close. Yes, the dark lines were rows of letters and words, within Strix's skin. If she squinted, she could even read them: "'. . . brown or speckled trout may be taken with angleworms or red worms, crickets, grubs, portions of beef or pork cooked or raw, the liver of . . .'"

"It's from a book about fishing," Strix said. "I'm also made of tax rolls, broadsides, a pamphlet by a mad Englishman who claims you can square the circle, and some love letters."

"Love letters!"

Strix smiled and nodded. "The best one is from a comptroller of stamps to a woman who I *suspect* was not his wife. It's quite passionate and lewd. I have to use two mirrors to read it, because it's on my butt. Do you want to look at it?"

Lizbet shook her head in horror. "I don't want to look at your butt!" For a moment, she had been charmed by the idea that Strix was partly made of love letters, but the offer to examine her bottom was appalling.

It was too late. Strix had already hoisted her layered skirts above her waist and bent over. Her gray wool stockings were such a mass of knots and darns that there was hardly any normal stocking left. They were held up by garters made of rope as thick as a ship's hawser. That's all Lizbet saw before she threw her hands over her eyes and shrieked.

When she dared peek between her fingers, Strix had reversed her dishabille and was standing in the road pouting. She caught Lizbet's eye, stuck out her tongue, and made a rude noise.

Lizbet could take no more. "I can't abide you any longer!" she yelled. "You are coarse, you are boorish, you . . . you . . . you eat mice! You lift up your dress in the middle of the road and show people your butt! I can't stand being with you another minute. I don't want to see you ever again. Good-bye!"

With that, Lizbet turned and stamped up the road, away from Strix.

She had expected an outburst of abuse. None came. After a minute, Lizbet looked behind her.

No Strix. The road was empty, except for some trash: scraps of paper, some rusty wire, a brown tangle of twine. A breeze wrapped the twine around Lizbet's leg.

Anxiety lanced through her. What had she done? She still had to go over the Montagnes du Monde, and she knew no good way to do it. She wasn't dressed warmly, and Strix was right, it was getting colder the higher she went. She had almost no food left, and little prospect of getting any, up here in the lonely mountains. She probably shouldn't have sent Strix away. Although—Strix wasn't going to fly her over on a broom, and didn't seem to have any good ideas of how to get over the mountains. Maybe it didn't make any difference.

The road became increasingly steep, rocky, and tiring to climb. A trickle of water came down its center, and it gradually began to seem less like a road and more like a streambed. The alpine meadows on either side gave way to a dark forest of fir and hemlock.

Around noontime Lizbet stopped to rest. She was exhausted. No sooner had she sat down than the urge to sleep came over her, and she had to fight to stay awake in the hazy light of the forest and the turpentine smell of the conifers. She had meant to hoard the little food she had, but found she was ravenously hungry. She quickly finished the rest of the meat and bread, and she was still hungry.

Through the trees, she could see glimpses of the peaks of the Montagnes du Monde. They looked no closer.

Besides hunger and exhaustion, Lizbet had another problem: her feet. Despite her practical, clunky boots, she had developed large and painful blisters. She was unused to hiking. The distance and the roughness of the road had beaten her feet badly. When she finished eating and got on her feet again, the pain came back with full force. She squeaked out a little cry of pain.

For the first time she thought about giving up.

What then? Well, then her father would languish in prison until he died.

Also, Strix had encouraged her to give up. The nerve. How dare she? Mrs. Woodcot had sent her to *help* Lizbet.

Anger with Strix, coupled with pity for her father, drove her on. Lizbet again trudged up the road into the fir and hemlock forest, on painful, blistered feet.

The pain worsened through the afternoon. The road only became more steep. As she climbed higher, the trees became shorter, but the forest remained thick and impenetrable. The air was raw and cold, even in the April afternoon, and here and there were patches of snow still on the ground. Lizbet worried what the coming night would be like. She had heard that woodcutters lived in the high forests, and hoped she would come across the house of a woodcutter's family with whom she could spend the night, and who might advise her on the road ahead. And even give her a bit of food? One could hope.

But hope was all she had. An occasional boot print could be found in the damp earth where water trickled down the road's center. There was no other sign of human life.

Evening came on, and exceeding cold. Lizbet shivered miserably. Between the cold, exhaustion, and the pain in her feet, she was close to turning around and trudging down the mountain in defeat. How had she ever expected to cross the Montagnes du Monde by herself? But even if she gave up, she would have to survive the night here, high on the mountain. Could she endure the cold and exposure?

It occurred to her for the first time that she might not even be able to get off the mountain. That she might die here.

Until now, death had been a safely abstract danger, comfortably distant in the future. It dawned upon Lizbet that death might not be far off at all. It might be now, soon, this very night, if she didn't find some place out of the cold.

For the first time since Carl had pursued her through the Grove of Frenzy, she felt fear. Cold and death now stalked her as Carl had. Where was there a Mrs. Woodcot, however witchy, however evil, to save her?

Lizbet immediately felt ashamed. She was a Christian maiden. If anyone should save her, it would be God. At least, she should give Him one more chance.

In the icy darkness, Lizbet seated herself on a patch of the furry moss that covered the rocks in this place. She felt in her pocket for the hosts and slipped one into her mouth. Dry and slick to her tongue, it slowly melted.

Time passed.

"God?"

"What is it? Hurry up."

God sounded rushed. "God? It's me, Elizabeth."

"Yes, yes, Elizabeth, what is it you want? Please make it quicker than you usually do."

In the background, Lizbet heard shouts, explosions, and the ringing of steel on steel. "If you're too busy," she said, "can I talk to Jesus instead? It'd be okay."

"Jesus! Hah! Talk to him if you can find him. Here I've got devils coming out my wazoo, and the Galilee Kid is running around turning the other cheek, going the extra mile, whipping moneychangers. I said to him, 'You couldn't have whipped a devil instead?' He turned one devil into an olive tree. One single devil. That was his contribution to the war effort. I raised such a klutz."

Lizbet said, "I've gotten myself into a fix. It's a long story—"

"You're stranded on a mountain in the cold, I know. I advise prayer. And hurry off the mountain as quickly as you can. Go to confession and confess all the sins you've been piling up. Is there anything else?"

"But I don't want to get off the mountain! I've told you why. I'm trying to cross the Montagnes du Monde to find the Margrave's book to save my father!"

Nothing, for a minute or two. Lizbet thought she heard screams in the distance. And *billowing* sounds. The beating of wings? Flames?

"God?"

"Are you still here? What is it? I'm busy."

"I'm scared, Lord. Will I die?"

"Could be. Try not to though. If you die now, it's either Purgatory or Hell for you. Those sins, you know. Lies, theft, consorting with witches. What's next? Murder? High treason? I'm disappointed in you, Elizabeth."

Without thinking, all her pain, frustration, and fear poured out. Lizbet yelled at God, "And I'm disappointed in you!"

She held her breath. What had she said?

"God?" she whispered.

Confused noise in the background. Yells, explosions, the clang of bells.

"God, I'm sorry, I didn't mean . . ."

No answer came. After a few minutes, the host dissolved completely and contact with Heaven was lost.

So everything was in the balance. Really everything. Not just life and death, but Lizbet's eternal salvation as well.

In the gathering darkness, Lizbet stared at the road ahead. Someone must live up here, to have built a road. To have left a bootprint. There must be a house somewhere ahead. There must be. She rose. On painful feet, she struggled forward, up the mountain, into deepening darkness and cold. Every step felt like walking on knives.

Chapter 7

If it hadn't been almost night, Lizbet might not have seen the cabin. Light from a window shone from off to the right, deep in the forest. A footpath led to it, but where the path joined the road was inconspicuous. Fir branches stung her face as she picked her way along the footpath, headed for that yellow glow that promised warmth, blessed warmth, perhaps food, perhaps a safe bed for the night.

The cabin was more crudely made than any building Lizbet had ever seen, walls of undressed logs. Its single window was oiled paper, not glass, and she couldn't see inside. With a hand numb and trembling from cold, she pounded on the door.

She pounded again. Was there a sound inside?

The door cracked open. An eye peered out. A man's voice said, "Who're you? What d'you want?"

"I'm Lizbet," Lizbet said. Her voice was shaking from cold and exhaustion. "I'm climbing the mountain. I'm cold, and I need a place to rest for the night. Can I . . . can I stay in your house?"

"Who's with you?"

Lizbet shook her head. "No one, I'm alone."

"What's your business up here?" The voice was suspicious.

"I'm trying to cross the Montagnes du Monde. I . . . it's complicated. Can I come in? I'm really cold."

A long pause. The door was flung open. "Come in, then."

A man stood framed in the lighted doorway. Canvas trousers and wool shirt, ragged at the edges and none too clean. His short grizzled beard was in the same condition. His eyes were bloodshot, and his gaze wary. He had long bangs that hid his forehead and almost got in his eyes. Behind him, Lizbet could see no one else in the cabin.

When Lizbet hoped to find a woodcutter's cabin, she had assumed she would find a family: man, wife, children. She hesitated. This situation was not proper, according to how Lizbet had been raised. An icy gust of wind blew some bits of paper and other trash around her, into the cabin.

"If you're coming in, then do it," the man growled, "before the wind blows in more dirt." He started to close the door.

"Wait!" Lizbet squeaked. She dashed into the cabin. The man grunted and closed the door behind her. *Thunk!* He lowered a heavy wooden bar down across the doorframe. *What is he protecting himself from, way up here?* Lizbet wondered. *Wild animals? . . . Monsters?* For the moment, she was glad she had made the decision to come inside.

The cabin was blessedly warm, but smelly. A fire crackled and popped sparks onto the hearth, its flames providing the room's only light. Shadows filled the corners. The air reeked of smoke, spoiled food, and unwashed flesh. Lizbet tried to keep herself from wrinkling her nose. She was a guest here, and that would not be polite.

"You're shivering," the man said. He got her a heavy wool blanket and draped it over her shoulders. The blanket was heavy and felt greasy, but within its folds, Lizbet slowly warmed.

The man seated her at a rough-hewn wood table, grimy like everything else. From a pot over the fire he ladled an untidy pile of root vegetables—potatoes, parsnips, or turnips, Lizbet couldn't tell—onto a chipped plate, along with a hunk of boiled meat. "Go on," he said. "Eat."

He produced a cigar, lit it from the fire, and smoked it as he watched Lizbet eat, tapping the ashes onto the floor.

The meal was filling, but bland. Lizbet, ravenous, cleaned the plate in a minute. The man smiled for the first time. His teeth were mostly gone; the ones remaining were rotted brown pegs. "You're a hungry, sturdy girlie, ain't you?" he said. He fetched a stoneware jug from somewhere in the shadows and poured a libation into a mug. "Whiskey," he said. "Want some?"

Lizbet shook her head quickly. Whiskey was part of a far-off, perilous world of card-playing, fiddle music, thievery, fortune-telling, atheism, and the woman in the pothouse whose white thighs showed when she danced. Lizbet wondered whether Strix drank whiskey. She decided that she really wished she hadn't sent Strix away.

The man poured the mug full, and took a long drink. He wiped his mouth with his hand. His fingernails were cracked and had arcs of black grime under them.

Lizbet realized she hadn't introduced herself yet. She stuck her hand out of the blanket. "My name is Lizbet Lenz," she said. "I'm very pleased to meet you. I'd like to thank you for the food, and for letting me stay in your house."

"Uh," the man said. He took her hand in his and roughly shook it.

"May I ask your name?" Lizbet said.

"Uh-uh," the man said. "You can ask, but I ain't tellin'. It's dangerous."

Lizbet had not expected this response. "Oh. I see. Actually, I don't see. Why is it dangerous?"

"None of your business!"

The man's shout hung in the air. Lizbet hugged herself, not sure what was safe to say. After a minute, the man spoke again. "So why is a young girlie like you coming all the way up here where no one but—no one but folks like me live?"

Lizbet told him the story of her father's magical misadventure, his imprisonment, the Margrave, the witches, and her quest to get the Margrave's book of magic. The man nodded through the story. He finally said, when she was done, "What happened to the witch girl who came with you?"

"I don't know," Lizbet said. "She disappeared."

Perhaps her story made the man more willing to talk. Or perhaps it was the whiskey. "Your father's got it bad," he said, draining his mug in noisy slurps. "Being in the Houses of Correction. I been down in the Houses. Glad I ain't there now. Though being out here ain't good either."

This wasn't what Lizbet wanted to hear, that this man had been in trouble with the law. She told herself that perhaps he was still a nice man. If her father had been imprisoned undeservedly, perhaps this man had been too. She wondered whether she should ask him, but decided against it. She had never been taught the manners of asking new acquaintances about their criminal past, but suspected it was something one didn't do. Also, she was afraid of what she might learn.

She was going to leave first thing in the morning, anyway.

The man didn't offer to talk about why he had been in the Houses of Correction, but he wasn't shy about condemning those he said were responsible for putting him there. The rich. The poor. The priests. Judges, lawyers, gypsies, foreigners, Hebrews. Pretty much everyone, it seemed, was responsible for the man's troubles. But most of all, Hengest Wolftrow. Wolftrow this, Wolftrow that, Wolftrow had hated him and plotted his downfall since the day he was born to his mother, the goodest woman what ever breathed, despite her habit of smothering her houseguests and selling their bodies to doctors at the university. Hengest Wolftrow was a blackguard, a villain, a bounder, a knave. A devil in human form. He should be deposed from his position and hung in irons at the Plaza of Fear.

Lizbet, feeling the effects of a wearying climb, the late hour, and a pleasantly full stomach, had been fighting off sleep. The horror of the man's words brought fully her awake. "That's high treason!" she exclaimed. "Surely you can't mean that."

The man glared down at the table sullenly.

"Surely . . . ," Lizbet pleaded. No crime was worse than high treason. To revolt against a ruler was to war against God's law. It was an offense against the Great Chain of Being, that gave structure and order to all creation.

The man took a deep gulp from his pot of whiskey. Instead of retracting his words, he changed the subject. He complained about the rigors of living up here at the timberline. The harshness of the weather, the scarcity of game, the unceasing labor of keeping up the house, digging the garden, working his traplines. He needed someone to help him. It wouldn't be so bad if there were two to do the work. It wouldn't be bad at all. He stared at Lizbet. She thought there was a hopeful look in his eye.

"It must be so hard living here alone," Lizbet said, as cheerfully as she was able. "I do hope you find someone to help you. When I get back to Abalia, I promise I'll make inquiries."

The man grumbled, and stared at the table again.

"I'm most grateful for your hospitality," Lizbet said. She drew the greasy blanket more tightly about her, and yawned. "But I'm very tired. I need to sleep." She looked around. Perhaps she could just curl up in a corner? "I won't be any more bother. I'll be leaving first thing in the morning."

She rose from the table—and gasped in pain, and almost fell.

"What's that?" the man said.

Lizbet lowered herself back into the chair, biting back a sob. When she put weight on her feet, it was like standing on burning coals. Painstakingly, she undid the laces on her boots and peeled off her socks.

Her feet were raw, red, and so swollen she could barely get her boots off. The blisters had broken, and the raw flesh oozed sticky yellow fluid. There were even open sores at her ankles where her boot tops had rubbed off the skin. Walking even a few steps was unbearably painful.

"You ain't going nowheres on those feet," the man said with satisfaction. "You'll be staying awhile. A good long while. I'll make a bed for you in the loft."

The loft was at the other end of the cabin. It was open on the side away from the wall. Barrels, skeins of rope, firewood, and other odds and ends mostly filled it. A rickety ladder gave access from below. Lizbet scaled it with difficulty and pain. The man shoved some of the clutter aside and put blankets on the loft floor.

"Sweet dreams, girlie," he said. "I'm thinking that the pair of us can work out some arrangement to our mutual benefit while you'll be stayin' here."

He backed down the ladder. When he reached the floor, he took the ladder away.

Lizbet lay her head as low as she could and still see over the edge of the loft floor. The man had returned to the table and was continuing to drink.

Movement, deep in the shadows in a corner of the room, caught her eye. Did the man keep a dog she hadn't noticed? Or maybe it was a mouse. But when fire crackled and flared up for a moment, the object was revealed to be just a ball of crumpled brown paper, and a wad of twine.

How long would it take her feet to heal? Days? A week or more? Lizbet was willing to wait, although she feared what might happen to her father if she delayed.

Once healed, she could start up the Montagnes du Mondes again. Maybe this man would even give her a little food to travel with? But he was rough spoken, and his thoughts of treason against his lawful lord were shocking.

Before she went to sleep, Lizbet fished a host out of her pocket and put it on her tongue. She sneezed. She wasn't looking forward to an earful of recriminations about her recent behavior, but surely God could at least advise her on how to deal with this odd man. She hoped he wasn't still too busy to talk.

"God?"

She heard nothing but a soft hissing and popping. A faint whistling noise rolled slowly up and down the musical scale.

"God? It's me, Elizabeth."

The sounds were oddly soothing, or perhaps Lizbet was simply exhausted beyond reckoning. If God were present, He never said a word, and Lizbet fell asleep with the host still dissolving on her tongue, and her unspoken questions still unanswered.

Chapter 8

Lizbet woke to the man's hand roughly shaking her shoulder. He had put the ladder back against the edge of the loft. Lizbet rubbed her eyes. The cabin was still dark. "Time to rise, girlie!" the man's voice yelled in her ear. "There's no sleeping late here, like fine folks do in town. Go throw the dinner scraps to the chickens and pigs, and gather up any eggs you find. Don't step on none, or there'll be trouble."

"What sort of trouble?" Lizbet asked, imagining being pecked by an angry hen.

"Trouble like a strap on your backside, for wasting food," the man barked. "Quit your stalling! Get out of that bed and earn your keep."

Lizbet knew some parents beat their children, but Gerhard had never beaten her. The man's words made her mind go numb.

Lizbet's feet were so swollen that she could barely get them into her boots. Even though she left the laces loose, her feet throbbed. When she tried to descend from the loft, every step down the ladder caused such agony that she nearly cried.

"Hurry up!" the man yelled at her. He was at the table, and had already started on his jug of whiskey.

Lizbet limped around the table, gathering up the plates and combining the scraps of food. "Quicker!" the man snapped at her. "I want my breakfast." Lizbet tried to hurry, but bearing weight on either foot made it feel like it was being squeezed in a red-hot vise. Carrying the table scraps, she hobbled to the door.

The sky above the Montagnes was just beginning to lighten. Numbing cold air bit Lizbet's cheeks and fingers. A cock crowed in the near darkness, and a couple of runty pigs, scenting the scraps, butted her legs with their wet noses. Lizbet scattered the scraps around. While chickens and pigs clucked and oinked and fought over them, Lizbet strained her eyes to look for eggs in the predawn light. She discovered four eggs in nests the hens had made in the fallen fir needles.

"Only four?" the man snarled when she came inside. "You must have missed some. No, don't look again! Cook the ones you got for me. I'm starving while you're loafing around."

Lizbet's stomach rumbled. "Any . . . ?" She hesitated.

"'Any' what?"

"Any for me?"

"No! Not until you're done with cooking and cleaning and chores."

Cooking and cleaning *and* chores? How long would that take? Lizbet's stomach rumbled harder.

She stoked the cast-iron stove with firewood. She found a skillet caked with grease and burned food, and cleaned it as best she could. Soon the eggs and slices from a dried ham were sizzling away, releasing a delicious scent. Hunger overwhelmed Lizbet. Perhaps if she sliced off just a tiny bit of the ham . . .

"Greedy, lazy thing!" the man yelled at her. "I fed you last night for nothin', and now you better feed me!" So Lizbet piled the food on a plate and watched while the man wolfed it down. When he noticed her watching, he sent her out back of the cabin to chop firewood, her stomach still rumbling and cramping.

It was afternoon before Lizbet was allowed to eat, and then only a mouthful. Her feet were hurting enough to bring tears to her eyes, but the man made her spend the rest of the afternoon scrubbing the cabin floor, hauling water from the spring, and washing his filthy clothes and dishes encrusted with grease and dried food.

Throughout the day, the pain in Lizbet's feet worsened rapidly. By evening her feet were so swollen that she could not fit them into her boots at all. Yellow fluid seeped from the blisters. The skin was an angry red all the way up her calves and shins. She struggled back into her bed in the loft, almost lifting herself up the ladder with the strength of her arms, barely able to touch her feet to the rungs.

Before she slept, she said her prayers, for herself, her father, for all the people in Abalia. She prayed for every person in the Holy Roman Empire, Empress Juliana, and for heathens and pagans in foreign lands. Last, and hardest, she prayed for the man below who tormented her, because Christians pray for their enemies.

Sleep came quickly, but it was shallow and fitful. Lizbet woke in the dark, clammy all over with sweat. Even her single blanket was too warm, and she threw it off. She touched her hand to her brow. She was burning up with fever. Her legs were swollen to the thighs, and so exquisitely tender she couldn't bear even to touch the skin or roll over on her pallet.

She was terribly thirsty. Could she struggle down the ladder and find the water pitcher? But when she tried to sit up, everything spun around, and she had to lie down or she would faint.

In the morning, the man would expect her to do his chores again. What would he do to her when he found she couldn't?

Beset by pain, fear, and fever, Lizbet lay in the near dark, breathing heavily. She could not see a way out. Despair broke over her like a black wave. When she had fled from Carl, Lizbet had found an even more dangerous person to help her, a witch. But who could help her now? She wished Mrs. Woodcot were here. Or even the awful Strix.

Lizbet wished she hadn't sent Strix away.

Hours passed. Lizbet drifted in and out of a troubled sleep. Her fever waxed and waned. At last, groaning sounds below as the man rolled from his bed. His boots thumped onto the floor. "Girlie!" his hoarse voice called. "What are you doing still in bed? You know better than that by now. Get down here, and get to work."

"I can't," Lizbet called back. "I'm sick. My legs . . . I can't even move them. It hurts too much. I have fever. Please, can I stay in bed just one day? Maybe I'll get better."

A roar of inarticulate rage came from below. Lizbet flinched. The sound of boots stamping. The man swarmed up the ladder. His face was flushed with rage. He brandished a leather belt in his hand. "Malingering still!"

"No . . . ," Lizbet cried.

He raised the belt. "Sick, are you? Well, I've got the cure for that." The belt came down, like a whip of fire.

All thought dissolved in a haze of agony. All Lizbet wanted was for the pain to stop. "Please," she begged of the man, of God, of the empty air. "Stop. Don't. Help me. Please help me. Please. I beg you. Help me!"

A new voice, beside her: "You heard her! Stop hurting her now!"

Strix's voice.

The blows stopped. Lizbet focused her eyes. Strix crouched in the loft beside her, forcing the man's arm back with all her might.

But Strix was made of paper and sticks and twine. The man was bone and muscle. With a roar, he shook Strix off, and shoved her away. Strix teetered, yelled, and fell from the edge of the loft. From below, a muffled thud.

For an instant, Lizbet almost forgot her own pain and danger. She even forgot she hated Strix. Strix had tried to help her, and instead, Strix had been hurt too. It wasn't *right*.

The man's hand rose again to strike her, but this time, instead of flinching away, Lizbet raised her arm and grabbed his wrist. Her fingers barely fit around it. "You hurt Strix!" she yelled in his face.

Pat-pat-pat coming up the rungs of the ladder. A bare brown arm circled the man's neck, and Strix's face appeared over his shoulder. Strix grabbed the man's hair and yanked his head back.

The man's bangs parted. For the first time, Lizbet saw his bare forehead. A pink scar puckered his skin, in the shape of an 'M.'

M meant 'murder.' Outlaws were branded like that. This man had been outlawed for murder.

"Strix . . ."

"Help me!" Strix yelled. "I can't do this alone!"

The man was already reaching behind him to grab Strix and throw her off. Gritting her teeth, and bracing herself against the pain she knew was coming, Lizbet swiveled her hips, put both of her red, swollen feet against the man's chest, and pushed as hard as she could. She cried out as agony hit her. Strix yanked back on the man's head.

The ladder rocked, and tilted back. Ladder, Strix, and Outlaw all toppled to the floor with a crash.

Wiping away tears from the awful pain in her legs and feet, Lizbet peered over the edge of the loft. Strix was standing nonchalantly, dusting off her hands. The Outlaw lay, unmoving, on the floor beneath the ladder.

"Strix," Lizbet said urgently, "we have to leave. We have to escape *now*. That man's an outlaw. And a murderer. Did you see how he was branded? We've got to get away, or I don't know what he'll do to us when he wakes up."

Grunting with the effort, Strix rolled the ladder off the Outlaw. She examined him with narrowed eyebrows. "He's not doing much of anything right now," she said.

"Really?" Now that the ladder was out of the way, Lizbet saw that the Outlaw's head was twisted on his neck at an angle she wouldn't have thought possible. Looking at it made her feel queasy.

"In fact, he's not even breathing," Strix said.

"Oh. He's not, is he?"

"I don't think he'll be a danger to us anytime soon." Strix put her hands on her hips. "Lizbet," she announced, "the trail of bodies in your wake has grown longer by one."

"What?" Lizbet said, shocked. "I didn't kill him! You killed him!"

"Me?!"

"You pulled his head!"

"You kicked his chest!"

They both stared at each other.

Silence, broken at last by a cockerel crowing outside.

"On the other hand," Lizbet said after a while, "in a way, I guess, I'm relieved that *somebody* killed him. If you know what I'm saying."

Strix nodded. "You wouldn't have lasted very long, being beaten like that." She cocked her head and examined Lizbet. "In fact, you still don't look too good."

Lizbet shivered and wrapped her arms around herself. A chill shook her. Her forehead was still sweaty from fever. "It was lucky you showed up," she said. She had no doubt she would have been dead at the Outlaw's hands, save for the timely appearance of Strix.

Save for the timely appearance of the hateful, arrogant, irritating Strix.

How could she still hate Strix, after Strix had saved her? How could Lizbet be that awful? Something broke into pieces inside her.

"Strix," Lizbet said. "There's something I need to tell you." Strix stared at her with those mismatched brown eyes. "I want to . . ." Lizbet swallowed hard. "I want to thank you. For coming back. For ignoring me when I told you to go away. For saving me from that awful man."

"Thank me?" Strix was incredulous.

"Yes. For saving my life. For being . . ." She hesitated, then plunged on: "For being a friend. The best possible friend I could have, right when I needed one the most."

Strix rolled her eyes. Her lip curled. "There's no such thing as a 'friend,'" she said. "Friendship is a lie, made up by mortals."

If someone had stuck a red-hot knife into Lizbet's heart and twisted it, it could not have hurt more.

"It's not a lie!" she exclaimed. "It's not, it's not, it's not! How can you say such things? Take it back! Friendship is not a lie!"

"You're hyperventilating," Strix observed.

"How can you say that," Lizbet whispered.

"Friendship is a lie," Strix said, "that mortals use to manipulate each other. There are no 'friends.' There are the strong and the weak, the ruthless and the timid."

That could not be true. That must not be true. Friendship was so important that Lizbet would not let herself be friends with anyone, because it hurt so much when it was taken away.

"Why did you come back, then?" she asked. "When I'd sent you away? If if wasn't because you wanted to?"

"You didn't send me away," Strix said. "You said you never wanted to see me again, so I knit myself into the shadows."

"But—" There was still a mystery here. She felt as if Strix were tippy-toeing around something big and awkward, and Lizbet had the sudden feeling that it was very important to find out what it was. "But why did you help me? If he killed me, you'd be free to return to Mrs. Woodcot. You said you didn't want to come with me to begin with."

"You know why." Strix's voice was poisonous.

She knew why? Lizbet said, "No, I don't."

Strix clenched her teeth.

Wouldn't she answer unless Lizbet asked directly? "Strix," Lizbet said, "tell me why you helped me."

Strix stared at the ground. "Because I had to."

"Why did you have to?"

"Because I am enthralled to you." Strix spat out the words.

Enthralled? "What does that mean? Why are you enthralled to me? Does that mean that Mrs. Woodcot told you to help me?"

"Because of the egg!"

The egg? What egg? Lizbet tried to think. At the pothouse, she had given an egg to Strix. Strix had acted strangely after eating it. "The egg I gave you at the pothouse?"

Strix was beside herself with frustration and anger. "Why are you doing this? Why are you making me humiliate myself?"

"I'm not trying to humiliate you," Lizbet said, as gently as she could. "I just don't understand."

Strix spoke slowly, as if each word caused her pain. "Mortals fall under the power of witches if they tell the witch their true names, or if they let the witch have a part of their body, like a lock of hair or a fingernail paring. Or if they accept food from the witch."

Lizbet nodded. "I'd heard that."

"I didn't know it also worked the other way around!"

Lizbet tried to make sense of this unexpected turn of events. "You're under my power, then? Because you accepted the egg from me?"

"Yes," Strix said miserably.

Did that mean that Strix had to do what Lizbet said? "Um . . . Lie down?"

Strix just looked at her warily. Maybe Lizbet had to give a direct order. "Lie down, my good and faithful servant."

Strix stretched herself out on the ground.

"Get up!"

Strix got up.

"Hop on one foot."

Strix hopped.

Lizbet watched her, wondering at this strange development. Strix glared at her with palpable venom.

"Okay, you can stop hopping," Lizbet said.

Strix stopped, and bent, bracing her hands on her knees. "So you see," she said, "there's no such thing as friendship. It's all a lie. I am your thrall and minion. Not your 'friend.'" She spoke the word as if it were a curse.

It's awful to have one's life owned by someone else, Strix had said, back in Abalia.

"You really hate it, don't you?" Lizbet said. "Being my . . . thrall."

"I hate it, and I hate you!"

"Strix," Lizbet said, "even if you think there are no such things as friends—wouldn't you like there to be?"

Strix looked at her suspiciously.

"I'm going to play a game. It's like a pantomime. I'm going to pretend that you are my friend, and I am yours. I'm going to pretend that you helped save me from the Outlaw out of friendship. In return, I will treat you as a friend would."

"This is ridiculous," Strix said, rolling her eyes.

Lizbet said, "Friends are kind to each other. For example, if I were your friend, I would want to free you from servitude."

Strix's voice was bitter and resigned. "It's mean of you to tease me. No one ever frees a thrall."

"But if I were to do it, how would I go about it?"

Strix said, "You'd have to grant me equal dominion over you. Each opposing power voids the other. All bonds are released."

"Suppose I were to tell you my true name?"

Strix's eyes locked with Lizbet's. She barely nodded.

"I was christened, Elizabeth Theresa Isabel Lenz."

Nameless emotions fled across Strix's face. She held up her hands in front of her and stared from one to the other, as if seeing them for the first time. "The spell is broken," she said softly. "You've freed me." She gazed at Lizbet. "Why? Why did you do that?"

"Because I believe in friendship," Lizbet said.

"I still don't believe in it," Strix said. But she said it softly, and without rancor.

Lizbet believed in it, but would not let herself have it. To Lizbet, friendship was a thing as glorious and necessary as the sun. And as distant, and unattainable.

Sweat ran down her brow. Her fever still raged. Her exertions and emotional turmoil of the past hour caught up with her. She was burning up. Her head spun, and whirlpools of black sparks choked her vision.

Lizbet fainted back onto her pallet.

Chapter 9

Lizbet woke, shivering so hard she could barely speak. Her teeth hammered together.

Strix had knelt beside her, her face an emotionless mask. "You fainted," she said. She put her hand on Lizbet's forehead.

"My feet," Lizbet said to Strix. "They really hurt." Yellow and green pus oozed from the raw spots on her feet. The angry red color on her legs had spread up to the thighs. The skin there was broken out in blisters filled with dark fluid.

Strix said, "I think it's blood poisoning. Your legs have gangrene."

Gangrene. Blood poisoning. A boy named Offa whom Lizbet knew in third grade had it, once. A tradesman's horse had stepped on Offa's foot with its iron shoe, crushing it. The foot became infected, the infection spread up the leg, and the leg turned black and terribly swollen. Offa died.

"I know some medicines for infection," Strix said. "Poultices, unguents. I'll search in the forest for herbs." But Lizbet heard doubt in her voice.

Lizbet's fever raged on through the morning and afternoon. Strix returned from the forest with spruce needles, fern fiddleheads, moss, and lichen, which she pounded into a wet green paste and applied to Lizbet's legs. The cool sensation felt good on on her burning skin, but her swollen legs and fever did not improve.

She could not eat. She tried to take sips of water, but her stomach rejected even that. She dozed fitfully, a troubled sleep that brought no relief from pain or fatigue. Toward evening she woke confused, forgetting where she was. Delirious, she thrashed and fought with Strix for half a minute, until she woke enough to recognize her.

"Strix," Lizbet said. "I'm sorry. I don't know what I'm doing. I feel like I'm burning up."

"You're very sick," Strix said. "My remedies aren't working."

"Am I . . . dying?"

"I think so," Strix said.

Lizbet's head swam, and she realized she was sinking into a faint again. She felt for Strix's hand. "Strix. I don't know what's going to happen. If I die, I just want to thank you again for trying. For doing your best. For helping. For being . . ."

She couldn't tell whether she had touched Strix's hand or not. She lost the thread of thought. Her soul tumbled away into realms of fever and delirium.

From that point on, Lizbet was never fully aware of where she was, or even who she was. She had vague memories of waking once and finding Strix kneeling by her pallet like a tawny sphinx, watching, listening, holding Lizbet's hand in silence. In moments of wakefulness, Lizbet babbled confusedly about her father, about their life fleeing from town to town, about her fears, her dreams, the tiny tragedies and hurts a child endures in a world not made for children. She freely shared with Strix her most intimate, embarrassing secrets, things she would be ashamed to tell anyone.

Strix listened to it all with utter seriousness and concentration, as if she were a prince trying to parse the ravings of a god-drunken sibyl.

Lizbet woke.

She knew she had to get up soon, but for now the bed was so warm and comfortable, and she was still pleasantly muzzy with sleep, so she thought she'd just roll over, pull the blanket over her head, and catch a little more—

She rolled over, and the thought came her: *My feet don't hurt.* That brought her fully awake. The movement should have caused exquisite pain. But it hadn't.

Experimentally, she wiggled her toes beneath the blankets. No pain. She swiveled her ankles. She flexed her knees and hips. No pain. A wave of relief washed over her. At last, she was getting better! Her cheeks weren't hot either. The fever had broken. Somehow, she had survived the crisis.

Lizbet sat up, rubbing her eyes. She was still on her blanket pallet in the loft. "Strix!" she called. She looked over the edge of the loft.

The cabin door was open. Strix came in from outside, carrying eggs in one of her skirts. She looked up. "I think I'm better," Lizbet said. "My legs. They don't hurt. I think they're okay again."

Strix nodded. "You like them?" She set the eggs on the table.

"Oh yes! Isn't it true that you never appreciate something until—" Lizbet threw off the blanket.

Her legs were different.

Lizbet was pale-skinned, but her legs were even paler than before. Except for a few horizontal brown seams. Her toes were like round white pebbles. Her toenails were painted with little designs: a red heart, a diamond shape, a bumpy thing, an upside-down black heart with a handle. Her right big toenail displayed a colored drawing of a bearded man sticking a sword through his head.

No blisters, broken skin, pus, or any sign of disease, unless the brown marks were scars. How had she healed so fast?

Or had it been fast? How long had she been asleep? "Strix," Lizbet said, "did you paint my toenails?"

"Nope," Strix said. "They came that way."

When Lizbet lifted her legs up, she found them curiously heavy. Not weak, but heavier than she was used to. When she went to swing her right leg onto the ladder, to climb down from the loft, it moved more ponderously than it should. Lizbet cautiously climbed down the ladder. Walking proved to be awkward and off-balance, like walking after your foot's been asleep, but without the numbness. She would have to take it slow for a while. But there was no pain, and her legs felt strong and well.

Clunk, clunk, clunk went her footsteps as she crossed on the wooden floor in bare feet.

Clunk?

Lizbet stared and stared at her feet. Something else was different, and not just the clunking.

Her feet were reversed. The big toes were on the outside, and the pinky toes on the inside. It was as if her right and left feet had been switched.

She must have shrieked. "What is it now?" Strix said.

"M-m-my feet! What, what, what—"

Strix's brow furrowed. "I thought you said you liked them?"

"They're, they're on backward! What . . . how . . . ?"

"They're not on backward. They're on the way they should be." Strix sat down on the floor, unlaced her black boots, and pulled off her darned and knotted wool stockings. She kicked her brown feet in the air.

Strix's feet were on backward too.

"See?" Strix said.

So that's what had bothered Lizbet about Strix's feet when she first met her. The toes of Strix's boots went in the wrong direction.

"But, my feet. How? Why?"

"I fixed them," Strix said proudly. "Your legs were dying, and they were killing the rest of you. So I made new legs for you. And as long as I was fixing things, I thought the feet might as well go on the right way."

"New legs . . ."

Witches made things, Strix had said. Strix could make little horses that walked on their own. Mrs. Woodcot had made Strix. So Strix had made human legs for Lizbet.

Or were they human?

Almost afraid to ask, Lizbet said, "What did you make them out of?"

"Oak, and strap iron from an old wagon I found behind the cabin," Strix said. "You beat up the legs you had so badly, so I made the new legs stronger. The skin's birch bark. You're so pale, it was the best match I could find. The toes are stream pebbles. I cut the toenails from playing cards."

"They're witch's legs," Lizbet said.

"I thought about replacing them with the Outlaw's legs."

Lizbet's heart went ba-bump. "You didn't . . ."

"No, I didn't. See? You're throwing a conniption just thinking about it. I didn't want to hear you complain endlessly, so I didn't do it." Strix stared at Lizbet closely. Her voice softened. "Are you sure you like them? They're better than human legs, really."

No, I don't like them! Lizbet wanted to shout. *I don't want witch's legs! They're peculiar and scary. I don't want to be like the Outlaw, or like a witch, or like anything but myself. And now I have them, and I can't get rid of them, because my old legs are gone forever. And having witch's legs makes me different. And strange. And I'll never be able to go back and be a normal girl again, no matter what happens.*

I'm changed. Forever.

But how could she say that to Strix? Strix had saved her life. She had saved it twice. Strix had done the best she could think of for Lizbet: she had given Lizbet legs like herself.

Lizbet looked at Strix in that moment of silence and tried to read her face. She heard a new note in Strix's voice that she had never heard, different from all the smugness and superiority and insults. Something hesitant and vulnerable. The need for Lizbet's approval.

She could hurt Strix with a word, if she wished.

Instead, she forced herself to smile as widely as she could, and said, "They're perfect, Strix. They're just going to take some getting used to, that's all. See?" Stomping and thumping her new legs on the puncheon floor, Lizbet hobbled around the tiny room as fast as she could go, teetering and tottering this way and that, wheeling her arms to keep her balance, until she heard Strix laughing.

There was still the matter of the Outlaw's body. It lay where it had fallen, sprawled on the cabin floor.

"We ought to bury him," Lizbet said.

"Typical mortal thinking," Strix said. "Here you have a perfectly good dead body, and all you can think of to do is throw it away."

"Burying is what dead bodies are for. What else would you do with it?" Lizbet remembered the fate of Carl. "Were you thinking of squishing him in a press? But we don't have a press."

Strix shrugged. She knelt beside the Outlaw's head. "It's too late for that, anyway," she said. "They have to be alive when you squish 'em. When they die, the affections evaporate like ether. However, he has other things we can use."

Delicately, Strix inserted the tip of one index finger into the Outlaw's left nostril.

"Ewww," Lizbet said. "What are you *doing*?"

Strix pushed. Her finger slid in up to the third knuckle. Her brow furrowed in concentration, Strix squished and squeezed the tip of her middle finger into the nostril as well.

Could the man's nose really be large enough to admit two fingers?

But a moment later, Strix had her ring finger inside too. And a moment later, her thumb and little finger. Strix took a deep breath and braced her free hand on the floor. She gave a determined grunt, flexed her arm, and shoved. Lizbet watched, biting her lip.

Strix's entire right hand squeezed into the Outlaw's nostril.

"Ew, ew, ew!" Lizbet cried.

Strix ignored her. The muscles in her temples worked. She continued to push. By inches, her hand, wrist, elbow, and finally her entire arm slid into the Outlaw's nostril, up to the shoulder.

The thing was impossible, of course. It was like a dream, where you could fly, or monsters ate you but you were still alive. Except that Lizbet was wide awake. It was Strix. Being with Strix was like being in a waking dream.

"Got it," Strix said with satisfaction. When she withdrew her arm and hand, dangling from her fingers was a mass of iron-gray material that twitched and moved.

"What's *that*?" Lizbet said.

Strix sniffed at it, poked it with her finger, and said, "Courage."

Courage was one of the cardinal virtues. Lizbet balked at the idea that the Outlaw had any virtues at all. "He wasn't courageous, was he?" she said.

Her tone of voice must have revealed her thoughts. Strix snorted. "If you don't like 'Courage,' call it 'Recklessness.' Is that better?" She was now squeezing her fingers into the opposite nostril.

"'Recklessness' is different," Lizbet said.

"Is it? People call it one thing when they like it, but call it something else when they don't." Strix forced her arm all the way inside again. This time she drew out something sea-green, no bigger than a grain of barley. "'Empathy,'" she pronounced it.

Lizbet reluctantly admitted it must have taken courage, or something like it, to live up here, alone, depending only on oneself to survive day to day and year to year in the wilderness. "I thought you said that the affections disappear when you die?" she said.

"These aren't affections," Strix said. "They're virtues. Or vices, depending on how you look at them. They're woven into your heart. They go with you to your grave. Unless a witch harvests them first."

Next came a bright red mass that quivered and bounced. "'Rebellion,'" Strix said. "Or 'Independence.'" Whatever it was called, the Outlaw had a lot of it.

Again and again, Strix delved into the Outlaw's body, drawing out masses of material that that she named 'Kindness' (a tiny amount), 'Cruelty' (quite a lot of that), 'Treachery' (slithery, bile colored), and others.

When she was finished, Strix said to Lizbet, "What do you think? Do any of these suit your fancy?"

"What do you mean?"

"What came out of one, can go into another," Strix said. "With these, I can patch up your character any way you like. Need more Courage? No, you've almost got too much of that already. Any more and you'd start picking fights with bears." She eyed Lizbet like a dressmaker sizing up a bolt of cloth. "How about taking some of his Rebellion though? I think you must have had your hands in your pockets on the day they handed out Rebellion."

"I don't want to be more rebellious," Lizbet said, thinking of all the things she'd done in the past week. "I'm plenty rebellious already."

"Oh, goblin poop," Strix said. "If you were rebellious, you would have asked Mrs. Woodcot to overthrow the Margrave, or call down an army of devils to break open the prison and free your father. *That's* being rebellious."

Lizbet was speechless.

Strix went on, "Not that she would have done it. But the idea didn't even enter your head. Instead, you're off on this loopy journey over the Montagnes—"

Lizbet broke in, "You can just stop, because I don't want any of that stuff. I wouldn't want to be like that man, at all. Even a little."

Strix shook her head. "Mortals are so vain. No one ever really wants more virtues or vices than they already have, even if they need them badly. Still, I'm hanging on to this stuff. In case you change your mind."

Strix rummaged through the Outlaw's possessions until she found a bandoleer and some spent shotgun shells. She stuffed the squirmy vices and virtues into the empty shells, and the shells into the bandoleer. Slinging the bandoleer around her chest, she strutted about the cabin like a Barbary pirate, waving the Outlaw's shotgun at Lizbet and threatening to pepper her with Sloth or Whimsy.

Together they dragged the Outlaw outside and dug a grave for him in the stony, unforgiving earth. It was exhausting work. Strix helped, but most of the labor fell to Lizbet. For all of Strix's restless energy, she turned out not to be very strong, perhaps because she was only made of paper and string and pocket fluff. Lizbet's new wood and iron legs were still unsteady for walking, but they were powerful and able for digging.

"Do we really have to dig down six feet?" Strix complained, leaning on her shovel and panting.

"That's how deep a grave is," Lizbet said.

"Who makes this stuff up?" Strix said. "Would anyone care if we stopped at five feet and six inches? Or four feet? Or three? Why don't we just leave the Outlaw's body on a crag, for the vultures to eat? That's what the Zoroastrians would do."

"Because we're not Zoro-whatever-you-said," Lizbet said. Hip-deep in the grave, she shoved her spade into the earth and heaved out another shower of earth and pebbles. Her breath came in pants. Her shoulders and back burned with fatigue.

She needed to dig the Outlaw a proper grave, every inch of six feet down. A proper grave and a proper burial were the least she owed him. Because of guilt. Guilt for having killed him.

It didn't matter that he had almost killed her. It didn't matter that he was a murderer himself. He was an adult, who had given Lizbet shelter and food. For Lizbet to disobey him—let alone kill him—was called "petty treason." It was a crime, and a sin. Adults were the natural masters of children. For a child to turn her hand against an adult, even an evil adult, was an offense against the natural order of things, against God, against the Great Chain of Being itself.

Lizbet tried to explain the Great Chain of Being to Strix. "At the top is God," she said. Her breath came in huffs as she forced her spade into the stony soil. "The angels answer to God. The Pope answers to God. The bishops and priests obey the Pope. Nobles obey the Pixie Queen. Commoners obey the nobles. Children obey adults. Horses and dogs obey people. Everyone has their proper station." In her imagination, Lizbet could almost see the Great Chain of Being, like an immense glittering cathedral as high as the sky, a precise mathematic of privilege, obligation, order, and law. "If you defy the Great Chain of Being, you're rebelling against all the world and the heavens."

"Your queen is a pixie?" Strix said, leaning on her shovel.

Lizbet made a noise of exasperation. "You haven't heard a word I said, have you?"

"Children obey adults or they get beaten," Strix said with a shrug. "Commoners obey nobles or they're hanged. The Great Chain of Being is obviously just an excuse for the strong to exploit the weak, dressed up in fancy language. It's funny that humans would be ruled by a pixie though."

"Empress Juliana isn't really a pixie," Lizbet said. "She's called the Pixie Queen because she's delicate and beautiful, and all men fall madly in love with her the moment they lay eyes on her."

"Sounds like a pixie to me," Strix said. Exerting all her strength, she dug her shovel an inch into the earth and heaved a spoonful of dirt onto the pile beside the grave. "This would be easier if we were Zoroastrians," she said.

Evening gloom was creeping fast beneath the firs and hemlocks by the time they had the grave deep enough to suit Lizbet. With a dull thump the girls rolled the Outlaw's body in. In far less time than it had taken to dig it out, they shoveled the dirt back in and made a tidy mound across the top.

Lizbet felt she should say something over the grave. "Sleep tight," she said. "Get some rest. On Judgment Day, God will sort things out between us, okay?"

"What's Judgment Day?" Strix asked.

"That's when God brings the dead back to life," Lizbet said.

Strix nodded. "Oh, I get it. Like zombies."

"No, not like zombies! For heaven's sake."

Lizbet explained to Strix about the Second Coming, and the Beast, and the Seven Seals. Strix's Bible knowledge was spotty at best. "It's dangerous to read the Bible," Strix said. "You can burst into flames. I once heard of a witch who read the Bible by wearing gloves made of asbestos and isinglass. Even so, she scorched her eyes and had to put wet rags on them for a week."

Dinner was hens' eggs collected from beneath the trees, and ham, with biscuits fried in a pan over the fire. Exhausted by the day's grim labors, Lizbet had barely crawled into her loft and covered herself with blankets before she fell asleep.

She woke from troubled dreams of crashing thunder and a bolt of lightning that set the Outlaw's house on fire. Still only half-awake, she found that the house was not on fire after all. But she still smelled smoke. Cigar smoke.

Terror gripped her. Cigar smoke? *The Outlaw's alive*, she thought. He must not have been dead after all, but only stunned. He's crawled out of his grave. He's come back to kill us.

Pausing, first, to relax with a cigar?

That didn't seem likely. As Lizbet shook off sleep, the hammering thunder of her dream resolved into just plain hammering. She pushed herself to the edge of the loft and risked a peek over the edge.

It was morning again. On the opposite side of the cabin, the oiled paper window glowed yellow with daylight. Strix stood on the floor of the cabin, a hammer in her brown fist, pounding away at wooden sawhorse taller than she was. The sawhorse had a head, neck, and tail. As she worked, she puffed at a cigar clamped between her teeth.

"Strix? What are you doing?"

Strix turned, and blew a smoke ring directly at Lizbet. The smoke rolled through the air, like a serpent with its tail in its mouth.

Lizbet coughed as the smoke ring hit her. "That's disgusting."

"It certainly is," Strix said. She removed the cigar from her mouth and examined the cigar band. "Poor tobacco stock, grown too quickly, cured indifferently. Still, even a bad cigar is better than no cigar." She took another mouthful of smoke and blew a smoke ring shaped like a figure-of-eight on its side.

"I mean, it's disgusting because girls shouldn't smoke." Because it wasn't ladylike, but Strix wouldn't understand that. What else did people say? "It will stunt your growth," Lizbet said primly. She eyed Strix's boy-like figure. "And if you will forgive my saying so, a little growth wouldn't hurt you in the least."

"I don't grow."

Every time Lizbet thought she had Strix figured out, Strix came up with some new eccentricity. "What do you mean? How can you not grow? Everyone grows."

"I told you, Mrs. Woodcot made me. When she wants me bigger, she makes me bigger. She adds new gallows rope, weasel's ears, mechanic's waste, whatever she likes. Smoking doesn't enter into it." She filled her cheeks with smoke and blew another smoke ring, a complicated knot this time. It unwound itself as it traveled through the air, dissolving into twisting smoky strands.

"Oh. I see. I guess that explains why you don't have ... why you aren't more ... you know. Filled out." Lizbet was beginning to feel sorry she'd started. "If witches don't have babies in the usual way, of course, then you wouldn't need ..."

"Breasts."

"It's more delicate to say, 'a bosom.'"

"When I'm big enough, Mrs. Woodcot will create breasts for me," Strix said. "They will fill with gall and wormwood. At Satanic Masses on the blasted heath, I will give suck to fallen cherubs and the fierce spawn of demons."

"Strix, quite frankly, that's far more than I really wanted to know." Lizbet searched for a way out of this line of conversation. "Whatever are you hammering at? It looks like a horse."

"It is a horse. It's a witch horse. To carry us over the Montagnes."

Its skeleton was wood. The joints were articulated with leather. Its tail was a spray of broomstraw.

Midway through the day, they maneuvered the witch horse through the door, into the clearing in front of the cabin. "Soon it will be too big to get out," Strix said. "It would have to kick down a wall."

Lizbet watched while Strix worked. Strix sent Lizbet to fetch things she needed: dried lima beans for teeth, chestnut hulls for eyes, papers for stuffing. Lizbet was gradually getting used to her new legs. By evening, she had taught herself to walk about without holding her arms out for balance, although she wobbled a bit. Running or jumping were still out of the question.

Strix had her do little tasks, like unraveling rope to make the horse's mane, or cutting up the Outlaw's clothing and stitching the pieces together to make a patchwork hide. It fascinated Lizbet to watch Strix make the witch horse's muscles out of straw. It was like watching a master seamstress: Strix's fingers danced, tucking, twisting, knotting, folding, pinching. Lizbet tried to follow, but Strix's nimble fingers moved too fast. Strix noticed Lizbet's look of concentration. She said, "What is it?"

"It's you," said Lizbet. "That's clever. What you're doing."

"Uh-huh."

Lizbet's fingers were already moving in imitation of Strix's. "Can you teach me how to do it?"

"No."

"Please?"

"You're a mortal. Only a witch can do this."

Lizbet already had an answer. "It's pretend, again. Pretend I'm not a mortal."

Strix rolled her eyes.

"Thank you," Lizbet said. "You're really nice to do this."

"I am not 'nice'!"

You twisted the straw *here*, Strix said, and then you held the twist tight with two fingers while you tied *here*. Then you doubled it, and bent *here*, to keep it all snug. There was a special secret turn, and a mysterious inside-out knot, then several twirly loops that went in directions that Lizbet had never seen before. The first time Lizbet did it, the tightly twisted knot of straw flew out of her hands and shot across the clearing. Strix barked out her contemptuous laugh for just a moment. Then she stopped. Lizbet's cheeks blushed hotly. "Try again," Strix said in a half-strangled voice.

The next time didn't work either. "Again," said Strix.

The next one at least held together, but—

"It won't work," Strix said. "You made Mme. Minglefinger's Loop go widdershins twice. It's supposed to go widdershins once and sunwise once. Do it again."

"Who is Mme. Minglefinger?"

"A famous witch. She invented that loop. She said it came to her in a dream, of a snake revolving with its tail in its mouth. Or so she claimed."

"She didn't really?"

"Gossip is that Minglefinger actually learned it from a fallen angel in exchange for a sexual tryst so violent that it tore her into two halves, straight up the middle. Her apprentice had to sew Minglefinger together again with carpet thread and a darning needle. Do you want to try this or not? We don't have all day."

And so it went, Lizbet's inexperienced fingers failing again and again to make the subtle knots correctly, until Strix gave up on her and went back to making the witch horse herself.

Lizbet kept on trying though. She failed repeatedly, until she was ready to yell in frustration. However, she did not give up. Somewhere around mid-afternoon, after uncounted failures, she finally made a bundle of straw with every knot and twist correct.

"Strix. Look." With shy pride and trepidation, Lizbet held it up: a sloppy fascicle of twisted and knotted straw, the thickness of a pencil.

Strix glared at it. She took it from Lizbet and poked it with a fingertip. The bundle of straw twitched, just a little.

"It's not well done," Strix said.

"But it moves!"

Strix nodded. She frowned and glared at Lizbet suspiciously. "A mortal shouldn't have been able to do this."

Lizbet thought about that.

"Now make me twenty more like it," Strix said.

"*Twenty?*"

"If it's much for you, I'll do it."

"It's not too much for me," Lizbet said quickly. The hint of a smile crossed Strix's lips.

Lizbet's next three attempts failed, before she made another straw bundle so that it twitched when she poked it. She worked through the afternoon and into the evening. Her stomach growled. She ignored it.

By early evening, she had a pile of of twenty straw bundles by her side. The first were clumsy, but the last ones she made looked almost as good as Strix's. Her fingers ached and were covered with little cuts from the straws. Strix, meanwhile, had twisted and knotted dozens of times as many, and had already bound them together into muscles and attached them to one of the forelegs. When she stroked the horse's neck, it raised its leg and stamped its hoof on the ground. The hoof made a ringing sound, because Strix had made it of spoons and forks, braided together. The hoof glittered red and gold in the last rays of the setting sun.

"Now give me yours," Strix said.

Lizbet handed over her little pile of straw bundles. "What's it going to be?" she asked eagerly.

"The coccygeus," Strix said.

"The cox-what-y-us?"

"A tail muscle."

"Oh."

Strix laughed. "What's wrong?"

"I don't know. I guess I was hoping that it would be more important. Than just a tail muscle."

"If you were a horse, you'd think the tail's important. Chases the flies away."

"But this isn't a flesh and blood horse," Lizbet said. "It won't have flies . . . will it?"

"Maybe it'll have clockwork flies," Strix said. She was whipping Lizbet's bundles of straw together with string. Next, she nailed the joined bundle to the horse's wooden frame with tacks.

Strix scratched the horse's flank with a fingernail. The tail slapped back and forth. Lizbet gave a little gasp. *Her* bundle of straw was moving the tail!

They broke off work to eat supper. Afterwards, Lizbet and Strix sat together on the cabin's doorstep in the chilly darkness. Crickets and spring peepers made the darkness noisy. Strix was smoking one of the Outlaw's cigars. The ember glowed in the dark.

"How much longer?" Lizbet asked. "Until the horse is done?"

"Days," Strix said. "Maybe a week or more."

That long! With her father still languishing in the Margrave's prison. And no telling what they'd run into on the other side of the Montagnes, or how long it would take to find the Margrave's book.

"I'll help," Lizbet said. "It'll go faster with both of us."

Strix took the cigar out of her mouth and examined the glowing tip. "Are you sure you wouldn't like a puff or two of this? It's not so bad, once you get going."

The change of subject made Lizbet pause. She said, "I told you, it's not healthy—"

"I think it would be okay for you."

Lizbet couldn't decipher Strix's tone of voice. "No, Strix," she said. "No."

Despite her fatigue from working all day long, Lizbet could not get to sleep. Nameless anxieties bedeviled her. Every tiny noise in the night brought her fully awake again. Maybe it was just the uncertainty of the task to come, and the peril her father was in. She turned over and over, counted sheep, did the times tables, and tried to conjugate the verb "to love" in Latin: *amo, amas, amat. Amamus, amatis, amant* . . . Finally, after hours, she slipped into troubled and anxious dreams.

In her dreams she was riding the witch horse. A swarm of clockwork flies was biting the horse's flanks. The horse's tail slapped at them. The flies bit Lizbet's legs, because they were witch legs. Then they bit her waist, chest, arms, and neck. They buzzed around her face. Lizbet batted at the flies. Her arms were white and silky as birch bark too, like her legs. The birch bark covered her chest and went up her neck, and as she touched her cheeks she found that her face was covered with it as well. She caught one of the mechanical flies between her fingers and squished it. *Timor* flowed over her fingertips, clear and chemical. She licked up a tiny, bitter drop with her tongue. Fear filled her.

She was wide awake. Her heart was beating fast. She lay quietly on her pallet, her thoughts racing as fast as her heart. Her thoughts went, *No, no, no, no, no, no, no, no!*

Lizbet sat up. The fire had decayed to embers. Lizbet wrapped her blanket around herself against the cold, and descended the ladder. The Outlaw's canvas cigar bag was on the table where Strix had left it. Lizbet took out a cigar. It smelled pleasantly spicy when she put it to her nose. You were supposed to cut off one end before you lit it, weren't you? Lizbet picked an end, and bit it off with her teeth. The cigar didn't taste as nice as it smelled. Crouching on the hearthstone, she held the cigar tip among the coals until it smoldered. She put the other end between her lips and inhaled deeply.

It was like inhaling a cocklebur. Lizbet coughed violently, almost retching. She thrashed back and forth, gasping for air. Her head swam.

"You're not supposed to breathe it in," came Strix's voice from the loft. "Just fill your mouth with smoke."

Lizbet's coughs resolved after half a minute. Strix climbed down from the loft and sat at the table. "You don't have to smoke cigars, you know," she said.

"What else do witches do? Do they partake of inebriating spirits?"

"Mrs. Woodcot drinks mushroom and calamus root brandy," Strix said. "And she takes snuff."

Lizbet found the Outlaw's jug and poured out a mug of rancid red whiskey. It was even more awful than the cigar: it stung her mouth and even the inside of her nose as it went down, and left her gasping.

After several more swallows, Lizbet's head felt light and heavy at the same time. She liked the feeling, and to celebrate she tried dancing with her new witch legs and fell on the floor, giggling uncontrollably. Strix rolled her eyes. Lizbet next decided she could convert Strix to Christianity by singing her all the Christmas carols she knew at the top of her lungs.

She was belting out the second verse of *Adeste Fideles* when she realized she didn't feel so good any more. The room was spinning, and her stomach was—

"Strix, I'm going to be . . . uh . . ."

Lizbet barely made it to the door. She spent the next hour spread-eagled across the doorsill, vomiting onto the stone doorstep, while Strix alternately giggled over her and tried to express sympathy. Strix was not good at this.

"Say 'there, there,'" Lizbet said.

"Why?"

"Because that's what people say, that's why."

"Why?"

"I don't know . . . oh, I'm going to be sick again."

"There, there," Strix said, patting Lizbet's heaving back. "There, there."

When she was finished, Strix put Lizbet to bed. She awoke that afternoon with the strong impression that her head would explode all over the cabin if she moved a muscle. Gravity had gone haywire too, and seemed to be pulling her in every which direction.

"Do I have blood poisoning again?" she asked Strix in a whisper.

"No, I think there's another explanation," Strix said.

In the misery of her hangover, Lizbet clung to this tiny consolation: she had tried to sin like a witch, and failed. She hated both cigars and liquor. She hoped that meant she hadn't really turned into a witch. Please let it mean that. *I'm not becoming a witch*, she told herself fiercely. *I'm not, I'm not.*

Chapter 10

The witch horse took four days to complete. Lizbet's skills slowly improved, although she still lagged behind Strix. It was a large beast that looked like a dappled horse if you didn't look too closely. If you did, you could see the patchwork pieces of the Outlaw's clothing and bed linens that Lizbet had sewn together to make its skin. In its way, it was as mixed-up as Mrs. Woodcot's house, which seemed to be the way witches did things. That didn't make it any less impressive or horse-like. It neighed and whinnied, and reared up on its hind legs most grandly, browsed on the first shoots of spring grass, and in all ways acted like a great big beautiful horse.

They threw blankets over the horse's back to sit on. Dried hams and whatever other food they could find went into a couple of bags, along with a jug of water. Strix insisted on bringing the last of the cigars, and wore the Outlaw's bandoleer around her chest.

In the half-light before dawn, the air was cold and damp. The sky above the Montagnes had just begun to turn pale. The witch horse shivered and clinked its silverware hooves, as if it were eager to be off.

"I think we're ready," Strix said. She linked the fingers of both hands together. "Step here, and I'll boost you onto Violette's back."

"Who?"

"The horse."

"But 'Violette' is a girl's name. He's a stallion."

"I like boys with girls' names," Strix said. "It makes them seem more masculine."

"It violates the natural order of things," Lizbet complained.

"There isn't any natural order of things," Strix said. "We just make up stuff. Are you getting on Violette or not?"

"Wait," Lizbet said.

She hadn't tried to talk to Heaven in days, and her need to hear God's familiar voice had been growing. She said grace before every meal (while Strix fidgeted and stuck her fingers in her ears) and said her prayers every night before bed, but it wasn't the same. Things hadn't gone well the last few times she spoke with God, and she was scared to try, but also scared not to try. What would He think of her witch legs? But despite her recent problems with Him, He was a dear old friend, she missed Him, and she couldn't simply give up on Him without trying one more time.

She fished a host out of her pocket. "What's that?" Strix asked.

"It's a cracker that the priest blesses," Lizbet said. "It becomes the body of Christ."

Strix took this concept in stride. She put out her hand. "Can I see?"

Lizbet handed her the host, but the moment it touched Strix's fingertips, Strix shrieked and dropped it. Tendrils of smoke arose from her fingers. She stuck both hands in her mouth.

Lizbet retrieved the host from the ground. It seemed the body of Christ and the flesh of witches did not get along. "Are you okay?" she asked. Strix glared at her.

Lizbet, with trepidation, put the host on her tongue. It tasted more brackish than she remembered. Maybe that was the witchy part of her rejecting it. Or maybe dirt had gotten on it when Strix dropped it. But at least Lizbet's tongue did not burst into flame. She felt encouraged by this.

"God?" she said. "Hello, God?"

"Lizbet!" boomed a cheerful voice. "What's cookin'?"

God always called her 'Elizabeth.' Always.

"Who *are* you?" she said.

"It's God, darlin'. Who else would I be? I'm here in Heaven, resting my butt on a golden throne, surrounded by Powers and Principalities, all flappin' their wings and singin' to beat the band. Chowin' down on ambrosia, bouncing the cherubs on my knee. Not as special as it's cracked up to be, but not bad, not bad. How you doin', kid? How's tricks?"

"You're not God," Lizbet said. "You're not fooling me. Who are you really? Where's God? I want to speak to Him."

"The name's Belial, kid. I'm sort of helping God out for now. He's indisposed. You might say."

"What do you mean by 'indisposed'?" Lizbet said. "Is He okay?"

"He's fine. Now, what's your beef? I haven't got all day."

"I don't want to talk to you, I want to talk to God," Lizbet said. "I'm not leaving until I hear from Him."

A deep sigh. "Sweetheart, no can do. The old man's in the pokey, and the boys aren't in a mood to let Him have visitors. We got a history with Him, and there are a lot of hard feelings."

God was in jail? Lizbet tried to grapple with this idea.

"Let me talk to Jesus, then," she said.

"Hah! We'd like to talk to him too. The kid's on the lam. Hell is offering a reward of ten thousand silver talents if you catch Christ and hand him over. You'll have to steal the talents yourself, of course, but we'll keep the constables off your tail.

"Anyways, babe, I'm better than God or Christ. They had all these rules and restrictions, thou shalt not this, remember that, honor something else. Every damn thing you wanted to do was a sin. But Hell's in charge now, and you can forget that crap. You get to do whatever you want. See? It's gonna be great."

"Whatever I want?"

"The sky's the limit. Go nuts."

Lizbet thought about this. "Can I steal someone's horse?" she asked.

"You bet!"

"But you said that everyone gets to do whatever they want."

"So?"

"So I get to steal a horse, but the man I steal it from doesn't get what he wants."

"He just has to steal it back from you. See how it works?"

"Then I don't get what I want."

"So steal it from him again!"

"That's ridiculous," Lizbet said. "No one's going to want to spend their time stealing each other's horses back and forth. I liked it the old way."

"All right, maybe we haven't thrashed out the details yet," Belial said. He sounded peeved. "I guess there'll have to be some compromises, for practicality's sake. In the meantime, just figure out stuff for yourself. Check back with us, we'll probably have some rules posted in a week or two."

"I'll do that," Lizbet said. "And when I do, God had better be okay. Or you'll have to answer to me!" She swallowed hard, and contact with Heaven was lost.

Uh-oh. She had spoken out of emotion. Had she really threatened to storm Heaven and rescue God? As if she didn't have enough to do already.

"How's God?" Strix said.

"That wasn't God," Lizbet said. "Someone named Belial. I think Hell won its war with Heaven. The devils are in charge." She shook her head. "They have no idea what they're doing."

"Devils aren't much for organization," Strix said. "They like having a good time, they play too rough, and won't clean up afterward."

"It's funny," Lizbet said, "but I don't think this changes anything. For me, I mean. My father's still in prison. I still have to get over the Montagnes."

"Right. Let's go, then."

Lizbet put her foot into Strix's offered hands and struggled onto Violette's back. Strix vaulted on behind her. Lizbet stroked Violette's neck, whispered in his ear, and they were off.

The air was chilly and smelled of spring. The brilliant edge of the sun crept over the mountaintops. The sky was blue for ever and ever. It was a fine day for a journey over the edge of the world, and at this moment, whether the Powers of Evil or the Forces of Good ran the universe seemed to matter very little.

As Violette toiled up the mountain road, the evergreen trees covering the mountain became shorter and more wind-blown, until they were little more than masses of needles and twisted branches hugging the ground. The road grew steeper and more rugged. In another hour, they had left the evergreens behind, and Violette's silverware hooves clinked on windswept granite. Vast crevasses filled with snow and ice yawned on either side. The only route upward was along a spine of fissured rock that snaked up the mountainside. In a wilderness of ice and stone, Lizbet and Strix were the only living things. If you counted Strix.

The wind, which had been a fresh spring breeze down in the fir and hemlock forest, now whipped around them in a gale. Lizbet's skirt fluttered behind her like a flag. Her arms were numb from cold. After another hour of this, Lizbet and Strix agreed to cover themselves with the blankets, instead of using them as a saddle. That kept them warmer for a bit, but the higher they went, the harder and colder the winds blew, and before long even being covered with blankets didn't count for much.

"How much longer?" Lizbet yelled. Even right next to one another, they had to yell to make themselves heard over the roaring of the wind.

"How should I know?" Strix yelled back. "I've never been here before."

Someone had been here though. The precipitous ledges of rock on which Violette struggled up the mountainside were not just a path found by luck. They traveled on a road that someone had built. Switchbacks had been cut into the steep cliffs, voids had been filled with rubble, obstructing boulders had been rolled aside. Who could possibly live up here to do this? Had the route been cut by trolls, or giants? The work was years or decades old: where stone was broken, lichen had crept over the cut edges. Lichen grew undisturbed on the rocks beneath Violette's hooves. Whoever built this high and perilous route no longer used it.

The wind blew without rest. As Violette climbed ever higher, Lizbet and Strix found themselves surrounded by bare rock. Even the snow could not resist the wind, and lingered in white rivulets only in cracks between the stones. When Lizbet looked down, Abalia was lost in haze and distance. Above, the sky had become so dark blue that it was almost black, but the sun was brighter than ever.

Lizbet shivered constantly in the cold. The blankets weren't enough. The wind cut right through them. It felt as if it were cutting through her own body as well, as if the wind were ripping her apart. The sensation was unpleasant and frightening. Lizbet turned her head to yell at Strix, but instead of words, something else came out of her mouth. A pale white mass bubbled out of her throat like a balloon, filling her mouth and nose, choking her.

Her soul.

Frantically, Lizbet tried to swallow it. She pushed at her soul with her hand, trying to shove it back down her throat. It must be the wind. They were near the heart of winds that blew down from the Montagnes. The winds were so strong here that they could even tear out the soul of a girl Lizbet's age.

Lizbet's soul filled her mouth. She couldn't speak. Only her frantic eyes begged Strix for aid.

Strix threw herself on top of Lizbet. One hand covered Lizbet's mouth and nose. With her other hand, she pulled the blanket over them both.

The effect was immediate. It was if someone had buried Lizbet beneath fifty pounds of fallen leaves and crumpled paper. The force of the wind lessened. The sensation of Lizbet being torn in two receded. Her soul slid down her throat and melted into her body. For now, Lizbet was whole again.

She was warmer as well. Strix was good insulation against the awful wind.

"Thank you," Lizbet whispered through Strix's fingers. She thought of something. "But isn't your soul in danger as well?"

"I don't have a soul," Strix said. "All I have is a body. Souls are nothing but bother."

Lizbet decided this was not a good time to argue with that idea.

Clink-clink, clink-clink went Violette's hooves on the stones.

"I suppose I'll just have to cover you up the rest of the way over the Montagnes," Strix said. "Mortals are so frail."

Beneath the blanket, and beneath Strix, it was dark, and oddly cozy, with the wind howling without. It reminded Lizbet of autumns when she was little. People swept fallen leaves from their dooryards into piles. It was fun to hide underneath a big pile of leaves, concealed yet still able to breathe, and still able to see scraps of sunlight coming through the crevices. Children played hide-and-seek in the piles, covering themselves up. Lizbet remembered how the dry leaf dust in her nose always made her sneeze, and gave her away.

She sneezed.

She waited for the automatic 'God bless you,' that people said when you sneezed. Strix was silent.

"You should say 'God bless you' when someone sneezes," Lizbet said.

"I told you," Strix said. "I don't like God. I wouldn't wish his blessings on anyone."

"You're overthinking this, Strix. It's just to be polite. People say all sorts of things to be polite, without worrying about the theological implications."

"What do mortals say when someone farts?" Strix asked.

"Nothing! The very idea."

"Do they say something when someone pees?"

"No!"

"When they poop?"

"No! No, no no!"

"How about when they—"

"Strix, stop! Whatever you're going to say, I'm scared to hear it. We only say something for a sneeze."

Higher and higher they climbed. Lizbet's breath came fast in the thin air. Gusts of wind that found their way through the blankets and through Strix bit into her flesh like iron needles.

Violette halted. He restlessly clinked his hooves on the stones.

Had the path given out? Had they reached a dead end? "What's happening?" Lizbet asked anxiously. "Is everything okay?"

"I think so," Strix said. "We're at the top."

Lizbet's heart thumped. The top of the Montagnes du Monde? "Can I see?" she asked.

"No," Strix said. "It's too dangerous."

"Just for a moment?"

"No."

Lizbet struggled upward, shoving her head between Strix's arm and body. She pushed the blanket aside with her face.

"Why do I even try?" Strix said. She covered Lizbet's mouth and nose again with her hand to hold in Lizbet's soul.

Icy wind lashed Lizbet's skin, as if it were trying to tear out her soul through her very pores. Her eyeballs were cold when she blinked her eyes. After only moments her cheeks were numb and nerveless. She would not be able to withstand it long. She looked around.

On either side, the crests of the Montagnes stretched to the north and south horizons, an archipelago of granite islands jutting through clouds that concealed the world below. Steep mountainside fell away to the east and west. Above, the sky was black as night, the sun hot and almost white. Strangely for midday, the stars were out.

There was a hole in the sky.

Lizbet almost didn't see it: a black void in the black firmament. But if she looked closely she could see sunlight glinting on its broken edges. It was large, three or four times the size of the moon. And was the hole moving across the sky as she watched, just a little, from east to west?

She had little time to consider this. In only moments the gale winds chilled her so much she could barely move. Lizbet pulled her head back under Strix and curled herself up against Violette's back. Strix whispered encouragement to Violette and he walked forward, down the rocky mountainside. For the first time since the journey's start, they were descending rather than climbing.

Into a world unknown.

Chapter 11

The winds that roared against the eastern slopes of the Montagnes du Monde were no less cold or perilous than the winds on the western side. Lizbet huddled beneath Strix and the blankets for hours, listening to Violette's hooves going *clink-clink, clink-clink* down the rocks, feeling the stallion's muscles move beneath her. By the time Strix shook her shoulder and told her it was safe to sit up again, they had come far down the mountainside.

Lizbet sat up, rubbed her eyes against the light, and looked around. Violette was walking on a downward trail through dense forest, but the forest trees were . . . odd. They wouldn't quite come into focus.

One sort of tree looked like a spruce from a distance, but the closer you got, the more you realized that it wasn't a spruce at all. As Violette walked underneath, Lizbet stretched up and plucked off a shoot to examine it.

Instead of needles, the twig was clothed in soft azure feathers. The stem was not a twig of green wood, but a steel buttonhook. When Lizbet looked closely at the other forest trees, they proved to be equally odd. One had branches made of rakes. On tips of their tines, tiny umbrellas were opening. Another tree, that at first looked like a willow, was not covered with dangling leaves and branches but paper streamers. Out of the forest floor, instead of fiddlehead ferns, curled rods of black iron erupted, like the tops of wrought-iron fence staves. Yet, now and then, Lizbet saw a real, ordinary tree, a larch or a fir, and here and there a real fern poked its green whorl from the ground.

Once Lizbet might have been simply astonished and charmed by such a curious forest. Now, though, she recognized something familiar in it. Like Violette, or Strix herself, the forest was cobbled together out of all sorts of different things. Like Lizbet's legs.

"It's a witch forest," she said to Strix. "It's like a forest a witch would make."

"I like it," Strix said.

"So there are witches here?"

Strix nodded. "Mrs. Woodcot knows some of them."

A faint trail led between the trees. Lizbet spotted a footprint in the soft earth near a puddle and jumped off Violette to examine it. But it was only the three-toed splay footprint of a goblin.

After they had descended for several hours through the witch forest, the trees abruptly gave out. They emerged from the wood into a wide alpine meadow broken by rocky outcrops. Strix brought Violette to a halt. It was mid-afternoon. Sunlight fell from behind, casting their shadows onto the rutted road in front of them. The road ran between the falling hills, disappearing into a valley, then emerging again, until it was lost to the eye.

Lizbet's gaze followed the hills down. Far away, at the foot of the mountains, half seen in the cloudy distance and shimmering air, the land turned flat. A broad plain stretched eastward to a blue and hazy horizon.

"There's a whole world here," Lizbet said uncertainly. Might it be as large as the world she'd left behind? The wide sky and the endless earth made Lizbet feel tiny. How was she to find the Margrave's lost book in all this immensity?

Twilight began early on the eastern slopes of the Montagnes but lingered a long while: the sun, declining in the west, disappeared behind the mountains hours before daylight left the sky. When the sun was long gone, and the sky had finally begun to grow dim, the girls stopped for the night. On a hilltop near the road they found a copse of shrubby trees that looked suspiciously as if they had been constructed of worn-out brooms. The ground was littered with fallen broomstraws and made a tolerable seat or bed. Lizbet and Strix spread out the blankets on top.

They had no way to build a fire. For supper they gnawed off bites of dried ham as tough as leather and chewed handfuls of dried pod beans until Lizbet's jaws and temples ached. She envied Strix her razor-sharp teeth. She wondered if Strix could replace her teeth with stronger, sharper witchy teeth.

No! she told herself. What was she thinking? She didn't want to be any more of a witch than she was already.

Besides being tough, the dried ham was intensely salty. It left Lizbet dry-mouthed and thirsty. They had already finished the jug they had brought along, so she set off across the meadow in search of water. The meadow grasses, just now springing from the dead brown mounds of last year's growth, resembled the braid on soldiers' epaulets and banknotes scissored into leaf shapes. Lizbet plucked one. It had an engraving on it of an elegantly dressed woman with three chins, and tall white hair hung with strands of beads. Here and there a pink or yellow paper pinwheel thrust out of the turf, spinning on its stick in the dusk. Stars were beginning to appear on the eastern horizon.

The sound of water rattling over stones led Lizbet to a stream. It was clear, and bitter cold. Lizbet found a pool where minnows darted among misty clumps of roots. She lowered the jug into the pool. Water gurgled in.

One clump of roots circled the jug, feeling and exploring it.

Alarmed, Lizbet lifted the jug out of the water and brushed the roots off with her fingers. Immediately the roots whipped back and forth, and vanished. The muddied water cleared. Nervous, but curious, Lizbet reached in and touched another root. It, too, thrashed about, then vanished. This time Lizbet saw that it had pulled back into the streambank. "Come look at this!" she called to Strix.

As Strix looked over her shoulder, Lizbet reached into the water and flicked one root after another with her finger. As she touched them, they pulled back into the bank. Soon the pool was empty.

"You shouldn't bother strangers," Strix said.

"Strangers?"

"Witches."

Lizbet frowned. "Witches? Those are witches?"

"Those are witches fingers," Strix said. "There are witches that are made of roots, grubs, clay, pebbles, and badger holes. They're slender, crooked, and hard like wood or stone. They burrow through the earth. Sometimes they stick their fingers out of riverbanks, like willow roots, and tickle the fish. They eat corpses they find in graves and steal bags of coins that misers bury in their gardens."

Lizbet thought about witches burrowing through the earth beneath everyone's feet, and shivered. "There are really witches underground?" she said. She stamped her foot on the ground. It seemed solid enough.

"Don't do that," Strix said.

The ground began to rumble and shake. Pebbles danced. Alarmed, Lizbet drew back.

Not a moment too soon. The earth fissured. Dirt sprayed into the air, and amidst the geyser, something thrust up and regarded Lizbet with black depthless eyes. It was terribly thin and twisted and brown like a root and seemed to have four or five arms with dozens of spidery fingers that stretched and branched into tiny threads.

"What have you got for me, sweetie?" she said.

"I . . . ," Lizbet said. She turned to Strix, expecting help. Strix was gone.

"Did you bring me a present, dearie?" The witch turned her head to regard Lizbet. Her joints creaked as they moved. "You called me out of the earth to give me a present. What's my present? What is it, honey? Where's my present? I want my present." She swayed forward until her mouth, a yawning dark blot, was only inches away from Lizbet's face. Her breath smelled of soil. Tiny white grubs crawled over her.

"I don't have . . . I didn't know . . . ," Lizbet said. She backed away.

The earth witch dived back into her hole and vanished. Relief washed over Lizbet. She turned and walked away as quickly as she could without stumbling.

Beneath her feet, a rumbling and shaking. The ground rolled beneath her. Lizbet barely kept her balance. In front of her the earth fountained up. There was the witch. Her bottomless eyes and mouth regarded Lizbet. Lizbet's heart rattled in her chest. The witch could dig through the earth faster than Lizbet could walk. "You're rude to run away so fast, honey," the earth witch said. "You haven't given me my present yet. I want my present. Are you my present? Should I take you down into the earth with me? I like corpses. Can you be my corpse?"

"No!" Lizbet said. "No! I'm not your corpse. It was a mistake, I didn't—"

The earth witch's crooked arms reached out for her. Lizbet swallowed a shriek as cold tendril fingers brushed her skin.

"Here's a corpse for you!"

Strix's voice.

An object came hurtling out of the twilight. The earth witch reached up and caught it. It was one of the hams.

"Thank you, baby," the earth witch said. She cackled. "Come back someday. Bring me another present!" She bent double, dived into the earth, and was gone.

Cicadas and spring peepers, with voices like the brass reeds of spring-wound music boxes, filled the twilight with their singing. A breeze rustled the banknote grass. The evening had returned to normal. Save for the circle of disturbed ground where the earth witch had vanished, there was no sign that anything unusual had happened.

"Thanks," Lizbet said, her voice shaking.

Strix shook her head. "It's never good to disturb people you don't know," she said.

By the time they got back to the copse of broom trees and Violette, it was almost fully dark. "Oh, Strix, look," Lizbet said. She pointed down the hillside.

On the distant plains to the east, twinkling lights had appeared.

The dangers and worries of the last day fled in a moment. Lizbet threw her arms around Strix from behind and bounced up and down. "Look, Strix, look! Lights! There must be people here! Maybe even a town. I was so afraid this whole world didn't have anyone in it. But there are people! If the Margrave took this same route over the Montagnes, maybe he passed through there. We can ask them. We'll search for clues. We'll be like inquisitors. We'll find the Margrave's book. We'll save my father. We can do it!"

"You make it sound so easy, all of a sudden," Strix said.

"Not exactly easy," Lizbet said. She stopped bouncing. "I know it's still hard. But it's always better to be hopeful than despairing. You can at least be hopeful, can't you, Strix?"

"Uh-huh," Strix said glumly.

Sunlight woke them on their bed of broomstraws. After a jaw-breaking breakfast (dried ham and dried beans again), the girls set forth. The morning was cool and fair. Towers of white cloud cast vast shadows that crawled across the land below. Strix bounced along atop Violette, singing doggerel:

"One boy wondering,
Two scolds yelling,
Three storms thundering,
Four bells knelling,
Five dogs fighting
Six ships sinking,
Seven swords smiting,
Eight pens inking,
Nine whores bedded,
Ten kings beheaded . . ."

Lizbet thought she'd walk instead of ride. This gave her the chance to practice the fine points of balance on her new legs. They still wobbled, just a little. The last margin of skill, to learn to walk as gracefully as ordinary people walk, eluded her. Through the morning, as they traveled down out of the foothills of the Montagnes toward the plains beyond, Lizbet struggled to relearn the easy gait that she had always taken for granted.

After a while, understanding bubbled up from the secret parliaments of the soul where our decisions are made before we know we have made them. Why did she especially care about walking gracefully, at this moment?

It was the opinions of strangers.

They'd be coming to where those lights had been the night before. She expected houses, people, maybe a country crossroads village, maybe even a town. If she stumbled, or walked awkwardly, the people there would snicker at her. Or, if they didn't, they would treat her with the too gentle, over-courteous manner that the well-bred reserve for the crippled, that serves in place of an insult.

The thought stopped Lizbet in her tracks. Strix halted Violette and looked back. "Hurry up," she said. "Or do you want to ride for a while?"

"Strix," Lizbet said, "isn't it awful that we care about the opinions of strangers more than those of our friends? I don't care if I'm awkward on my legs around you, but I'd be all blushes if some stranger I don't even care about saw me, and smirked. It's such a shame, isn't it? I suppose it's because . . ."

She had been about to say, ". . . because friends trust in each other's affection, so moments of awkwardness or foolishness don't matter." But then she remembered that Strix wasn't a friend. Lizbet had been acting like a friend to her, because it was the proper thing to do, since Strix's timely appearance had saved her from the Outlaw.

But now she was thinking of Strix as a friend even when she didn't mean to.

"It looks like a town built by toddlers," Lizbet said.

"If toddlers were as big as grown-ups," Strix said.

It was early afternoon. The road had led them down out of the foothills and onto the plain, where it followed beside a river that meandered through meadows and fields. The road finally brought them to the outskirts of a town, where it turned into the town's main street. Perhaps this town was the source of the lights Lizbet and Strix had seen the night before.

Lizbet, Strix, and Violette walked warily down the street. Such a town, Lizbet had never seen. Building stones were piled up helter-skelter, ends jutting out. Every wall was askew. Every window was crooked. Not a single angle was square. The town looked like it had been built by a child playing with blocks. Perhaps the streets and sidewalks were supposed to be cobblestone, but instead of being properly laid, the stones had been simply dumped onto the roadway. To walk down the road was to constantly bruise one's feet on the upturned stone corners. Only the wrought-iron sewer grates were square, soundly constructed, and normal looking.

"Do you think this town was built by witches?" Lizbet asked.

Strix shook her head decisively. "No witch would ever build anything this sloppy."

By the time they had traveled several blocks into the town, they had not seen a single soul.

"That's funny," Lizbet said. "It's the middle of the day. Where is everybody?" She yelled, "Hello! Anyone here?"

"We are travelers from over the Montagnes du Monde," Strix yelled. "We have wonderful tales to tell, of thrilling adventures in our strange, foreign land!"

"We do?" Lizbet said.

"You almost had your soul blown out of you, remember? We fought off a murderer?"

"Those weren't thrilling," Lizbet complained. "They were terrifying and horrible."

"'Thrilling' is when awful things happen to someone else," Strix said. "'Horrible' is when they happen to you."

Their voices echoed against the buildings. Otherwise, nothing broke the silence, save for the twittering of birds as they dug for stray seeds between the jumbled paving stones. When Lizbet looked at the birds closely, they appeared to be made of quilted calico.

"This is eerie," she said. "I don't like it."

"Maybe there was a plague," Strix said.

"Strix, I can always count on you to say something cheerful." Lizbet shook her head. "It can't have been a plague. There aren't any bodies or skeletons. And anyway, the town hasn't been abandoned. Weeds and trees would cover an abandoned town, and this town still looks like people live here. Suppose it's a town of vampires? Maybe they're all asleep in their coffins or something." She shivered.

"Don't be superstitious," Strix said. "Vampires are just popular folklore."

Farther up the avenue they came upon a town square framed by lopsided buildings. At the square's center, water gushed over a pile of rubble that Lizbet supposed might be a fountain. A ridiculous yellow sandstone cathedral tilted to one side so badly that it surely would have fallen over had it not been propped up by an adjoining building that leaned the opposite way.

"Well, hello, little ladies!" a cheerful voice called out. "This must be my lucky day. I never expected a rescue party of beautiful maids like yourselves."

In front of the cathedral stood a man, his neck and wrists confined in wooden stocks. He was fat-bellied and very tall, seven or eight feet at least. Coarse brown fur, ticked like a hound's, covered most of his body. He had goat's legs with hoofed feet, a snuffly wet pig's snout, floppy ears, and curled horns. His naked pink tail lashed back and forth.

All right, maybe it wasn't a man after all.

He smiled, displaying a multitude of fine white teeth in a large mouth. His tongue, as round and pink as his tail, nervously groomed the fur on his face. "Silly me," he said. "As you can see, I've stumbled into the most absurd predicament. Thank goodness you two arrived, just in the nick of time. I seem to have gotten myself trapped in this cantankerous device." He shook his wrists in the stocks, making the hardware rattle. "You're probably asking yourself how such a thing could have happened?"

"Actually," said Strix, "I have a pretty good idea."

"What *is* this?" Lizbet said.

"It's a Common Lesser Furry Devil," Strix said. "What's your name, bunky?"

"They call me Toadwipe," said the devil. He grinned toothily again. "Obviously you are a young lady of uncommon perception and learning. It's a delight and an honor to make your acquaintance, Miss—?"

"Strix."

"What a lovely name. The perfect decoration for a witch maid as charming as yourself. And your mortal companion would be?"

"Lizbet," Lizbet said.

"What a cute sobriquet! But it's surely a nickname?" He winked. "I'll wager your real name is a hundred times more lovely. I'll perish of curiosity if you don't immediately tell me what it is?"

"Don't tell him," Strix said quickly.

Toadwipe sighed deeply and dramatically. "Isn't it sad that we all can't be more trusting with each other? These are suspicious days. Everything is at sixes and sevens. God Himself is absent from His throne, the stars and planets are topsy-turvy. Here I am, the harmless boulevardier, just minding my own business, and look what happens.

"See, I was having my customary postprandial stroll to aid the digestion, when I set eyes upon this contraption. I said to myself, 'This is a scientific device for improving the physique.' I want you to know, I am a fanatic for physical culture. Strength. Fitness. Vitality. *Mens sana in corpore sano.* I imagined this was a device for the muscular development of the neck and shoulders. I resolved to give it a spin. But I had barely touched it when the tricky thing sprang closed, and la! I find myself trapped."

"And this?" Strix said. A brass padlock secured the two halves of the stocks. Strix rocked it back and forth with her finger. "I suppose you managed to slip the shackle through the hasp and close the lock accidentally too?"

"What a fine mind you have!" Toadwipe exclaimed. "You instantly seize upon the heart of the problem. What's wrong with locks is that they're too hard to open. What we need is a file. Or a mallet and chisel. But best of all would be a key. And do you know, I know just where we might find one."

Strix crossed her arms. "You don't say."

"And the moment I'm free, we'll be off, the three of us, jolly companions on fantastical adventures beyond the imagination! We'll ride across the sky on white stallions. We'll visit far kingdoms over the mountains and the seas. I know a pair of brave, gentle, and handsome young men who would fall in love with you if they but laid eyes on you. Princes, both, who will lay their hearts at your feet." Toadwipe's eyes twinkled. His tongue licked eagerly at the fur on his cheeks and ears.

"I don't think I would want a prince's heart at my feet," Lizbet said. "Ew."

"So! Not for you the mawkish insincerities of a decayed and foppish aristocracy? I knew you were made of better stuff the moment I set eyes on you. What then, lovely Lizbet, is your heart's desire?"

"Lizbet," Strix said, "don't even—"

"He's the first person we've run across," Lizbet said. "It can't hurt just to ask."

Strix groaned.

"I'm looking for a book," Lizbet said. "It belongs to Margrave Hengest Wolftrow of Abalia. He lost it, here, someplace, on this side of the Montagnes du Monde. Have you heard anything about it?"

"What a happy coincidence!" Toadwipe said. "I know of exactly the book you mean."

"You do!" Lizbet's heart turned over and went *thump!*

"I used to read it all the time when I was a boy. Wonderful stories and pictures it had. Free me now, and I shall fly like the wind and fetch it in a trice."

Lizbet was suddenly doubtful. "Are you sure? I don't think it's likely to be a picture book. More like a book of magic."

"Yes, that was it, it was chock-full of magic, no stories or pictures at all," Toadwipe said with great decisiveness.

"And it had a bright red cover," Strix said.

"It did?" Lizbet said. "How do you—"

"Yes, red!" Toadwipe said.

"No, wait," Strix said. She propped her chin on her fist. "I think it was green."

"Perfectly green," Toadwipe said. "Not red at all."

"Or perhaps yellow."

"Now that you mention it, it was yellow as a daffydill," Toadwipe said. "Only release me, and I will fetch it at once!"

"Maybe he's colorblind," Lizbet said hopefully.

"Maybe he can't tell the difference between the truth and his bare butt," said Strix.

"He has a bare butt?" Lizbet looked behind Toadwipe. "My goodness, he does." Toadwipe's bottom was as pink and naked as that of a Barbary baboon. Except where it was covered with red welts.

"He must have accidentally backed into a bailiff with a whip too," Strix said. "I'm wondering about the story behind this. I've never heard of mortals capturing a devil."

"They surprised me while I was sleeping," Toadwipe said. "A simple case of mistaken identity."

"A moment ago you were saying this was all an accident," Lizbet said.

"It's the heat of the midday sun," Toadwipe said. "It addles the brains. I hardly know what I'm saying. I fear my health may be in danger. Free me now, so that I may seek respite in the shade. Oh, the fierceness of the sun!"

Lizbet had an idea. "Toadwipe, how would you like something to drink to slake your thirst?"

Strix said, "Why play pothouse wench to this hellmouse?"

"Yes, yes," Toadwipe said. "Bring me the cooling draught, lest I shrivel with thirst. If I die, it will be on your conscience!"

Chapter 12

The first building abutting the square that they looked into proved to be a grocery, with bins of shabby root vegetables and a regiment of doubtful-looking sausages dangling in rows from the ceiling. The next was a draper's, piled high with bolts of coarse cloth printed in ugly patterns. With the third building, though, Lizbet struck paydirt: a brewery.

The kegs of beer were heavy, but Lizbet and Strix were able to manhandle one out the door and, with much grunting and straining, roll it across the town square to the stocks. It sloshed noisily as it rolled.

Strix broke open one end with a paving stone, dipped their jug inside, and lifted it to Toadwipe's rubbery lips. He drained it in one continuous gurgling swallow. "Ah!" he said, sputtering beer foam from his lips. "By Hell, that hits me where I live! My shrunken tissues are restored." He tried to peer into the keg. "Almost . . ."

"More?" Strix said.

"I am positive that just a trifle more would make a new devil of me."

Another jug of beer was forthcoming.

"My former good health is all but renewed," Toadwipe declared. "Just one more sip should do it."

Another jug followed. And another, and another, and another. And several more after that.

What Lizbet had remembered was Mrs. Woodcot's advice that it was helpful to get seraphim and incubi drunk when entering into negotiations with them. Toadwipe wasn't a seraphim or incubus, exactly, but—

Before long, the keg was empty. Toadwipe's head hung limply from the stocks. A string of drool slowly dripped from his mouth to the street.

"Toadwipe."

"Yuh?" Toadwipe's eyelids slowly lifted. His bloodshot eyes took a while to focus on Lizbet's face. He pointed at her with a curled black fingernail. "You're cute, you are."

"Toadwipe." Lizbet grabbed one of his floppy ears and shook it. "Pay attention."

"Whazzat? Leggo my ear."

"If I release you from the stocks, will you fetch the Margrave's book for me?"

"The who what?"

"The book. That the Margrave lost. You said you read it when you were a boy. If I let you go, will you get it for me?"

"An'thing f'r a cutie like you. Where's it at?"

Strix burst out laughing.

"I don't know where it is!" Lizbet yelled. "You said you did!"

"I dunno any books. Hate books. Hate readin'. Hate ever'thing." He paused. "'Cept beer. Beer good." A hopeful note came into Toadwipe's voice. "More beer?"

"Beer gone. I mean, the beer is gone. The keg is empty. Oh, Toadwipe, you are worthless," Lizbet said, shaking her head. "Do you know what?" she said to Strix. "It's awful to say, but he reminds me of my father."

"Your father . . . ," Toadwipe mumbled.

"He means well, Toadwipe, but he makes too many promises he can't keep, and that gets him into trouble. He's in prison right now." She rattled the stocks. "Sort of like you are."

"Prison? Oh, the poor devil." Toadwipe began to bawl. Tears gushed from his eyes, and transparent phlegm poured out of his snout.

"He's a mortal, not a devil. But thank you for your expression of sympathy." Lizbet patted Toadwipe's furry hand, still trapped in the stocks.

It was a little past noon. The sun was high and bright. The surrounding stone buildings radiated heat. "Strix," Lizbet said, "I want to let Toadwipe go."

"What?"

"I feel sorry for him. Toadwipe will die of starvation and thirst if no one comes back for him."

"Devils can't die," Strix said. "They're spirit, not matter. Toadwipe, stop that drooling, it's disgusting."

"But what if this town is really deserted? He'll be trapped here until the stocks rot apart. That might be years."

"The worst that will happen to him is boredom."

"There's such a thing as mercy. And Christian charity."

"Mere human weaknesses," Strix said. "Fables that the guilty concoct to exploit the innocent."

"They are not!" Lizbet said. "Strix, we're all sometimes guilty. And sometimes we're all innocent. We all need each other's love. Even Toadwipe."

Strix's eyes narrowed. "Is this another game of pretend?"

"No," Lizbet said. "This is real as anything. And, and . . ." There was something tormenting her that she had to say. ". . . and I'm no longer pretending you're my friend either."

Strix's face fell. "Really? I was just getting used to it. Sort of."

"I want to be your friend for real," Lizbet said. She swallowed hard. She grabbed Strix's shoulders and squeezed them. "As long as you want me to be. We've been through too much not to be friends. Is that okay?"

Strix nodded. "It's okay. Being with someone who isn't going to beat you, and who you can't beat either, it's different, and strange. But . . . I've gotten used to it." Her lips formed a small, awkward smile, the smile of someone who hasn't had much practice at smiling. "I . . . kind of like it, in fact."

"Thas ver' sweet," Toadwipe said. "Thas nice. Nice girls 'r' fren's. Now I wan' more beer. Beer is my fren.'"

"Shut up!" Lizbet said.

"You keep out of this!" Strix said.

"Uhhhh. No yellin'."

Lizbet lifted one of Toadwipe's hairy ears and yelled directly into it. "Toadwipe! TOADWIPE!"

Toadwipe jerked. "Wha!"

"The key," Lizbet said. "You said you knew where the padlock key was?"

"Uh," Toadwipe mumbled. "In there." He jerked his head backward. Lizbet looked.

Behind him, a teetery-tottery granite building abutted the square. A shield, sloppily painted with an unrecognizable beast rampant and unreadable words, hung beside the door. Lizbet said, "In that building?"

"Uh-huh," Toadwipe said, and again lapsed into a stupor.

The building's door hung open. Lizbet couldn't see into the dark room beyond. She took a deep breath. She said, "I'm going in there, then."

"Be careful," Strix said. She frowned. "Is that right?"

"Perfect," Lizbet said. "Exactly what a friend would say."

She scaled the tumble down stone steps and peered into the doorway. Tables, chairs, in poor repair. Trash littered the floor. Bones, gnawed clean of flesh, piled in the corners.

She stepped into the room. Tools hung from pegs on the walls: whips, manacles, knives, axes. Oh dear. What sort of a place was this? Lizbet did not want to go any deeper into this building.

But she had promised herself she would. She had resolved to free Toadwipe, and she was not the sort of person who could go back on a resolution once she had made it. Lizbet had crossed the Montagnes because she had promised herself that she would free her father. She had been feeling more and more dismayed that despite all her struggle and hardship, she seemed no closer to her goal. Freeing Toadwipe was a toy version of freeing her father, practice for her larger task still unfinished.

She searched the room, but the padlock key was nowhere to be found. A dark hallway opened through an archway on the room's far side. Steeling herself, Lizbet crossed the floor and tiptoed down the hall as quietly as she was able.

Portraits in crude wooden frames lined the walls. Smoke and dust begrimed the portraits, and in the dimness—the only light came through the outside door—Lizbet could barely make out the faces. Bug eyes, saggy jowls, mouths like buckets. The faces in the portraits were as ugly as goblins.

The hall ended in a wooden door. From behind it came a faint cacophony of wheezing and buzzing noises. Lizbet hesitated. Fear battled with curiosity.

Duty won. She turned the doorknob as gently as she could, and eased the door open.

In the room beyond, a bright glint in the dimness. The glint rose and fell, with a tinkling sound. Yes! It was a ring of brass and iron keys that shimmered in the faint light.

It hung from the belt of the biggest goblin Lizbet had ever seen.

The goblin was as big as a man, or bigger. It tilted back in a chair, asleep, its three-toed splay feet up on the table in front of it, its forepaws clasped over its belly. The goblin snored loudly. With each wracking, bubbling snort, its immense round belly moved in and out. The ring of keys rose and fell, and jingled.

A dozen other goblins lay sleeping on the floor. They slept in piles, like piglets, goblin piled on top of goblin. Their snoring made the air shudder.

So that was why the town was deserted. It was a goblin town. Of course, goblins slept during the day. Come evening, they'd be out and about and making trouble. But all the goblins Lizbet had ever heard of slept in basements and sewers. They didn't have towns. Goblins didn't wear clothing, and these goblins had belts and trousers. One wore a slouch hat. The goblin with the keys wore a blue coat with brass buttons like a constable.

The snoring continued uninterrupted. Lizbet tried to calm herself. She had promised to release Toadwipe. She had *promised.*

She strained her eyes to see in the near darkness. The keyring hung from the goblin constable's belt, secured by a leather strap that fastened around the belt with a big wooden button. Could Lizbet undo it? Without waking the constable? Doubt assailed her.

She retreated up the hallway to the first room, where weapons hung on the wall. By standing on tiptoes and reaching up as high as she could, Lizbet just managed to shove a big black knife off its wall peg. She grabbed for the handle as it fell. For a terrifying second, it eluded her grip, and she juggled to grab it, fearful it would fall and wake the goblins.

She caught it at last. Taking a deep breath, and willing her racing heart to be still, Lizbet crept down the dark hallway again and into the goblin common room.

In the dimness, goblins surrounded her. Hairy, stinking, floppy piebald flesh, in heaps and piles. All Lizbet's nightmares of falling into a goblin sewer came back to her. She wanted to scream and run.

Instead, she inched forward. The knife grip in her hand was slippery with her sweat.

She crouched by the goblin constable's chair, only inches from his sleeping body. His stink was in her nostrils, and she fought not to sneeze. Her trembling fingers explored the button. Gripping the knife, she sawed at the stitches that secured the button, over and over.

At last, the button popped free. It struck the floor with a loud *click!* "Huh, duh," one of the sleeping goblins moaned. It stirred, and turned over.

Lizbet crouched down as low as she could. She held her breath.

Minutes passed before she dared raise her head and peer around the room again. The goblin had gone back to sleep.

She eased the strap out from beneath the goblin constable's belt, a fraction of an inch at a time. Remembering what had happened to the button, she supported the keys with her other hand while she worked.

It took ages, but she was scared to work any faster.

At last the strap came free. The ring of keys was hers! Relief washed over over her. Now to get out, release Toadwipe, and hightail it out of this goblin town before sundown, when all the goblins would—

"Lizbet!"

Oh no.

Careless, noisy footsteps coming down the hall. "Lizbet, where are you?" Strix yelled. "Are you okay? I got tired of waiting, so I picked the lock with a hairpin."

Toadwipe's voice, farther away: "Hey, lookit all these sharp things. We could have fun torturing sinners. Who do you want to torture? I got some ideas."

The door opened wide. "Toadwipe is sobering up already and getting rowdy," Strix said. "We need to ditch him. There you are! What's taking you so . . . Oh. Goblins."

The goblin constable's eyes popped open, rolled around, then focused on the girls.

Strix put her hands on her hips. "Sure are a lot of goblins. Really big goblins. You know, I think we should be going."

"Sally toot!" the goblin constable exclaimed. "Dumpty winkle snool?" He jumped to his feet, his chair clattering over behind him. He yelled, "Ap! Jeek! Zoop!" All around, goblins began to stir and open their eyes. One by one, they tumbled off one another and pulled themselves to their feet.

"I was just, um, borrowing," Lizbet began. The ring of keys was suddenly very heavy in her hand. She tossed the keys onto the table with a clatter. "It's okay, it looks like our problem's solved, so we'll just be taking our leave, you can all get back to whatever you were doing, like sleeping . . ." She edged backwards toward the door.

"Nabby! Stabby! SPLAT!" the goblin constable yelled, pointing at Lizbet. However the words translated, their meaning was clear. The awakening goblins smacked their lips and flexed their stubby fingers. They got to their feet and waddled in Lizbet's direction. They snapped their jaws and growled deep in their throats.

Lizbet reached the doorway. She braced her feet wide and thrust out the knife, point first in front of her. "Strix!" she called over her shoulder. "Run! I'll hold them off!"

"Don't be ridiculous," Strix said over Lizbet's shoulder. "You can't fight a roomful of goblins." She took Lizbet's free hand in hers. "I'll knit us into the shadows."

Strix faded away, but only halfway. Unlike the time in Abalia-Under-the-Hill, Strix didn't disappear completely. She remained a transparent, ghostly figure. "Strix," Lizbet said urgently, "I can still see you. Sort of. It's not working."

"That's impossible," Strix said. "I'm doing it right." Strix pulled her backward, down the hall. The goblins waddled after them.

Somewhere high above, a bell began clanging thunderously.

In the front room, Toadwipe was taking practice swings with a cat-o'-nine-tails. "Salutations!" he said. Toadwipe could see them? Toadwipe's eyes lighted on the troop of goblins pushing down the hallway. "Uh-oh. Company coming. Good luck, best regards, look me up sometime." He dropped his cat-o'-nine-tails and leaped into the air, coming down in a swan dive. Lizbet braced herself for the crash as he hit the floor. Instead, the wooden boards cracked and split noisily, a dark hole yawned open, and Toadwipe vanished into it. The floorboards snapped shut behind him.

"Off to Hell," Strix whispered in Lizbet's ear. "Good riddance."

The goblins were almost on top of them. "Grappy spool!" one yelled almost in Lizbet's face.

Lizbet shrank away. She said, "Strix, I think he can see us."

"He can't see us. I don't think . . ."

The goblin's fist hit the side of Lizbet's head and knocked her off her feet.

As the goblin bent to seize her, Strix's boot caught its immense round stomach. It stumbled backward, gasping for air.

Dazed, Lizbet clambered to her feet. The knife had fallen out of her hand. "They can see us!" she gasped to Strix.

"Just run, then!" Strix yelled.

Together they piled through the door and down the steps. Goblins waddled behind.

Out of the doors of every building on the square came goblins. Big, man-sized goblins, bigger than Lizbet or Strix. Above, the bell continued to clang. Hundreds, thousands of goblins must have been snoozing in the cool darkness of their back rooms during the day. Now they were awake. And angry.

Lizbet scanned the square. They were surrounded by goblins. Scores of goblins continued to pour from the buildings. They ringed the square, and the ring was closing. "What do we do?" she yelled to Strix.

"Run!" Strix pulled her toward the center of the square.

"Where? There's nowhere to go!"

"I don't . . . Wait. I know. Down!"

Down?

Strix stopped at a sewer grate near the square's center. She crouched and grabbed the bars. "Quick! Help me lift it!"

Down a sewer?

But that's where goblins lived. Or were supposed to. Lizbet's years of nightmares about falling down into a goblin sewer came back to her in a rush. Terror filled her.

"I can't . . . ," she whispered. "I just can't."

"There's nowhere else to go," Strix yelled. "Help me lift the grate!"

Falling, tumbling helplessly, through uncounted goblins . . .

"No . . . !" Lizbet wailed.

"It can't be any worse than what's up here!"

Couldn't it? But wouldn't a sewer in a goblin town have even worse goblins in it? The goblins of goblins.

"Noooooo!"

"Lizbet! Please!"

Lizbet stared at Strix. "Please help me," Strix pleaded. "Please?"

It may have been the hardest thing Lizbet had ever done: to kneel, grab the sewer grate in her fists, and nod to Strix. Her teeth chattered. When Strix yelled, "One! Two! *Three!*" Lizbet's part in heaving up the grate was more moral than physical, but she still yanked as hard as her trembling muscles would allow.

The sewer grate squealed as metal ground against stone. It tilted up, and fell backward onto the cobbles with a clang. Strix shrieked. An open shaft gaped, its bottom lost in darkness. Metal rungs led downward.

Lizbet gulped. She had not overcome her fear. She had given in to it, and in despair, accepted whatever was to come. "Strix—"

Strix knelt by the sewer, her mismatched eyes wide, her mouth open in horror. She gripped her left shoulder with her right fist. "What's wrong?" Lizbet said.

Then she saw: Strix's left arm was gone.

From just below the shoulder, there was nothing but torn bits of paper and dangling string.

"My arm," Strix gasped. "It . . . b-broke. It just came off."

The arm lay beneath the overturned grate, the fingers still gripping the metal bars.

"Strix," Lizbet said, trying to still her chattering teeth and numb lips, "Strix, we have to go. Down. Now." The first of the goblins from the constable barracks was almost upon them, waddling so fast it threatened to lose its balance. It waved a spiked hammer with its paw.

"My arm. I need my arm."

"Strix, we can't wait—"

"My arm!"

Strix wouldn't budge without her arm.

From all directions, the goblins were closing in.

Straining and panting, Lizbet dug her fingers beneath the grate. Using her utmost strength, she levered it up enough to grab Strix's arm from beneath it with her other hand, before she let it drop again.

"Now go down the sewer! I'll follow!"

The look on Strix's face broke Lizbet's heart. But there was no time to wait, to talk, to console her. Lizbet pushed Strix toward the edge. "Go down! Please. Now!"

Rung by rung, Strix clambered down into darkness. As soon as Strix was below the edge, Lizbet followed.

The goblin with the hammer waddled up and peered over the edge. "Wazoo!" it yelled. "Zaxtax shimmelninny! Blap!" It swung its hammer down into the well, as far as it could reach, hitting the brick wall inches from Lizbet's head. Shattered bits of brick stung her face.

"Hurry!" she yelled downward.

Would the goblins follow them?

Down into the depths of the sewer shaft they descended.

Chapter 13

Nightingale,
Milk pail,
The Devil lives in Hell.
Huckleberries,
Queen Anne cherries,
Ask him how he fell.
Peacocks,
Cigar box,
A fib he'll likely tell:
Chicken bones,
Kidney stones,
He tumbled down a well.
　　—a rhyme of Strix

As they climbed downward, the air around Lizbet and Strix became damp, and chilly enough to raise goose bumps on Lizbet's flesh. Angry goblin faces ringed the shrinking circle of sunlight above. Goblin yells echoed off the wet brick walls. But the goblins didn't follow the girls down.

That was good. Unless the goblins weren't following because they knew something even worse lurked below.

Lizbet, like Strix, climbed down with one hand. In the other, she gripped Strix's severed arm. Poor, poor Strix! Strix was made of paper, leaves, strings, fur, and other stuff that just wasn't very strong. Not as strong as human flesh and bone. Too much strain, and Strix would break.

Lizbet had been in awe of Strix: her witchy skill of making creatures that moved, the way she could knit into the shadows.

Her talent of pulling vices and virtues out of a dead body might be icky, but it was more than Lizbet could do. The unexpected revelation that Strix was physically fragile was unnerving. Traveling with Strix had been reassuring, because Lizbet thought, deep down, that Strix was the equal of any crisis.

But she wasn't.

That knowledge made Lizbet cringe with guilt. Because if she had pulled at the grate a little harder, if she had borne her fair share of the effort, if she hadn't let fear overthrow her, they would have been able to lift the grate together. Instead, Strix lost her arm to save them both.

Strix, mean and witchy and arrogant Strix, had been a better friend to Lizbet than Lizbet had been to Strix.

"Strix," Lizbet said. "Stop for a moment. I'm going to climb over you and go down first." Being the first into danger was the least Lizbet could do.

Strix didn't protest. She didn't say a word. Lizbet wondered whether she was still shocked by the experience.

They had gone down a few yards more, Lizbet in the lead, when the wavering light of flames appeared below, and the smell of smoke rose around them. The lights hadn't been there a moment before. Looking down, Lizbet could see figures standing below, holding torches.

Lizbet stopped climbing. Fear swallowed her up. Were these the sewer goblins she had dreaded?

"Get the spears and axes ready!" a man's voice yelled from below. "Hack 'em to bits as soon as they get close!"

They didn't sound like goblins. But they didn't sound friendly either.

Daring to descend a rung or two farther, Lizbet finally made out upturned pale faces.

Human faces.

"Please don't hurt us," she cried. "The goblins are after us!"

A babble of voices: "It speaks!" "I've never heard a goblin talk sense before!" "More torches!"

The light below became brighter. "It's not goblins," said a man's surprised voice.

"I think it's two girls," said a woman's voice. "But they're dressed so strangely."

"We're from over the Montagnes du Monde," Lizbet called down.

For a moment, the people at the bottom of the sewer shaft fell silent.

"Is it General Wolftrow?" another man's voice yelled up. "Is he here? Has he returned at last?"

"It's not the Margrave, it's just us," Lizbet called down.

"He's a Margrave, now, is he?" a man said. Another laughed bitterly.

She reached the bottom of the sewer shaft. It was wider than the top. Brick archways led away on all sides. Black water trickled across the center of the floor. Men and women holding torches surrounded her. They were dressed in old-fashioned clothing, the kind Lizbet thought only grand-mothers and great-uncles wore, although these people were of all ages. Lizbet used her free hand to help Strix down the last few rungs. Strix half fell, dazed, into Lizbet's arms. "We're escaping from the goblins," Lizbet said. "Can you help us?"

"Are you really from over the Montagnes?" a man asked. "Can that be true?"

"What's wrong with the other girl?" a woman said. "She looks ill. Is she all right?"

"She's hurt," Lizbet said. "It's her arm."

"Poor child," the woman said. She looked closely at Strix, then drew breath sharply. "Her arm—it's gone!"

A gasp of shock and anger from the others. "Damned goblins," one said. "They'll pay for this," another said.

"Oh, the poor, dear thing," the woman said. "Well. We must do what can be done." She was a sturdy dame, with short legs and muscular shoulders. She swept up Strix into her arms, and exclaimed, "Why, your friend's no heavier than a sack of feathers. She must be all skin and bones."

"Actually . . . ," Lizbet began.

"Jean! Go run for the barber-surgeon. I'm taking this little angel to the Women's Commons." A boy nodded and scampered off. His footsteps echoed off the wet brick walls. "The rest of you men, clear out. Dear," she to Lizbet, "I'm Kate."

"I'm Lizbet," Lizbet said.

"Lizbet, come with us."

She bustled away down one of the tunnels, Strix limp in her arms. The women and girls from the group followed. Lizbet ran to keep up.

From one tunnel they passed to another, and another, until Lizbet lost track of where they might be. The lamps that the women carried were the only light, a tiny moving pool of illumination in an underground universe of darkness.

They ran up a stone staircase slick with fungus, water rushing down both sides. They descended into a black well on iron steps that creaked alarmingly with each footfall. The women and girls hurried through intersections where a dozen sewer tunnels converged, over chasms bridged by iron grates swaying on iron chains, through cavernous storm sewers as wide as the nave of a cathedral, where they had to hop nimbly over water flowing down the center. Some tunnels stank of decay and filth so that Lizbet could barely catch a breath; others smelt as fresh as rain.

"The goblins' sewers are bigger and better than their whole town," Lizbet exclaimed to Kate, panting as she hurried.

"Goblins do things upside down, dear," Kate replied.

They finally emerged into an arched chamber of stone and tile that Kate said was the Women's Commons. Flickering candles and oil lamps lit the room dimly. The sound of running water dashing against stone echoed from somewhere near. Curtains partitioned part of chamber into alcoves. Within the alcoves, Lizbet glimpsed beds and trunks. Kate laid Strix gently on one of the beds.

"At least she's not bleeding too much," Kate said.

"I don't bleed," Strix said. Her voice was steady and serene, but terribly quiet. Lizbet wished Strix would say something sarcastic or mean.

Running footsteps. Jean hurried up, accompanied by a middle-aged round-faced man wearing a floppy black tie and frock coat. The man's clothes were splattered in blood from collar to knees.

"Bernard!" Kate said sternly. "You're a sight. You haven't been trying to shave customers with a straight razor again, have you?"

"No, ma'am," Bernard replied cheerfully. "I drained old Kasper's wen for him this morning." He held up one sleeve of his coat. "It ain't all blood—there's some pus too."

"This girl is hurt, Bernard," Kate said. "It's her arm. It's, oh, it's come off." A sob lurked just beneath her words. "Can you do anything for her at all?"

"Lost an arm . . ." Bernard's smile faded. "Oh dear, I don't know—"

"I have her arm," Lizbet said. She held Strix's arm up.

A couple of the women gave out little cries. Bernard flinched. He shook his head. "I'm sorry, missy, but I can't do anything with the arm. Once it's off, it's off. An arm can't properly be put back. The best I can do is to tidy up the amputation. That means cutting and stitching. We'll dope her up with whiskey first, but there'll still be screaming and carrying on. Afterwards, she'll be okay if the gangrene don't set in. But her poor arm's lost for good, I'm sorry to say." He sat down on the edge of the bed. "Let me reconnoiter a trifle." From a coat pocket, he produced a pair of silver spectacles with a cracked lens. He bent and peered at the stump of Strix's arm. "Something's peculiar here. Did you try to mend this with a paper bandage? Jean, fetch another lamp. I don't see—"

He drew back abruptly. He stared at Strix. The corners of his mouth and his eyebrows all pointed toward the center of his face, like an X. "What is all this? This ain't a natural arm, it's all papers and leaves and string and whatnot." He pushed up Strix's sleeve. "Ain't artificial too—it's part and parcel of the girl." He looked anxiously about the room. "What's this about? What kind of girl is this?"

Kate stared at Lizbet. They had been found out. "She's a witch," Lizbet said. "She's not flesh and blood, she's made of papers and letters and teabags. It's all perfectly natural. For a witch."

Bernard stood. "I don't know anything about cutting on witches," he said.

"Who can help her, then?" Lizbet said. "Is there a witch who could help her?"

The women murmured and drew away from the bedside. The atmosphere in the room grew noticeably more chilly.

"I wouldn't know," Kate said. "There are certainly no witches here." She looked at Lizbet sharply. "You wouldn't be a witch yourself?"

The other women whispered to each other more loudly. Bernard crossed himself. "Lord save us," he said.

"No, I'm not!" Lizbet said. Her voice was high-pitched with anxiety. She advanced on Kate faster than the other woman could back away, grabbed Kate's hand, and held it to her cheek. "See? Feel how I'm a mortal. I'm warm, and sensible." She took Kate's hand and wrapped the fingers around her forearm. "See? See?"

But her legs weren't mortal. What about her legs?

Her skirt came to just above her knees, her thick wool socks to just below. The chamber was poorly lit. Maybe Lizbet's birch-white witchy legs would escape notice. She hoped.

Lizbet tried to direct their attention elsewhere. She took another woman's hand and pressed it to her other cheek. "See?"

Kate gently squeezed Lizbet's arm up and down. Her fingers caressed Lizbet's cheek, and with an impulsive, motherly gesture brushed an errant lock of dark hair behind Lizbet's ear. "Why are you in the company of a witch, then?" she asked in a gentler tone. "Are you ensorcelled?"

"I'm not ensorcelled," Lizbet said. "Strix is my friend."

"Witches are no one's friend," another woman said. She was a head taller than Kate, skinny except for her tummy, with a nose like a bunion and anxious eyes. She wrung her hands together and rocked right and left on the balls of her feet. "Maybe she's a spy for the Pope of Storms."

"She's not a spy," Lizbet said urgently. "She's just a girl. I don't know anything about any Pope."

"If she were the Pope's spy, he wouldn't have set the goblins after her, Maglet," Kate said.

"I dunno, I dunno, witches are tricky ones," the woman called Maglet muttered. "I dunno about that. It might be a ruse. It might be a plot."

Kate seemed a little assuaged, but the other women and girls still murmured to each other in tones of suspicion and discontent. Casting anxious glimpses back, they drifted away. The room emptied, until only Kate, Lizbet, and Strix were left.

"How did you come to be in such a fix, dear?" Kate asked.

Lizbet told her story, from her father's being arrested, her trip to Mrs. Woodcot's, the journey over the Montagnes, until Lizbet and Strix got to the goblin town and accidentally woke up the goblins. She left out her injured legs and how Strix made her new ones.

Kate shook her head again and again through the story. "Such an awful burden for such a young girl to bear," she said when Lizbet was done. "Such terrible hardships." Her voice flattened, and the words came like a penitent making a reluctant confession to his priest. "I see it was all General Wolftrow's doing. He was the one who put the idea in your head."

"He didn't ask me to do this," Lizbet said.

"No, he didn't. And yet, somehow, you are doing all this for him, putting yourself in danger of losing your life and your soul, consorting with witches, nearly captured by goblins. And it started with things Wolftrow said or did." She smiled, barely. "He plays skittles with men, and the pin that goes flying may be three pins away from the one his ball hit."

Lizbet walked to Strix's bed, sat on the edge, and laid Strix's severed arm on the bed beside her, where it would have lain if it were still attached. "Strix," she said. "There's no one here who can help you." Strix nodded silently. "I don't know what to do," Lizbet said. "Can we keep your arm, and when we get back over the Montagnes, maybe Mrs. Woodcot can put it back on for you? Since she made you to begin with?"

Strix stared at the ceiling. A new look played across her features. It looked like fear. It was the first time Lizbet had ever seen Strix look fearful. "I don't think that's a good idea," Strix said.

"Strix, what's wrong?" Lizbet said. "You're too quiet. It's not like you. I know, your arm, but—does it hurt?"

Strix shook her head. "It doesn't hurt."

"It must be a shock . . ."

"It diminishes me."

Lizbet thought about this. "I suppose that's what losing part of your body would do."

"It diminishes *me*. The me that's talking to you."

Lizbet's skin went goosebumps.

"It's like missing part of your soul. Witches don't have souls, but the part of us that's *us* is spread throughout our bodies. Our bodies are our souls."

"Oh, Strix . . ." The horror of it gripped her. And Strix had covered Lizbet with her own body to save Lizbet's soul from being blown away in the Montagnes. "What can we do?"

Strix shook her head. "Only a witch could help. Only a witch can put me together again."

Only a witch. Only a witch could build things that lived and moved from inanimate materials. "Only a witch can do this," Strix had said when she was building Violette.

But Lizbet had helped build Violette, hadn't she?

"I'm going to do it," she said.

"What?"

"I'm going to fix you."

Lizbet begged a candle from Kate and inspected the stump of Strix's arm. The stuff Strix was made of poked out: rolled and folded papers, leaves, twine, pocket fluff, brown duck feathers, rattlesnake skin, cattails. Her arm bone was a bundle of twigs lashed together with string. "I'll need kindling," Lizbet said to Kate, "and if you have old letters, bits of leather, maybe an old pillow leaking feathers, that would help. And flour and water. And ink."

In a way, it was easier than building Violette, because Lizbet didn't need to create anything new. She just had to reattach everything, stuff fluff and feathers in the holes, and patch it all together. But in way, it was harder too. Because it was Strix. It had to be right. It had to be perfect.

But it also had to be done. Even if it wasn't perfect.

Thus, Lizbet was torn between what her beginner's skills allowed, what she wanted to do, and the need to do *something*, even something flawed, when there was no one else there to do it.

Her palms were sweaty as she worked, and her fingers shook. Strix could offer little help. She did not remember her own creation, any more than Lizbet remembered hers.

As Lizbet worked, she learned. How to shape paper and feathers together into firm flesh. How to string it all together with strips of leather and lengths of twine, so that Strix could move her fingers. How to tension the twine properly by twisting it around twigs. As Lizbet worked, she grew more confident. Her hands no longer shook. She finished up by patching Strix's skin with papers and flour-water paste, like papier-mâché. She stained it with oak-gall ink to make it brown, to match the rest of Strix.

Hours went by. When Lizbet was finally done, Strix twisted her arm back and forth, and drummed the fingers on the bed. She lifted her hand in front of her face and swiveled her wrist around.

"How is it?" Lizbet asked anxiously. "Does it feel okay?"

"It feels good," Strix said. Her voice was surprised, but pleased. "It all works."

"Oh! I'm so glad. But how do *you* feel? Is it really you again? Do you feel . . . whole?"

Strix nodded. "I'm me again." She shivered. "That was awful. I'm glad it's over."

"Are you sure you're okay?" Lizbet's voice was still worried.

Strix frowned. "Yes, I'm sure. What do you mean?"

"Strix," Lizbet said, "I think you're sweetest, gentlest girl I've ever known. And to prove it, I'm going to give you a big hug and a kiss." She leaned down, threw her arms around Strix, and planted a noisy, sloppy kiss on her right cheek.

Strix exploded. "I am not sweet! I am not gentle!" She wiped her cheek with her hand. "My cheek is wet! I'm utterly disgusted. There's wet human spit on my cheek. Ick!"

"That's better," Lizbet said. "Kate, can we borrow a wash-rag for Strix? Kate?"

"What's better? What are you talking about!"

"You're back to your old nasty self. And do you know, Strix, I really wouldn't want you any other way." Lizbet looked around. "Kate must have left when I was busy with you."

"She can bring me supper when she returns," Strix said. "I'm starved."

"Me too," Lizbet said. "We've had a day, haven't we. Oh, that reminds me. Before Kate gets back . . ." She undid her bootlaces, removed her boots, and put them back on, but on the opposite feet, the way boots go on a normal mortal. They pinched her feet. It would do for now, but Lizbet hoped she didn't have to conceal her witchy feet too long. She checked her knees. The skin was paler than the rest of her, but as long as she kept her socks pulled high, none of the brown birch-bark seams showed on her exposed skin. Maybe her legs would pass muster long enough.

But how long was "long enough"? They had escaped the goblins, but where were they to go now?

She had barely got her shoes on opposite when she heard Kate's decisive footsteps approaching. She appeared from the mouth of a tunnel. "It's become late," she said. "You've been busy with your . . . friend all afternoon. Corporal Tiermann has commanded your presence at supper. He wants all your news from over the Montagnes. Is something wrong? You look disappointed."

A corporal? "It's just . . . ," Lizbet began uncertainly, "Corporal Tiermann is good to want to dine with me. But maybe I can also meet with someone older, who knew Margrave Hengest Wolftrow, and might know something about his lost book?"

Kate smiled slightly. "Dear, Corporal Tiermann is High Lord of the Sewers. His rank is the greatest of any in the sewer city, and his age is nearly the oldest. He was in General Wolftrow's army that the crossed the Montagnes thirty years ago. If anyone can help you, Corporal Tiermann can."

Chapter 14

Corporal Henrik Tiermann was a scrawny middle-aged man with a straggly gray beard that went everywhere. Dinner with the corporal proved to be dinner with the whole colony of sewer-dwellers. They placed Lizbet at the opposite end of the dining table from Tiermann. Between them on both sides of the table, six old men slurped and smacked their lips as they ate. They wore army uniforms so tattered that they were little more than rags. Boys brandishing knives and forks ran up and down behind them, cutting each man's food into bites. Younger men and women dined at a score of other tables set up on the floor of a great stone sewer plenum. Rows of pipes on both walls poured forth steaming gray sewage that splashed in noisy cataracts to the floor and drained away into stone and brick channels.

The noise and stink were almost unbearable to Lizbet. The others didn't seem to notice, and put away their food with vigor and enthusiasm.

The main course—the only course, it turned out—was chunks of meat and vegetable matter in an oily gray sauce. It smelled like a badger caught in a trap, if you'd thrown away the badger and cooked the trap. Lizbet wondered whether it was polite to ask what it was she was eating. Instead, she asked one of the serving boys, "Can the cook give me the recipe for this?"

The boy shrugged. "There's nothing to it," he said. "It's just rat. It's always rat. And fungus." He pointed with his knife at a pale globe on Lizbet's plate. "That's a blind cave fish eye. You must have done something to deserve that."

"I can't think of what. It's an honor, then?" Lizbet said.

"Not much. They give fish eyes to people who are under suspicion, to let 'em know that they're being watched."

"Suspicion of what?"

"Polyandry or barratry, mostly. Or sometimes Gnosticism or flirtatiousness."

"I don't believe I've done any of those," Lizbet said.

"Maybe the eye's because you're a stranger, then."

"Do they usually give them to strangers?"

The boy shrugged. "Who knows? I've never seen a stranger here before."

"Not ever? Really?"

"Uh-uh. Where would a stranger come from?"

"Well, I came from over the Montagnes," Lizbet said.

"Are you sure?" The boy's voice was skeptical.

"Of course I'm sure!"

"The old folks say they came from over the Montagnes," the boy said, "but there's younger people who don't believe it." He lowered his voice. "They say we've always lived right here. They say we're all lost parts of the Universal Sewer, and with the Universal Sewer our souls long to rejoin."

The old man seated at the table to Lizbet's left interrupted. "Enough, boy." He fixed the boy with a rheumy gaze. "Hold your tongue before you get an eye on your own plate." His gaze darted between the boy and Lizbet. "And maybe a second one as well." He returned to his food.

The boy blushed. Lizbet blushed. The boy made himself busy elsewhere at the table.

What must it be like, Lizbet thought, to have always lived with the same people you'd known all your life, and never meet anyone new? After spending her childhood being dragged from town to town by her father, she had longed for a settled life. But if this were an example, it didn't seem like it would be very much fun. And it seemed to give rise to peculiar ideas about a world that the people here had never seen. Of course, things might be different if you didn't have to live in a sewer and eat rat every day too.

"How come there are people living in this sewer?" Lizbet asked the old man at her left.

The old man looked at her suspiciously. "Are you flirting with me?"

"Certainly not!"

The old man slurped up a spoonful of rat stew and gummed it noisily. "We're down here 'cause of the goblins," he said. "Can't go up top long. Goblins are hostile. You saw."

"But there must be another way out?" Lizbet's heart sank. Were she and Strix trapped?

"You can get out," the old man said, "only there's nowhere to go."

Nowhere to go? "But there's mountains, and rivers, and plains," Lizbet said. "I've seen them. I've never been over the Montagnes before, but it looks to me like there's a whole world over here. Why do you have to live in a sewer?"

The old man shook his head. "The world on this side is filled up with goblins and witches and worse. There's no place for us."

A whole world of goblins and witches?

"We wait for Wolftrow to return for us," the old man said. "He said he'd return."

Between noisy gobbles of his bowl of rat stew, the old man told Lizbet his story.

Thirty years ago, fresh from his victories over the Catalans and Berbers, and looking for new worlds to conquer, General Hengest Wolftrow (not yet Margrave) had crossed the Montagnes du Monde with an army of a hundred thousand men. Trailing behind came thousands of others, the sort who follow after armies: tinkers, brewers, musicians, and women. ("You mean the soldiers' wives?" Lizbet asked. "Not exactly," the old man said.)

The crossing had been nightmarish. There was no road over the Montagnes, so Wolftrow built one. Cutting through the living rock, moving vast boulders, the Grande Armee labored two months to build the road that had taken Lizbet and Strix over the top of the Montagnes in a single day.

The army was unprepared for the high reaches and perilous cold of the Montagnes. Many froze to death. Those who survived lost fingers, toes, whole limbs to the cold. The horses all died. Still Wolftrow drove his army on. "Wolftrow was mad with dreams," the old man said. He had a patent from Empress Juliana to subdue the lands over the Montagnes du Monde and add them to the Holy Roman Empire. But many suspected Wolftrow lusted after a kingdom of his own. Some said he was seeking magic with which to depose the Pixie Queen and set himself on the ancient throne of Charlemagne.

Whatever Wolftrow secretly desired, he was ruthless in his pursuit of it. As his army perished around him, he drove the survivors onward up the mountain with undiminished fervor. When they reached heights where the etheric winds began to rip men's souls from their bodies, Wolftrow marched in front, blocking the wind with his own body. Wolftrow's own soul seemed indissolubly knit to his flesh, a heroic soul in a heroic body that no wind, however fierce, could tear asunder.

Many were desperate to quit this journey of horrors. Under another commander, they might have mutinied. Wolftrow persuaded them to march on. He was a man of messianic personality. A few words from General Wolftrow to a despairing soldier made the man believe that it was he, and he alone, whom Wolftrow counted on to save them all through strength and steadfastness. At night, he was everywhere among the troops, striding from campfire to campfire, coaxing, encouraging, giving hope to the despairing. The soldiers loved him as a father is loved. His frown was more feared than death.

The army's numbers dwindled each day. At the last, a half-frozen, horror-stricken handful of survivors stumbled over the Montagnes' crest and down the eastern slopes into the unknown lands beyond. Out of a hundred thousand men and women who left Abalia, Wolftrow's great army was reduced to a few score by the time they found the goblin town.

Like Lizbet and Strix, they had accidentally woken the goblins, and a battle ensued. But Wolftrow's tattered ranks, exhausted and half starved, had no fight in them. The goblins chased Wolftrow's soldiers down into the sewers.

There they had refuge. They ate rats and offal, and eked out a precarious existence by raiding the goblins above.

Wolftrow quickly became restless. He still had grander dreams than ruling over a sewer. One day he set out alone, vowing to cross back over the Montagnes. He swore he would bring a new army to rescue the sewer-dwellers. He swore he would return.

But he never did.

"He's Margrave of Abalia now," Lizbet said. "He's been margrave for years." She remembered how Margrave Hengest Wolftrow seemed to her: hollow, filled with shadows. She could not imagine him having the strength of body, or will, to cross the Montagnes again. "I don't think he's coming back," she said.

The old man shook his head and sighed.

At the table's opposite end, Corporal Tiermann turned his tin plate over and banged his spoon loudly on the bottom. The diners became quiet. Tiermann rose, slowly, assisted by two boys.

"There is a stranger among us," he said. His voice was a croak, except where it wheezed. "Lizbet"—he nodded at her—"who comes to us from over the Montagnes." Tiermann motioned for Lizbet to rise, and bid her to tell her story.

Lizbet told the assembly the version of her story that she had told Kate. She had to raise her voice so that everyone in the room could hear over the background roar of falling columns of sewage. Her words rang off the dripping stone floor and the great arch of the roof. Every time she spoke Hengest Wolftrow's name, there were whispers in the room, and sometimes low curses. But there were also sighs.

"And so," she finished, "I'm looking for the Margrave's book, that he lost. Can you help me?" She looked around the room. "Has anyone here heard of it? Have you seen it?"

Sounds of puzzlement. People whispered to each other, and shook their heads. "I have never heard of such a thing," Tiermann said. "General Wolftrow is friends with bullets and bayonets, with muskets and mortars. Not with books. He cared little for reading, or writing."

"But he buys books from all over the world," Lizbet said. "He has filled a palace with books."

Murmurs from around the room, and a few snorts of disbelief.

"Why have you brought a witch among us?" a woman's screechy voice yelled out. It was Maglet. She pointed at Lizbet with a skinny finger. "She has a witch, with a crippled arm. She has it in the Women's Commons."

"We're traveling together," Lizbet said. "We're helping each other. She's my friend."

Again, mutters of disbelief.

Lizbet returned to the Women's Commons carefully carrying a plate of rat chowder for Strix. Strix devoured it, but not without complaints.

"Not gamy enough," she said around a mouthful of rat. "They should use a wild strain of rat. Needs more salt too. Also, the fungus is wrong." She gestured in the air with her fork, a gobbet of rat still impaled on its tines. "For proper rat dishes you really need the Purple Turksnose toadstool, grown in a compost of aconite and hellebore."

"I'll run tell the cook right away," Lizbet said. "I'm sure he's eager to accommodate your refined palate."

Strix stopped eating. "Are you being sarcastic?"

"Am I? I suppose I am." Lizbet frowned. "Sarcasm is a venial sin. It's untruthful and uncharitable. I apologize, Strix."

Strix shrugged and speared another hunk of rat. "Better a venial sin than no sin at all." She popped the rat into her mouth. "Keep working at it."

They washed their faces and hands in a basin and undressed down to their undershirts. Kate had assigned them beds side by side, separated only by a muslin curtain. The curtain was crudely printed in pictures of hunks of red meat with the bones sticking out. Lizbet guessed it had been made from cloth stolen from the goblin town.

The other women and girls who slept in the Women's Commons avoided Lizbet and Strix, except for curious or worried glances, and spoke only in murmurs. Everyone took to their own bed. Good-nights were exchanged. Before she slipped beneath the sheets, Lizbet surreptitiously removed her wrong-feet-on boots and her socks. Her poor pinched feet felt better immediately.

The oil lamps were extinguished. The darkness of under-ground, without even the faintest glimmer, a darkness more perfect and absolute than Lizbet had ever experienced, filled the room like earth being poured into an open grave. In the dark, the water nearby seemed to rumble more loudly, and Lizbet could hear every drop drip from the wet stone walls.

Lizbet didn't like this place at all. She didn't like the wet, the foul sewage smells, the smothering darkness, the suspicious people. She was disappointed that no one had heard of the Margrave's book. She had no idea where to look next. She began to worry about the dangers of blundering through a world where she didn't belong, a world, if the old soldier at her dinner table were to be believed, chockablock with goblins and witches.

Despite these worries, she was exhausted by the day's events and quickly fell asleep.

She awoke to flickering light, cold air on her bare feet, and Maglet's voice, screeching and triumphant: "This one's a witch too! I knew it! I knew it!"

Chapter 15

Lizbet jerked upright in bed, clutching the covers to her breast. Maglet crouched at the foot of the bed. She held a flickering oil lamp in one hand. With the other hand she had pulled the covers off Lizbet's feet. No longer could it be concealed: illuminated by the lamplight, Lizbet's feet were obviously on opposite the way they should be.

Instinctively, Lizbet pulled her feet back and tried to shove the covers down over them. Maglet yelled, "Oh, no, you don't!" She grabbed at Lizbet's ankle and pulled it free of the covers. She leaned over the foot of the bed and shoved her lamp in Lizbet's face with the other hand. "Hold still, or I'll make you taste fire, witch!"

"I'm not a witch," Lizbet said desperately. "I'm not really a witch at all. It's just my legs. I'll tell you all about it, if you'll let me—"

"Lies, lies, witches are all lies!" Maglet shrieked. "You've lied enough, no more of your lies! Wake up!" she called. "Wake up, all of you! Come see the witch!"

Grunts and stirrings around the room, and the sound of mattresses groaning, and bare feet thumping onto the stone floor. Women and girls in their nightclothes appeared one by one behind Maglet. They stared at Lizbet's feet, looked into her eyes, then back to her feet. Lizbet's blood rose to her cheeks. She told herself she had nothing to be ashamed of, but it didn't help whatever secret part of her was embarrassed.

"It's just my legs," Lizbet said quickly, stammering. "I had blood poisoning and gangrene, so Strix had to make me new ones. I'm not really a witch . . ."

"Gretchen, Isabelle, Sophie," Maglet said to another of the women, "run for Gregor and Hansel and the Glucks, and tell them to bring rope to tie up the witch. I'll bet she's a spy from the Pope of Storms. And some of you, grab the witch girl beside her, before she escapes—"

Lizbet, in her shock and fear and sleepy confusion, had forgotten about Strix. "Strix!" she screamed toward the curtain that separated their beds. "Run!"

"She's gone!" came a woman's voice. From across the curtain, the sound of bedclothes being torn apart. "The bed's empty," the woman said. "She's not here."

Strix had escaped! Thank heavens for that, at least. But Maglet's bony fist gripped Lizbet's ankle even more firmly. Having lost Strix, she was determined not to let Lizbet get away. "Don't try any tricks, witchy," Maglet said. "And don't get your hopes up. We'll find the other spy soon enough. There are miles and miles of sewers. We know 'em all, and she doesn't. We'll catch her, you'll see."

Maglet's smile was so smug, and she sounded so sure of herself, that Lizbet's hopes sank.

lizbet a tiny voice whispered in her ear. It was so low Lizbet could barely hear it.

"What?" Lizbet said.

"You heard me," Maglet said.

"I wasn't—" Lizbet began.

hush, silly, it's me.

It was Strix's voice. Lizbet glanced toward it. There was Strix, crouching by her bed. Only she was transparent, ghostly. It wasn't good enough. Maglet would be able to see her.

you have to get free, Strix's whisper said. *just for a moment. then i can knit us into the shadows.*

"It's still not working," Lizbet said, trying not to look at Strix's half-seen form.

Maglet looked at her sharply. "What are you talking about?"

it is *working,* Strix's voice whispered.

Lizbet had to admit that was true: Strix was right beside her, and Maglet obviously didn't realize it. How could Lizbet see Strix and Maglet couldn't?

She had no time to worry about that now. She had to find a way to make Maglet let her go. People were coming back with rope to tie her up, soon, and then getting loose would be hopeless.

"Uhhhhhhh," Lizbet groaned loudly. She put both hands on her stomach. "My insides! The pain! I think it's that rat I ate." She sat up and leaned toward Maglet. Her eyes rolled back in her head. Her mouth opened, and a thin drool of spittle fell onto Maglet's hand that gripped her ankle. "Uhhhhh, I'm going to be sick. I'm going to throw up all over." She made gagging noises deep in her throat and swayed her body toward Maglet.

"You disgusting thing!" Maglet screeched. She flinched back. She didn't let go of Lizbet's ankle, though, but gripped it harder than ever. "You get one drop on me, and I'll beat you senseless!"

"Okay," Lizbet said, "I won't then." She drew back her fist and punched Maglet on the nose as hard as she could.

Maglet howled. Blood spurted from both nostrils. She let go of Lizbet and shoved both index fingers into her nostrils to stanch the flow. Blood dribbled down both fists. "You've hurt me!" she screeched. "I'm bleeding!"

Lizbet, her ankle free, hopped from the bed. She felt Strix's crackly, leafy hand grasp hers. Her body faded to ghostliness. "Nicely done," Strix's voice whispered.

"Thanks," Lizbet whispered back. "What now?"

"Get your clothes," Strix whispered.

Lizbet's socks, boots, and dress turned ghostly as she touched them. Strix pulled her toward the center of the room, where the women and girls, still in their nightclothes, milled about, talking, and casting anxious glances into the room's dark corners. "What are you doing?" Lizbet whispered. "We need to hide."

"We *are* hiding," Strix whispered back.

Lizbet felt exposed and helpless, standing in the center of the room with the others all around her. She feared that at any moment someone would touch her and know where she was.

But she discovered that in a crowd of people, no one notices every time they brush against someone else. Also, Maglet soon had the braver women poking beneath the beds and into the corners with broomsticks. Odd as it seemed, it was safer to be the room's center, right in the midst of your enemies.

But it didn't solve their larger problem. Where were they to go next? Maglet was right. Without knowledge of the maze of sewers, Lizbet and Strix would quickly become lost.

The girls who had been sent for help returned, with men carrying weapons and rope. "They're gone?" one man said when he heard the news. "Then good riddance."

"They're not gone," Maglet said. "I saw the one disappear. It's some witchy trick. They might still be here, invisible. I tell you, if they're witches, they're probably spies for the Pope of Storms. If we capture them, we can ransom them back to the Pope. That's what you do with captured spies." Maglet's tongue licked her lips eagerly, and she rocked back and forth from one foot to the other.

"I don't know how we're supposed to find invisible people," another man said doubtfully.

"We'll go hand in hand through all the sewers, covering every inch," Maglet said. "No one will get past us. We'll beat every inch with sticks."

Lizbet liked the sound of this less and less, but Maglet, obsessed with the idea of finding and holding them for ransom from the Pope of Storms, whoever he was, gradually had her audience nodding and agreeing.

Kate had been standing back from the crowd, silent. She had a pensive look. She had not taken part in the broomstick search beneath the beds. When the women and men seemed to be agreeing with Maglet's plan, Kate loudly announced, "In that case, I'll guard the boats. If the witches wanted to escape, all they'd need to do is steal a boat and take it downstream and out the Grand Cloaca Ostium. In fact," Kate almost shouted, "I'm going to the boats right now."

"You do that," Maglet said. "You were being a little soft on the witch girl earlier. I'm glad to see you changed your mind. Now, the rest of you . . ."

Kate loudly stomped off, through a stone arch at one end of the commons room.

"C'mon," Lizbet whispered to Strix, "let's go." She squeezed Strix's hand and pulled her across the room, toward the stone arch.

"Where are we going?"

"We're following Kate to the boats. That's our way out."

"She's pretty strong," Strix whispered. "Are we going to fight her? Maybe we can slip past her. What if she comes after us?"

"Kate's not going to stop us," Lizbet whispered. "Didn't you hear her?"

"She said she was going to guard the boats," Strix whispered.

"No, she said, 'If Lizbet and Strix are listening, I'll show them where the boats are so they can escape.'"

"Is there something wrong with your ears? She didn't say that."

"Oh, Strix," Lizbet whispered. "So smart, and yet so dumb."

Strix looked puzzled. "Why would she help us? Is she your friend?"

"No, she's just . . . well, maybe she is, in a way. People are supposed to help other people in trouble. If we were among witches, wouldn't they help you?"

"No."

"Really?"

"Really. Why would they do that?"

Because it's nice, it's good, it's kind, it's how people would want themselves treated, Lizbet thought. Witches didn't understand that? "It's every witch for herself, then?"

Strix's ghostly head bobbed. "Of course."

Lizbet remembered Mrs. Woodcot's most beautiful and peculiar house. How could you make a house like that and not want to share it with anyone? She squeezed Strix's hand more tightly. She resolved to be the best possible friend to Strix that she could be.

Under the stone arch, a rocky wet tunnel spiraled downward into darkness. The girls hurried, anxious not to lose the glow of Kate's lamp as it disappeared down the tunnel ahead of them. The sound of rushing water that could be heard in the Women's Commons grew louder the deeper they went.

The tunnel opened into an immense arched sewer channel, twice as tall as Lizbet or Strix. A rushing river of sewage filled it almost halfway up. The roar, echoing off the tile walls, was deafening. At a tiny stone wharf at the sewer's edge, a few flat-bottomed skiffs bobbed up and down on the roaring tide of black sewage, straining at their painters.

"So here are the boats," Kate said. She was nearly shouting, and even so, her voice was scarcely audible over the noise of the rushing sewage. Her gaze searched about, as if straining to see something hidden in the darkness. "If the witches should happen to steal them, they would find that the Cloaca Maxim empties into the river in a few hundred feet. That place is dangerously close to the stronghold of the Pope of Storms. The witches would be well advised to go in the opposite direction, westward toward the Montagnes du Monde, traveling only by day to avoid goblins, and cross the Montagnes du Monde back into their own country.

"And," she added (was it only the flickering of her oil lamp, or did Kate's eyes become brighter, as if there were tears ready for release?), "if the two witches do cross the Montagnes, I hope they seek audience with General Wolftrow, and plead our plight, his army and their descendants, the ones he led on that terrible journey. Tell him we still love him, we are still faithful, and we wait steadfastly for him to return."

Dragging Strix behind her, Lizbet approached Kate and, bending down (the woman was a little shorter than she was), squeezed her shoulder and kissed her cheek. She tasted salty wetness. "We will," Lizbet promised.

"Tch," Kate said, half laughing and half sobbing, "the place is afflicted with ghosts, I hear them talking to me."

Lizbet and Strix slid into one of the skiffs. Lizbet unshipped the oars and swung them in their oarlocks into the roiling tide of sewage. Strix loosened the knot that secured the skiff's painter to the wharf and pulled the painter into the skiff's bottom. Immediately the current of sewage swept them out into its stream. "Farewell!" Lizbet called. "And thank you!"

At this moment, Maglet appeared at the tunnel entrance. She sized up the situation in a moment. "The witches!" she yelled. "They're escaping!"

"Are they?" Kate asked innocently. "Did they slip past me? Oh dear. How could that have happened? Why don't we discuss it at length, over a hot rat sandwich?"

"No, you froppish trull! We have to chase them! I'll get a skiff. Get out of my way!"

As Maglet tried to push past the shorter but sturdier Kate, Kate did something with her foot, and Maglet's legs went out from under her. Maglet's feet flew up, her head went down, and she fell onto the stones with a *whoof!* "Oops!" exclaimed Kate.

The river of sewage rapidly bore their skiff away. The current swept them around a curve in the tunnel, and wharf, Kate, and Maglet were gone.

Lizbet and Strix were plunged into blackness. Their only light had been Kate's oil lamp. In moments, even the last faint glow of that light upstream faded, and the darkness was complete. Lizbet had thought she would control the skiff with the oars, but when you couldn't see, it was pointless to row.

"Where are we?" Lizbet yelled over the roar of the current.

"We're being swept helplessly through a sewer in utter darkness," Strix yelled back.

The stink was intolerable. The roar of waters beat on Lizbet's ears like a solid thing. She felt one of her oars touch a sewer wall. She shoved as hard as she could, to push them back into midstream. If they struck something solid here, the force of the rushing sewage would surely capsize them, and it would be all over.

The dark. The stench. The danger. Lizbet had surely been in no more awful situation in her life.

She almost regretted it would end soon.

And it was ending already. Ahead, a faint glow of light, becoming stronger. The current swept them around a curve, and the circular end of the sewer pipe, bright with pink dawn light, rushed at them.

Through it, Lizbet could see nothing but sky. Uh-oh.

"Strix!" Lizbet shouted. "Sit beside me! Face backward! Grab one oar! Pull as hard as you can! We need to go faster!"

"Why?" Strix seated herself on the thwart beside Lizbet.

"Because we're coming up on a drop, and I'd rather fly than fall! But don't pull so hard you lose your arm again."

Straining and grunting at their oars, the girls pulled for all they were worth. The skiff sped over the filthy tide. Lizbet squinted as pink daylight swept over her. Looking up, she saw the end of the sewer pipe pass above her head. With all her strength, she gave one last pull on her oar, and they flew into empty space.

Chapter 16

For one dizzy, breathless moment the skiff was airborne. Then they were falling. Lizbet got out one shriek before the skiff hit water in a splash that sent vile glops of sewage spewing everywhere.

When she caught her breath, Lizbet looked about. The skiff spun around on a fast-flowing river. Taking the other oar from Strix, Lizbet struggled to orient them to the current. The sewer emerged high above the riverbank, between the columns of a marble temple. On both sides of the opening, where a waterfall of sewage cascaded into the river, a statue of a goblin woman emptied a ewer with one hand, while she held her nose with the other. Downriver, reeds and grasses grew in jungle-like abundance on both banks. And farther to the east—

A fortress rose into the pink and blue dawn sky. Twisty, wavy towers, buttresses like soaring wings. Windows, too many to count, pierced every wall, so that the entire building looked like latticework.

Spinning windmills sprouted from the building's towers. Lizbet could hear their steady *thum-thum* even at a distance. Square sails like a four-masted schooner's fluttered from one roof, triangular sails like those on a Mussulman dhow fluttered on another. Hundreds of banners, scarlet, purple, pink, azure, all furled and flapped in a ceaseless wind. The entire building seemed to be in movement.

The river was carrying them straight toward it.

"That has to be the stronghold of the Pope of Storms," Lizbet said.

Strix nodded. "This is where we're supposed to turn back and go in the opposite direction. We'd better land now and start walking back before we get any closer."

But . . . Lizbet thought. "A pope would have knowledge of everything in his domain," she said. "Wouldn't he? If anyone knows where the Margrave's book is, he would. We have to ask him."

"You're not really going to dare the wrath of the Pope of Storms?" Strix said.

"I don't even know who the 'Pope of Storms' is. Do you?"

"Mrs. Woodcot knew of him," Strix said. She frowned. She looked more serious and less bratty than usual. That worried Lizbet. "He is a witch lord, powerful, subtle, and ancient."

"Is he good, or evil?"

Strix rolled her eyes. "Haven't you learned *anything* about witches by now?"

"All right. Forget 'good' or 'evil.' Do you think he'll be helpful, or dangerous?"

"All witches are dangerous," Strix said. "No witch is ever helpful."

"Mrs. Woodcot is helpful. She sent you to help me."

Strix squeezed her lips tightly together and looked down into the water.

Lizbet was distracted by a sudden commotion from upstream, like a yell followed by a splash. "What was that?" she said. She turned to see, but the current had already carried them downstream, and Lizbet could no longer see the sewer mouth. She listened, but heard nothing more.

Lizbet wanted to have Strix along. The thought of leaving Strix behind made her feel uncomfortable and lonely. She knew that she could goad Strix to come with her. If she wanted. All she had to say was something like "If you're afraid to come with me . . . ," and Strix would come. Because Strix could not admit weakness.

But Lizbet wouldn't do that. Not anymore. Not after all they'd been through. It wasn't fair to Strix. It wasn't what a friend would do.

"I'm still going to the Pope of Storms," Lizbet said. "I really want to have you with me. You don't have to come, if you don't want."

"I'll come with you," Strix said. "I have to."

They beached the skiff on a mud flat amid dense reeds, took off their boots and socks, hiked up their skirts, and waded through the deep squishy mud toward solid shore. The "reeds," when Lizbet looked at them closely, were actually rolled-up newspapers, copper lightning rods filmed with verdigris, and mildewed leather buggy whips. The mud was plain old mud, though, and felt delicious between the toes. Lizbet stopped for moment, to enjoy it. "Maybe it's just that I'm really tired, or we're about to do something dangerous and I'm looking for an excuse to stop for a moment, but have you ever noticed how nice mud feels between the toes?" she said to Strix.

Strix shrugged. "Feels like mud to me," she said. "It's okay, I guess. Maybe it's your legs."

"My legs?"

"They're mostly oak and birch. I'm sure they love soaking up the nice mucky mud. Like all plant life."

Lizbet could almost feel the moisture and richness of the river mud soaking into her legs, feeding their vegetable tissues. She felt stronger already, and less tired. She spread her arms and lifted her face to the sky. "I could just stand here forever," she declared.

"If you don't start moving soon," Strix said. "Your legs will put down roots, and you *will* be there forever."

"Eeee!" Lizbet yelled. She sprinted through the mud as fast as she could go, beating Strix to the riverbank.

Strix came up behind her, laughing.

"It's complicated being a—I mean, having witch legs," Lizbet said accusingly. "You should warn me."

From the top of the riverbank, Lizbet could see the edge of the goblin town to the west, clusters of tumbledown buildings clinging to high ground above the river. To the east, no more than a quarter mile away, the stronghold of the Pope of Storms fluttered its banners and spun its windmills. But who was that between them and the stronghold?

On flat ground in front of the stronghold, a grove of cages, stocks, gibbets, and gallows had been erected. Each held a prisoner. As they came closer, Lizbet noticed that one of the prisoners resembled Toadwipe. Another had a head like a goat, only with long, curling tusks and a dozen horns pointing in all directions. Others looked like half-starved naked women. Others were even worse.

As they approached, the first prisoner Lizbet and Strix passed was an immense maggot, as thick as Lizbet's middle, but with the face of a prosperous middle-aged man with puffy sideburns and an extravagant mustache. It wore a smart black silk bow tie and pince-nez. It was confined in a cage of iron slats, in which it constantly crawled up and down, to and fro, restlessly weaving figures-of-eight with its body. As Lizbet and Strix approached, it started to chatter, without pausing its endless crawling.

"Hello ladies or girls I should say how are you sweet things today I wonder if I might trouble you to undo the latch on this cage where I have been confined cruelly on account of perjurious accusations or you could at least put in a good word with the proprietor of this establishment who is in gravest danger of destruction if my mistreatment ever comes to the notice of His Infernal Majesty whom I serve eternally with perfect love and boundless energy although my views are flexible and I could serve your Christian God instead if it please you to release me—"

Lizbet and Strix passed by the cage. Despite its seeming solid, Lizbet gave it a generous berth. The slats rang as the creature inside banged against them.

"—only do not forsake me and leave me here in vile confinement and betray your Christian charity which commends your mercy to miserable persecuted wretches such as myself or you risk losing the love of your God and the delights of Heaven and instead being condemned to the furnaces of Hell where devils will cut your pretty white flesh with knives and burn you with pitch!" Frothy white spittle flew from its mouth.

Behind them, Lizbet could hear it continuing to curse her. She tried to ignore it. "These are devils?" she asked.

"That's what they are," Strix said. "Lesser sorts."

"That one is pretty much what I expected a devil to be like."

"Not very nice, is he?"

"Half-mad, I'd call him. But Strix, don't you like devils? You're a witch, after all. They say witches consort with devils. At black masses and such. There's supposed to be revelry. Mad pipes and timbrels. Reckless dancing. And"—Lizbet felt her cheeks growing warm—"licentiousness."

"That's what they say."

"All a fib?"

"I've never been. Mrs. Woodcot says it's something like that. Afterwards, she comes home and has a sinking spell, takes to her bed for a week, and makes me fetch her root tea and casserole of baby's fingers to restore her strength."

Lizbet said, "I just don't see how you could bear to be licentious with a man-headed maggot who is out of his wits.

Or with something that looks like a giant boiled crayfish."
The crayfish may have overheard her. From inside the stocks
that restrained it, it clacked its scarlet pincers and waggled its
antennae. "Even if you ignore the sinfulness of it, I wouldn't
think it would be much fun."

"You can't judge someone by their appearance," Strix said.

"Even if they have the head of a goat?"

"I am a free-thinker," Strix said.

"But if they're a devil," Lizbet persisted, "they're not very
nice inside either. You've said so yourself. A couple of times."

"It's what you do if you're a witch. They say . . ." Strix
paused for the tiniest fraction of a second. "They say you get
used to it."

"Oh, Strix."

"What?"

"Poor Strix . . ." Lizbet took Strix's hand and squeezed it.

"'Poor Strix' nothing! Is that pity? I don't want your pity!
I might . . ." That pause again. "I might enjoy carnal relations
with a giant boiled crayfish. You never know."

"I don't want to happen to you what happened to Mme.
Minglefinger."

"I'll be fine," Strix said. She squeezed Lizbet's hand tightly.
"You don't have worry about *me*."

They passed a naked woman dangling from a gallows. She
was so thin that her ribs stuck out of her chest like sprung barrel
staves. Her mop of hair was bright orange. Her left hip bore
a large black stain. "Hello, girls," she called out as Lizbet and
Strix approached. "Might I have a word with you?" Her voice
was a throaty purr, perhaps made harsher than intended by the
action of the rope noose around her throat. "Would either of
you have a pair of tweezers I might borrow for a moment? My
eyebrows are like wild animals." Her eyelids fluttered.

"Who is this?" Lizbet asked.

"This is a Temptress," Strix said.

"She doesn't look very tempting to me," Lizbet whispered in Strix's ear. "She looks half-starved."

"I heard that," the Temptress said. "You aren't very tempting yourself, sweetie, spattered with sewage, with a face like skim milk and a figure like a fence post." Lizbet flushed.

"She's not supposed to tempt *you*," Strix said. "She tempts holy men, mostly. Eremites. Prophets. The odd parish priest. What happened to your hip, hon? Did someone throw an inkpot at you again?"

"Mind your own business," the Temptress said.

"Who confined all of you devils out here?" Strix asked. "Was it the Pope of Storms?"

"Find out for yourself," the Temptress snapped.

"You know," Lizbet said as they walked on, "you might get more cooperation if you were a little nicer."

"It hurts to be nice," Strix said. "It gives me a stomachache."

"You should take a bicarbonate of soda," Lizbet said.

The stronghold of the Pope of Storms, close up, was less a building than a cluster of slender towers jammed into each other like the cells in a honeycomb. Each tapered sharply, coming to a point hundreds of feet above. There were scarcely any real walls. Each tower was a skeleton of stone, its ribs adorned with bits of broken glass and pottery. Although, on account of the hundreds of flags and pennants fluttering from every prominence, and the streaming drapes blowing out of every window, Lizbet could make out the underlying building only in glimpses.

A wide moat surrounded it all. Lizbet was beginning to worry about how they were going to cross it, when a drawbridge descended in front of them.

Lizbet thought drawbridges were usually supported by chains or ropes. This drawbridge came down on gray beating goose wings. The drawbridge itself was made of tiny twigs glued together with mud.

"It looks like a bird's nest," Lizbet said.

"The Pope of Storms is in love with all things of the air," Strix said.

"It doesn't look very strong. Do you think it's safe to cross?"

Strix put her hands on her hips. "You're the one who insisted that we barge into the stronghold of a mighty witch lord. I'm happy to turn around anytime."

"I never said anything about *barging*. But . . . all right. Let's go." Lizbet grabbed Strix's hand and pulled her along behind.

"Anyway, it's not the drawbridge you should worry about," Strix said. "It's what comes next. This drawbridge obviously came down just for us. It's always dangerous when someone else has plans for you, but you don't have plans for them."

The drawbridge bounced a little as they stepped onto it, and loosened twigs fell off into the moat below. Lizbet peeked over the edge.

The moat was crawling with crocodiles. They cut serpiginous paths through the water, only their noses and eyes visible. They made throaty roars when they yawned, and you could see every one of their scores of teeth. Their teeth looked like paring knives and broken bottles. Their scales were hunks of smashed crockery and shattered wine glasses.

Lizbet and Strix had scarcely gone a few steps when the gray goose wings came to life again, flapping noisily, and the drawbridge began to tilt up. Open air appeared between the drawbridge and the bank.

"Which way?" Strix yelled. "It's not to late to jump back!"

"I'm not going back!" Lizbet yelled. "Come on!" She pulled Strix forward. As the drawbridge tilted higher, they started to slip, and finally lost their footing, skidding the last few yards on their backsides. They arrived at the stronghold's gates in a dusty heap of Lizbet, Strix, and a pile of twigs and mud.

A man strutted out to meet them. No, it was a bird. No, it was a man.

His frame was tall and spare, his hair white and closely cropped. His nose was so long it almost curled around into his mouth. He appeared to be wearing a brown morning suit with a white ruffed collar, but when Lizbet looked closely, suit and collar proved to be feathers.

A second man hopped up behind him, only half as tall as the first man, and plumper, with a tiny nose and bright eyes. He was dressed in a brown and white striped frock coat, red cravat, and feathery breeches. Actually, he was feathers all over too. "Welcome!" he cried. His voice was a cheerful chirp.

"Are they?" the first man croaked sourly.

"Of course! They are expected!"

"Catarrh is expected in the spring, and the ague in winter, but neither is welcome."

"We aren't catarrh or ague," Lizbet said. She pulled herself to her feet and brushed herself off. "We are a girl and a witch."

"I might have a touch of the ague," Strix volunteered. "From the cold river."

Lizbet glanced back and forth between the two men. She curtsied, and tried to remember the proper way to speak to a Holy Father. "Do I have the pleasure of addressing His Witchy Holiness, The Pope of Storms?"

The smaller man chuckled. "No, neither of us is anything of the sort," he said. "But your mistake is charming in its innocence."

"The Pope will undoubtedly have you hung for it," the taller man said.

"This is Griffon, I am Cupido," the smaller man said. "Come with us. Let's not keep the Pope waiting!" He turned and made off through the entranceway with a hopping, skipping gait. Griffon followed, stiff-legged, tilting from side to side as he walked.

Inside the stronghold was like the outside. Every wall, every surface was pierced with windows and archways, and

Lizbet could see bits of the morning sky if she looked up. Clouds of steam and fog blew constantly down the corridor, teasing Lizbet's hair and fluttering her skirt.

Lizbet followed Cupido and Griffon somewhat hesitantly. "The Pope of Storms wouldn't really hang us, would he?" she said.

"He might chop off your head instead," Griffon said dolefully.

"Ignore him," Cupido chirped. "You have nothing to worry about. The Pope is a mild and genial fellow."

"Except when he's on a murderous rampage," Griffon said.

"I was wondering why he has so many devils held prisoner?" Lizbet asked.

"They were molesting the good citizens of Slattern," Cupido said. "That's the goblin town, up the hill to the west? The goblins are the vassals and thralls of the Pope of Storms. He takes his responsibilities to them seriously. No misbehavior in the Realm of Storms! As soon as there was trouble, he rounded up the devils and confined them, lickety-split. Curious thing, the devils. They never used to be a problem. Lately they've become bolder."

"Maybe it's because God has been deposed from His throne, and devils are running the universe?" Lizbet said.

"Is that so?" Cupido said. "I don't follow politics."

They marched down and then up several flights of stairs, coming at last to a wide and airy chamber two stories high. Gusty winds howled down its length. Lizbet's hair fluttered out behind her, and her skirt stuck to her legs. The wind stung her eyes, and she had to squeeze them almost closed. Drops of rain pelted her face. The scent of ozone made her sneeze.

"God bless you," yelled Strix.

"Thanks," Lizbet yelled back.

At the head of the room, through boiling fog and vapor, Lizbet glimpsed a figure ten feet tall or more. A tattered great coat, high boots, and black wide-brimmed hat. A scarf fluttered between coat and hat, its ends so long that Lizbet could almost touch them. But within the coat, the hat, the scarf, no person could be seen, save for the swirl of cloud and steam that, if Lizbet used her imagination, might be said to momentarily look like a face, a body, an arm, or a leg before dissolving again in the blowing wind.

"Your Holiness," Cupido proclaimed, his high chirping voice cutting through the roar of the winds, "your guests have arrived!"

"Is this . . . a witch?" Lizbet said to Strix.

Strix nodded. "The Pope of Storms is made of airs and vapors," she said. "He's made of mist, fog, the smoke of forest fires, steam from volcano vents, blizzards, tempests, hailstorms, and whirlwinds."

Lizbet tried to calm herself. She leaned forward a little, as if steadying her body against a gale. She tried to curtsy, and barely escaped falling over. "Your Highness!" she yelled into the wind. "My companion and I thank you for granting us audience! Our journey here has been difficult, and fraught with danger. We have come over the Montagnes du Monde to find a book that belongs to Margrave Hengest Wolftrow. The Margrave has my father imprisoned, and I hope that—"

What mischief have you been doing to my goblins?

The Pope of Storms' voice whistled, whispered, boomed, and howled. It was the midnight wind hissing across the grass. It was the tempest roaring through the oaks. Lizbet felt a sense of helplessness and futility when she spoke. As if she were pleading with the wind.

"I . . . we . . . ," she stumbled.

You trespassed in the goblin city. You burgled shops and stole a keg of beer. You freed a criminal whom I had confined for his crimes. You pilfered the keys of the goblin constable.

"Uh-oh," Strix said.

"He'll behead them for sure," Griffon said. "Probably after hanging them first."

"No, I think he's in a forgiving mood," Cupido said. "Maybe he'll just have them flogged."

"It was an accident!" Lizbet yelled into the wind. "We didn't know . . . we couldn't find . . . I felt pity for Toadwipe . . . I'm very sorry. We'll make amends . . ." The wind carried her words back to her. She didn't know whether the Pope of Storms even heard her.

For your crimes, I order you confined in my dungeon for a thousand years, to be whipped daily, and take no nourishment save for your own tears.

"A thousand years . . . !" Lizbet exclaimed.

"An unusually lenient sentence," said Griffon. He shook his head, and his feathers fluttered mournfully "I fear such soft-heartedness will only encourage future lawbreakers."

But on account of your tender years, and because your crimes were the result of ignorance and youthful folly rather than a hardened criminal mind, I will strike five hundred years from your sentence, have you scolded instead of whipped, and allow you a diet of tea and shoes as well as tears.

"The sentence cut in half!" Cupido chirped. "Truly, the Pope of Storms is made out of mercy!"

"But—my father! Five hundred years! It's still too long! He'll die before I get out. I'll die." Lizbet shook her head, shocked by this dismal prospect.

Strix. You have no more to do here.

The tattered greatcoat spread wide. The blustering winds pushed Strix forward, toward the cloudy figure of the Pope of Storms. Strix's layered dresses and rusty hair fluttered out before her. She bent backward, fighting the wind, almost losing her footing.

Embrace me. The whirlwind will be our steed. I will repossess you to the house of Mrs. Woodcot. And none too soon. Your actions have been suspicious. Why didn't you leave the mortal girl to die in the Montagnes? Though it mattered not in the end. Come, Strix.

Fighting the winds which forced her toward the embrace of the Pope of Storms, Strix cast one look back at Lizbet. In Strix's brown eyes, the turn of her head—what was that look? Fear, loss, longing, and guilt: Lizbet saw all of these, in an instant.

She leaped forward, threw her arms around Strix, and held her tightly against the winds. "She doesn't want to go!" she cried. "She doesn't *want* to!"

Strix! Come to me without delay.

Ferocious winds dashed against her. Lizbet's clothes whipped her skin painfully. She gasped to breathe. She struggled to hold on to Strix.

"I'm not going!" Strix yelled. "If you're going to put Lizbet in a dungeon, put me in one too!"

Cease your folly. You risk dissolution.

"I don't care! Lizbet is my friend!"

The winds reversed. Lizbet and Strix were violently thrust in the opposite direction. They lost their balance and fell. Still clinging to each other, they were rolled across the floor by the tempest, out the door, and (both of them shrieking in shock and relief) down a staircase, to fetch up at the bottom, bruised but whole.

Lizbet released Strix. She tried to push herself up on her hands.

Strix did not let Lizbet go. Instead, she grabbed her more firmly, and hugged Lizbet to her. "I'm in trouble," she said in a shaky voice. "I'm in really, really bad trouble. Worse than I've ever been in. What's going to happen to me?"

"Right now, you're going into the dungeon," croaked Griffon, tottering down the staircase one step at a time.

"Don't worry, we don't even have a dungeon," chirped Cupido, hopping down behind him.

"We'll build one just for you," said Griffon.

"But in the meantime, we'll put you up in a guest room," said Cupido.

"Tiny and bare, with a heavy bar across the door," said Griffon.

"It has a beautiful view!"

"Of the hungry crocodiles in the moat."

"They're fed daily, Griffon. If they want second helpings, they should speak up."

The guest-room-dungeon, several floors higher in the stronghold, proved to have a beautiful view indeed. As it seemed with every room here, there was more window than wall. Immensely long curtains blew through the open spaces and out into the sky. Below, Lizbet could see crocodiles cutting through the waters of the moat. Somewhere nearby and above, a windmill made a continuous *chuff-chuff-chuff* noise.

The bar clunked down outside the door, and they were locked in. The room was not quite "bare," as Griffon had threatened. Two gray hammocks made of woven grass and vines, bits of yarn and loose threads, hung from ceiling. Lizbet thought they looked quite like oriole nests. Strix immediately flopped down in one, and by the time Lizbet had arranged in her mind all the questions she wanted to ask—why was the Pope of Storms suspicious? Why was Strix in trouble?—Strix was sound asleep.

They had both gotten no more than an hour of sleep in the last two days—that brief time in the sewers, before Maglet woke Lizbet. Exhaustion claimed her. She crawled into the remaining hammock, and despite everything she was feeling, excitement, fear, and despair, she was asleep almost before she closed her eyes.

Hours later, Lizbet awoke to the sound of the bar outside the door being slammed back, the squeak of the door opening, and Griffon's lugubrious voice: "Tiffin is served. Prepare for your scolding."

Lizbet rubbed her eyes. Griffon and Cupido stood in the doorway. Cupido held a steaming teapot. Griffon held a platter with a boiled boot, artfully presented in a garnish of hobnails, shoelaces, and grommets.

Chapter 17

While Lizbet and Strix ate, Griffon and Cupido scolded them.

"Don't be so slovenly."

"Chew each bite twenty times, else you'll get colic."

"You wear your dresses too short."

"You're lazy, you'll never amount to anything."

"That's not fair," Lizbet protested. "You've only just met me—how do you know whether I'm lazy or not?"

"This boot isn't bad," Strix mumbled through a mouthful of half-chewed shoe leather. "For a cooked boot, that is. Watch out for nails though."

"You're too kind," Cupido said. "I'll be sure to tell the cook you enjoyed it. Lizbet, you ought to eat more, you're too skinny."

"You're a greedy little pig, Lizbet," Griffon said. "If you eat that much you'll get fat."

When the scolding was done and the meal finished, and Griffon, Cupido, pot, and platter had departed, Strix said, "We have to escape."

Lizbet nodded. *But even if we succeed in escaping the Pope of Storms,* she thought, *what then?*

The awful truth was that Lizbet had failed. She had not found the Margrave's book. She had run out of ideas where to look for it, in all this immense world. Even if she escaped, she would return empty-handed. She had no way of releasing her father from prison. Her struggles, her pain, the loss of her legs—all had been for nothing.

Despair drained the strength from her limbs and dragged her down, as men drown in quicksand.

Strix didn't notice. She was already making escape plans.

Strix stuck her head out a window and craned her neck around. They had slept through most of the day, and it was nearing sunset. The horizontal light through the windows was orange-red and dim. The winds had died to almost nothing, and the long draperies that had fluttered out the windows like banners now hung almost vertically. "We're about a hundred feet up," Strix announced. "That's our first problem. We could try knotting the draperies together to make a rope. That might get us to the ground."

"And the moat? And the crocodiles?" Lizbet said.

"I read a story about a man who used crocodiles as stepping stones to cross a river," Strix said. "He had to walk very quickly across their heads. I think it helped that all the crocodiles were in exactly the right spots."

"I think that kind of thing works better in stories than in real life," Lizbet said.

"Let's start on the draperies," Strix said. "Crocodiles later."

There were lots of draperies, and they were very long, but even after Lizbet and Strix had knotted them all together, they weren't quite long enough to reach the ground. "Is it hopeless?" Lizbet said. At that moment, she was feeling it was quite hopeless. Everything was hopeless.

"No!" Strix said. She balled up her fists. "We have to get out. We *have* to. I am in such trouble, you don't know."

"We're both in trouble," Lizbet said.

"Yes, but—"

"Wait," Lizbet said. She had an idea. "I know the ropes of draperies aren't long enough to reach the ground, but they must be long enough for us to reach one of the windows below. And there are lots and lots of windows." The stronghold was practically nothing but windows. "I'll bet we could climb down outside and get back in through an open window. Maybe we could find a room that wasn't locked."

"Even if it weren't locked, we'd still be trapped in the stronghold," Strix said doubtfully.

"We could lower the drawbridge to get out."

Lizbet knew the plan relied too much on hope and luck (how did you lower a drawbridge that flew on goose wings?), but it was the best she could think of at the moment.

Saying "I'll bet we could climb down" was easy. Actually doing it was terrifying. Lizbet went first, gripping the taut velvet drape between white knuckles, wrapping the fabric around one ankle, squeezing it between her legs. The rope of draperies swung gently back and forth in the still air of early evening. The sun had just set, the sky was still light. The dark waters of the moat were hundreds of dizzy feet below. Lizbet could hear the distant splashings and bellows of the crocodiles. To fall spelled death. Lizbet quailed. Had they made enough knots when they tied the drapes to the window frame? She wished they had doubled up the drapes for strength, instead of just tying them one to one. What if Griffon and Cupido came back? Would they cut the drape and let her fall to her death?

"Hey." Strix's voice, right above her. "Are you actually going to climb down, or are you just going to hang there with your eyes closed?"

Inch by inch, hand over hand, Lizbet let herself slide down the rope of drapes. But when she came to the first window below, she found it was covered by a lattice of stone bars. She grabbed at it with her hand and yanked. It didn't budge. She yanked at it harder, until the rough stone scored her skin and made it bleed, but the stone bars refused to yield. She looked up. Strix, leaning out the window of the guest-room dungeon, was fifteen feet above. Lizbet didn't think she had the strength to climb up there again.

The next window down was also protected by stone fretwork. Through the bars, enticingly, Lizbet could see light falling through an open door. A door she could not get to.

She slid down fifteen feet more. Another window of crisscross stone bars confronted her. Lizbet's fear of height and falling was overtaken by another fear: maybe there was no window below that she could enter. Had the Pope of Storms planned it this way? Had he anticipated his prisoners' escape plans and ordered them confined in a room that he knew had only barred windows below? Maybe Lizbet would descend to the end of the drapes and be stuck there, with no way to reenter the stronghold, too tired to climb back up, and nothing to do but fall into the waiting jaws of the crocodiles below.

"Can you speed it up?" Strix called from above. "This is taking a long time."

"Shut up!" Lizbet yelled. In anger and frustration, she hauled back her foot and kicked at the stone bars with all her might. She didn't care if it hurt. She wanted it to hurt.

With a sharp crack, and the crunch of falling masonry, her foot smashed through into the room beyond.

"Maybe the bars aren't stone after all," she called out to Strix, amazement in her voice. "I think I can break through them." She aimed another kick at the grate, and another chunk caved inward.

In a minute, she had made a hole big enough wiggle through. Behind the window, she found herself in a dim, dusty storeroom. Immense pottery jars stood along the walls, each taller than Lizbet, narrow at the bottom and bloated at the top. Names were painted on them: "Zephyr," "Boreas," "Sirocco," "Harmattan," and others. Lizbet thought she heard noise from inside the jars. She put her ear to the one marked

"Boreas." The ceramic was icy cold against her face. From within, a distant roaring, a sound like winter gales whipping through the fir trees.

"Don't open that jar," Strix said. She slipped through the hole Lizbet had made and dropped to the floor.

"I wasn't going to," Lizbet said.

"I just worry that you're too brave for your own good," Strix said, shaking her head. "Or mine." She stooped and with both hands picked up a chunk broken off the window grill. She rolled it back and forth. "It's stone," she said. "Just as I thought. Catch!" She tossed it to Lizbet.

Lizbet caught it. It was, indeed, solid stone. How had she ever broken it? When she scraped it with a fingernail, the nail chipped. She dropped the chunk of stone to the floor and stamped on it as hard as she could. It shattered to pieces.

"Witch legs," Strix said with satisfaction.

Of course. Lizbet's legs of oak and iron straps. Like battering rams, they had broken through the stone grill.

It's lucky that I have witch legs, she thought. Instantly, she hated herself for thinking that. But then she put the hatred aside as well and just let the first thought remain, unjudged. Because it was true. Like it or not, her witch legs had saved her.

An unlocked door led from the storeroom to an interior hallway of stone struts studded with baubles. Lizbet took Strix's hand and pulled her down the hall. The front of the stronghold, with the main gate and the drawbridge, faced east. Lizbet headed down the hallway in the direction she thought must be eastward and looked for stairways down. Also, she kept a lookout for doors into which they could dodge into if they heard someone—

"Hi! You must be the new prisoners. Trying to escape, I see?"

Lizbet's heart clenched in her chest. She spun around.

In the hallway behind them stood a goblin. Shorter than the average goblin. Fatter than the average goblin. Uglier than the average goblin, if such a thing were possible. Green, gray, and pink piebald fur. A mouth full of rotten teeth.

"Bon soir, mais bon filles," the goblin said, spreading his paws in greeting. "That's French! What can fudge do for you?"

Fudge? But Lizbet preferred any subject of conversation besides "prisoners escaping."

"Fudge!" she said brightly. "It's, um, tasty. It's nice to give to your sweetheart on St. Valentine's Day. It can make you deathly ill if you eat too much."

"There was once a boy," Strix said, "whose name was Alf. Alf loved a girl, Meg. Meg was so thin you could read the newspaper through her. Meg loved everything sweet, but she didn't love Alf. To win her heart, Alf brought her fudge every day. At the end of a year, Alf had spent his last penny on fudge, but Meg had fallen in love with him."

"I'm going to guess the ending," Lizbet said. "Meg was now as big as a circus tent from eating all that fudge, and Alf no longer loved her?"

"Actually, Meg was still as thin as moonlight," Strix said. "She had a tapeworm. They married, and lived no more or less happily than other couples. Why are we talking about fudge?"

"Not fudge, but Fudge," said the goblin. He pointed at his chest with both thumbs. "I'm Fudge! My name's Logofudge, actually, but they all call me Fudge. One syllable being easier to remember than three, and the incongruity and humor of a goblin being named after a confection is also a mnemonic advantage. What's your name, little lady?"

"They call me Lizbet," Lizbet said.

"I'm Strix," Strix said.

"Hajimemashita! That's Japanese." He offered a hairy elbow to each girl. "Shall we be on our way, then? By the way, how do you two intend to lower the drawbridge?"

Lizbet's cheeks flushed. "I'm positive I have no idea what you're talking about."

"But you can't escape without crossing the drawbridge," Fudge said. "It's the only way past the crocodiles. You two are trying to escape, aren't you?"

"No!" said Lizbet quickly.

"Never crossed my mind," said Strix.

"What a bitter disappointment!" Fudge exclaimed. He clutched his chest. "My new-born hopes perish upon the Tarpeian rocks! My spirit founders in the storm-wracked seas of expectations dashed. It sinks beneath the waves of despair." He began to bawl. Tears, faintly green in color, soaked his furry cheeks.

"Why is your spirit foundering and sinking and so on?" Lizbet asked. She dabbed his tears with her sleeve.

"I'd hoped to come with you," Fudge said between sobs.

"Why can't you just leave by yourself?" Lizbet said. "Although, I have no idea what you're doing here in the first place. And how a goblin is able to talk sensibly."

"Maybe he swallowed a scholar, and the scholar is inside talking for him," Strix said. She grabbed Fudge's jaws in her hands, pulled them wide apart, and yelled into the wet and smelly opening, "Anyone in there?"

"Umph! Mmmmph! Urrrk!" croaked Fudge. His arms and legs flailed.

"Strix, stop," Lizbet said. "I don't think that's it. A scholar wouldn't say that his spirit founders in the storm-wracked seas of something-or-another. Men of learning speak concisely, without overwrought melodrama."

Strix released Fudge, who sat down roughly on the floor, rubbing his jaw. "No one answered anyway," she said.

"The sad truth is that I am a prisoner like yourselves," Fudge said. "The Pope of Storms won't let me depart while I am under suspicion."

"Suspicion of what?" Lizbet asked.

"There have been some, um, disappearances. Missing, ah, things."

"This is all very vague," Lizbet said.

"Well, books. Or, actually, words. And they blame me. It's not my fault. Exactly. Or rather, it's not something I could help—"

"Books!" Lizbet exclaimed. "Books?"

"I am the Pope of Storms' Master of Libraries," Fudge said.

Lizbet knelt down, grabbed Fudge by his furry shoulders, and stared him in the eye. "Fudge. Listen to me. I am looking for a book that belonged to the Margrave Hengest Wolftrow of Abalia. He lost it, somewhere, on this side of the Montagnes du Monde, years ago. Do you know anything about it?"

"Oh, yes," Fudge said, "that book is in the Great Library. I know it well."

"Fudge! I love you!" Lizbet threw her arms around the smelly little goblin and hugged him as hard as she could.

"Oof!" went Fudge.

"See?" Strix said. "You never know where passion will strike. Personally, I'd rather have intimate relations with a giant boiled crayfish, but there's no accounting for taste."

"I didn't mean *that,*" Lizbet said, releasing Fudge. She brushed hair and goblin dander off her clothing. "Fudge, may I see it? Please? The Margrave's book?"

"Of course," Fudge said. "Are you *sure* you two aren't trying to escape?"

"Actually," Lizbet said, "I'm not sure. We could be. Just a little."

"I eagerly await a decisive resolution of the issue," Fudge said. "Meanwhile, follow me."

He waddled out the door, Lizbet and Strix on his heels.

Fudge led them through halls of stone ribs and struts, and up and down a dozen twisting staircases. They passed no one. Save for their footsteps, the stronghold was silent. Even the whoosh and whisper of the constant winds had subsided. Lizbet asked Fudge, "What if the Pope of Storms discovers we've left our room?"

"The Pope and all his servants take repose at this hour," Fudge said. "Winds die down at dawn and sunset, you know. It's all due to the tiny angels who sort Democritus's atoms of air into piles of warm ones and cool ones. That's why winds blow. The angels stop for breakfast and supper, of course, and no work gets done at those times."

"I'd heard it was done by demons," Strix said.

In the silence, Lizbet thought her footsteps sounded as loud as drumbeats, each one announcing: "The prisoners are loose!" "I'm still worried we'll be caught," she said. "Strix, can you knit us into the shadows, just in case?"

"Won't do any good," Fudge said. "That only works with mortals. Everyone on this side of the Montagnes can see you plain as day."

"So that's why the goblins could see us," Lizbet said, "but the sewer people couldn't. Fudge, you know all sorts of things."

Fudge halted. At the end of a hallway, they stood before two high doors of woven twigs. "And here," Fudge announced, "is the Great Library." He threw open the doors. Lizbet and Strix drew their breath.

Great it was. A cathedral of books, fifty feet wide, a hundred long, six stories high. Bookcases covered the floor like standing stones, and climbed the soaring walls. Bookcases made of brass rods like birdcages hung from the ceiling. Thousands of bookcases, hundreds of thousands of books.

Lizbet walked among the stacks, straining to read the titles in the deepening twilight. Each book had a name on it: Jorge, Louisa, Sven, Chaim, Georgette, Archibald. Some books had titles written in the inscrutable characters of Araby or Siam. Lizbet picked a book from the shelves at random, a volume in an elegant red leather binding, titled *Johan*. She opened it. No title page, no table of contents, no first chapter . . . She riffed through the pages. Every one was blank.

Lizbet replaced the volume and picked another, this one with two foreign characters on the spine. It was also filled with blank pages from end to end. A book titled *Ysabet* was likewise empty. So were *Vladimir*, and *Sylvie*, and *Kemal*.

"Fudge . . . ," Lizbet said.

Fudge was halfway across the library floor. By dint of vigorous jumping, and bouncing like a ball on his round belly, he propelled himself high enough to grab a book from an upper shelf. He waddled back to Lizbet, eagerly holding up the book for her to take. It was bound in black silk, its cover stamped in gold leaf with a design of crossed cannon and furled flags. Its spine read *Hengest Wolftrow*.

Lizbet stretched forth her hand to receive it coldly and reluctantly. She should have felt joy, and hope: at last she had found the object of her desire. Her mission was half-accomplished. Her goal was within sight.

Instead, Lizbet was filled with foreboding. She took the book from Fudge and opened it.

As she had feared, every page was blank.

"This is it?" she said doubtfully. "Might there be another book? A book of magic, or something of the sort?"

Fudge shook his head. "Nope, none other. One book for each person."

"But why are they all blank, Fudge?"

Fudge scratched his belly with one broken, yellow fingernail. He stared upward. "Well, they might not *all* be blank. Maybe I haven't investigated every last one, in fact . . ." He snuffled at the air with his wet rumpled wet nose, like a truffle pig scenting out a truffle. "In fact, I think I can smell some words right now, some exciting, savory, magical words." His tongue darted about his lips, wetting them. "There might be a book I missed. Where could it be?" His voice was suddenly happy and eager.

Lizbet looked around at the myriad of bookcases. She sniffed the air. What was Fudge talking about? Something poked at her leg. She looked down. Fudge was sticking his wet goblin snout into the pocket of her skirt.

Lizbet shrank back. "What you doing? Stop that!"

"It's a book!" Fudge said. "A book with words in it. I can smell the words. Sumptuous, heady, delicious words! You have a book on your person. Please, please, Lizbet, let me sniff—I mean, let me see it. I love words, surely I do."

"Fudge, I don't have a book," Lizbet said.

"You do, you do, I can smell it, ooooo, it smells delicious, I can smell it in your pocket, please, Lizbet, please!"

Fudge was slobbering in his eagerness. Lizbet said, "Look, Fudge, there's nothing in my pocket. I'll show you." She stuck her hand in her pocket, intending to turn the pocket inside out, to prove it was empty. But her hand touched papers. She pulled them out.

It was the pages of her father's grimoire that she had torn out and stuck in her pocket the day she fled from the marshals of the Magisters of Children. She had forgotten she still had them.

Seeing them, Fudge was in a frenzy. He leaped up and down, he pawed at her, his wet snout went in circles. "Please let me taste them," he cried. "Please, just a little, just a little taste, please, please, please!"

"Strix?" Lizbet said.

Strix shrugged. "Do what you like. I don't know what to make of this."

Lizbet took the spell about how to turn dust motes into gnats and handed it to Fudge. She stuck the others back in her pocket.

Fudge grasped the piece of paper with reverence. "Thank you, thank you, kind child," he mumbled. He held the spell to his snout and inhaled from it. Deeply, more deeply. His eyelids fluttered. Fudge was in ecstasy. The paper vibrated madly. Harder and harder Fudge panted, in and out, his belly and chest working.

As Lizbet watched, something black peeled off the paper and shot into Fudge's nostril. And again, and again. A steady stream of tiny black curlicues, flying off the paper, into Fudge's nose. Lizbet realized they were letters, and words. When they finally stopped, Fudge drew a deep sigh of satisfaction and collapsed to the floor, his eyes half-closed. Lizbet took the paper from his limp hand. It was blank.

Chapter 18

"Well," Strix said, "now we know what happened to all the books."

"And why Fudge is under suspicion," Lizbet said. "And rightfully so."

"And why a goblin is able to speak sensibly."

Lizbet hadn't gotten that far in her thinking. "Why?"

"Fudge must have absorbed all the stuff in the books he's inhaled," Strix said. "How to talk like people. Things about winds and weather. Terrible purple prose." She tickled Fudge's belly with her toe. Fudge sighed happily and fell over on his side.

Lizbet looked around. "But what was in all the books?" she said. "Why do they all have only a person's name as their title? Were they all diaries? Or novels? What an odd sort of library. If it were my library, I'd have some histories, some elevating biographies of individuals of virtue and piety, books of self-improvement, the works of Homer, Horace, and Virgil—"

"Ovid, Juvenal, and Sappho," Strix suggested.

"No, because they are indecent. Having a library of nothing but novels seems terribly frivolous, even for a witch lord. Could they be biographies? But why would the Margrave care about losing a biography? Father seemed to think it was a book of magic, or something."

Strix nudged Fudge with her toe. "Fudge! Snack's over. Sit up. Time for some answers."

Fudge opened his eyes, rolled over, and trundled himself to his feet. "Thank you, Lizbet! That was delectable." His nose edged toward her skirt pocket. "I can smell a little more in there too . . ."

Strix boxed him on the snout. "Not now. Maybe later."

"Hunger for knowledge is admirable," Lizbet said, "but why can't you just *read* books like everyone else?"

"Fudge," Strix said, "what are all these books about? What was in them? Before you snorted them up your nose?"

"Oh, they were all sorts of people," Fudge said. "Explorers and adventurers, mostly, because they're the ones who cross the Montagnes and get captured by the Pope of Storms. One man from Lombardy came in a lighter-than-air ship. He was a natural philosopher. Some were churchmen, seeking heathens to proselytize. Others were mere brutes, looking for gold, or glory."

"You mean these were biographies, then?" Lizbet said, still puzzled. "Or fiction?"

"Oh, no, not fiction, and not just stories," Fudge said. "These were real people."

Silence.

"'Real people'?" Lizbet said at last.

Fudge nodded. "They were written there by the Pope of Storms himself."

"You can't write a 'real person' in a book," Lizbet said. "Can you?"

"If you're the Pope of Storms, you can," Fudge said. "Do you know that a high wind can blow your soul right out of your body?"

"Yes," Lizbet said. "It almost happened to me."

"That's what the Pope of Storms does. Mortals who cross the Montagnes fall into his hands. His winds blow and blow, harder and harder, until a person's soul rips loose from his flesh. The Pope of Storms catches it, squeezes it into his fountain pen, and writes it out into a book."

"And then Fudge snorts it off the page," Strix said.

"I don't think he's supposed to," Lizbet said.

"You inhaled the Margrave Hengest Wolftrow?" Strix said.

Fudge looked guilty. "He was unusually tasty. A powerful personality. A paradox of a man. Ferocious in war, ferocious in love, both egoistic and self-sacrificing. A brilliant mind, driven by the crudest of desires. Gentle and ruthless at the same time."

"Like a witch?" Lizbet said.

"Should I be pleased or insulted by that?" Strix said. "Pleased, I think. Except for the 'self-sacrificing' part."

"Not really like a witch," Fudge said. "Witches are mercurial creatures, of capricious and unpredictable impulse. Hengest Wolftrow doesn't have a shred of whimsy in him. All business, that one. No witch will ever conquer the world. She'll get halfway prepared to do it, then suddenly develop an interest in making marmalade out of porcupines, and spend a century honing her skills, until she makes the best darned porcupine marmalade in the universe. Meanwhile, the world rolls on, unconquered as before. Wolftrow, though . . ." He looked wistful. "Wolftrow might have done it. General Wolftrow is a man of indomitable will."

"'Was' a man of indomitable will," Lizbet said. She remembered the hollow man of shadows in his palace in Abalia, compulsively collecting books, but never finding the one book he truly needed. "You needn't speak of him in the present tense after you've snuffled him up your nose. He might as well be dead."

"But he's not dead," Fudge said, tapping his round belly with a fingernail. "He's right here."

Lizbet crossed her arms. "Are you sure?"

"I contain multitudes," Fudge said. "Adventurers and rapscallions, bluestockings and churchmen, their boyhoods and girlhoods, their dreams, their sins, and what they ate for breakfast on the twenty-third of June."

Lizbet thought about this. An idea began to take form. "Fudge," Lizbet said, "If I gave you pen and ink, could you write out Margrave Hengest Wolftrow's book, as it was before?"

"Of course!" Fudge said. He looked sad. "Although I'd probably sniff it up again, as fast as I wrote it down. I can't help myself! Everyone is so delicious. Oh, would that I were tied to the mast, like wily Odysseus, to protect me from my own unquenchable desires!"

"Suppose we just tied your nose to a mast, and left your hand free to write?" Strix said. "Come to think of it, suppose we trussed up all of you and presented you as a prisoner to the Pope of Storms, with the story of your guilt? He'd be delighted that we'd caught the person who made his library vanish. In return, maybe he'd forgive us for the stuff we did at the goblin town and let Lizbet go. I like that idea."

"Oh no!" Fudge cried. "Who knows what the Pope of Storms would do to me for my crimes! Have mercy!"

"You'll have to speak to Lizbet about that," Strix said coldly. "I am a witch! 'Mercy' is not a word I know."

"Suppose we don't report you to the Pope of Storms," Lizbet said, "and in return, you help us escape, and come back with us to Abalia? I need to return the Margrave's book. Now we have both the book and its contents. That is, you. Maybe that will be good enough."

But once they had escaped from the Pope of Storms, what was to prevent Fudge from just wandering off?

"Fudge, you're all out of books," Lizbet said. "You've inhaled all the words in all the books in this library. But I know where there's a lot more. A huge library of books. A palace jam-packed with tens of thousands of books from all over the world."

"That would be heaven!" Fudge exclaimed. "Where, oh, tell me where!"

"It's in Abalia. It belongs to the Margrave. I'll bet he'd let you sniff up a book or two from his library if you wrote his soul back into his book for him."

"He might even tie you to a mast while you did it," Strix said. "Or maybe a chair."

"Do you think?" Fudge hopped up and down in eagerness. His wet snout wiggled back and forth. "Oh, let me come to Abalia with you! Please, please, please!"

"Good work," Strix said to Lizbet.

"But first," Lizbet said, "we have to escape."

"Fudge," Strix said, "there's no way to lower the drawbridge?"

The little goblin shook his head dolefully. "I'd hoped you knew how. It won't obey me. It only obeys the commands of Griffon or Cupido. They will not help us. They were made by the Pope of Storms, and their souls are in thrall to him."

The library was entirely dark by now. Through the fretwork walls of the stronghold, the moon could be glimpsed as it rose over the eastern horizon. A breeze blew through the library stacks.

"The winds are moving again," Fudge said. "All the stronghold will soon be up."

"We need to hurry back to our room before we're missed," Lizbet said. She stuck Hengest Wolftrow's book in her skirt pocket.

Fudge led them back through the stronghold, waddling as fast as his squat legs could carry him. "I'll come back at dawn," he told them, "when the winds are quiet again."

"Be sure you do," Strix said. "We have to escape soon, before the Pope of Storms decides to remit his sentence of five hundred years—"

"But that would be good," Lizbet said.

"—and blow Lizbet's soul from her body, and write it into a book instead."

"Oh. That would be bad."

"Hm," Fudge said. He stared at Lizbet with sudden interest, and his nose snuffled back and forth.

Strix glared at Fudge. "I'm sure she'd be horribly dry, bland, and tasteless," she said.

"I wasn't even thinking about that," Fudge protested. "I swear I wasn't!"

1. Montgolfier balloon sewn out of drapes and hammocks. [Canceled: no way to get it out the window.]

2. Parachutes. [Canceled: same problem as climbing down ropes made of drapes: they'd still wind up in the moat with the crocodiles.]

3. Make wings out of the drapes, fly across the moat. [Canceled by Strix: even if the wings worked, none of them would be able to fly without any practice. Falling to their deaths would be more likely.]

"All of these escape plans have the same problem," Lizbet said. "There's only so much you can do with some drapes and a couple of hammocks. Maybe Fudge can find us enough drapes to get to the bottom, or even some real rope. But then how do we get past the crocodiles?"

"Things would certainly be easier if we had an army of the living dead at our disposal," Strix said. "They could fight the crocodiles while we escaped." A look of surprise and pleasure crossed her face, as if she had eaten an especially delicious mouse. "Wait, I've got an idea. Suppose we kidnap Griffon and Cupido? We'd tie them up and throw them to the crocodiles as a distraction. Then we'll climb down the drapes and swim across the moat before the crocodiles know what we're doing."

"Strix, that's an awful idea!"

Strix looked crestfallen. "Do you think Griffon and Cupido are too strong for us to overpower? That could be a problem."

"No, the problem is that it would be an awful thing to do to poor Griffon and Cupido. It's too cruel. I simply won't hear of it. We'll have to find some other way."

"In other words, the real problem is that you're too soft-hearted," Strix said. "I can fix that." The Outlaw's bandoleer that Strix had carried with her over the Montagnes still hung around her chest. She plucked out several shells and peered into them. "You need a big squirt of Ruthlessness, and a dribble of Treachery. And while we're about it, an ounce or two of Rebellion wouldn't hurt you in the least." She pulled something crimson and squirmy from one of the shells and held it up to Lizbet's face.

Lizbet shrank back. "No! I told you before, I don't want that."

"But if you were more ruthless, you'd be happy to throw Griffon and Cupido to the crocs. And we could escape. See?"

"I don't *want* to be ruthless," Lizbet protested. "Or rebellious. If I were like that . . . I'd be a person who didn't deserve to escape."

"I'd rather be a person who escapes," Strix said, "and worries later about whether she deserved it." But she stuffed the bubbling red Rebellion and the slithery, bilious Treachery back into their shotgun shells. "I'm still keeping these," she said. "Someday, you might change your mind."

"Never."

"As in, 'you never know what the future might bring,'" Strix said.

For hours, Lizbet and Strix dreamed up plan after plan for escape. For hours, they discarded every one as unworkable, impractical, or madly dangerous. By midnight, their ideas spent and the wells of inspiration dry, they still had no clear idea how they might escape. Strix, with her usual insouciance in the face of impending catastrophe, gave up and threw herself into a hammock, and soon was fast asleep.

Lizbet, still beset by worry, leaned out a window. Below, the silvery waters of the moat rippled in the moonlight. To the east, dark plains disappeared to an unseen horizon beneath a deep and starry sky.

On every map of the world that Lizbet had ever seen, the Montagnes du Monde were drawn as a closed circle of peaks. All around the Montagnes were mortal lands: the Duchies of Moscow and Kiev, Lizbet's own Holy Roman Empire, the Caliphate of the Turks, the Hindoo Indies, Cathay, and then back to the Duchies of the Rus. Inside the circle of the Montagnes, only blank white paper, and the words *Terra Incognita*.

But the lands over the Montagnes were not *incognita* to Lizbet. She was here, in them, right now. And what lay beyond, farther than she could see? If you went on and on toward the east, across this world, would you eventually cross the Montagnes again and find yourself in Cathay or the Indies? The world being round, and all.

Lizbet had a sudden vision, shocking in its clarity, of the world as a sphere divided into two halves. One half was Lizbet's ordinary mortal world. The other half was this world of witches, and goblins, and who knew what else. The Montagnes du Monde ran around the world like a wall, separating the two halves. Keeping them apart.

Only they weren't staying apart. Witches and goblins from the trans-Montagne world had gotten into the mortal half of the world. And Lizbet remembered seeing a few real ferns and firs amid the rake-and-umbrella trees and pinwheel wildflowers the day they had come down the eastern slopes of the Montagnes. And what about Wolftrow's lost army of the sewers? Things from the mortal lands were seeping into the witch world too. Witch things and mortal things were beginning to mix together.

Like Lizbet herself.

Perhaps she had been thinking about escape plans all along, without realizing it, while she stared into the darkness. In her mind, all the plans began to mix together too, into something only a witch could have thought of, and only a mortal could execute. A plot that required both trickery and bravery.

Lizbet couldn't bear to let Griffon and Cupido be eaten by the crocodiles. So she'd let herself be eaten instead.

Hip-deep in the moat, Lizbet wrapped her arms around herself and shivered. Suppose Griffon and Cupido didn't get to her before the crocodiles did? Suppose they just didn't care, and let her be eaten?

Serpentine ripples cut through the water. Lizbet had climbed down ropes of drapery and dropped into the moat with a splash. The crocodiles hadn't known what to make of her at first, but now they were swimming closer.

A commotion in the window of her guest-room-dungeon, far above. Cupido's face peered out. Fudge's voice from inside: "They're trying to escape! Lizbet's in the moat!"

"Oh, my stars and garters!" Cupido squawked.

"Oh, help!" Lizbet cried as loudly as she could. "I have acted rashly! I am being eaten by crocodiles! Come save me!"

"You two were supposed to keep Lizbet safe!" Fudge's voice yelled. "If she comes to harm, the Pope of Storms will turn you both into feather dusters!"

Gasps and shrieks from above. The faces in the window disappeared.

A crocodile's tail swatted Lizbet's leg, nearly knocking her over into the water. From far above, the crocodiles hadn't looked nearly as big as they did when you were right next to them. Another one brushed her thigh. Its jaws yawned wide as it passed. Moonlight glittered on its broken-bottle teeth. Lizbet instinctively winced away, but bumped into a crocodile on her other side. It thrashed, opened its jaws, and bellowed.

With a great beating of wings, the drawbridge descended. In the moonlight Lizbet could make out three figures crossing it, one hopping madly, one tottering behind, one waddling. And a ghostly figure tailing them.

Would they reach her in time?

By now Lizbet was surrounded on all sides by crocodiles. The crocodiles swam closer, jostling her back and forth, threatening to knock her off her feet. She tried to kick one away, but the water slowed her kick to nothing and almost made her lose her balance.

A crocodile lunged for her, its jaws wide. Teeth closed around Lizbet's thigh and bit down. Lizbet yelped, and beat on the crocodile's head with her fists. Another closed its jaws around her other leg. Sensing a kill, the remaining crocodiles thrashed madly. Spray and foam filled the air.

"Back, miscreants, back!" came Cupido's voice across the water.

A skiff lurched over the waves toward Lizbet. It pulled up beside her. Cupid stood up in the skiff and beat at the crocodiles with an oar. He reached a feathered arm down and clasped Lizbet's waist. "Upsy-daisy!"

Cupido pulled. Lizbet jumped. In a shower of spray, she tumbled head over heels into the rowboat, nearly capsizing it.

"Oh, my heavens, are you safe?" Cupido said. He peered at Lizbet's legs. "Thank goodness you're not bleeding much.

Or bleeding at all, actually. What luck! I saw a crocodile with your leg in its mouth." He took the oars, swiveled the skiff around, and headed for the opposite bank.

"I have some nasty scratches and gouges," Lizbet said, looking over her legs. "Maybe some paint or furniture polish would help."

"Paint?" Cupido said.

"My legs are made of oak and strap iron, with birch-bark skin," Lizbet said. "It's a long story."

The outside bank of the moat drew near. "Griffon will be waiting for us," Cupido said. "To escort you back to your room. You should never have tried to escape. The Pope of Storms will be so upset."

"You have no idea," Lizbet said.

The skiff grounded on the bank. Cupido hopped out. "Griffon!" he said. "I've rescued Lizbet!" He peered into the darkness. "Griffon, why are you lying on the ground?" Around Griffon stood a half-starved naked woman with ribs like sprung barrel staves, a Common Lesser Furry Devil, and a giant boiled crayfish. "And who let all you devils out of your restraints?"

"Mmmmmfffff!" said Griffon through the gag in his mouth, struggling against the ropes that bound his ankles and wrists.

"I made the devils promise to help us if I set them free," Strix said, "but a lot of them ran off anyway. Devils aren't much for keeping promises. The rest are headed into the stronghold to have a word with the Pope of Storms."

Griffon and Cupid both fit into the birdcage of iron slats that once held the man-headed maggot. "I'm sorry," Lizbet said to them. "You've both been good to us. As gaolers go, that is. You're both a lot nicer than the gaolers keeping my father. Even the cooked shoes were okay, if a trifle bland. Cupido, you were just wonderful about saving me from the crocodiles. Griffon, I think you'd be happier if you cultivated a more positive attitude toward life."

"That's a tautology," Strix said.

"You can call it names all you want, it's still a good idea," Lizbet said. "I'll remember you both in my prayers." She said to Strix, "The Pope of Storms will release them soon, won't he?"

"As soon as he deals with the escaped devils. I'm hoping they'll slow him up long enough for us to put some distance between us."

"So long, then," Lizbet said.

"Mmmmfffff!" said Griffon.

"Not so fast," a voice behind them said.

Maglet's voice.

A figure stalked out of the gathering darkness. Maglet. She was wild-eyed. Her hair and clothing were matted with sewage. She carried an oar like a weapon.

Chapter 19

Strix's back was turned. She hadn't noticed Maglet yet. "Strix!" Lizbet yelled.

Strix had half turned as Maglet swung her oar. The blade cut through the back of Strix's right thigh. Strix staggered, and fell to the ground. She faded to a ghostly outline. Maglet stared right and left. "Where'd she go? Damned witchy tricks."

She raised her oar high and smashed it down where Strix had been, but Strix had rolled aside. The oar missed her by inches.

"Fudge!" Lizbet yelled. "Grab Strix's hand! She's knit into the shadows!"

Fudge ran to Strix, and they joined hands. Fudge, too, faded away.

"Ah-ha!" Maglet yelled. "Now I know where you are." She raised her oar to strike where Fudge had been.

Lizbet launched herself toward Maglet, yelling. Maglet turned and swung the oar. Lizbet tried to dodge. The oar glanced off her left shoulder.

Now what? If Lizbet took Strix's other hand, Maglet would know where everyone was. Lizbet's shoulder, numb at first where the oar hit, began to hurt badly.

"I've been waiting," Maglet croaked. "Two days. I'll not be made a fool of again, by a pair of spies."

She began to stalk in circles, sweeping the oar in front of her, feeling for the invisible Strix and Fudge. Strix tried to stand, but couldn't. Maglet's oar had cut her leg almost in half. "What's wrong, witch?" Maglet yelled at Lizbet. "Why don't you disappear too? You'd do it, if you could. Not much of a witch, are you?"

"I—" Lizbet began.

She wanted to say, "I am too!" For the first time, she wanted to mean it. At that moment, Lizbet wished with all her strength that she were a witch. She wished she were a witch with whatever magic it took to stop Maglet.

Maglet's oar bumped against Strix. "Ha!" she yelled. Her oar came down, crushing Strix's foot. Maglet cried, "I hit the witch! I felt it!" She raised the oar over her head again. Strix tried to twist away. Fudge cowered, whimpering.

As soon as Strix's legs were broken, Maglet could smash her to bits, even if she couldn't see her. Was there nothing Lizbet could do?

If Lizbet had to have witch legs, why couldn't she have witch magic to go with them?

Wait, she thought. *I do have magic.* Awful, stupid magic. The spells from her father's grimoire were still in her pocket. She drew them out. Fudge had snorted up one, but there were two left. A gold-conjuring spell that actually made it rain mice. A spell to make noses bigger. In desperation, Lizbet began to chant the nose spell. In the near darkness, she squinted to read her father's swirly handwriting. It was rumpty-thump dog Latin:

Naso Maximus!
Naso Cumlulo!
Naso Laxio!
Fiat!
Vide!
Naso Deformis!
Naso Horribilissimus!
Naso Formidolosissimus!

Fiat!

Vide!

"Shut your mouth, witch!" Maglet yelled.

Was Maglet's nose any larger? In the deepening twilight, Lizbet couldn't tell. She tried again.

Naso Maximus!

Naso Cumlulo . . .

Maglet's nose seemed larger. A little. Or was it just Lizbet's imagination?

Naso Maximus!

Naso Cumlulo . . .

Maglet's nose was definitely larger. The tip of the oar dropped to the ground. Maglet's gaze jerked back and forth, as if she realized something was wrong, but didn't know what.

Naso Maximus!

Naso Cumlulo . . .

Maglet's hands flew to her face. Her fingers fiddled with her nose. "Wha, wha—" she stuttered.

Naso Maximus!

Naso Cumlulo . . .

"My nose! Wha—what's happening to my nose!"

Naso Maximus!

Naso Cumlulo . . .

Maglet's nose was immense. It spread from cheek to cheek. It erupted from her face like a hummock, a hill, a Vesuvius of swollen pink flesh.

Naso Maximus!

Naso Cumlulo . . .

"Shut up! Shut up! SHUT UP!" Maglet lifted her oar and charged at Lizbet.

Lizbet ran, and dodged. On defense, she had the advantage, being smaller and more agile than Maglet, and not burdened with an oar. But she couldn't chant the spell and run too. Now what?

From the twilight, a voice:

Naso Maximus!

Naso Cumlulo . . .

Strix was chanting.

Maglet screamed in frustration. She stopped chasing Lizbet. Her nose was now larger than her head. She was barely able to keep her head erect on account of the weight of her gargantuan nose.

Together, Lizbet and Strix chanted:

Naso Maximus!

Naso Cumlulo . . .

"You know," Strix yelled out the twilight, "this is really bad Latin."

"Shut up and chant!" Lizbet yelled back.

With a dull thump, Maglet toppled into the dirt.

Lizbet and Strix fell quiet. Lizbet approached Maglet cautiously.

Maglet's nose was larger than her whole body. It was red and oily, lumpy and misshapen. Its warts were the size of Lizbet's fist. Its blackheads were like molehills. Coarse brooms of hair erupted from cavernous nostrils. It pinned Maglet's head to the earth with its awful weight. On her hands and knees, she strained to lift her head from the ground. She failed. She groaned, and out of the corner of her eye stared fearfully at Lizbet.

Strix became fully visible. She lay on the ground a few yards away.

Lizbet said to Maglet, "We're not spies. Really. We were prisoners of the Pope of Storms. You didn't have to do this. None of this had to happen."

"Lies!" Maglet hissed.

Strix said, "Some people just won't listen, no matter what."

"What can we do with her?" Lizbet said.

"Huh?" Strix said. "We don't need to do anything with her. We need to get going, before the Pope of Storms figures out we've escaped."

"We can't leave her like this," Lizbet said.

"It's her own fault," Strix said.

"I don't care," Lizbet said. She thought. "I've got an idea."

Ediv!

Taif!

Sumissisolodimrof osan!

Sumissilibirroh osan!

When she finished chanting the spell backward, Maglet's nose had shrunk an inch.

"Good," Lizbet said. She went over to the hanging cage of iron slats that held Griffon and Cupido. She slid the paper with the spell on it through the slats. "When the Pope of Storms releases you," she said, "I want you to say this spell backward, a lot, until Maglet gets her normal nose back."

"Urrrmmmphh!" said Cupido around his gag.

"What happens if they say it backward too often?" Strix said. "Will Maglet get a nose-shaped hole in her face?"

"Strix," Lizbet said, "you have the weirdest ideas. Can you walk?" She bent a shoulder under Strix's arm and helped her up.

With a thigh slashed almost in half and a crushed foot, Strix couldn't walk unless she had one arm over Lizbet's shoulder, with Lizbet bearing half her weight. Lizbet found that Strix weighed much less than a mortal, but they still couldn't go very fast. They had a long way to go, all the way back over the Montagnes du Monde.

First, though, they had to get past the goblin town of Slattern. It was almost full night. They had no hope of avoiding the goblins, who would be awake and active. Night was their day. To circle the town, though, would add miles and hours to their journey.

Lizbet had another idea. *It's always dangerous when someone else has plans for you, but you don't have plans for them,* Strix had said. This time, Lizbet decided, she would be the one with the plan.

The rutted track away from the Pope of Storms' stronghold led up a slope, directly into Slattern. The stars were out, the moon was bright. Off-key music, shouts, and sounds of raucous merry-making issued from the goblin buildings ahead.

"Are we really going through Slattern?" Fudge asked. His voice was worried. "They don't like me there. They say I put on airs."

"Sometimes the safest place is in the middle of your enemies," Lizbet said. From an alleyway, a goblin was staring at them. Then it ran into a building. A moment later, the goblin reappeared, a dozen more goblins behind it. After a minute or two of vigorous debate (basically a shouting match punctuated by fistfights), they started toward Lizbet, Strix, and Fudge.

"Our current situation feels insecure to me," Fudge said. "You'll forgive me if I retire from the lists until the passage of time lends clarity to events." He tried to slink backward, but Lizbet caught him by the scruff of his stubby neck. With her other hand, she drew the mouse-rain spell from her pocket.

Plurat mus muris!
Aetherius pluvius!
Celebritas!
Exercitus,
Hastatus,
Mus multis partibus . . .

A light rain of mice began to fall from the sky. A mouse hit Lizbet on the top of the head, squeaked, and bounced off. Lizbet stifled a shriek and kept on reading the spell. *Plop, plop, plop!* Mice fell into the dirt, shook themselves off, and scuttled away. Lizbet reached the end of the spell and started again. Strix picked up a sleek black mouse by the tail and dropped it into her mouth. "Stop that," Lizbet said. "The mice aren't for you, they're for the goblins. Fudge, you too. If you eat so many you can't walk, I'm not going to carry you."

The mice pelted down with increasing fury, great dark sheets of mice sweeping across the land. "I hope we're not going to get mouse hail," Strix said, looking at the sky doubtfully.

Still chanting the spell, supporting Strix with one arm, kicking the reluctant Fudge forward with a boot, Lizbet led them into Slattern. As she had hoped, the goblin posse barely noticed their presence. Overcome by greed and gluttony, they scuttled to and fro, grabbing mice by the handful and stuffing them into their gaping mouths.

Among the crooked streets of crooked buildings, they walked as quickly as they could through the rivers, pools, and eddies of mice. Guided by the moon behind them, Lizbet headed west, hoping they would come out in the right direction, on the side of the Montagnes du Monde.

She spotted cathedral towers leaning drunkenly above the crowd of mean buildings. A thought came to her. Might it be . . . ? She led Strix and Fudge toward the cathedral, hoping.

In the town square by the cathedral they found Violette still standing where they had left him, the first bit of real luck they'd had since Lizbet couldn't remember when.

"Oh, Violette, you are a sight for sore eyes!" Lizbet exclaimed.

They arranged themselves on Violette's back, Strix in front, Lizbet in the middle, and Fudge last, a chubby parcel rolling back and forth atop Violette's haunches, trying to hold on to Lizbet's skirt tails.

Strix urged Violette to a trot, and they were off, up the street they had come down days ago. In a few minutes they were out of Slattern.

The mouse rain ended. Moonlit fields and meadows flanked the road. Lizbet sometimes glimpsed the river off to the right, sparkling silver. Ahead, the dark masses of rising hills, and beyond them, the Montagnes du Monde, a ragged black blot rising high against the stars.

All through the night they rode. By the time the dirt track began to climb into the foothills of the Montagnes, the eastern sky had lightened, and the stars were beginning to go out. Ahead, in the dim predawn, Lizbet could make out the dark line on the slopes of the Montagnes where alpine meadow yielded to forest. It was near there that she and Strix had made their first camp after they had crossed the mountains, and where Strix had saved her from the earth witches. Lizbet had the comfortable feeling of a traveler who returns from foreign parts and first catches a glimpse of familiar landmarks.

For the first time in days, she felt hopeful. She had faced danger time and again, and escaped every time. She was halfway to her goal. All they had left to do was to retrace their footsteps over the Montagnes. She felt more than hopeful. She allowed herself to feel a little smug. She had run from the goblins, from the sewer people, and from the Pope of Storms, but she hadn't run from Maglet. With magic and courage, she had defeated Maglet. She had made a plan for passing through the goblin city safely, and her plan had worked.

For the first time in a long, long time, Lizbet felt smart, and strong, and capable of anything. The steady rhythm of Violette's body beneath her had the effect of the drum that stirs men to battle. Lizbet threw her arms around Strix's waist, laid her face on Strix's shoulder. A breeze sprang up behind them and blew Lizbet's hair around her face, to mingle with Strix's rusty curls.

"We did it," she said, raising her voice over the sound of Violette's pounding hooves. "Strix, we really did it. We're through the worst of it. We got what we came for." The Margrave's book was a solid lump in her skirt pocket that bumped her thigh with Violette's hoofbeats.

"*You* got what *you* came for," Strix yelled back.

"You did too," Lizbet said. "Mrs. Woodcot sent you to help me, and you did. I couldn't have done it without you." She hugged Strix tightly. Strix's left thigh squeezed Violette's flank tightly, but her right leg swung loose. Lizbet gingerly touched Strix's thigh. Her fingers probed over the cut edge, where Maglet's oar had slashed it. The feel of the loose papers and string, fluttering in the wind, made her shiver. Strix's thigh was cut all the way to the bone. Or whatever Strix had for bones. "Your poor leg," she said. "And your foot too. As soon as we get back, we'll go straight to Mrs. Woodcot's and have her mend you. You've had just terrible injuries, and all for me. Strix, you've been like a hero to me. I know you're going to say something sarcastic, but I don't care, you really have been."

"I can't go back to Mrs. Woodcot," Strix said. "I can't go back ever."

The wind behind them whistled louder. It whipped Strix's words away, and Lizbet had to strain to hear her voice.

"Why?" she yelled.

"Because I wasn't supposed to be a hero to you!" Strix yelled back. "It was all a lie! Mrs. Woodcot didn't send me to help you. She sent me to stop you! None of this was supposed to happen."

"Why? Why didn't you—?"

"I was trying to be your friend." She dug her good knee into Violette's flank and shouted encouragement in the horse's ear. "Listen, we're in trouble. Hang on tight." Violette shook his head and broke into a gallop.

"My goodness gracious, I'm bound for such a spill!" Fudge exclaimed. He hiked up his grip on Lizbet's skirt.

"Don't you dare touch my butt!" Lizbet yelled.

"I'm going to fall, I'm going to fall!" Fudge yelled.

Lizbet turned to yell at him. The words died in her throat. Behind them, blotting out the dawn, came the whirlwind.

A swirling funnel of darkness descended from an angry sky. It whipped back and forth across the land. Where it passed, trees tore out of the ground and spun into the air. A false twilight descended. Lightning crackled in the clouds. A fine stinging rain spattered Lizbet's cheek.

"Strix!" Lizbet yelled. "Is it the Pope of Storms?"

"Yes!" Strix yelled back.

"What . . . what can we do?" Lizbet felt sure a spell about noses or mice wouldn't stop a whirlwind.

"We can't do anything but run," Strix yelled. "I'm trying to get us up into the forest. Maybe it will block the wind."

Higher they galloped up the twisting road through the foothills, ever higher, ever steeper. Violette's muscles strained. His joints squeaked and groaned. His nostrils blew steam that was torn away by the winds. Sheets of rain turned the road to mud and soaked Lizbet to the skin.

Fudge had Lizbet by the waist. He tried to yell, but all Lizbet heard over the howl of the storm was "Eeep!" or "Oooo!"

Gusts of wind blasted against them, rocking them back and forth. Could Violette even keep his feet" Lizbet wondered. Then, as she watched in shock, a square of muslin from Violette's skin ripped loose, peeled from his body, and was swept away by the wind. Beneath, feathers and sawdust erupted through the hole. Another patch of skin popped its stitches, ripped away, and was lost. The wind worked its way under Violette's patchwork hide. Huge sheets of it were torn loose and sailed away in the wind, until Violette looked like a flayed horse, all his muscles exposed to the wind and rain.

Straw began to fray from his straining muscles beneath Lizbet's legs. Larger chunks tore off. Violette's gait slowed, from a gallop to a canter to a limping trot. The funnel cloud roared closer. Crooked lightning played about the column. The tornado's tip swerved across the hills, as if it were seeking them.

Slowly, more slowly Violette walked as parts of him blew away, until at last he stopped, and Lizbet, Strix, and Fudge were sitting atop only an unmoving sawhorse of naked wooden beams. With a screech, its joints gave way, and it collapsed into a pile of timbers, spilling its passengers into the cold mud.

Fudge struggled up and tried to stand. The wind bowled him over, squealing. Over and over he rolled, like a furry ball, faster and faster, the wind pushing him before it.

Lizbet helped Strix to her feet. "Come on!" she yelled in Strix's ear. "We've got to hurry!" Up the slope, the dark line of trees marking the forest seemed very far away. Strix's lips moved in reply, but in the howl of the wind, Lizbet couldn't hear her words.

Then, in horror, Lizbet watched Strix's upper lip peel back, tear off, and fly away. Then a strip of her forehead. Part of her neck. The skin of her cheek.

"STOP!" Lizbet screamed into the wind. She desperately tried to cover Strix's face with her hands. She feared her own soul might be blown away, but she squashed that fear down. She had to save Strix.

She tried to cover Strix with her own body, but there was too little of Lizbet. The whirlwind was almost upon them. All the world turned to roaring and darkness. Muddy rain dashed against her. Blowing twigs, bits of wood and pebbles, filled the air. Something struck Lizbet's ear and bloodied it.

She shouted defiance, but her words made no sound above the roaring of the wind.

From out of the whirlwind, the voice of the Pope of Storms.

Perfidious Strix. You have betrayed your mistress again and again. You are good for nothing. Come to me, Strix. Come and be dissolved.

The wind screamed. As if grasped by an invisible fist, Strix was pulled out of Lizbet's grasp. Lizbet desperately tried to hold on, but her fingers tore through Strix's clothing and flesh. Strix's skin sloughed away against her.

As Lizbet cried in horror and loss, Strix's body pulled free and sailed up into the whirlwind.

Her strength sapped by despair, Lizbet sank into the wet grass. The front of her dress, her arms, her face were covered with wet brown papers, teabags, and string that had been Strix's skin.

Strix's naked body rose into the air, into the storm. She hung limply in the sky, illuminated by lightning, her ripped flesh fluttering madly.

Dissolve, said the Pope of Storms.

The screaming wind rose to a frenzy. As Lizbet watched in horror, Strix came apart.

Her body disintegrated into uncountable tiny scraps. Something small and hard struck Lizbet on the chest and bounced off. Lizbet grabbed it out of the grass. For an instant, a flash of lightning illuminated it. Lizbet stuck it in her pocket.

Lizbet.

"What!" Lizbet screamed into the storm. She couldn't even hear her own words. She screamed anyway. "I don't care what you do! I don't care anymore! Damn you!"

Dissolve.

The furious wind dashed branches and stones against her. Lizbet cried out in pain. Her flesh was more solid than

Strix's, but even a human body would be reduced to lifeless pulp if battered by windblown debris for very long.

Strix was gone. Strix, the best friend Lizbet had ever had. The only friend she had allowed herself to have.

The object in her pocket, that she had glimpsed for a moment in the lightning flash, was an oval seashell with a smooth, rounded top and a toothy seam on the underside. It had a lustrous brown center, with white around the edges.

Lizbet recognized it as one of Strix's eyes.

She did care what happened. Despite what she had screamed at the Pope of Storms, she did care. All she had left was the memory of Strix. Of friendship. Lizbet wanted to live. She wanted to live for that, if for nothing else.

Could she save herself? She couldn't fight a whirlwind. The forest up the mountainside was too far away. When her father had been imprisoned, she had gone to the Margrave for help. When he wouldn't help, she went to Mrs. Woodcot. Who could help her now? Who could stand up to the Pope of Storms?

Fighting the wind, Lizbet knelt, balancing on her hands on the muddy earth. It was perilous. The winds threatened at any moment to knock her off her feet. Flying debris hit her like stones from a sling. Blood seeped through her clothing in a dozen spots, and there was clotted blood in her hair. She lifted one foot and kicked with her toe as hard as she could on the ground.

She saw something immense and dark out of the corner of her eye. She dropped flat. A tree swept over her, its branches scraping her flesh. She struggled up again. She kicked the ground as hard as she could. "Help! Help me! I . . . I have something for you!"

Beneath her, a rumbling that Lizbet felt more than heard. Before her, the muddy earth swelled, cracked, and fountained up. A figure like a twisted tree root thrust up through the hole, its eyes and mouth bottomless dark blots.

"Well, howdy-doo, sweetie!" The earth witch craned her head around. It creaked. Her voice wasn't especially loud, but it cut through the storm as if the storm weren't there. "Quite a spot of unsettled weather we're having, ain't it? But spring's like that, don't you know." She surveyed Lizbet. "What'cha got for me, sweetie, hm?"

"I have . . . myself," Lizbet shouted into the wind. "Please. Take me with you. Take me underground. I will be your corpse."

The earth witch bent close to her. Her myriad fingers, like twitching white worms, played over Lizbet's body. Where they touched her wounds, Lizbet flinched. "But you ain't a corpse, sweetie. You're wood and iron from the middle down, and flesh on top, but you're still alive and kickin'. Get it? Kickin'? You had to kick the ground to fetch me? Oh me, oh my, I'm so droll." She tittered.

"I'll be a corpse soon," Lizbet pleaded. "I'm half-dead now. See how I'm bleeding all over? Please, please, just take me. You can have my corpse if I die."

"So it's a gamble, now, is it?" the earth witch said. "Maybe you'll die, maybe you won't, la-di-da. If you don't, no corpse for me. I'm less interested all of a sudden. A sure thing is more my style."

Leave her. The mortal girl is mine.

The earth witch stared into the sky. "Is that you, Stormy? Are you the one what beat this child half to death?"

She is a thief, old grannie. She stole a book of mine. She is the spy of a mortal general over the mountains.

"Oh, stop your prattle," the earth witch said. "Everybody knows there's nothing on the other side of the mountains but the sky!"

She is my prisoner, escaped with her confederate, who is now dissolved. It is time for Lizbet to come to me.

The winds screamed. Lizbet felt her body lift up off the ground. She was about to be pulled into the whirlwind. She shrieked and grabbed for the earth witch. It was like grabbing a dirty, twisted root, crawling with grubs. Lizbet squeezed her eyes shut and tried to hang on. She felt herself, and the earth witch with her, being lifted into the air.

The earth witch shouted, "Lemme go! You've got some nerve, you big bag of wind!"

The earth witch plunged into the ground, dragging Lizbet with her. Down, down, down into the earth they fell, into blackness and wet and the smell of soil and decay. With a smash, dirt and rock closed above them.

The wind and rain were gone. In their place, silence. Utter darkness. Stillness. Lizbet sat in a puddle of cold slimy stuff. Mud?

If Lizbet had sought her own grave, she could have found no place more like it.

"That's better," the earth witch's voice said in the darkness. "There's no place like home, I always say." Lizbet felt the earth witch's threadlike fingertip wrap around her nose and tweak it. "Are you a corpse yet?"

"No," Lizbet said. "I don't think. Not quite, anyway."

"Work on it," the earth witch said. Her laughter cackled in the darkness. "Better be a corpse when I come back, sweetie, or there'll be trouble!"

Chapter 20

Exhausted, in pain all over, entombed in cold subterranean darkness with nothing better to do, Lizbet curled up on the muddy floor and slept.

She woke to thready fingers wrapping around her arms and shaking her rudely.

"Aw, rats, she's still alive," a creaky voice said.

Lizbet yawned. She was undoubtedly alive. In fact, to her surprise, she didn't feel that bad. She filled her lungs and swiveled her arms around. No pain. No pain from the wounds made by sticks and stones in the whirlwind. Even in her shoulder, where Maglet's oar had struck her, the pain was gone.

Another voice said, "She'll die of starvation and thirst soon, anyway. I say leave her."

Lizbet did not feel hungry or thirsty though.

"I'm starved," a third voice whined. "Can't we start eating her now?"

"No," said another voice.

"No," said another.

"It's against the rules," said another.

There were an awful lot of different voices. "Who are you all?" Lizbet asked.

"Matilda!"

"Bertha!"

"Hildegarde!"

"Viola!"

"Winifred!"

"Lucille!"

And on, and on, for a minute or longer.

"There are so many of you," Lizbet said.

"It's boring under the earth," the voice who had called herself Bertha said. "So we make more of us for conversation."

"But then there are so many of us," Winifred complained, "there aren't enough corpses to go around. Are you sure you aren't a corpse yet? It's been hours."

"How many hours?" Lizbet asked.

"Ten!"

"One!"

"Fifty!"

"Eleventy-sevenths!"

Lizbet guessed that when you lived beneath the earth, without sun or moon, day or night, precision in measuring the passage of time was not of great concern. "Actually," she said, "I think I'm feeling a little better."

"Awww!"

"Shucks!"

"Curse the luck!"

"Look," Lizbet said, "I've got an idea. Why don't you put me back on top of the earth again? That way, the Pope of Storms could finish killing me with his whirlwind, and I'd be a nice fresh corpse for you to eat." She hoped the Pope of Storms had given up and gone away by this time, but if the earth witches weren't good with time, maybe they wouldn't think of that.

"We don't like fresh corpses. We like corpses all rotted and maggoty," Hildegarde's voice said.

"Don't be picky, dear," Winifred reprimanded her.

"There's something funny going on," Bertha said. "Still, it's true you're not becoming a corpse very fast just sitting around down here."

Bertha's hard roots wrapped around Lizbet. Scrabbling sounds in the darkness. Clods of dirt rained upon her. In the grasp of the witch, Lizbet flew upward. *My goodness,* she thought, *the earth witches dig fast.*

Moments later, they burst through into blinding sunlight. Lizbet was roughly thrust up out the earth, to tumble onto mud and wet grass. "And don't come back 'til you're dead!" Bertha said. She dived back into the earth, which closed around her, and was gone.

It was broad day, under fair skies. Not too much time could have gone by while Lizbet was underground. A day at most. The earth was still wet. The dirt road was half muddy puddles. The land had been scoured by the whirlwind. Downed trees and broken branches lay everywhere.

Lizbet herself was all mud from her toes to her waist. She undid her boots, removed her stockings, and stepped into a puddle to wash off. Just sinking her feet into the cold squishy mud at the bottom felt so good that she didn't wash, but stood there for minutes, enjoying it.

Wait. Strix had warned her about her wooden witch legs. About putting down roots. Still, it felt soooo good . . .

Lizbet forced herself to step out of the puddle. She lifted a foot to examine it. Was that a little white root coming out near the big toe? Or just a corn? She decided it was a corn. The foot still looked pretty normal. Except that it was on the wrong side, of course, because Strix had made it that way.

Strix.

Strix.

Strix had said this. Strix had done that.

Everything reminded her of Strix.

She looked down at herself. Bits of brown paper were still stuck to the front of her dress, and even her forearms. Parts of Strix that had rubbed off on Lizbet as she tried desperately to hold on to her while the Pope of Storms dragged her out of Lizbet's arms. Lizbet stuck a fist into her pocket and squeezed it around the seashell that had been Strix's eye.

Burning hot tears filled her eyes and ran down her cheeks. She sat down, put her arms around her knees, and cried until her face ached with crying and her chest hurt with sobs.

When she couldn't cry any longer, Lizbet stood up, wiping her eyes and her nose with her fist. As she stood, a scrap of paper fell off her skirt. She bent and picked it up. Another fell off. They were drying out and coming loose.

She carefully peeled all the bits of paper off herself and stacked them in a little pile. That was all there was left of Strix. Wait, there was another piece of paper in the grass nearby. She added that to the rest, and an old teabag near it. She found a bundle of broken sticks, tightly lashed with twine, that must have been part of Strix's arm or leg. Spirals of rusty wire clung to the splintered stump of a bush.

Before long, Lizbet was methodically crawling on hands and knees, back and forth through the flattened grass and splintered tree stumps. She moved slowly, her eyes inches from the ground, not wanting to miss the tiniest bit.

Over the course of the day, her pile grew: papers, used teabags, twine, scraps of tawny fur. Delicate curved lunules of isinglass that must have been Strix's fingernails and toenails.

When she found Strix's teeth, they proved to be broken bits of straight razor and sharp-edged chunks of milk glass. Although she handled them with care, she still pricked her finger on one. She stuck her finger in her mouth with a peculiar sense of happiness. *Oh, Strix,* she thought. *You were always like that.*

By the time darkness fell, Lizbet discovered that she had a considerable pile, and she was still finding pieces. What now?

She had been content to collect Strix's remains just for the comfort of doing it, without thought of what she would do with them.

She forced that problem from her mind. She did not need to think about it yet.

The pieces were light and flimsy, and Lizbet feared a breeze might scatter them. She needed a bag or a sack, but she had none. After a moment's thought, she removed her dress, unbuttoned it down the back, and laid it on the ground. The serge was double thickness, so she popped a seam on one side, using one of Strix's teeth to cut the stitches, and unfolded the fabric, making it twice as big as it had been. She piled the pieces of Strix on the remains of her dress and tied the fabric up by four corners, like a beggar's bindle. The night air was chilly. Lizbet hugged her arms around herself. It was improper to be seen in only undershirt, bloomers, and stockings, but there was no one here to see her and be shocked, and anyway, she had to have something to keep Strix in.

She lay on the ground to sleep, pulling the bundle of Strix over herself like a comforter. As she had when Strix covered her with her own body on the journey up the Montagnes, Lizbet immediately felt warmer and more secure. Her last thought, as she drifted toward sleep, was that the rustle of the papers and sticks and leaves in the sack was Strix's voice, talking softly to her, although she could not make out the words.

She awoke at dawn, ravenously hungry, and there was no food to be had. Lizbet sat on the edge of a puddle left by the Pope of Storms and let her bare feet dangle into the cold mud. By the time the sun was halfway up the sky, she was no longer feeling hungry. She pulled up her undershirt and examined her chest, where she had been bleeding from wounds. The bleeding had long since stopped. The wounds were pink, and hurt only a little. They seemed to be healing. Lizbet decided there were definite advantages to being partly composed of vegetable matter and able to take nourishment from the earth like a plant.

But what did it mean that her toes were pebbles, and her toenails playing cards? If she jumped into a brook, could she roll down the streambed to the sea? If she walked into a gambling den, could she beat the cardsharps at their own game? She hadn't done very well with cigars or alcohol, but perhaps vice required practice.

It was time to face facts: Lizbet was a witch. Or, half a witch, anyway. And not just in her legs. The witchy legs Strix had given her weren't staying put. Their influence was seeping into the rest of her. Making animals out of straw that moved as if they were alive that was something only a witch could do, Strix said. Yet, Lizbet had done it. Only people from the trans-Montagne world could see you if you were knit into the shadows, Fudge said. Yet Lizbet had been able to see Strix.

But only partly. Lizbet was still not entirely a witch. Instead, like the world itself, she was half witch and half human, with the two halves slowly melting into each other.

She crawled on hands and knees across the ground all day long, finding parts of Strix in the grass and between the stones. At intervals she would have to cry. She stopped until the tears passed. Then she started again.

Sometime after midday, she spotted something colorful wedged in the branches of a bush that had been snapped by the wind. When she freed it, it proved to be a vessel of exquisite workmanship. It was the size of Lizbet's fist. It was crafted of hedgehog quills, nettles, broken brown bottle glass, and black briar root. In it were strings and gobbets of stuff: red, green, yellow, blue, all moving and twisting restlessly. Vices and virtues of the sort Strix had harvested from the Outlaw.

Lizbet realized she was holding Strix's heart.

That night, she crawled under the sack of Strix's parts and fell asleep beneath the stars, Strix's heart under her arm.

The next day passed the same, and the days after that. The amount of Strix Lizbet had collected grew large, and heavy, and filled the remains of the dress like a taut ball. It was too heavy to sleep under anymore, and almost too heavy to carry.

One day Lizbet heard footsteps. She looked up and saw a squat muddy figure waddling towards her. "Fudge?"

"Lizbet, may you be lucky at dice, and your womb ever fruitful!"

"Thanks, I guess," Lizbet said. "I'm glad you're alive. Where have you been?"

"I got caught by the wind," Fudge said. "And I rolled, and rolled and rolled, and rolled, and rolled—"

"I see."

"—and rolled, and rolled and rolled, and rolled—"

"Yes, yes, I get it."

"—and rolled, and rolled, and—what's this?" He stooped and picked something from the ground. "It's a piece of paper."

Lizbet held out her hand. "Fudge, I'm looking for those. It's all that's left of Strix."

"It has words on it," Fudge said. He took a long, snorting breath through his nose. His voice became dreamy. "Mmm, they smell delicious . . ."

Lizbet leaped to her feet, charged at Fudge, bowled him over, and straddled his round belly. She pried the piece of paper from his paw.

"Thievery!" Fudge cried, banging his feet and fists on the ground. "Robbery! Brigandage! Finders keepers! Salvage rights! Possession is nine-tenths of the law!"

"Think of it as kidnapping and rescue," Lizbet said. "You tried to kidnap Strix, and I rescued her."

"I suppose our dispute could be construed according to that theory," Fudge said. "Now please get off? I can't breathe."

Lizbet made no move to comply. "Fudge," she said, fixing him with her gaze and wagging her finger at him, "hear me, and hear me good. If you inhale so much as one iota of Strix, one comma, one period, one jot or tittle, I will rip you open from nose to toes to get her back."

The violence of her words, and the feelings from which they sprang, shocked and surprised her. Had she really said that?

"And I mean it!" she added. So she must have.

Fudge nodded miserably. Lizbet climbed off him. Fudge rolled to his feet. Brushing twigs and dirt off his generous hindquarters, he said, "So when are we going to Abalia? Where there's a huge, delicious library? You promised."

When were they going? Was Lizbet going home at all? She still had to free her father, but how was she to get over the Montagnes du Monde with no witch horse, carrying a fifty-pound bag of Strix? And what was she going to do with Strix when she got there?

Strix deserved a proper Christian burial. In Lizbet's view, that was the bare minimum that a well-lived life was owed at its end. Although, she reflected, Strix would have *hated* a Christian burial.

Whatever did one do with the remains of a witch? A witch would know, like Mrs. Woodcot. But Strix had said she couldn't ever go back to Mrs. Woodcot. Strix had betrayed Mrs. Woodcot by being a friend to Lizbet. Lizbet had taught Strix friendship. Lizbet was responsible for Strix's fate.

Lizbet squeezed her eyes shut, trying to hold back tears. The black dog of guilt seized her and shook her like a rag.

Lizbet's need to talk with God was acute. She hadn't tried the hosts since that time the devils answered from Heaven. She wondered if she could wheedle the devils into letting her have a word with Him. The hosts were still in the pocket of her dress. The dress was pulled tightly around Strix's remains, but Lizbet, with effort, squeezed her hand into the pocket.

Her fingers touched cold sticky goo. Oh no. Her heart sank. Along with everything else, her dress had been soaked in the storm. The hosts had dissolved into mush.

But when she drew her fingers out, something on them sparkled. Lizbet bent close to look. Red threads, tiny green pearls, and glowing blue-white strands stuck to the tips of her fingers, mixed with the cracker mush. They looked like the material Strix had harvested from the Outlaw's body, only in tiny amounts.

Of course. When the priest consecrated the host, it became the body of Christ. It would have vices and virtues, like anyone's body. On the tips of Lizbet's fingers was the nature of Christ.

Not quite knowing what to do with it, but feeling it would be impious simply to throw it away, Lizbet picked through the mess of soggy crackers and separated the character traits into tiny piles by color. Strix's cartridge belt, though battered, had survived the storm. Lizbet stowed the tiny samples of Christ's virtues into empty cartridges. Some she recognized from the Outlaw: iron-gray Courage, the tiny sea-green pearls of Empathy. The glowing blue-white strands were unfamiliar to her though. When Lizbet touched them, she felt a sweet, fleeting pain in her bosom, as if an angel had pierced her with a golden spear.

"I want to go to Abalia!" Fudge whined. "When can we go? I want to go now!"

"So do I, Fudge," Lizbet said. "But we have to find all of Strix first. I'm not going without her."

Lizbet had no way to get over the Montagnes. And you couldn't go around the Montagnes: they circled the world. Could there be a way through the mountains? A cave, or a tunnel, or—

A tunnel?

Lizbet sent Fudge to hunt for the last errant bits of Strix, threatening him again with riot and mayhem if he even thought about snuffling her up. Meanwhile, she made a plan. It was a little tricky. But that was okay. Lizbet felt trickier than she had been before, and was learning to feel all right with it.

She stamped her foot on the ground.

After a moment, she felt a deep rumble beneath her feet. She stamped on the ground again and stepped back. The earth cracked and opened. An earth witch popped halfway out of the hole, squinting her knothole eyes against the daylight. She regarded Lizbet with reproach. "What!" she said. "Still not a corpse?" Lizbet recognized her voice as Matilda's. She peered up and down at Lizbet. "And looking healthier than ever. You're good for nothing!"

"What have you got for me, baby?" Lizbet said.

"What have I got for you? Hah!" Matilda put all her six or seven hands on what Lizbet supposed were her hips, but looked more like knotty stumps. "Mortals don't make demands of the earth witches. The nerve!"

"I hear you steal gold that misers bury in their gardens," Lizbet said.

"The world is full of tales," Matilda said airily. "Who knows what is is true?"

"If that tale is true, the earth witches must have gold to spare. I want some. I want you to give me ten thousand gold pieces, be they thalers, francs, lira, pounds, or whatever the coin of these realms might be," Lizbet said.

Matilda tittered. "Away with you and your delirious fantasy!"

"In return," Lizbet said, "I shall give you all a present."

"You owe us a present already," Matilda said indignantly. "You owe us your own corpse! That was your promise, though now I suspect it was all a trick. I ain't making any new deals until you deliver your corpse, safe and dead."

"Suppose I give you two corpses, instead of one?" Lizbet said.

"Wild and nonsensical promises! You can't even provide one, how can you possibly get two?"

But in her cracked voice, Lizbet heard a note of interest. Of greed. Reason said, 'No', but greed said, 'I want . . .'

"I know," Lizbet said, "where there are millions of corpses in the earth. Free for the taking."

"Poppycock! Flapdoodle! Delusions! Daydreams!" Matilda paused. "So . . . where are these corpses, exactly?"

"Ten thousand gold pieces first. Then I'll tell you."

"Not a twice-clipped counterfeit bronze beggar's penny will I give you!"

"Five thousand, then. The rest later."

"Usurious skinflint!"

"One thousand."

Lizbet let herself be bargained down to a single gold piece, with another nine hundred and ninety-nine on credit. Matilda disappeared into the earth to fetch it. Lizbet didn't actually have any interest in money—at least, no more than the rest of humankind, who on the whole prefer riches to poverty—but she wanted to convince the earth witches that she was offering something valuable. And also to give them something to cheat her out of.

To some people, the tang of larceny makes a bargain irresistible. Lizbet hoped witches might be like that.

Matilda popped out of the earth and thrust a muddy coin into Lizbet's hand. Lizbet spat on it and rubbed the mud off with the heel of her thumb. It glowed yellow.

"Now tell me where all these millions of corpses are, sweetie," Matilda said, longing in her voice.

"They are in graveyards and burying grounds on the other side of the Montagnes du Monde," Lizbet said.

Matilda balled up all of her fists and shook them in the air. "Liar! Thief! Give me back my gold! There is nothing on the other side of the Montagnes du Monde!"

"You are misinformed," Lizbet said. "There's a whole world over there. With millions of people who live and die and fill the churchyards and the cemeteries with their corpses."

"No!" Matilda yelled. "It's all lies. The earth witches tunneled through the entire world, long ago, and there's nothing over the Montagnes du Monde, just empty sky."

She sounded very sure of herself. "How long ago?" Lizbet asked.

"What does it matter? A year, a hundred, a thousand years, a thousand thousand. Long ago. Before the sun and moon and stars."

"I don't know how you could have missed it," Lizbet said, "but there's a world there now. A world of mortals and dumb beasts, dismal forests with bandits, howling deserts full of camels and Mussulmen, oceans with ships sailing, and all sorts of things. The Holy Roman Empire and the Pixie Queen, the heathen Northmen, the Hindoos, wild Americans across the sea who wear feathers in their hair."

"You're making it up," Matilda said suspiciously.

"Am not. I came over the Montagnes myself. Look at me." Lizbet spread her arms. "I'm half-mortal, half-witch. Have you ever seen anything like me before?"

"You're a peculiar creature, that's for certain," Matilda said. "Maybe you come from where you say. Maybe you don't."

"The only way to find out is to tunnel beneath the Montagnes," Lizbet said. "On the other side you'll find proof that I'm right." She held her breath.

"It's an awfully long way," Matilda said. "And through rock and stone."

"It's too hard for you, then?"

"I didn't say that!"

"I understand if the earth witches are unable to do it."

"The earth witches can do anything!" Matilda said angrily. "As the roots of the oak break apart granite, we pass at will through the hearts of mountains! If we feel like it."

"If you can't do it, you'll be missing out on a ghoul king's banquet of corpses," Lizbet said. "Brimming with maggots and rot, shoulder and hip bones falling from their sockets, swollen with the gases of decomposition or liquefied to black pools of decay. Yum! I should imagine, that is. If you enjoy such things."

Matilda said sharply, "You swear you're telling the truth?"

"If I'm not," Lizbet said, "you need not pay me a single gold piece more."

"I'll fetch my sisters," Matilda said, and dived into the ground.

Shortly earth witches began to pop up through the soil, knotty black and brown root like women, scores, hundreds of them. They pointed at Lizbet, complained about the harsh sunlight and the ugly blue sky, and chattered to each other. "Where?" Matilda asked. "They want to know where? Where do we dig?"

Lizbet decided it was best to have a corpse ready for them. The nearest corpse she knew was the Outlaw that she and Strix had buried a few weeks ago. She tried to figure in what direction the Outlaw's cabin would be. She pointed at the side of the Montagnes, mostly west, and a little south. "There. Dig there."

Within minutes, a dark hole appeared in the mountain slope. First earth, then cracked stone poured from the opening and tumbled down the mountainside in a vast midden. All day, without cease, Lizbet heard the clatter of stones rolling as the earth witches delved ever more deeply into the living rock of the Montagnes. The heap of stones below the hole grew and grew.

The earth witches cared nothing for time of day. Into the night they worked. The last thing Lizbet heard before she fell asleep, and the first noise that wakened her in the morning, was the rattle and bang of stone chips pushed out of the deepening tunnel through the mountain.

While the earth witches dug, Lizbet and Fudge continued their search for the last bits of Strix. Eventually they could find no more. Days passed. The midden of debris stretched half a mile down the mountainside. At last, Matilda reported that her witches were almost through to the other side.

Lizbet and Fudge rolled the ball of Strix encased in Lizbet's dress up the mountain to the tunnel mouth. At the dark opening, Lizbet hesitated. The tunnel roof was barely high enough for her to stand upright. An invisible river of cold, damp air poured from the tunnel and made her skin go goose bumps, even in the sunlight. Childhood fears of the dark assailed her. What would happen to her, deep under the mountain? She had tried to stoke the greed of the earth witches, but what if they had tired of digging? What if they decided not to bother with the tunnel, but eat Lizbet herself, "rules" or no rules, deep within the mountain, with none to know?

Steeling her nerves and gritting her teeth, Lizbet rolled the ball of Strix before her through the dark opening and into the blackness and cold inside the mountain.

The floor was rocky and uneven. Rolling Strix, whose parts must have weighted fifty pounds in all, was heavy work for a skinny teenage girl. The light from the tunnel mouth faded. All was muffled blackness. Behind her, Fudge muttered to himself.

They walked for what seemed an endless time. In the darkness, who could tell the hours? Lizbet's arms and shoulders grew numb and ached with pain from rolling the bundle of Strix over the rocky floor. Her breath came heavy, and despite the tunnel being cold, her undershirt was damp with sweat. What would she do with Strix when they emerged? She thought and thought.

When her effort and pain and exhaustion had gone on so long that Lizbet thought she would surely fail in her task, she told herself, *Just another step. Just one more. And one more.*

In this dream of fatigue and pain, she at last heard a sound: the cracking of rocks like muskets going off, the sarcastic chatter of the earth witches. "Almost through, sweetie," came Matilda's voice in the blackness. The witches' eager voices rose in a din, and Lizbet glimpsed a ray of daylight ahead, through a rock crack. The witches all complained—"Hateful light!" "Nasty, naughty sun!"—but they continued to dig their fingers into the hole. Rock shattered and fell away, and the hole widened until Lizbet could step through.

She squinted in the sudden daylight. The earth witches pushed out around her. Lizbet stood on the rocky western slopes of the Montagne du Monde, just above the tree line. The day was clear, and although the details of the land below were too distant to see, an occasional tendril of smoke from a chimney rose through the still air, telling of human presence below.

In her exhaustion and despair, it came to Lizbet, at that moment, what she must do with Strix.

"Now where's our corpses, honey?" Matilda said in her creaking voice. "You promised millions of corpses!"

"A deal, a deal, we have a deal!" the other earth witches cried.

"Follow me," Lizbet said.

After a little exploring, Lizbet discovered the path she and Strix had taken on their trip up the Montagnes, the road cut by Margrave Hengest Wolftrow's army decades ago. She set off down the mountain. The earth witches followed her and flanked her, diving in and out of the earth like a school of leaping fish. By the time Lizbet found the side path that led to the Outlaw's cabin, the witches had already scented his corpse. With little cries of excitement, they vanished into the earth. The earth churned as they swam through it. Trees tilted back and forth on their roots.

The door of the Outlaw's cabin was open: Lizbet and Strix had not bothered to close it when they left. Lizbet squeezed the bundle of Strix through the doorway. She found the Outlaw's flint and steel, and after she and Fudge had gathered tinder, she started a fire in the fireplace. She needed fire for what she was going to do.

The floorboards creaked, cracked, and broke. Matilda thrust up her body up through the hole. She wiped her mouth with her hand. "That was delicious!" she said. "More, please!"

"There are no more corpses in the neighborhood that I know of," Lizbet said, "but there are churchyards and burying grounds all over the earth. There are some in Abalia, which is just down the mountain. And now, the rest of my thousand gold pieces?"

"The gold, eh? Oh, someday, someday," Matilda said. She cackled, and laughter echoed from under the earth. "We promised to pay you later, but we never set a date. Not as clever as you thought you were, sweetie?"

"Clever enough though," Lizbet said. "Farewell, then."

Matilda regarded Lizbet out of her depthless black eye sockets. She tilted her head back and forth. "Hmmm. Farewell, baby. You're a strange one, half witch and half mortal. Come, girls! We've a world of sweet corpses to find and eat, yes, we do!" She dived into the earth beneath the cabin. The cabin trembled on its foundations as the witches swam off through the earth. Gradually the trembling died away.

In making her deal with the earth witches, Lizbet had worried whether having the world's corpses eaten by witches might cause problems on Resurrection Day, when the earth was supposed to give up its dead. However, she reasoned, if God were able also to raise the dead from the sea, and raise martyrs after they had been burned by Mussulmen or Protestants, surely He could raise a dead man eaten by a witch.

Of course, now that God was confined in the devils' prison, having any Resurrection Day at all was looking less certain. People might be obliged to stay dead indefinitely. It would cause complaints.

Fudge waddled up and tugged at her undershirt. "The Margrave's library in Abalia calls to me!" he exclaimed rapturously. "Biographies! Travelogues! Cookbooks! Diaries! Plays! Poems! Belle lettres!" His feet danced on the floor and his furry toes curled. "I surely shall die in a frenzy of anticipation if we do not expeditiously make our way with all due speed! I can almost smell the great library from here. Why do we tarry? We must be off!"

"Soon, Fudge, soon," Lizbet said. "There's something I have to do first. I have to burn Strix."

Chapter 21

I am the rose you cut, that soon must die,
The letter that you penned, and threw away,
And every time you told your friend a lie,
And burning tears upon your wedding day.
—a rhyme of Strix

Lizbet had decided what to do with the sack of Strix. Strix wouldn't have wanted a Christian burial. And she had denied being an atheist. Perhaps she was more like a heathen, or a pagan. How did the heathens dispose of their dead? By fire.

The great war chiefs of the Northmen, it was said, were burned in their own longboats. The Hindoos burned their dead on wooden pyres. Strix was rather like a Northman, Lizbet thought, fierce and proud. She would appreciate a fiery end.

Lizbet's plan was to set fire to the Outlaw's house, with the bundle of Strix inside.

"Gather more tinder," she said to Fudge. "Put it in all around the house, inside and out. I am going to burn everything down."

All that would remain of Strix were Lizbet's memories.

Maybe those should burn as well. In the Indies, they said, people put a man's wife on the fire alongside him when he died. As she imagined the fire to come, Lizbet felt a terrible urge to stay in the house and join Strix in the flames. There would be the agony of burning, but then there would be release. Release from the pain of friendship found, but lost. Release from the pain of guilt for not having been able to save Strix. Release from the guilt of having caused Strix's destruction by teaching her friendship, friendship that had led her to betray her masters.

Lizbet sat at the table, her cheeks damp with tears. She took Strix's seashell eye from her pocket and placed it on the tabletop in front of her. It was a thing of shocking beauty, lustrous white and umber, with a pupil of the deepest jet. Lizbet caught one of her own tears on a fingertip and touched it to Strix's eye. It trickled down the pearly shell. Was this the first time Strix had been able to cry? The thought made Lizbet's tears come harder.

She untied the sack and took out Strix's other eye. It was a white china drawer knob with a brown and black tortoise-shell center. She put it beside the first one. No wonder Strix's eyes hadn't matched. Lizbet found herself laughing through her tears.

How many times had she looked into those brown eyes? This was the last time she ever would.

They didn't look right without eyelids or eyebrows though. Lizbet found, mixed in with the pile of Strix, two arcs of fur that she remembered as Strix's eyebrows. Weasel or mink, perhaps. She placed them on the table above the eyes, in the position they would have had in life. Eyelids? One of the scraps was cloth from a gunny sack, the frayed edges making eyelashes. Lizbet arranged it atop the left eye. The other eyelid was the dried brown petal of a rose, with curled bristles from a worn-out paintbrush glued to it. A draft fluttered the right eyelid, almost as if Strix were winking.

With eyebrows and eyelids in place, the effect was remarkable. Looking into Strix's eyes, disembodied and sitting on the table, was almost like looking into them when Strix had been alive. Memories poured over Lizbet. She angled the right eyebrow up, as Strix had used to do when she was being skeptical. Oh, it so reminded her of Strix. The right eyelid fluttered again. Where was that draft coming from? Lizbet got up and checked the door. It was tightly closed.

Wink, went the eyelid. *Wink.*

Lizbet wet a finger in her mouth and held it up. No movement of the air.

Wink.

Wink.

Lizbet stared into Strix's eyes. She held her breath.

Wink.

Trembling so hard she could barely speak, Lizbet said, "S-S-S-Strix?"

Wink.

"Um . . . if you can understand me, wink once for 'yes' and twice for 'no.'"

Wink.

"You're really there?"

Wink.

"You're . . ." She scarcely dared say it. "You're . . . alive?"

Nothing.

"I mean, in the sense that Strix could ever be said to be alive, given that she was made of paper and string and whatnot."

Wink.

"OH MY GOD STRIX!!!"

"Strix," Lizbet said, "I was planning on burning you, and myself as well. Can you forgive me?"

Wink-wink.

"But I didn't do it. Doesn't that count for something?"

Long pause.

Wink.

Two-sided conversation was almost impossible. Lizbet tried to get Strix to spell words by winking once for *A,* twice for *B*, and so forth, up to twenty-six times for *Z*, but Strix didn't have the patience for it. Lizbet would just have to guess Strix's side of the conversation.

"What can we do, Strix? Is there . . . is there some way to get you back together again?"

Wink.

"If I take you back to Mrs. Woodcot, can she—"

Wink-wink.

"You didn't let me finish."

Wink-wink.

"You *really* don't want go back to Mrs. Woodcot."

Wink.

"All right. Is there another witch who could remake you?"

Wink.

"Really? Who? Certainly not the Pope of Storms. I wouldn't trust the earth witches to do it either—they'd turn you into a root or something. Who? It's not like I can guess, because I don't know any other witches."

Wink-wink.

Lizbet had an idea. Out of the pile of Strix's parts, she found Strix's lips: two wads of oakum molded and shaped. Lizbet had to guess what bits of paper or leaves had covered them. She placed them on the table where she thought Strix's lips should go. Without mouth, voice box, windpipe, or chest, Strix still couldn't really talk, but if she could form words with her lips, Lizbet might be able to lip-read. A little.

"Strix," Lizbet said, "who can we get to remake you?"

The lips pursed briefly.

"Yes, 'who.' That's what I said."

Wink-wink.

Strix's lips drew back, then formed what Lizbet thought was an *s*, then a *p* or *b*, and a spitting motion, like a *t*.

What was she trying to say? Lizbet tried to imitate the motions with her own mouth: *ssbt.*

Oh no. Not 'Lizbet.' Strix hadn't said 'who.' She had said 'you.'

"Me?"

Wink.

"Strix . . ."

Wink.

"It's one thing helping make a horse . . ."

Wink.

". . . or repairing your arm, where at least I had something to work with and I could just darn together stuff that was already there, but how could I possibly make a whole person from pieces, so that you'd work as good as new, and not make any mistakes, when I've never done it before . . ."

Wink.

Lizbet stared into Strix's eyes for long minutes.

Strix's right eyebrow raised.

"You really want me to do this?"

Wink.

"Okay," Lizbet said. "Okay. I'll . . ." She had been about to say, 'I'll try.' But instead she said, "I'll do it. I swear I'll do it. I'll make you whole again. However hard it is. However long it takes."

Wink.

Fudge put his paws on his roly-poly hips. "What do mean, we're not going to Abalia?" he said. His tone was one of virtue outraged.

"Not until I rebuild Strix," Lizbet said.

"But . . . the library! The books! The Margrave! Your father!"

"Are you trying to make me feel guilty?" Lizbet asked.

"No! Is it working?"

"Fudge, move back. You'll kick Strix's arm out of place."

Lizbet had spent the last day spreading out Strix's parts on the cabin floor, arranging them in what she hoped was the proper order. Strix's skull, made of snapping-turtle shells, was at the top, with her eyes, her teeth of glass and razor shards, and her nose (carved from a brown water-lily seed pod). Her ribs were all sorts of things: bent willow switches, basket withies, discarded chair slats. A few were still intact, but most had been snapped by the violence of the whirlwind and would have to be repaired or replaced. The long bones of her limbs were whittled sticks, or bundles of twigs tied with twine, or (in the case of her right thigh bone), the shaft of an umbrella, with its knobby handle pulling duty as the hip joint. Every bone had been broken, most in several places. At the center of where the chest should be, Lizbet carefully placed Strix's heart.

At least Lizbet could figure out where the bones went. Muscle and skin were harder. Strix had never been brawny: her muscles were twisted fascicles of brown butcher's paper, packed between with excelsior. Her skin had been torn into a thousand pieces of paper and parchment. It was impossible to tell how they had all fit together originally. Lizbet would have to improvise. She did find the page from the fishing manual that had been Strix's cheek, and a love letter that made her blush furiously to read. She knew that it was supposed to go on Strix's bottom.

"It's no good trying to make me feel guilty," Lizbet said to Fudge. "See, if you want, you can speed things up by helping. I need new upper arm bones—"

"Humerii."

"Whatever they're called. Go find a couple of sticks the right size and whittle them into shape. Not too thick, but not too delicate. Make sure they're sound, with no rot. Hardwood is better than pine. And they mustn't have any big knots to weaken them. And they should be a little springy. Bouncy. Saucy."

"No trouble at all," Fudge said dryly. "Anything else?"

"Why, yes," Lizbet said brightly. "There's lots else to do. Shall I make you a list?"

"No," Fudge said. "I'll just start looking for saucy hume-rii." He trundled himself toward the door.

"And after that, ribs," Lizbet called after him. "And make them perky!"

Abalia was only a day's hike down the mountain. She could have left Strix in parts and gone down to try to solve things with the Margrave and her father.

But she couldn't bear to leave Strix alone, a helpless pile of papers and sticks. And she suspected that fixing things with the Margrave wouldn't be simple. Lizbet would do her best for her father. But she wanted Strix by her side. She needed Strix by her side.

Day by day, Strix came together. Bones, muscles, organs. Some things were missing entirely, and Lizbet had to make them up using her own ingenuity. A dish sponge for the liver. Stockings, their toes cut out and sewn up end to end, for bowels. Masses of yellow morel mushrooms, gathered in the woods, for the lungs. Rebuilding Strix's head and face was especially hard. Lizbet had to work from memory. She was ruthless with herself. Twice she undid a whole day's work because it just didn't look like Strix.

The day she was about to close up the chest, lash the ribs to the breastbone, and pull the muscles over the top, Lizbet paused for one last look at Strix's heart. She held it in her hands: a dark, exquisite vessel, seething with vices and virtues, like a den of serpents. *I could make her more gentle,* Lizbet thought. Among the vices and virtues she had saved from the hosts, and even in the ones Strix had harvested from the Outlaw, there were a few tiny sea-green pearls of Empathy, and a few pale threads of

Humility. If Lizbet added those to Strix's heart, maybe it would make Strix a little nicer. Less caustic. Less cynical.

Less like Strix.

Hot sweat prickled on Lizbet's forehead. "I'm sorry," she whispered under her breath, to no one but herself. "I'm sorry, I'm sorry, I'm sorry. I didn't mean it."

Strix must be Strix. Nothing but Strix. Without blush or apology.

Inside and out.

Topside to bottom.

For good or ill.

For ever and ever.

Every morning, before she began her work on Strix, Lizbet plunged her feet into a mud puddle, or a pile of leaf mould, and let her legs soak up nutrients for a few hours. Fudge hunted for spring peepers and crickets among the larches and uncurling ferns. Twice Lizbet cast a shower of mice to add variety to his diet.

Every other moment of her day was spent rebuilding Strix. Long after the sun had set, and the fire guttered down to embers, long after Fudge was snoring in the corner, Lizbet still knelt on the floor over the remains of Strix, knotting muscles, carving joints, pasting skin. More than once she fell asleep at her work and didn't wake until morning, to find her head cushioned on Strix's breast as if it were a pillow.

Every day Strix came together a little more. Every day she looked a little more like Strix. Two weeks and a few days after Lizbet began, Strix was complete. Lizbet helped her sit up. "How do you feel?" she asked.

Strix shrugged her shoulders, bent her knees up, and put them down again. She swiveled her neck around, rotated her wrists, and wiggled her fingers. Her movements squeaked and groaned like a chair whose joints have loosened. "Not bad," she said. "A little creaky. It'll work out with use."

Together they sewed up the tatters of Strix's layered dresses as best they could. The result was enough to keep Strix decent, although she looked more like a patchwork girl than ever. Lizbet stitched her own dress together again at the split seam. It covered her adequately, but its days as a sack had stretched it to shapelessness.

Strix refused to wear the Outlaw's cartridge belt though. "What's wrong?" Lizbet asked. "You've been wearing it all along."

"There's something wrong with it," Strix said, making a face. She held the cartridge belt up to her nose and sniffed. "Something . . . icky."

"Icky?"

"Holy."

"Holy is not the same as icky."

"It is to me," Strix said, dropping the cartridge belt. "I'm going to go wash my hands."

Lizbet picked the cartridge belt up and examined it. It seemed fine to her. She guessed Strix was sensing the nature of Christ that she had extracted from the mush of communion wafers. Oh well. She would wear the belt herself, then. She slung it over her shoulder and chest.

The next morning they set off down the mountain road, Lizbet and Strix, with Fudge waddling after, panting and puffing and trying to keep up.

Lizbet had long since lost count of the days and weeks. The morning sun was high and warm. The ferns on the forest floor had uncurled fully. The birches by the creeks were leaved out. Lizbet thought it must be almost June. She and Strix had been gone from Abalia more than a month.

The Margrave's book in Lizbet's skirt pocket was considerably worse for wear. Like everything else caught in the Pope of Storms' tempest, it had been rains oaked. Although Lizbet had dried it out as best she could, the pages were wavy and wouldn't shut properly, and its black silk covers were water-stained. On top of all that, of course, it was blank. As they walked down the mountain, Lizbet struggled with what she would say to the Margrave, what sort of deal she could make to get her father back.

Lost in these thoughts, it took her a moment to notice Strix tugging urgently at her sleeve. "What?" Lizbet said, slightly perturbed at having her thoughts interrupted.

"She comes," Strix said. There was a tremor in her voice.

They had left the forest behind and were descending a switchback dirt road through rolling hills. A white goat trotted toward them up the road. A fluttering covey of pure white doves lighted on a bush. In a field by the road, a white cow chewed its cud beside an Andromeda shrub decked with trusses of glistening white buds. Lizbet's gaze darted from one to another. If you looked at them a certain way, they almost formed a pattern, like puzzle pieces. She stepped back, forward, tilted her head to the side. She closed one eye and squinted.

Goat, doves, cow, flowers all came together, into a shape. The shape of a pale and beautiful woman.

Lizbet started back. Mrs. Woodcot stood in the road before them.

She wore a white silk gown that glistened in the morning light. It hissed when she moved. She had a white hat with a wide brim, decorated with a long white ribbon that half wrapped around her. "Good morning, my dears," she said brightly. "Lizbet, whatever are you doing here? You were supposed to quit your silly trip over the Montagnes in failure and despair."

"I figured that out," Lizbet said. "But I didn't."

"That was rude of you. And you somehow escaped the Pope of Storms as well. You can't do anything right, can you?

I declare, Lizbet, you are the most irritating and incompetent mortal child I've ever met."

There were about a thousand things Lizbet might have said. Instead, she held her peace.

She had learned something of witches in the past few months. They followed rules. They couldn't do just anything. Mrs. Woodcot couldn't put Lizbet in her press as she had threatened, because she had already done that to Carl. The earth witches couldn't eat you if you weren't already dead.

As far as Lizbet knew, she didn't owe Mrs. Woodcot anything. If she left Mrs. Woodcot alone, maybe Mrs. Woodcot would not be able to harm her.

Trying to keep her voice from shaking, and choosing her words carefully, Lizbet said, "I beg pardon if I gave offense. Perhaps we can discuss the matter more fully another time. You will forgive me if I don't stop to chat, but my companions and I have a full day's journey ahead of us."

"And you will find that journey easier if I relieve you of an unnecessary burden," Mrs. Woodcot said. Before Lizbet knew it, Mrs. Woodcot was inches from her, close enough for Lizbet to smell lavender and lilies on her. Mrs. Woodcot's hand darted into Lizbet's skirt pocket and emerged clutching the Margrave's book. She held it triumphantly above her head. Her smile was like a heartbreak.

Lizbet yelled, "Give that back! It's mine! You can't just take it!" She leaped to grab the book from Mrs. Woodcot's hand, but missed. Mrs. Woodcot was inches taller, and the book was out of reach.

"Such twaddle," Mrs. Woodcot said. She retreated a few steps, still holding the Margrave's book over her head. "What a little liar you are, Lizbet. The book's not yours at all, and you know it. You stole it from the Pope of Storms. As his agent, I will take charge of it, and return it in due time to His Holiness, the Triple Tyrant of Wind and Rain."

Mrs. Woodcot worked for the Pope of Storms? "But it's not his either," Lizbet said. "It belongs to the Margrave. I'm just returning it. It's not fair of you to take it!"

"Oh, the book is disputed property, then," Mrs. Woodcot said. She put her index finger to her chin and made a moue. "That makes it an affair of the law. There must be a trial! We need judges and lawyers and witnesses, gavels and benches and wigs, depositions and motions and testimony. Go get all those things, little Lizbet, and we shall have the best trial ever. It will last a hundred years. It will be in all the papers. It will settle everything. Meanwhile, the object in dispute will be kept in safe hands. Which is to say, mine."

Lizbet tried one more gambit: "You might as well give the book back to me," she said. "It's not even the book you want."

"Oh, I think it is," Mrs. Woodcot said. She turned it around in her hand. "A trifle water stained, but it has the right name on its spine, you see, and inside . . ." She riffled the pages. "But where are the words? This book seems to be empty." Her wingy eyebrows narrowed, and she glared at Lizbet. "What mischief have you been up to? Where is Hengest Wolftrow's soul?"

"The Pope of Storms got it all wet," Lizbet said "Maybe the rain washed the ink out."

"Oh, I think not. Hengest's soul is not one to be unmade by a little rainwater." Mrs. Woodcot did something with the book, and it vanished. Perhaps she hid it in her bosom. "I don't quite know what happened here," she said, "but my commission from the Pope of Storms is to prevent Hengest from getting his soul-book back. Book in hand, I have fulfilled that duty."

Lizbet wondered whether Fudge could write out the Margrave's soul in any blank book. She hoped he could, because she didn't see any way of getting the original book back from Mrs. Woodcot.

And maybe that was for the best. If Mrs. Woodcot were convinced that the blank book was all she was going to get, then maybe she would be satisfied and go away.

Lizbet heaved a sigh as deep and dramatic as she could make it. "Mrs. Woodcot, it seems you have the victory. I have failed in my purpose. I bid you farewell and set my melancholy foot homeward toward Abalia and whatever fate awaits me there." She forced out a sob, hoping that it sounded convincing. "Let's go, Strix."

"Go where you like," Mrs. Woodcot said, "but go there alone. Your companion's journey stops here. Strix! You faithless wretch! Quit hiding behind the mortal girl. Come out and give an account of yourself."

Lizbet stepped in front of Strix. She held out her arms to block Strix's progress. "She doesn't want to," she said fiercely. "She doesn't ever want to see you again."

"I'm sure she doesn't," Mrs. Woodcot said, smiling. "And I will pleased to grant her wish. In just a little while, she will never, ever see me again." Her curled finger beckoned. Her finely pointed fingernails glinted in the sunlight. "Come, Strix. Come and be dissolved."

"What!"

"It is time for Strix to be unmade. From her parts, I will build a new Strix, a better Strix, a Strix more obedient to her maker. Strix, I have word from the Pope of Storms that he dissolved you himself, but it seems His Holiness is misinformed. I am so disappointed in you. All you had to do was leave the mortal girl to die in the mountains, or crawl home in failure. So simple. And yet, you could not do even that."

"She freed me," Strix said. "I accidentally took food from her—"

"What a fool I raised!"

"—and she freed me from thralldom to her."

"So, Lizbet was no less of a fool than you."

"She said . . ." Strix's voice cracked, and Lizbet thought she might have cried, if she were capable. "She said she wanted to teach me what friendship meant."

"An illusion, an affectation, a lie that mortals tell each other."

"It is not!" Strix cried. "It is not! It's real. It's true as light and air, as the sun and the earth. Lizbet is my friend!" She clutched at her chest. "When Lizbet is with me, it hurts, right here. That's how I know it's real."

"Are you certain it's not just heartburn?" Mrs. Woodcot asked.

"No, I'm pretty sure it's friendship," Strix said.

"I've heard enough of this," Mrs. Woodcot said. She swept down upon Strix in a blizzard of hissing white silk. She seized Strix by the arm. "Strix," she said, "it is time to say good-bye to all things."

What could Lizbet do? Her mind raced. She had left the nose spell with Griffon and Cupido. But maybe—

Naso Maximus! she chanted. Could she remember all of it?

Naso Cumlulo!

Naso Laxio!

Fiat!

Vide!

Naso Deformis—

But that's as far as she got. Mrs. Woodcot would not be subdued as easily as Maglet. She chirped, "Hush, child! Be seen and not heard." She thrust out her index finger. Her fingertip exploded into shining white threads, which flew through the air, straight at Lizbet.

Lizbet got out one shriek before something stung her lips as if she had bitten into a hive of bees. Fighting the pain, she tried to open her mouth to continue the spell, but her lips would not open. The harder she tried, the more it hurt. She reached up to touch her mouth.

Dozens of threads dangled down her chin. Lizbet's lips had been sewn shut.

"And now for you, treasonous child," Mrs. Woodcot said to Strix. "I'd unmake you here and now, but then I'd have the bother of carting your parts down the mountain. Come, Strix." She pulled Strix's arm. "Follow me. I will take you to pieces when we get home."

But Strix dug her heels into the dirt and twisted away from Mrs. Woodcot. "I'm not going!" she cried. "I'm not going to be unmade again! Not by you!"

"Strix!" Mrs. Woodcot said. "Follow me. I *command* you."

The word *command* resonated like an explosion of thunder. Every pebble in the road, every tree and bush, the very sky and mountains sang it back. The world itself seemed, for a moment, to tremble and bow down. Lizbet quailed. How could Strix resist? She threw her arms around Strix and dug her feet into the dirt too.

"I won't!" Strix yelled.

"Come!"

"No!"

All things hung in the balance. Lizbet squeezed Strix as tightly as she could. A drop of blood ran down from her lips to her chin.

After an endless moment, Mrs. Woodcot released Strix's arm and took a step back. When she spoke, her voice wavered. "This can't be. You can't defy me. It isn't possible. You are my thrall. I made you. My command is law to you. It must be obeyed, as the leaf falls from the tree."

Strix's face was a mask of defiance. She bared her teeth. She balled up her fists. "Go command some other Strix," she growled. "I'm not the Strix you made. You heard right: I *was* dissolved by the Pope of Storms. But I was made again." She pointed at Lizbet. "By her. She is my creator now! Lizbet can command me, if she wants. You can't. Not any longer."

"Piffle. Mortals cannot make witches."

Untangling herself from Lizbet's arms, and dropping to one knee, Strix yanked down Lizbet's stockings and lifted up her skirt. Lizbet's birchbark skin shone white in the midday sun. Strix said, "What part of this looks like a mortal to you?"

"Unnnggh," went Lizbet, trying to push her skirt down. "Nnngg!"

"The part above the waist, mostly," Mrs. Woodcot said, "which obviously still possesses a most unwitchlike modesty. However, your point is well-taken." A slight smile played about her lips. "Well, this is a fine how-do-you-do. I have lost my thrall to a half-breed witch, and my own lord and maker is partly to blame. An embarrassing blunder on his part.

"I collect such blunders. When I have enough, I will challenge the Pope of Storms for mastery, and his blunders will fight on my side against him. Such will have to be my consolation for losing my thrall. Ta, then. I'm off. I'll make myself a new Strix when I arrive home. Or maybe a tabby cat would be less trouble." Mrs. Woodcot twirled the long ribbon on her hat around one finger. The whirling white ribbon sliced through her like a sword, cutting her to pieces, and when Lizbet blinked, there was nothing left but a white goat in the road, a white cow chewing its cud in a field, and a white Andromeda bush. Doves' wings beat the air like departing laughter, until they vanished into the sky.

Strix rose. Her voice was drained, but at peace. "I knew Mrs. Woodcot would show up sooner or later," she said. "I knew I'd have to face her, but I didn't know what would happen. I was worried that I might still belong to her. You have no idea how good it felt, the moment I discovered I could refuse to do what she said."

"Nnng," Lizbet said.

"Hold still," Strix said. She placed her hands on Lizbet's shoulders. Her face approached Lizbet's. Lizbet closed her eyes. She felt Strix's breath on her face. Strix's lips brushed hers. *Click!* went Strix's teeth as they severed a knot. Then a brief jab of pain as Strix yanked a thread out. On and on it went, stitch after stitch, pain and joy mixed together until Lizbet could not tell which was which.

Chapter 22

As they started down the road again, Fudge reappeared from hiding and waddled along beside Lizbet and Strix. He chatted about this or that: the botany of flowers and shrubs they passed on the road, the history of the Holy Roman Empire, the quarrels and amours of angels. It was rather like being in the company of a talking encyclopedia that randomly flipped from page to page.

A good bit of Fudge's chatter, though, was private memories: what someone Lizbet had never heard of said to someone else she had never heard of, years ago. Sometimes it was a clever remark, or a stinging insult, or a declaration of love in a moment of private passion. In the memories of people whose souls Fudge had snuffled up his nose, it was odd how personal moments of high emotion, of no consequence to anyone but those who experienced them, loomed larger than the grand march of history that swept the lives and fates of millions before it.

The closer they came to the outskirts of Abalia, the more Lizbet's thoughts turned to the Margrave and what she would say to him. In her mind's eye, she saw him in his quarters, a dim and spectral presence like a living shadow. A table before him was strewn with tiny decanters and caskets from which he sometimes took a swallow.

With a little gasp, Lizbet understood for the first time what she had seen: without his soul, the Margrave had to drink the distilled emotions of others to maintain the illusion of a self. Those moments of strong feeling that breathe life into mortals were denied to him. If he were unable to consume the emotions of others, would he fade away entirely?

But where was he obtaining them? From a witch, surely. The most likely suspect was Mrs. Woodcot.

"Strix," Lizbet said. "What do you know about Mrs. Woodcot and the Margrave? Mrs. Woodcot works for the Pope of Storms?"

"She's the thrall of the Pope of Storms," Strix said. "He made her, like she made me. The Pope of Storms considers Hengest Wolftrow to be dangerous. He sent Mrs. Woodcot over the Montagnes to guard him. She's supposed to prevent him from ever crossing the Montagnes again, or regaining his soul."

"But she's also sustaining him? With distilled emotions?"

"She plays more than one game," Strix said. "If it weren't for her, Hengest might dwindle to nothing. But then the Pope of Storms would call Mrs. Woodcot back. She doesn't want that. She prefers living in mortal lands, where she's powerful and feared. And, as you heard, she has designs on her master's realms. It's safer for her to carry on her plots against him at a distance."

"So if we needed the help of the Pope of Storms," Lizbet said, "we could offer to take his side against her. Or if we wanted her help, we could offer to help her betray him."

Strix stopped. She put her hands on her hips. "What is wrong with you?" she said. "Haven't you learned not to meddle in the affairs of witches? Don't you have enough excitement in your life already? Haven't both of us had enough catastrophes to last a lifetime, just in the past month and a half?"

"I guess we have," Lizbet said. "But we survived, after all. And if meddling in the affairs of witches doesn't go right, maybe the answer is not to stop meddling, but to learn to meddle better. Two months ago, I don't think I could have figured out how to get the earth witches to help us cross the Montagnes. But I did. I've learned some things."

"I never should have given you witch legs," Strix said, shaking her head. "That was my first mistake."

"Actually," Lizbet said, "I've learned to like them. I wouldn't give them up for anything."

They spent the night in the same barn loft they had used on the way up the mountains. The next morning dawned clear, and they took to the road early. By mid-morning Lizbet spotted the church spires and crooked stone chimneys of Abalia peeking above the descending hills. They were alone on the road. By the time they entered Abalia proper, where gray flint buildings jammed against each other and leaned over twisty cobble streets, they had not seen a single person.

"Such a wonderful city!" Fudge said. He craned his head around in wonderment. "So modern and scientific! Neat, square, every corner perfect, every stone aligned to its neighbor in perfect geometry and harmony!" He clasped his chest with his paw. "The multitudes within me knew of cities like this, but I never imagined I would see one myself."

"It's gray, and dreary, and boring," Strix said. "I like it."

"Also deserted," Lizbet said. "Something's wrong. Where is everyone?"

"Still abed?" Strix said. She stretched, and yawned. "Maybe they're too bored to get up. I would be, if I lived here. I'd love that. I'd sleep all day."

Lizbet shook her head. "It's nearly noon. Everyone should be on the street. Goodwives, servants, carriers, beggars." She looked around. In a dark window, she thought she saw the flash of a pale face. She ran up the steps to that house and rapped on the door.

But although she waited for minutes, and rapped the knocker again and again, there was no answer.

Had Abalia turned into a goblin town like Slattern, where people slept in the daytime and came out at night?

She led the others in the direction of the Margrave's Palace. As they neared the center of the city, streets widened and houses became taller and richer.

Lizbet heard a sound, and stopped to listen. "Who's doing all that screaming?" she asked.

A woman in a black day-gown and white bonnet came fleeing up the street, gasping and shrieking. A flying creature the size of a terrier batted about her. It looked like a man and a lizard mixed together, with a whip tail and tiny scaly wings. It held a pair of shears in each of its four clawed feet. As it fluttered after the woman, its shears flashed and clicked, and bits of the woman's clothing flew off and fell to the ground. The woman, screaming and crying, swiveled and danced about, trying to kick it away. Her clothing was already half cut to pieces. Through rents, her shift and even her pale naked flesh could be seen. Lizbet blushed.

The lizard-devil tittered. "Naked you were in the Garden of Eden, naked you will be again! Out, hypocrisy! Out, false modesty, that teases by concealing! God the Tyrant has fallen, and Hell will return the world to its former innocence!"

"Why, that's the biggest humbug I've ever heard in my life!" Lizbet exclaimed. "Hell doesn't care about innocence. You're just finding an excuse to torment this poor woman. Talk about 'hypocrisy.' Shame on you!"

The lizard-devil giggled. "Oh, look, another prudish girl who mistakes vanity for virtue. Why, I think you deserve my Snips of Truth more than the other." It fluttered toward Lizbet, clicking its shears. Its former victim scurried away, pulling the tatters of her clothing around her.

"You just can't keep out of trouble, can you?" Strix said to Lizbet.

Now what? The nose spell hadn't worked so well the last time. Lizbet doubted that a rain of mice would help. She put up her fists. How did boys fistfight? She had no idea. And she thought fistfighting a devil might not work, anyway.

The lizard-devil dived at her, its shears clicking. But at the last moment, it cursed and darted away. "What are you?" it snarled, fluttering over Lizbet's head. "You stink of Christ!"

"I do?" Lizbet said.

"Pah!" The lizard-devil flew away. "And you!" it cried out at Strix, from high over her head. "What is a witch-child doing, consorting with a saint?"

"She's no saint," Strix yelled upward. "Have you lost your mind?" Cursing, the lizard-devil fluttered off.

Lizbet was prepared to admit she had not been especially saintly lately. What was the creature talking about? Then it came to her: a tiny bit of Christ's essence was in shotgun shells in the Outlaw's cartridge belt that she wore. Maybe that's what the lizard-devil had sensed.

Toward them, two devils drove a column of schoolchildren down the street. In front was a Common Lesser Furry Devil acting as a beadle, at their rear a naked Temptress, playing the part of a beldame. The two devils passed a brandy bottle between them, and another bottle circulated among the children. The boys were all dressed in girls' dresses, and the girls in boys' jackets and short pants. As they went down the street, each child beat the child before them on the fundament with a wooden spoon. They sang as they walked. The brandy did little for their ability to stay in tune.

Hail, Father Satan!
Prince of all the nations!

Long live thy horns and teeth,
And save our souls when we sneeze.

"I've heard that all true poets are secretly of the Devil's party," Strix said, "but the reverse obviously isn't true."

The center of Abalia was a carnival of the damned. Men, women, and children fled through the streets, pursued by devils. Beaten, stripped of their clothing, their skin painted with insulting and impious words, hoisted on ropes, batted back and forth from devil to devil like shuttlecocks, mortals were the playthings of the devils. Everywhere devils, hundreds of them. Lizbet realized that this must be what happened in Slattern. She almost wished the Pope of Storms were here to set things right.

Chapter 23

At the Margrave's Palace, the insolent boy guard who had flirted with Lizbet didn't offer her any trouble this time. That was because he had been tied by the wrists and ankles, and hoisted upside-down above the gates. Without his pants.

"Hello, cute bottom," Lizbet called upward as they passed beneath.

"Lizbet!" Strix said. "So forward. For you, that is. Do you know this brat?"

"Hey!" yelled the boy. "Get me down? I mean, please? Can you . . . use magic, or something? I'm sorry about last time. Hey!"

The great wooden doors of the Margrave's Palace, which had been unlocked on Lizbet's first visit, were now shut. Lizbet pounded with her fist on the doors. A voice called faintly from within, "No admittance for devils! Go away!"

"Please let us in!" Lizbet yelled. "We're not devils! We're here to see the Margrave!"

"Can't open up. Orders of the Margrave. A devil might get in."

"But we have something the Margrave wants! It's a book."

"The Margrave's interest in book collecting has been overtaken by his interest in self-preservation," the voice inside yelled. "Come back in a few years, if the situation improves."

"This is different," Lizbet yelled. "This is a really special book." She pounded on the door. "Please let us in!"

"Are you sure you're not a devil? Go away, or we'll pour boiling oil on you!"

"An empty threat," Strix said. "This is a palace. Where are they going to get boiling oil?"

Two floors above them, a window creaked open. A battered black cauldron appeared in the open window. Lizbet, Strix, and Fudge hurriedly retreated. A voice behind the window shouted, "Heave away!" The cauldron tilted. A dark object crashed heavily down onto the slate step where Lizbet had been standing a moment before. Not boiling oil, but an immense book, as thick as it was broad.

Fudge sniffed eagerly. "Words!" he said. "I smell savory words!" He waddled up to the book and flipped open its cover. "It's an unabridged dictionary," he said, wonder in his voice. "'Aa. noun. *Petrog.* Rough, scoriaceous lava.' 'Aam. noun. A Netherlandish or German liquid measure.' 'Aani. noun. *Egypt.* Relig. The dog-headed ape, also called cynocephalus, beloved of the god Thoth.' It's all so wonderful!" His snotty nose twitched, drawing circles in the air. Bending over the dictionary, he snorted deeply and ecstatically. Tiny black letters lifted off the page and flew into his wet nostrils.

"A sorry excuse for boiling oil," Strix said.

Lizbet looked up. Somewhere high in the Palace, atop six stories of rococo windows and stringcourses of stone acanthus, was the Margrave's office. "If only we had a way to get to the Margrave," she said. "If only I could speak to him, just for a minute. Strix, it's a shame you never learned to fly a broom. But wait. That gives me an idea."

Lizbet approached the door again. She glanced upward nervously, but no more dictionary attacks were forthcoming. She pounded on the door. "If the Margrave wants to rid Abalia of the devils, we can help!" she yelled. "We are an emissary of witches. We seek an alliance with the Margrave against the devils."

"The Margrave is against witches too!" the voice from behind the door yelled.

Lizbet persisted. "But main his problem right now is devils. We are two witches—or a witch-and-a-half, actually—with a captive goblin. We offer our services against the devils. If the Margrave's situation is really that bad, he needs to speak to us."

"Captive?" said Fudge.

"Services?" said Strix.

"Shhh," Lizbet said. "Play along."

Lizbet knew she was promising far more than she could deliver. How on earth would she get rid of the devils? But that wasn't important. What was important was that after a perilous journey and great hardship, she was stuck outside the door of the only man who could free her father. She was so close to her goal. She brushed all other concerns aside.

A clanking of the latch mechanism, and the door cracked open. It was the bald, uniformed man with the huffing bellows laugh whom Lizbet had spoken to when she came to the Palace the first time. Bellows eyed her up and down. "I've seen you before," he said. "Huh. You're no witch, you're the fake magician's daughter. Fake father, fake daughter." He tried to slam the door, but Lizbet had stuck her foot in the opening.

"Move your foot, little girl, or I'll crush it," he said. He glared at her.

"You can't crush it," Lizbet said. "It's a witch's foot of oak and strap iron. I *told* you." As Bellows strained against the door, Lizbet said, "I'm half a witch, and this is Strix, who is a witch from top to bottom, and this is Fudge, a talking goblin—"

Fudge bowed, as much as his bulging stomach would allow. "I bid you good morrow, officer, and wish you godspeed in the punctilious performance of your constabulary duties." Bellows stared at him, his mouth gaping open. His grip on the door relaxed.

"—a talking goblin who the Margrave would like very much to meet, because he has an important book in his memory that the Margrave has been seeking, and as you can tell, we have traversed Abalia without having been molested by the devils, which demonstrates that we have power over them, so please take us to the Margrave, as soon as you can. Please." Lizbet paused for breath.

Bellows hesitated. Lizbet decided she might not get a better chance than this. She put her shoulder against the door, shoved it open before Bellows could react, and pushed her way past him into the Palace receiving room. Fudge followed, tottering to and fro as he struggled to carry the unabridged dictionary. Strix came behind. "Thanks so much," Lizbet said to Bellows. She headed for the stairs.

"What did I tell you last time?" Bellows roared. "Hans! Heinz! Hrothgar! Helmuth! Herzl! Heimlich!"

The receiving room was packed with soldiers and officials, but also scores of townspeople. The air smelled of stale human bodies, wood smoke, and cooking grease. Beds had been made on the floor with blankets, and two elegant fireplaces at either end of the room had been pressed into service as cooking fires. Townspeople were taking refuge here from the devils overrunning Abalia.

At Bellows's call, six soldiers wearing the Margrave's orange and blue livery and clanking curiasses separated themselves from the crowd and surrounded Lizbet, Strix, and Fudge. "Escort these three to the Margrave's office," Bellows said. "If they do anything suspicious, defenestrate them immediately."

They set off up the stairs. "What does 'defenestrate' mean?" Lizbet whispered to Fudge.

"It means to throw someone out of a window," Fudge said.

It was almost more than Fudge could bear to pass by four floors jammed with books. At each landing, his nose madly twitching, panting with desire, he tried to squeeze between the guards' legs and waddle off into the stacks. Lizbet had to run after him and drag him back to the staircase. "Stop it," she hissed, "or you'll get defenestrated."

"How do you defenestrate someone, anyway?" one of the guards asked another. "Never done that. Do they get a last meal? Do you have to call a priest, so they can get shriv, or shrove, or shrunk, or whaddyacallit?"

"Nah," said the other guard. "They don't get none of that. That's the beauty of it. You just unlatch a window and chuck 'em out. But there's an art to it, see. Some windows are better for defenstratin' than others. Bigger ones are better than smaller ones. It's best if the window is high up too. Defenestratin' someone out a ground-floor window is more trouble than it's worth."

"Huh. You know all about this stuff," said the first guard.

"I've read up on all the important defenestrations," the second guard said. "The First Defenestration of Prague. The Second Defenestration of Prague. The Defenestration of Lisbon. The Defenestration of Paris. If we have another defenestration"—he glared meaningfully at Fudge—"I'm ready."

The Margrave's doors were open. As they approached, Lizbet saw the Margrave inside seated at his table. Priests in black cassocks and captains and majors in gray wool and gold braid stood around him, arguing. The priests' voices were thin and high with anxiety. The officers' voices were low and unhappy. "Devils are a religious problem," a captain was saying. "The army has no way to fight devils. Why can't the Church do something?"

"We pray," said a priest, "but our prayers are unanswered. We fear that something terrible has happened in Heaven."

He wrung his hands with such nervous energy that Lizbet half believed his fingers would pop off and bounce along the floor.

"Can't you just throw holy water on the devils, or something?" one of the captains said.

A monseigneur shook his head. "There is no holy water," he said. "It cannot be made. Water remains ordinary water. Communion wafers can longer be consecrated. Babies cannot be baptized. Marriages cannot be solemnized. The sacraments are dead." His voice was almost a sob. "God has abandoned His Church," he said.

One of Lizbet's guards cleared his throat discreetly. All faces turned toward them. "This here girl," the guard said. "She says she can get rid of your devils."

The Margrave, Lizbet thought, looked even worse than before. His massive face was pallid as suet and seemed almost to be deflating and folding inward. His rich silk and fur robes seemed to be hung on a stick, not a man. His lusterless eyes slowly focused on Lizbet. "What girl? You? Lenz's daughter? Back again." He flicked his finger at Fudge. "Who let a goblin in? Get that vermin out of my palace." Then he noticed Strix. He braced his fists on the table in front of him and laboriously pushed himself erect. "A witch? A witch girl! How dare a witch come into my presence!"

The conversation was not going as Lizbet liked. "Margrave!" she said. "I have traveled over the Montagnes."

"Eh?"

"I have met the Pope of Storms—"

Hengest Wolftrow's mouth was an empty cavern.

"—and I have taken from his library a book. A book you have been seeking."

"Silence! Say no more now." Wolftrow swung his arm around the room. "The rest of you, leave. Leave!"

Confused, the prelates and officers babbled complaints and milled about, but Wolftrow would hear none of it. Pushing them and shoving with a sudden energy that Lizbet would not have thought him capable of, he herded them before him, forced them through the exit, and slammed the doors behind them. "The book," he said, panting, leaning his back against the closed doors. "You have it? Give it to me, now."

This was the difficult part. Because exchanging the Margrave's book for her father's freedom had all been Lizbet's idea to begin with. She had not actually made a deal with the Margrave.

But she had bargained with witches. Could she bargain with the Margrave?

With trembling hands, Wolftrow fumbled among the vials and caskets on his desk. He popped two of the white pills of *Spes* into his mouth, and a stick dipped into a jar of tarry black *Ira*. With a tiny silver spoon, like a doll's spoon, he placed on his tongue a single drop of clear liquid. Lizbet shivered as she got a whiff of its scent: *Timor*. Fear.

"In return for getting your soul book back, I'd like you to free my father," Lizbet said, trying to keep her voice from shaking. "I did a good deed for you, and in return, I'd like you to do a good deed for me."

Wolftrow's face, no longer pale, was flushed with blood. He seemed inches taller than he had been moments ago. "I do not dicker like a common tradesman," he said. "You are lowborn, and a child, sprung from a family of criminals." Lizbet flushed. "How dare you make demands on me?" Wolftrow said. His voice rumbled with the assurance of a man accustomed to having his will done without question. "If you have something of mine, yield it to me now, and receive such mercy as I see fit to bestow."

Lizbet hesitated, but Strix said curtly, "No deal, no book. Lizbet, let's go. Maybe Hengest will be more interested tomorrow. Or maybe we could sell the book and bribe your father's gaoler with the gold." She put her hand to the doorknob.

With a curse, Wolftrow seized Strix. His immense hand nearly fit around Strix's waist. Ignoring her struggles and yells, he bore her to the window in a few huge strides, threw it open, and defenestrated Strix.

Lizbet cried in terror. She rushed to the window and leaned out.

But she didn't see what she had feared: Strix's broken body on the ground, six stories below. Instead, Strix had twisted herself up so that one hand grasped an ankle, and the other arm and leg were entwined together, with the effect that as she fell, her free limbs whirled rapidly about her trunk.

Like a winged maple seed, Strix spun slowly to the ground.

She landed lightly on one foot and untangled herself. She looked up and waved.

"I thought you didn't know how to fly," Lizbet yelled.

"That wasn't flying, that was falling," Strix yelled back.

Lizbet turned on Wolftrow. "You threw my friend out the window!"

"No one has the right to hate witches more than I," Wolftrow said. "No one has suffered more at their hands."

"But Strix is a good witch! Well, sort of good, that is. In her own way. Or, actually, not good, but also not evil. Or, sort of good, and sort of evil, but mostly stuff that I can't figure out whether it's good or evil . . ." Strix was too much trouble to explain to a stranger. "But you didn't have to throw her out the window!"

Wolftrow stood in front of Lizbet, looking down at her. He grasped her shoulders with both hands and, steadying himself on her as if she were a cane or a crutch, slowly lowered himself to kneel on one knee. It was like a mountain lying down.

Lizbet stared into his eyes. "You cannot imagine," he said, "what it is like to have one's soul torn from one's flesh."

"Actually, I sort of can," Lizbet said. "It nearly happened to me. Strix saved me."

"A witch saved you . . . ?"

"She lost her arm for me. Then she lost her life. But I put her together again."

"You claim you crossed the Montagnes du Monde," Wolftrow said. "And you burgled the lair of the Pope of Storms? And returned? Impossible." He shook his head. "But—the Pope of Storms. How do you know that name? No one but myself has heard that name, on this side of the Montagnes."

"We did cross the Montagnes, like I said," Lizbet insisted. "Strix and me. We followed the road that you built."

"The road. Yes! Yes, we did build a road. It was a terrible ordeal. Tens of thousands died." To Lizbet's astonishment, Wolftrow's eyes brightened. Shimmering tears welled up, but did not fall. "So you found our path. And you followed it through the Montagnes?" His grip on her shoulders tightened. "Tell me more. Tell me what happened."

Lizbet told her story, leaving out Fudge for the moment. When she was done, Wolftrow said, "None but I knew of these things. Can it be true? You have been over the Montagnes. You have walked in my footsteps. In the goblin village. In the sewers. In the halls of the Pope of Storms. A child! A girl. Astonishing. To succeed where all before you have failed. You have heart. You have courage. You are a heroic girl indeed, Lizbet Lenz."

No one had ever called Lizbet "heroic" before. In fact, very few nice things had been said about her by anyone since the awful day her father was imprisoned. Her life had been one fight after another.

She blushed. To hear such a compliment from the Margrave was overwhelming. "Thank you," she said. "Strix helped. A lot."

"'Strix'? An evil name. The witch-child?"

Lizbet nodded. "She's the one you threw out the window."

"You have magic to control her, then? To bend her infernal nature to your will?"

"I wouldn't call her nature infernal, exactly," Lizbet said. "Although she can be frustrating, at times. And I didn't control her with magic. I taught her how to be friends."

"How Machiavellian of you. Lizbet—"

"'Machia—' What?"

"—Lizbet, you are a remarkable young woman. A promising young woman."

The door creaked open a few inches. The ghostly form of Strix slipped through. This time she had knit herself into the shadows. She waved at Lizbet and stuck out her tongue. Lizbet resisted the urge to wave back. A soldier opened the door wider and peered around, before shaking his head and closing the door again.

"So the remnant of my army still waits for me, over the Montagnes?" Wolftrow said. "They are still faithful. I am moved."

Lizbet frowned. "They thought you would come back for them. You told them you were going back over the Montagnes for help."

"I went in the other direction," Wolftrow said. "I went seeking magic. Magic enough to remake the world. We didn't cross the Montagnes to retreat in despair. The tens of thousands who died in the mountains didn't die for that. We crossed to make the two worlds one.

"Child, do you know where the Montagnes came from? Do you know why the world on the other side is all magic and witches and goblins?" Lizbet shook her head. "Few know this. Long ago, a thousand years and more, a dark planet filled with magic came hurtling from the outer voids, beyond the battlements of Heaven. It smashed through Heaven itself. It smashed through the crystalline spheres that hold the heavenly bodies in place as they rotate around the Earth. It passed through the sphere of fixed stars, and the spheres of Saturn, and Jove, and Mars, and the Sun, and crashed into the Earth itself.

"Our globe is now a world of two halves. That terrible collision raised the peaks of the Montagnes du Monde. When we cross the Montagnes, we cross into another world."

"The hole in the sky!" Lizbet exclaimed. "At the top of the Montagnes, I saw a hole in the sky."

"That is where the dark planet burst through the sphere of the Moon," Wolftrow said.

"The earth witches didn't know our side of the world even existed," Lizbet said, "even though they said they explored the whole world, digging underground. But they must have done it before their world crashed into ours."

"I crossed the Montagnes to subdue that dark planet and bring it under human rule and God's law," Wolftrow said. He gripped Lizbet's shoulders more fiercely. His gaze was hypnotic. His voice was filled with restless energy. "Lizbet, I need your help in this task. If you have the book that holds my soul, give it to me now."

"My father . . ."

"I will do the right thing by your father. Do you have my book, or is this all a ruse?"

"I have it."

Wolftrow released Lizbet's shoulders. He rose. His gaze locked with hers. "Then I command you, yield it to me now!"

Margrave Wolftrow's command was not the same as Mrs. Woodcot's. It was just a word. It had no more force than Lizbet chose to give it.

But Lizbet had no rebellion in her soul. The Great Chain of Being was as real to Lizbet as the sun and the sky: a magnificent, overarching truth that sustained the world. If the Margrave gave an order, Lizbet must obey.

"Your book is here," she said. "Fudge?" She looked around. "Fudge, where are you?"

While Lizbet and Wolftrow were talking, Fudge had seated himself in a corner with his unabridged dictionary, happily snuffling in line after line. "'Abat-jour,'" he said happily. "'Noun. A device designed to reflect light from a window downward. Also: a skylight.'" Strix, still knit into the shadows, flipped the dictionary cover closed and shoved Fudge toward the Margrave.

"That's not a book," Wolftrow said. His lip curled. "That's vermin."

Fudge put his hands on his roly-poly hips and tilted his neckless head back to survey the Margrave, towering above him. "I may be vermin, but I'm educated vermin," he said.

"This is Fudge," Lizbet said. "He reads books. Well, not 'reads,' exactly. More like 'sniffles.' He sniffled up the book of your soul. It's inside him, now."

Wolftrow stared down at Fudge with both fury and fear. His breaths came heavily.

Lizbet thought she'd better hurry. "He can write it out for you, in a new book," she said quickly. "All we need is blank paper and a pen." She searched the room. There was a pen and inkwell and a few sheets of stationary on the table where the Margrave had been sitting, among his vials and caskets. She lifted Fudge up, grunting with the effort, and plopped him down in the Margrave's chair.

Fudge's wet snout didn't even come to the tabletop. Fetching the unabridged dictionary, Lizbet shoved it under Fudge. That was better. "Fudge," she said, "can you do it?" She dipped the pen in the inkwell and pushed a sheet of stationary toward him. "Can you write out some of the Margrave's soul book?"

She held her breath. Fudge had never actually done this, although he *said* he could.

Fudge's pen poised over the paper. He stared upward for a moment and pursed his fleshy lips. Then he put pen to paper and began to write.

Wolftrow hovered over him. His eyes were wide his mouth gaped open. As soon as Fudge finished the first page, Wolftrow snatched it and held it up, his eyes jerking back and forth over the scrawls. "It's here," he breathed. "I'm here. By God. This is me. This is how I was. This is how I am. Old Margaret. Helmuth—how I feared him! Knuth-am-strand. The Gymnasium. Those terrible nights in Marberg forest . . ." He muttered on, a rush of names and events. Lizbet couldn't make sense of them, but to the Margrave they were like a tonic. The *Spes* and *Ira* and *Timor* had lent him the momentary illusion of humanity. But as he read the words Fudge scribbled down, Wolftrow became a man in truth. No longer a shock of dark clothes on a stick, but a man of strength and vigor, powerful shoulders, deep chest, incisive gaze. A man who, after years of wandering among shadows, had finally rediscovered who he was, and believed again that he had a mission in the world.

Wolftrow finished the first page and threw it down. He hungrily read the second, but when he picked up the third—

"It's blank," he said, flipping it over and over. He stared at Fudge. He tilted his head and leaned closer. "What's this?" A black scrawl of letters was stuck to Fudge's nostril. Wolftrow reached for it, but Fudge gave a snort, and the line of copy vanished up his nose.

Wolftrow's face went livid. He drew his palm back to strike Fudge. Fudge cowered.

"No!" Lizbet pleaded. "Don't! He can't help it."

"It's so delicious!" Fudge said.

"Don't hit him," Lizbet said. Wolftrow, still shaking, hesitated. "Help him," Lizbet said urgently. "He wants to be good, but he can't stop himself."

After a bit of experimentation, they decided to dispense with tying Fudge to the chair. Instead, Wolftrow called in one of the munifexes, who sat by Fudge's side as he wrote, rapping Fudge on the nose when the goblin's will weakened and his snuffly nostrils dipped toward the paper.

Papers black with scribble accumulated in a pile. Wolftrow pored over them greedily.

"I told him that if he wrote out your book," Lizbet said hopefully, "you might let him snuffle up some of your library?"

"All of it," Wolftrow said. "Every last word of it he may annihilate. All other books are worthless to me, now that I have the one I need."

"And my father?"

Wolftrow put down the papers. He looked her in the eye. His voice was pained. "Child, I want to release your father, but I cannot. I cannot even go to the Houses of Correction to give the order. You've seen how I am a prisoner in my own palace. The streets are ruled by devils. To venture out is to be at their mercy. My city is in the hands of an enemy. You said"—his voice took on a hopeful note—"you said to the guards that you could solve the problem of the devils."

Lizbet had hoped that the Margrave, in his excitement over having his soul book back, had forgotten the ruse she used to gain an audience with him. But he hadn't.

"Lizbet," Wolftrow said. His gaze fixed on hers. His voice was stern, confident, and respectful. It was a voice that made you want to square your shoulders and salute. "Lizbet. I believe that if any mortal can find a way to chase off the devils, it is you. You are a remarkable young woman. In crossing the Montagnes, overcoming untold dangers, burgling the stronghold of a witch prince, and returning safely, you have accomplished something no one else has, no one else could have. You have gifts of courage and imagination beyond any other of your sex. If anyone can chase the devils from Abalia, I truly believe it is you."

Hearing this, charmed, almost hypnotized by the Margrave's voice, Lizbet wanted believe he was right.

"Sometimes a woman can succeed where a man cannot," Wolftrow said. "Remember Joan of Arc, who chased an invading army of British shopkeepers off our continent?"

"But they burned Joan at the stake," Lizbet complained.

"And she is in Heaven now, among the saints."

Lizbet hoped that Belial and the devils weren't giving St. Joan a hard time. Heaven might not be a safe destination any longer. "You know something?" she said. "You remind me of God." Like God, the Margrave had a gift for making you want to believe him, and follow him. His voice, his gaze, the little compliments he paid you—he made you fall in love with him, after a fashion. But also like God, the Margrave was full of advice that steered Lizbet toward a fate that was not likely to turn out well for her.

But she could not bring herself to refuse him.

"Thank you, Lizbet," Wolftrow said. "That's quite a compliment."

It hadn't been entirely a compliment, but Lizbet decided not to clarify it for him.

So ridding Abalia of its devils was the only way she was going to get her father out of prison. But how on earth was she to do that?

Chapter 24

No sooner had Lizbet and Strix left the Palace than they heard the clip-clop of hooves on the cobblestones. A devil came toward them down the avenue. It had the head of a goat, the trunk of a goat, the legs of a goat—in fact, it looked very much like a goat, if goats were eight feet tall, entirely scarlet, and walked on their hind legs. A lolling tongue sprawled out of its mouth. It was almost upon them. Lizbet took off her bandoleer and swung it in the air.

The goat-devil squealed, threw up its forelegs as if to protect itself, and stumbled off, bleating curses.

"There," Strix said. "You've driven off one devil. Only hundreds more to go."

"Except he hasn't been 'driven off' at all," Lizbet said. "He just went around a corner. Oh, Strix, how am I supposed to drive hundreds of devils out of Abalia?"

"Find someone who knows how to drive out devils," Strix said. "Do whatever he does."

"But there isn't anyone who drives out—wait. Maybe there is."

"Really? I thought I was making a joke."

"Christ drove out devils," Lizbet said. "A couple of times, in the Gospels. But He's on the run from the devils right now. We can't go over to His house and quiz Him on His technique."

Wait, she thought. Christ did have a "house," so to speak.

She hadn't been to church in a long, long time.

It wasn't safe to go to the Cathedral of St. Dessicata. Someone there might recognize her as the girl who stole the hosts. After a while wandering through the streets, Lizbet and Strix found a humble little chapel in a fauberg half a mile from the Margrave's Palace. A few devils loitered outside, heaving paving stones at its stained-glass windows.

Strix refused to enter. "I heard of a witch who went into a church once. She turned to stone. The priest put her in his garden, plumbed her with lead pipe, and used her as a fountain. I'm not going in there." She gave Lizbet a worried look. "I'm not all that sure it's safe for you anymore."

"If I start getting stiff in the legs, I'll run out fast," Lizbet promised her.

The door was barred, but after Lizbet banged vigorously on it, a young priest opened it a crack, and she convinced him to let her inside.

"I'd like to take Holy Communion," she told him.

The priest let her in, but shook his head sadly. "There is no Communion, child. We have no hosts. Communion wafers cannot be consecrated, even by the Bishop." Lizbet remembered overhearing a priest in the Margrave's office saying that.

The moment Lizbet stepped inside the little church, her soul was at ease. The nave was high and narrow, and full of inviting dark recesses. A ray of light through the broken rose window struck the altarpiece, and its gilding glittered. Lizbet breathed deeply of the cool air. In a rush, memories of other churches came back to her. Soaring hymns, hours of quiet reverie, glowing stained-glass stories of the gospels, long, personal talks with God. In Lizbet's unsettled, lonely childhood, a church had always been a place of familiarity and comfort. She said, "At least the devils are afraid to come in here."

The priest shook his head again. "The devils are stopped by a stout wooden door," he said. "When the devils first appeared, we thought they wouldn't dare enter a church. But they came right in. They emptied their bowels upon the altar. They passed water on the floor. They painted tar on the portraits of the Virgin." He was near to tears. "The Church has lost all its power. God has abandoned us. Hell rules the universe."

Hearing this, Lizbet fought down anger. The devils had despoiled even this humble little church, just out of mean-ness. She *would* put them down. She wanted to put them down. "Even if I can't have Communion, I'm going to pray, anyway," she told the young priest.

She slipped into a pew and knelt. She knit her fingers and rested her forehead on her clasped hands. She whispered all the prayers she could remember. Then she prayed in her own words, for herself, her father, the Margrave, the Pixie Queen, all the priests and the Bishop, all the people of Abalia, and of the Holy Roman Empire, and in all the world. She prayed for Strix, and Fudge, and the earth witches and the goblins, even though none of them would approve. She prayed for Griffon and Cupido because she had promised to, and for the Pope of Storms and Mrs. Woodcot. She prayed as hard as she could. "What can I do?" she asked silently. "How can I get my father free? The devils are desecrating Your churches. The Margrave is counting on me to drive them out, but I don't know how."

It wasn't the same without the dry and starchy host melt-ing on her tongue. There was no answer. The gates of Heaven were closed.

But every silence has its voices. A breeze whispered through the broken stained-glass windows. A dry oak leaf scratched across the floor. A cricket beneath a kneeler chirped its insect blessing. The distant murmur of a priest, a half-heard shout from outside. As it had been when Lizbet lay beneath her dress full of rustling pieces of Strix, and dreamed she heard Strix's voice whispering to her, so she now imagined that all the church's faint and fitful sounds joined together like scraps of cloth in a crazy quilt. And within that maze of rustles and whispers, a distant voice, more imagined, more wished for, than heard:

. . . elizabeth . . .

It was the voice not of God the Father, but of Christ. She listened. She didn't dare reply.

. . . elizabeth . . . dear child. my blessings on you, such poor blessings as i can give. i would gladly help you, but i cannot even help myself. i am in hiding, dear heart.

o, elizabeth, have mercy on us.

But that was how mortals prayed: *Oh, Lord, have mercy on us.*

"Jesus?"

. . . have pity on us . . .

Lizbet's heart was about to break.

"Jesus," she prayed. "I have to banish all the devils from Abalia. I don't know how."

Silence.

Lizbet's heart squeezed painfully in her chest. Her teeth chattered. Had she broken the spell?

A still, distant voice, like a voice imagined in the patter of rain:

. . . only christ can banish devils . . .

And that was all. No matter how long she waited, no matter how hard she prayed, everything else was silence.

Strix was waiting outside the church door. "That took long enough," she said. "Did you have a nice pray?"

"I knew the answer all along," Lizbet said. There was wonder in her voice, but also fear. "Only Christ can banish devils. We need Christ."

"You said that already. We don't have one."

"We'll make one."

Strix raised an eyebrow. "Easier said than done?"

"I suppose everything is easier said than done," Lizbet said. "You can tell me afterward whether it was easy. Because you're going to do it."

"I'm going to do *what?*"

"Let's go," Lizbet said, taking Strix by the hand and dragging her down the street. "We need to find a blacksmith shop."

"We're going to make a giant, powerful, iron Christ?"

"No," Lizbet said. "A small, weak, fleshy Christ. That looks a lot like me."

Blacksmithing was a common occupation. They found a smithy within two blocks of the church. The shop was empty, the hearth cold. Like the rest of Abalia, the smith and his 'prentices were hiding from the devils, or had fled the town. Lizbet wrinkled up her nose. Everything was soot and grime. The floor was cinders underfoot.

She searched through the blacksmith's tools until she found what she was looking for: iron pincers. On the smithy's walls, different sizes hung from hooks. Huge pincers that would take both a man's fists to hold, all the way down to tiny ones with which the blacksmith might have wrought a delicate brass filigree for a lady's vanity table. It was these tiniest pincers that Lizbet picked. They were cold to the touch, and left traces of soot on her fingers. Lizbet shivered, thinking about what was next. She handed them to Strix.

Strix accepted them doubtfully. Lizbet sorted through the cartridges in the Outlaw's bandoleer until she found the one she was looking for. She pried back the cardboard flaps over its open end. Inside, tiny blue-white filaments of Christ's divine nature glowed in the darkness. She dropped the bandoleer on the floor and handed the cartridge to Strix.

Strix retreated an inch. "Ew."

"Take it," Lizbet insisted. "Don't touch what's inside. It might burn you. Grab it with the pincers instead."

Strix understood at last. Her expression softened. For the first time ever, Lizbet thought she looked gentle. She took Lizbet's hand. "You really want me to do this?" she asked.

Lizbet squeezed Strix's hand. She forced herself to nod.

"No one wants this," Strix said. "No one ever wants to be better or worse than they already are."

"I don't want it," Lizbet said. "I'm scared of it. I'm scared it won't work. I'm scared I'll get hurt. I'm scared you'll get hurt. I'm scared it's wrong, and I'll go to Hell because of it, although with the devils in charge of everything, I'm honestly not sure Heaven would be much different.

"But whatever the danger is, I still need to put down the devils. It's the last thing I have to do, to get my father free. After everything I've gone through, I'm not going to stop now."

On a grimy benchtop, Lizbet cleared away a space, and laid her body down. "Strix," she said, "it's time." She stared up into Strix's mismatched brown eyes. With her lips more than her voice, she said, "Do it."

Strix's face hovered above her. The glowing strands of Christ's divine nature, held in the black iron pincers, approached Lizbet's nose. She pushed her palms down against the workbench, trying to hold her body still, although all her flesh was shaking. Her body arched with fear and apprehension. Her nose felt strange, full, as Strix's hand slid in. There was a twinge of pain, and she jerked. "There, there," Strix said. "There, there."

Something touched the back of Lizbet's throat, and she wanted to cough. Tickling sensations deep in her chest. She realized Strix had her entire arm in her nose, up to the shoulder. It should have been terrifying, but the longer it went on, the less frightening it became. Strix's face, hovering inches from hers in an expression of intense concentration, was comforting.

Movement, deep within her. Turning, squeezing, pushing, rolling, aching. Then *expanding*, as if a white bird had spread its wings inside her. Lizbet gasped.

"It's done," Strix said. With careful slowness, she removed her arm from inside Lizbet.

Lizbet sat up and shook her shoulders. Strix eyed her cautiously. "How is it?" she asked. "How do you feel?"

"I feel . . . ," Lizbet said. "I feel . . . lighthearted."

"*Lighthearted?*"

"Fearless. I feel . . ." She shook herself again. She allowed herself to smile. "I feel as if everything is going to work out. As if, at the end of all things, all wrongs will be fixed, so there's nothing ever to be scared of. I think maybe it's the first time I've really felt that way."

Then the weight of all the world descended upon Lizbet, crushing her.

She screamed. She fell back onto the workbench, thrashing, her eyes wide with horror. Strix bent over her. "Lizbet! Lizbet! What is it? What happened? Did I do something wrong? Lizbet! What is it? Stop it, you'll hurt yourself. Lizbet!"

Strix had knotted into Lizbet's heart a tiny portion of Christ's divine nature. The sins of mankind that Christ was born to bear had descended upon Lizbet's own small shoulders.

Every cruel word, every lie. Every blow struck in anger, every burrowing maggot jealousy. Every murder, every theft, every war, every advantage taken of the weak by the strong. Every coldness where there should have been love. Every distance where there should have been closeness. Every stinginess where there should have been generosity of purse or spirit.

Every unkindness.

Large and small, mankind's flaws and crimes heaped themselves on top of Lizbet in that moment. Heavy as mountains, they crushed her. They chattered in a myriad of voices, some tiny, some roaring, endlessly talking about themselves. Recriminations, guilts unexpunged, petty grievances, resentment, smugness: a swarm of dirty, biting flies.

Lizbet struggled, trying to get away. Her body thrashed back and forth, her hands banged on the workbench, her head bounced up and down until the back of her scalp was bloody.

Strix held her, pleading with her to stop, trying to restrain Lizbet's twisting limbs and body, and cushion her head.

In all that dark night of guilt and sin and crime that had engulfed Lizbet, Strix's touch was her only comfort.

It came to Lizbet that she bore the merest tiny threads of divinity in her heart. If this was what came of having the barest trace of Christ's nature, what monstrously greater burden must Christ Himself have borne?

Yet Christ had carried that terrible weight without resentment or complaint—He who had been but a man born of woman Himself. Why couldn't Lizbet bear her own, far lesser burden, here, and now?

"Lizbet!"

Strix's voice called her back to the world.

Lizbet stopped thrashing. Her flesh went limp. "Are you okay?" Strix asked. She released Lizbet, reluctantly.

As if she were lifting the weight of mountains, Lizbet pushed herself up on her elbows. She forced her breathing to slow.

She swung her legs over the edge of the workbench and slid off to stand, trembling, on the cinder floor. "Are you okay?" Strix asked again.

"No," Lizbet said. "Not really." Every fiber of her wanted to fail, to fall, to crumple to the ground in despair, crushed by the sins of the world.

Instead, she lifted one shaking foot and took a step. Then she took another. Strix hovered over her, one hand at Lizbet's elbow, another at her back.

The Mussulmen say, "Take one step toward God, and God will take two steps toward you." Perhaps the white bird within Lizbet had been waiting for her to shoulder her share of the world's sins without complaint. Waiting for her to rise and move, and strive her best to do what needed to be done.

The white bird spread its wings. It spoke, with a woman's sweet voice: *All shall be well, and all* shall *be well, and all manner of thing shall be well.*

Lizbet stood. Her feet and legs stopped shaking. She turned and looked Strix in the eye. "Hold my hand," she said.

Strix came from outside humanity, uncreated by God, uninvolved in the endless mortal cycle of sin and guilt and redemption. Her laws were different laws. Whoever judged her, it was not God. Holding Strix's hand gave Lizbet strength. Like the white bird within, Strix's touch called to Lizbet from a place of certainty, beyond the boiling seas of sin and error through which she, and all humanity, plunged and foundered.

The Holy Spirit within her, the witch by her side, Christ Lizbet stepped forth into the world to do battle with the armies of Hell.

Chapter 25

"It shouldn't be hard to find a devil," Lizbet said. She and Strix walked hand in hand, down the street, away from the smithy.

Strix looked at her anxiously. "Maybe you should start with just a little devil."

But before they could find a devil, a devil found them. An eight-foot-tall scarlet goat clip-clopped around a corner on its hind legs. It held a whip in one cloven hoof. It licked its lips. "What have we here?" it bleated. "Two sweet little girlies. Some fun!" It cracked its whip. The sound echoed like a musket-shot off the stone buildings.

Lizbet strode forward, pulling Strix after her.

The goat-devil halted. "Who are you?" it bleated. "Not fair! You stink of Heaven!" It turned, and its hooves clattered off.

"That was lucky," Strix said, releasing a breath. "Now let's find one a little smaller, just for practice—"

"It's getting away!" Lizbet yelled. She ran after the retreating devil, dragging the protesting Strix behind her.

The goat-devil was faster, though, and quickly put fifty feet between them. Frustrated, Lizbet yelled at its retreating back, "Stop! Stop! STOP!"

The goat-devil stopped.

Lizbet approached it. The goat-devil trembled from horns to tail. It cowered as Lizbet approached. "Don't!" it bleated. "Don't touch!"

A few feet separated them. Its animal stink make Lizbet gag.

"Now what?" Lizbet whispered to Strix. "What do I do?"

"How should I know?" Strix said. Her tawny brows knit in thought. "It asked you not to touch it, so maybe you should touch it."

"Nooooo!" howled the goat-devil.

"Okay, you should definitely touch it," Strix said.

Lizbet approached the goat-devil. Cringing, she grabbed its chest, a greasy, rancid handful of matted red hair and loose skin.

The goat-devil screamed. Sudden thunder crackled overhead. Orange flames burst from beneath Lizbet's grip, enveloping her hand in a ball of leaping fire. Oily black smoke poured out between her fingers.

With a cry, Lizbet let go and jerked her hand back. She put her arm to her mouth, coughing from the smoke.

"That looked promising," Strix said. "Keep going."

"It burned my hand!"

But now that the initial shock was over, Lizbet realized that her hand didn't hurt. "I thought it did." She turned her hand over and back. Except for some soot, it seemed fine. "Maybe it didn't."

Flinching, again Lizbet grabbed a hunk of the goat-devil's hair and flesh. Flames and choking black smoke burst forth. Livid storm clouds swept down the sky, and thunder crashed. The goat-devil screamed for mercy.

In a minute, Lizbet's grip had burned the fistful of flesh to ash. She grabbed another hunk. The goat-devil cried, "Mercy, mercy upon us! The pain! The burning!"

"This is taking too long," Strix complained after a while. "Are you going to have burn it to ashes handful by handful? We'll be here all day."

"I'm hurting it too," Lizbet said. "I don't like that. Even though it's a devil."

"Can't you just banish it or something?"

"I don't know how!" Lizbet wailed.

"Calm down," Strix said. "Let's think this through. It stopped when you commanded it to. So maybe it has to obey you. Try telling it to go away. Go back to Hell or something."

"Don't you need sacred objects?" Lizbet said. "Bell, book, and . . . something. Bell, book, and skillet? You ring the bell, read from the book, and . . . beat the devil with the skillet? Oh, I can't remember. And isn't there a ceremony? I don't know what I'm supposed to say."

"Make something up," Strix said. "'Take thee away.' 'Begone.' 'Scram.' 'Adios.' Say anything you want. You're Christ. Who's going to question you?"

"Uh . . ." Lizbet pitched her voice down an octave and tried to sound commanding. "I abjure thee, in the name of my Father, Most High and Most Holy, betake thou to the Hell He hath consigned thee to, and never return hither to trouble the goodfolk of Abalia!"

Strix clapped her hands delightedly. "Not bad, if a little wordy. Oh, look, something's happening."

The light of leaping flames poured up from between the cobblestones of the street, beneath the goat-devil's black hooves. The cobblestones shook. One after another, they lifted from their beds and flew into the air. They whirled around the goat-devil's head like a swarm of angry bees.

A cobblestone swung high overhead, and fell like a comet. It struck the goat-devil on the top of its head. Another cobble followed it, and another. Blow after blow, they smashed down on the goat-devil's head as it cowered, whimpering.

Like sledgehammers, the cobblestones pounded the goat-devil into the ground as if it were a fencepost.

In less than a minute, there was none of it left. The ground rumbled one last time, and released a plume of sulfurous smoke. A wail from beneath the earth, diminishing into some unimaginable distance below. The cobblestones settled again into their beds, and the street was whole and empty once more.

"Holy crap," Strix breathed.

"Strix?" Lizbet blushed. "Your language."

Strix put two fingers in front of her mouth. "I'm sorry," she mumbled through the fingers. "But that was damn good."

Not all devils departed in the same highly theatrical fashion as the goat-devil. For some, the earth simply opened and swallowed them, as it had for Toadwipe. Some were drawn wailing up into the sky by a sudden whirlwind. Some were consumed on the spot by furnace flames, leaving not even ash behind.

One especially ugly specimen, all scales and horns, frantically jammed its head into its own anus, followed by its thrashing shoulders, arms, legs, and hips, its entire body falling into its bowels with increasing speed until, with one last, loud, malodorous fart, there was nothing left. Strix got the giggles and couldn't stop. For days afterward, she would periodically break out in giggles over nothing, and Lizbet had to shush her.

Lizbet tried to count the devils as she banished them, but lost her place somewhere after ten score and thirty. For six days, she and Strix walked the length and breadth of Abalia, from the rows of guillotines and black-iron gibbets at the Plaza of Fear, to the Hospital of St. Luke, at the center of a vast cemetery crowded with the tombstones of former patients.

Into the fleshpots and dives of Abalia-under-the-Hill they went. With torches they descended into the sewers, driving the goblins before them. Everywhere, they shouted for all devils to show their noses and be properly banished.

At night, they slept in Lizbet's former home, as abandoned as the rest of the town. Lizbet took Strix through the rooms where she had lived. In her bedroom, Lizbet showed Strix her dolls: Gertrude, Hedwig, Christina, Berta, Sophia, Margaret.

Strix walked a doll down a tabletop, moving its arms and legs with her hands. "They don't move by themselves?" she asked.

"Silly. I made them when I just a mortal."

In the cellar, they found hams and dry sausages hanging from the rafters, still sound, and a tub of fat with which to brown them. The bins of winter root vegetables had begun to sprout, but they salvaged what they could. Strix peered around the cellar. "There's no firewood down here?" she asked.

"No, the stove and fireplaces burn coal," Lizbet said.

"Your father beat you with a lump of coal?"

"What? No, of course not."

"What did he beat you with, then?" Strix asked.

"He didn't beat me with anything!"

"We kept firewood in the cellar," Strix said, "and when Mrs. Woodcot wanted to beat me, she'd tell me to go down in the cellar and pick the stick to do it. I hated the cellar."

"This cellar was still cool on hot summer days," Lizbet said. "I liked to take a lamp, a devotional manual or a book of poems, and go down to the cellar to read, when everything was hot and muggy upstairs. I liked the cellar."

"Your father really never beat you?"

Lizbet shook her head.

"Maybe that's why you're such a Goody Two-shoes."

Lizbet nodded. "Maybe."

"I wish . . ." Strix said. "I wish Mrs. Woodcot had maybe beaten me just a little bit less."

Lizbet, in a rush, threw her arms around Strix and hugged her as tightly as she could.

Nights were troublesome. By never-ceasing effort, by a constant fight against exhaustion and despair, Lizbet bore up under the weight of mankind's sins during the day. At night, though, when she tried to sleep, nightmares came. She would wake up, groaning and thrashing. Strix held her and comforted her until she was calm, and sleep came again. Sometimes in anxious dreams Lizbet thought she heard God calling to her, from an unbridgeable distance. His voice, once powerful and reassuring, was now faint and melancholy, as if He had lost all hope.

On the third day of Lizbet and Strix's anti-diabolic campaign, the citizens of Abalia began to emerge from hiding. A pack of street urchins followed behind them, shrieking when a devil was encountered, cheering and clapping when it was banished back to Hell. Other children and adults soon joined them, until a small mob tagged behind. Sometimes they helped to ferret out a devil which had hidden beneath a bridge or in a sewer. Once they brought forth from a basement an old woman in rags.

"A witch!" they cried, pushing her forward. "Banish her to Hell!"

"Stop 'cher selves!" the old woman cried. "I 'ent a witch none or other!"

"Come here, grandma," Lizbet said. The old woman shuffled forward reluctantly. Lizbet touched her withered cheek, her bony wrist. She was not a witch. The woman was all warm flesh and skin, not paper, cloth, feathers or other witchy material.

The old woman smiled toothlessly. "You're a good girl, 'ent 'cher," she said. "Your own hands, 'er be gentle through and through. You're warms my rheumatiz." She stroked Lizbet's hand with her bony, wrinkled one.

"No witches!" Lizbet shouted to the crowd. "Leave witches alone. We're only after devils. If you can't find any devils, then go about your business."

She had been afraid the crowd wouldn't listen, and that she would be faced with a surly mob. But to her surprise, the people nodded, murmured their assent, and dispersed. One or two faced her, knelt, clasped their hands, and prayed briefly.

"I think you could make them do whatever you wanted," Strix observed.

"I know," Lizbet said. "The sooner this is over, the better."

After six days, no more devils were to be found. Abalia's citizens emerged from hiding to reclaim their city. The streets once more filled with life, people coming and going, buying and selling, working and begging, gossiping, pickpocketing, shopping. Tunners and ankle beaters and draymen, featherdressers and fellmongers, postboys and poulters.

Through the streets and avenues Lizbet and Strix walked to the Margrave's Palace. As Lizbet passed by, people who had been arguing lowered their voices and found reasons to agree. Brawling boys became friends again. Beggars found silver in their bowls instead of copper. Butchers confessed to astonished customers that the "lamb" they had for sale was actually mutton.

But when Lizbet had passed, voices rose again in anger. Blows were thrown. The scheming, cheating, vanity, and lies of mortals reasserted themselves.

Lizbet knew this. Although she bore up under it, she never escaped the terrible weight of human sin pressing down on her slender shoulders. She longed to give up her godhead. Divinity, even a little, was too great a burden.

The guard boy was at the Margrave's gate again, in a new set of pantaloons which didn't match to the rest of his uniform. He grinned and made kissy faces at them.

"Be respectful, or I'll wither you like a fig tree," Lizbet warned him.

The Palace doors were open. The refugees were gone from the reception room. Bellows edged up to Lizbet in a servile manner and bowed so deeply his spine cracked audibly. "Your fame precedes you, Mistress Lenz," he said. "I, I want to thank you for clearing out the devils from Abalia. Please forgive any rudeness you've previously suffered from me. The Margrave will be wanting to pay his respects to you as well."

Guards again accompanied Lizbet up the staircase. There was no talk of defenestration this time. Strix followed behind, a ghostly presence knit into the shadows. A boy ran up the stairs ahead, shouting Lizbet's coming.

If the Margrave's presence had been powerful before, it was overwhelming now. Steel gray hair, vivisecting gaze, chest and shoulders like a mountain bear. Everything about him that had seemed hollow and empty when Lizbet first met him, now bespoke presence and strength and indomitable will.

The litter of vials and tiny caskets was gone from the Margrave's table. A pile of papers half a foot high sat there instead. They seemed to be blank, and Lizbet noticed a few tiny black q's and m's clinging to the Margrave's nostrils. Fudge sat happily in a corner, snuffling up fanciful colored lithographs of lions and peacocks from an illustrated atlas of natural history.

"Lizbet!" Hengest Wolftrow said. His voice reverberated about the room. He strode forward. He towered over her. "Lizbet Lenz! Beyond all hope, beyond all expectation, you have succeeded! You are as good as your word. I receive news that you have banished all the devils from our city. I have been going to and fro in Abalia, and walking up and down in it, and everywhere I hear the story of your deeds. The daughter outshines the father." He bent over Lizbet and seemed about to take her hand. Then his expression darkened slightly, and he took a step back.

"You are a remarkable young woman," Wolftrow said. His eyes narrowed. "Even more remarkable than before."

"Thank you for your kind words," Lizbet said. "Now, about my father. I'd like to have him out of prison. Please. As you promised."

Margrave surveyed her in silence. Then he said, "Lizbet, when I release your father from prison, what will you do?"

The question was unexpected. For a moment, Lizbet could think of nothing. All her hopes had been focused on the very moment her father would be freed. She had not let her imagination go beyond that.

"I suppose . . ." she began uncertainly. "I suppose we'll just live our lives. As we did before."

"I must warn you," Wolftrow said, "Abalia will not be safe for you, or him. Abalia's citizens have not forgotten their grievance with your father for covering their homes and fields with a plague of mice. Gerhard Lenz is safer in prison."

"Then we'd have to leave," Lizbet said. "In the past, we've traveled a lot."

Lizbet fretted. Why were they having this conversation? She had done everything the Margrave wanted. Why didn't he just release her father from prison as he'd promised?

"Come," Wolftrow said. He strode to the door, beckoning Lizbet to follow.

Out of the Margrave's office they went, Lizbet half skipping to keep up with Wolftrow's huge steps. Through the office filled with clerks, to the stairway. Hope bubbled up in Lizbet's heart. Were they going directly to the prison to release Gerhard Lenz?

At the head of the stairs, Wolftrow paused before the narrow iron-bound door that Lizbet had noticed on her first visit. From his robes he produced a key, and turned it in the lock.

The wards clinked and thumped, and the door swung open. Behind it, a corkscrew stone staircase, leading upward. But surely this wasn't the way to the prison? Wolftrow ascended the steps. Lizbet followed warily.

Light from above grew brighter as they climbed. The stairs emerged beneath a little cupola.

They stood at the highest point of the Palace's roof, on a sort of widow's walk ringed with a wrought-iron rail. It was a few dozen feet long and wide.

Lizbet turned around and around. She felt as if she were standing in the middle of the sky. This spot must be the highest in all Abalia, higher even than the bell towers of the cathedral. She could see nothing above or around her but the immense blue dome of the sky, sun, and ragged clouds. A warm breeze against her cheek carried the scents of late spring, apple blossoms and lilacs.

Strix, still transparent and ghostly, appeared at the top of the stairs and stepped out onto the roof, peering around. She spotted Lizbet, grinned, and put her finger to her lips.

From the roof's western edge, the Margrave summoned Lizbet with a crooked finger. As she approached, he swung his hand in a wide arc.

"Behold," Wolftrow said. "The kingdoms of the earth."

Lizbet turned her gaze downward. At the roof's edge, she could see out over the tilted red-tile roofs of Abalia, the rising threads of smoke from its chimneys, the tiny people moving on its streets far below. To her left and right, the end-less dark forested hills of the Piedmont. But before her, to the west, the land fell away, sloping down, and down forever. Beyond Abalia, falling hills, farms and forests, misty valleys and twisting shiny rivers diminished into distance and incalculable vastness, ever and ever wider, paler, dimmer, until the eye became lost in an unseen horizon.

"Bohemia. Pomerania. Saxony, Franconia, Thuringia." Wolftrow named them as a man names past lovers. "Beyond them, Normandy, Flanders, Gascony, Aquitaine, Provence, Aragon, Navarre, Lombardy, Venetia. All under the rule of our Pixie Queen." Wolftrow gazed down at her. "Have you ever dreamed that all these lands might be yours to rule? That they all might quake at your word? That they all might worship your name?"

"Well . . . no," Lizbet said. "No, not really."

"Juliana rules with might unassailable," Wolftrow said. "For now. But there are other worlds to conquer." He turned. Lizbet followed Wolftrow's gaze, toward the snowy Montagnes to the east, their peaks blinding white. "The world beyond the Montagnes is fully as large as our own. A world of marvels, riches, sorcery. He who masters it will rule an empire as large as all the known world. With the aid of powers and magics to be found there, he might conquer all this world as well. Such a man might be master of all the earth."

Strix, by Lizbet's side, whispered in her ear, "What's all this about? It's taking too long. What about your father?"

"What about my father?" Lizbet asked.

Wolftrow made a gesture, as if to put his hand on her shoulder. Instead, he halted halfway and withdrew his arm. A shadow passed over his face, but quickly vanished. "Lizbet," he said, "I have need of you. Your courage and imagination. Your spiritual strength. Think of it! You banished hundreds of devils from Abalia. The priests couldn't do it. The Bishop himself couldn't do it." His eyes were blazing. "The priests say that God has vanished. They say He has abandoned the world. Do you understand what this means?"

"I guess it means that Hell is going to rule the universe?" Lizbet said uncertainly.

"It means that *we* are going rule the universe. You and I."

Lizbet tried to absorb this.

"I . . . I don't think I want to rule the universe," she said finally. But in the vast immensity of the sky and the world all around, her words seemed faint and frail.

"We have an opportunity before us such as no mortal has had before, since the time of Adam in the Garden," Wolftrow said. "The greatest of kings has abandoned His throne. Now is the time to act, with decision and speed. All may be ours."

"God didn't abandon his throne, exactly," Lizbet said. "The devils won their war against Him. They rule in Heaven."

Wolftrow's voice was triumphant. "And you are the master of devils, Lizbet!" He clenched his fist. "Now that I am a man in full once again, there is none who can withstand me in battle. None can withstand your spiritual powers. If we join forces, how can we not prevail? Together, we will go forth and conquer the East, the West, and seize the throne of Heaven itself!"

Captivated by his fierce gaze, half hypnotized by his voice, Lizbet understood why a hundred thousand men had followed him over the Montagnes to their deaths. In that moment, she wanted to believe him. To go with him. To fight by his side, to share his victories. To be Queen of this world, and of Hell, and of Heaven.

She opened her mouth to say "Yes."

"That's the dumbest thing I've ever heard!" Strix yelled.

Strix's voice broke the spell. Lizbet shook herself. What was she thinking? "My father!" she said to Wolftrow. "All I want is my father back. I don't want any of the rest. You can do what you want, and go conquering anything you like. But please, please, release my father from prison."

"Who was that?" Wolftrow said. His gaze darted about the roof. "Who's there?"

Strix emerged from the shadows. She leveled a tawny finger at Wolftrow. "You never meant to let her father go, did you?" she said.

With a vigor and speed that belied his age, Wolftrow leaped for her. Strix, however, having been defenestrated once before, was ready for him. She knit herself into the shadows, ducked under Wolftrow's arm, and left him grasping air.

"You said you'd let my father go," Lizbet pleaded. "Please do it. I've done everything you asked."

"You and your father will rule kingdoms over the Montagnes," Wolftrow said, breathing heavily. "You will rule the very planets and stars in their spheres. But first, you must promise you will help me."

"Lizbet," Strix said from the shadows, "touch him."

"What?"

"Try to touch him." Wolftrow lunged toward her voice, but Strix was watching, and evaded him.

What was Strix talking about? Lizbet approached the Margrave and put out her hand. Wolftrow flinched and took a step back.

"You see!" Strix said triumphantly. "Two times he was about to touch you, and he couldn't. Lizbet, I think he's a devil. That's the whole problem. He's been a devil all along. Banish him!"

A devil?

"I am not a devil," Wolftrow said. "I am your margrave." His voice was sharp. "Do not lay hands on me. Do not commit high treason."

Treason.

The word hung in the air.

"I can't," Lizbet said. She shook her head helplessly. "I can't."

"Lizbet!" Strix pleaded. "He's never going to release your father. He's going to keep teasing you on forever! If there is one tiny bit of treachery or rebellion in your soul, this is the moment for it! Banish him!"

But there wasn't. Lizbet quailed. "I have no rebellion," she said. "I have no treachery."

"I often come to this rooftop," Wolftrow said. "To be alone. To think and reflect. I find a solitude here that steadies and focuses the thoughts."

He moved toward the cupola, and the stairway down. "I leave you here, then, in that splendid solitude, to do the same. When you have thought and reflected fully, I believe you will see the wisdom in my plan and embrace the glorious destiny that awaits if you join forces with me. I am willing to give you all the time you need. Whether it be hours, days, weeks, or years."

Each word rang like a bell tolling doom. Wolftrow was imprisoning her here, on the roof of the Palace.

On trembling and unwilling legs, Lizbet forced herself toward Wolftrow. She tried to lift her arms to seize him, but her arms would not obey her. Her knees gave way, and she sank to the rooftop. She could not assault her lord. Lizbet had no rebellion in her, or treachery, or rage.

But for the first time, she wanted these things. She needed them, and accepted that need. Her need was consecrated by her struggle and suffering over the past two months.

"Strix," she pleaded. "It's time. Help me. Change me. Use the Outlaw's vices. Make me a rebel. Make me a traitor. Strix! *Make me the monster I need to be!*"

But where was the stuff that Strix had harvested from the Outlaw? It was in the bandoleer that Strix had carried over the Montagnes, and Lizbet had carried back again. But Strix was not wearing it. Lizbet was not wearing it. Lizbet had left it lying on the floor of the blacksmith shop, days ago, not thinking she would need it again.

So there was nothing Strix could do. Lizbet had made her decision too late. "Strix!" she wailed. "The Outlaw's vices. I've lost them."

"Then take mine instead!" Strix yelled.

She emerged from the shadows in front of Lizbet. Her eyes were wide, her teeth bared. With both hands, in one motion, Strix ripped open her dress, baring her breast. As Lizbet watched in horror, Strix dug all ten fingers into the center of her chest and tore herself open.

She reached her hand inside, between her puffing yellow morel lungs, and drew out a fistful of slithering, bilious Treachery, and scarlet Rebellion. With a rising scream like a war-cry, Strix drew back her fist and smashed it forward into Lizbet's chest.

For a moment they stood, nearly motionless, Lizbet's chest impaled on Strix's arm.

The pain was blinding. Tears seeped from Lizbet's half-closed eyes. She felt Strix's fingers working within her.

The Margrave was upon them. He grabbed Strix and tried to pull her away. Lizbet raised one leg and kicked him in the stomach. He fell backward with an astonished grunt. His clothing smoked where Lizbet's foot had touched him.

Strix withdrew her hand. Blood covered it. Blood dribbled down Lizbet's chest and soaked her clothing.

Wrath filled Lizbet, and pride, and vengeance, blotting out all other thoughts. She hated the Margrave. Nothing else mattered. Screaming without words, she bore down upon him as he lay on the rooftop, grabbed him by the front of his robes, and hauled him to his feet with more strength than she had thought herself capable of. His clothing burst into flames in her fists. Wolftrow screeched and tried to bat at the flames. "Please, no, stop, oh, please, not me," he babbled.

"Begone!" Lizbet commanded. "Take thee to Hell, foul fiend!"

Stammering, tears pouring from his eyes, the Margrave pleaded for mercy.

"Tarry not! Flee! Away!"

"No, no, please, it burns," Wolftrow pleaded.

After a minute, Lizbet cried in frustration, "It's not working! I'm burning him, but he's not being banished."

"I'm not a devil!" Wolftrow cried. "Oh, please, it burns, please stop!"

Lizbet released him. He crumpled to the rooftop tiles, sobbing.

Strix said, "Maybe he's not a devil after all. Maybe he's just a man who acts like a devil."

Wolftrow rolled about on the rooftop, blubbering and batting at his smoldering clothing.

Lizbet walked up to him and aimed a solid kick at his chest. She wondered how many ribs she could break. Strix grabbed her from behind, and hauled her back. "Lizbet," she said, "stop. It's over. You don't need to do that."

"But I want to," Lizbet said.

"But still don't. It's not like you."

Lizbet thought about this. "It is now," she said, aiming another kick, at Wolftrow's head this time.

Strix, with difficulty, pulled her away before she knocked out the Margrave's brains with her oak and iron foot.

Chapter 26

Draw the long sword from my stone
Like in Avalon.
Drag me like a captive
Through the streets of Babylon.

Pray to me at dawnlight,
Like in Jenne-Jeno,
Paint my face with lapis like
An actor in Edo.

Murder me like Marlowe,
Whose blood did London stain,
I'll be your starry oracle
On Salisbury Plain.

I am the whitest of the brown,
The darkest of the fair.
At farthest Sekai no Hate,
Come and meet me there!
 —a rhyme of Strix

They made quite a sight, coming down the Palace stairs. In the lead, Margrave Hengest Wolftrow staggered, his face pale and drained, his clothing in rags, wisps of smoke still rising from him. The nauseous stink of burned silk and singed fur accompanied him. Behind Wolftrow came Lizbet, her face twisted by rage, an open wound in her bare chest, her clothing soaked in blood. Last was Strix, her own brown chest torn open, yellow lungs puffing out the front with each breath. She apologized cheerfully to people they passed. "Sorry about the mess," she said. "I know we must look alarming. We're having rather a bad day. If you feel lightheaded, please sit and put your head down. Sorry, sorry!"

When guards approached them at the entrance hall, Lizbet screamed, "Stay back! One step nearer, and I will send your Margrave to Hell with my divine power!" She grabbed Wolftrow by the back. Flames roared up to the ceiling. The guards fell back in panic. The Margrave screamed in pain.

"What have I done?" Strix muttered, shaking her head.

From the Palace, it was a quarter mile walk down the boulevard to the Houses of Correction. Palace courtiers, clerks, guards, and passersby on the street collected behind, and followed at a distance, whispering and pointing. Bellows the officer was among them, and the boy guard from the gate.

At the prison, a gaoler unlocked the iron doors at the Margrave's command. "Bring out Gerhard Lenz!" Lizbet ordered him.

When Gerhard stumbled through the doorway, he squinted against the sudden sunlight, shaded his eyes, and sneezed.

"Father?" Lizbet said.

"Lizbet?" Gerhard's voice was a hoarse croak.

How old he seemed! How stooped, and small, and ineffectual. Was this petty criminal and hoaxer the reason she had crossed the Montagnes, suffered terrible injuries, and narrowly escaped death again and again? Lizbet's lip curled.

Gerhard's eyes widened when he saw the wound in Lizbet's chest. His fingers reached to touch it, then retreated. "What happened, dear heart?" he asked. "You are terribly injured. Will you . . . ?"

"Will I what?" Lizbet said coldly.

"Will you die?"

Intoxicated by rage, Lizbet had hardly noticed her wound. Now that she was beginning to calm down, the pain was rapidly returning. Each breath sent agony stabbing through her. Blood continued to drip off her dress and fall between her feet. Her head spun. She sat down heavily on the hard flagstone walk in front of the prison. "I don't know," she said. She looked up at Strix. "Will I?"

"I won't let you," Strix said. It was the last thing Lizbet heard before she fainted.

Lizbet awoke staring upward into the pale blue and pink of a late afternoon sky. Her chest felt full, and heavy, but the pain was gone. Not daring to look, she reached down to touch her chest, not knowing what she would find. Her fingers went *clink* on her chest. Clink?

She strained her neck to look down at herself. Overlapping iron plates and leather straps encased her. She was horrified. So horrified she broke out into laughter. ·

Lizbet pried herself up on her elbows. The low western sun shone full on her face. Dark moving shapes crossed it. Larger than birds, but too far away to make out.

Strix sat on the ground nearby, as did Gerhard. The Margrave lay flat on his back, staring upward, still breathing heavily. A circle of townspeople stood around them at a distance. Lizbet found Strix's hand and squeezed it. "Thanks," she said. She pinged a fingernail on her chest. "What is this?"

The flying shapes against sun were larger. They were coming closer.

"Oh," Strix said, "I patched you up with whatever I could find. Papers and clothing, someone's armor, a watch, belts, bootlaces." She waved her arm to indicate the crowd around them. "They all helped. Everyone gave something." She raised her hands and made clapping motions in the air. The crowd cheered faintly from the distance. "They really like you. From your having put down the devils and all. They want you to be margrave. Or margravine. Or something."

"They don't care about Gerhard and the mice?"

"The mice are long past. That was just Hengest lying, of course."

"Still, I don't think I want to be argrave," Lizbet said. "Did you take out your vices you put into me? Rebellion, and Treachery? I don't feel that way anymore." She frowned. "Or only a little."

Strix nodded. "I took out Christ's divinity too. Ow." She inspected her hand. "I think I burned my fingers on it."

"Oh, Strix, poor Strix. Thank you."

Lizbet shaded her eyes. As they approached, the flying shapes resolved into immense scallop shells that sailed down the sky. Each was drawn by a team of dolphins in harness that leaped through the clouds as if they were crashing waves. Each shell bore a charioteer at the reins. The leading shell glittered pink and gold. Its charioteer was the smallest.

"It was awful having those things inside," Lizbet said. "I hated the Margrave. I hated myself. I hated the whole world. I wanted to hit everyone." She frowned. "Do you . . . do you really feel like that? All the time?"

"I only want to hit everyone sometimes," Strix said. "I just have to not do it." She shrugged. "Just because you feel like doing something, doesn't mean you have to do it."

"Are you sure you got every last bit?" Lizbet shrugged her shoulders and stretched her chest. It creaked, and the armor plates rang against each other. "I think I can still feel something I don't like. Something biting and restless, that wants to fight for no reason."

"I got it all," Strix said. "But while it's in you, it changes you. That can't be helped. Everything you do molds you, and squeezes you into its shape. Your heart always has the imprint of everything you've done, everything you've been." Her voice was pained. "Lizbet, I'm sorry, but you needed it. If only for just then."

Yes, she had needed it. And if Strix could live with such stuff in her heart all the time, Lizbet could figure out how to live with no more than the memory of it. However she felt, she didn't have to *be* rebellious or treacherous or angry. At least not most of the time.

From the heights of the sky, the armada of dolphin-drawn shells and riders descended. Holding the reins in the pink shell was a figure also entirely dressed in pink. A woman. A tiny woman.

Lizbet rose, went to Gerhard, and threw her arms around him. A little while ago, in her rage and rebellion, she had seen her father as a small, weak, crooked failure of a man. She still had to admit that he was all those things. But now she also saw him as she once had: a man inept but well-meaning, a father capable of warmth and generosity, who genuinely loved his daughter. All these things about Gerhard were true, the good with the bad.

The armada of shell-riders settled to earth, the great gray dolphins flopping onto the ground like legless dogs, rolling about in their harnesses and whistling musically to each other. The tiny lady in pink stepped delicately from her glittering shell. Her high-heeled boots seemed barely to bend the blades of grass she trod on. The other shell-riders were all bears and badgers who walked on their hind legs. They wore strappy leather armor. Each bore crossed swords on his back, or a bow and a quiver of arrows. They vaulted from their shells and arranged themselves around the lady in pink in the manner of an honor guard.

The lady could have been no more than four feet tall, but her body was voluptuous: a woman's, not a child's. Her pink dress clung to her form. Her shockingly short skirt fluttered about her hips. Her hair was so pale it was almost white, her eyes large, her ears pointed. Her smile was friendly, but knowing.

The pink lady and her badger-and-bear guards surrounded Wolftrow, where he lay on the ground. "Hengest," she said "Rise." Grunting, Wolftrow struggled to his feet. For a Margrave, he cut a miserable-looking figure, sooty as a chimney-sweep, clad in half-burned rags. His chin and shoulders slumped, his immense hands hung limp and defeated. "Your Highness," he said. His voice was a hoarse groan. He tried to bow, but staggered, and nearly fell.

"What happened here?" the pink lady said sharply. "Who did this to you?"

"It was her," Wolftrow said. He wagged his finger at Lizbet. "It was all her fault." The pink lady looked at Lizbet pointedly.

"I banished the devils from Abalia," Lizbet said. "I thought the Margrave was a devil, and tried to banish him."

The pink lady laughed, a carefree and musical sound. "He is only a mortal," she said. "You cannot banish him. However, you have certainly succeeded in making a mess of him. Hengest! Into my coach. I bid you come to court and dance attendance on your empress for a while. You have been useful in the past, despite your silly intrigues against me. Perhaps I can find some purpose for you in your mortal years that remain. But who will rule Abalia in your place? I seek a lad, neither a scholar nor a dunce, untroubled by imagination or ambition, who longs for a life of unappreciated drudgery. Something like an educated turnip." Her gaze searched the surrounding crowd. She pointed with an imperious finger. "You, there! Boy. Come to me."

A young fellow stepped forward. Lizbet recognized him as the kissy guard of the Palace gate. He sank to one knee in front of the pink lady. "Your name?"

"Francis Schnitzerzook, Your Highness," the fellow stammered.

"Francis, from this day forward you will be Margrave of Abalia, and of the Abalian Pale, from the Falls of the Nur and the Piedmont to the peaks of the Montagnes du Monde. Take this as your domestic policy: treat the people as a farmer treats his prize cow. Let them wax neither too fat nor too lean, and if you must use a switch, use it only to guide them from harm. This will be your foreign policy: keep the witches on both sides of the Montagnes occupied and distracted, but do not carry things to the point of war. Hengest went too far, and you can see the result."

"Your Highness!" Francis cried. "I adore you with all my heart! I pour out my soul to you. All that I am is yours! My life, my being, I pledge to you. Your eyes are like jewels. Your smile is like the sun—"

He went on like this, fevered oaths of romantic devotion mixed with extravagant but banal compliments. Lizbet blushed. The pink lady listened impassively for a minute or so before cutting Francis off.

"Yes, yes, of course," she said. "Francis Schnitzerzook, Margrave of Abalia, serve me well and faithfully. If you do so, in a score of years and ten, this will be your reward: you may place your lips here"—she indicated her cheek—"for the merest moment."

Francis trembled, and seemed about to explode. Instead, the blood disappeared from his face and he fainted to the grass. The pink lady pointed to his unconscious body and addressed the surrounding crowd. "This will be your new margrave," she announced. "Obey him as you would me, when he wakes up."

"Your Highness?" Lizbet said. "You are . . . Empress Juliana? You really are a pixie, then?"

Juliana's pale eyebrows rose. She indicated her followers. "My guards. Describe the men you see."

"I don't see any men," Lizbet said. "I see badgers and bears, Your Highness."

"Hm," Juliana said. She lowered her voice. "You are the only one. All others here see men-at-arms, and horses and coaches instead of flying scallop shells. When they look at me, they see a handsome mortal woman of middle years, as tall as you, dressed as befits a queen. 'Pixie' is thought to be no more than a fanciful compliment." Her gaze probed Lizbet up and down. "Who are you, to pierce my glamour? Who are you, to put down devils? Are you an angel, turned freelance?"

"I'm Lizbet Lenz," Lizbet said. "I used to be a girl. Then I became partly a witch. Then I was a little bit of Christ."

"What are you now?"

"Honestly, I'm not exactly sure," Lizbet said.

"I understand that's a common puzzlement among mortals," Juliana said. "My sympathies. You have my thanks for banishing the devils, which have been a problem since God was deposed from His throne. He and I have had our differences, but taken altogether, I still think He was a positive influence on the mortal world, while the devils have proven to be nothing but a nuisance."

"Your Highness, I have a project in mind," Lizbet said. "I want to release God from prison, drive the devils out of Heaven, and restore God to His throne. Will you aid me?"

For the barest second, Juliana was at a loss for words. When she regained her voice, she said, "I am in favor restoring the *status quo ante* in Heaven. However, I can't imagine how you could possibly accomplish such a thing."

"Ask Hengest Wolftrow what I can accomplish," Lizbet said.

"He and I have much to catch up on," Juliana said. She tilted her head and peered at Lizbet. "You are a child of unusual talents. We may talk again." She turned, clapped her hands smartly together. She raised her voice to her badgers-and-bears-at-arms. "We're finished here. Homeward!"

As Juliana and her entourage boarded their shells, the ground began to shake and fissure beneath Francis Schnitzerzook's unconscious body. As Lizbet watched, the grass and sod collapsed, and Francis fell into a dark hole.

But before anyone could move, Francis flew up out of the hole again, as if launched by a catapult. He landed on the grass with a thump. This brought him to his senses. He jumped to his feet, rubbing his bottom and yelling in pain. From the hole, the spidery, rooty form of an earth witch popped up. She craned her head around. "Rats!" she said. "He wasn't dead after all."

"He had just fainted," Lizbet said. "From love."

"A spurious hoax! Perfidious mortals!"

"You still owe me nine-hundred-ninety-nine gold pieces," Lizbet reminded her.

The earth witch cackled and spun something shining toward her. Lizbet caught it: a gold coin. "Patience, sweetie!" the earth witch said. She dived down into the ground, and the hole crashed shut over her.

All around, the dolphin teams flopped into the air, the whips of their drivers snapping above their gray snouts. The shells gently lifted into the sky. From the pink and gold shell, Juliana turned, waved, and blew a kiss.

Night was coming on. The sun sank below the house-tops, and long, chilly shadows crept across the green lawns in front of the Houses of Correction. Francis Schnitzerzook, Margrave of Abalia, was taken off by Bellows to be installed in the Palace that was now his. He was already giving orders and trying to sound imperious and official, and less like an adolescent whose voice tended to crack at inconvenient moments.

All Lizbet wanted was to go home. She wanted to be with her father, and talk, and laugh, like old times, and she wanted Strix there. Strix, who had held Lizbet's heart in her hands.

But the town of Abalia had other ideas. As they walked through the streets, the crowd that had followed them to the prison grew rather than shrank. Hundreds of townsfolk milled around, talking, laughing, cheering, pestering Lizbet for her story. How she had gone over the Montagnes, how she had fought the Pope of Storms and the Witch of the Grove of Frenzy, how she had banished the devils and deposed the Margrave. Lizbet was in little mood to talk, but Gerhard, once he saw which the way the wind was blowing, was happy to tell the tale, aided by whispered hints from Lizbet and Strix. Hints were all he needed, or wanted. By the time Gerhard was on the third retelling, a dragon and an ogre had somehow crept into the story, and Lizbet was fleeing across a rope bridge hundreds of feet above a torrent of boiling lava, bearing a book of magic with which to save Abalia from the tyrant Hengest Wolftrow.

Lizbet was astonished to see how much better Gerhard looked. His voice no longer croaked. His eyes twinkled. Even his stooped posture had improved. For some people, human regard is an essential humour, as necessary for life as blood in the veins or air in the lungs. Gerhard was like that. Alone in a tiny prison cell, he had withered into a stooped old man. But in the middle of a crowd, every eye on him, he blossomed like a rose in sunlight.

The mob found its way down the staircase in the Wall of Virtue and into Abalia-Under-the-Hill. It was in the mood for ale, which Abalia's churchmen and magistrates frowned upon. Lizbet now understood why the staircase in the Wall was so well-worn. Abalia-Under-the-Hill had no shortage of pothouses, and the mob found a drinking spot soon enough, filled it, and overflowed the tavern yard ten deep. Gerhard climbed atop an outside table. In a booming and dramatic voice and with many expressive gestures, he recounted Lizbet's story yet again, with new variations.

Lizbet found her way to the outskirts of the crowd. Strix shortly appeared, slipping in and out of the shadows as she made her way through the revelers. She carried a flagon of ale in each hand. She sat beside Lizbet, handed her one flagon, and slurped deeply and noisily from other. "Try it," she urged.

"It's sinful," Lizbet said.

"The sin's the best part," Strix said, drinking again.

Lizbet delicately sipped at the ale. The bubbles made her nose burn. Her ideas of what was a sin and what wasn't had turned upside down and spun around, and still hadn't come to rest. She sipped again. "Is the bitter taste the sinful part?"

"No, that's the hops," Strix said. She put her hand over the top of Lizbet's flagon. "That's fine for now. Slow down, or you'll be upchucking all night again."

Lizbet smiled. "My, a witch advocating temperance! Is there no end of wonders in the world?"

Strix stuck out her tongue. She had pulled her layers of dresses around herself to cover up her morel lungs, which still blew out the front of her chest with every breath. Lizbet reached to touch them, but drew her hand back. Strix said, "I hope you'll fix me, before . . ."

"Before?"

Strix stared into the darkness. "Before you leave."

Standing on the table, gesturing with a wine bottle someone had given him, Gerhard had his audience enraptured. He had finished with Lizbet's heroic tale and was now expounding on some dubious financial scheme that was going to make all of Abalia rich beyond the dreams of princes.

Lizbet knew what would happen next. In a few months Gerhard's schemes would come to nothing, everyone who gave him money would be ruined and angry, and Gerhard would have to flee yet again.

But not with Lizbet.

"Of course I'll fix you," she said to Strix. "Right now. Tonight. But I'm not leaving. Or at least, I'm not following after my father. I've had too many adventures. I'm too different from the person I was. Too different from what anyone is." She rapped a knuckle on her steel chest, to hear it ring. "I don't even know what I am, anymore."

"Like every other teenager," Strix said. "But I wasn't talking about your leaving with your father. What madness were you saying to the Pixie Queen, about storming Heaven and springing God from prison?"

"I've been thinking about it," Lizbet said. "We need to rescue God. Despite His faults, the world gets by better when He's around. And even you have to admit that the devils don't know what they're doing."

"And you're planning on getting into Heaven—how?"

"I've got this figured out." Lizbet drew imaginary pictures in the air with a finger. "You see, there must be holes in all the Spheres since the dark planet crashed through them into the Earth. We'll fly through the holes, one after another, until we get to Heaven. We'll build flying chariots, like the Pixie Queen's. We can make giant bats, like they have in the Torrid Zone, to pull our chariots through the sky. We'd make their wings out of India rubber. We'll use patented steel springs for their muscles."

"You have far too many ideas," Strix said, shaking her head.

"Strix, look," Lizbet said. She had been dreading this moment, but it was something she had to do. "I know you don't like God. And you're right, even if we get help from the Pixie Queen, rescuing Him is going to be dangerous. It's still something I want to do. So . . ." She took a deep breath.

"So if you don't want to come along with me, you don't have to."

Strix said, "I always have to do what you want." Lizbet couldn't read her tone of voice.

"'Have to'? No, you don't. Why? Because of the egg? But I freed you from that, a long time ago."

"It isn't the egg," Strix said. "Remember that Mrs. Woodcot thought I had to obey her command because she made me? But I didn't, because I had been unmade. And remade. By you."

The meaning of this went round and round in Lizbet's head. Finally she said, "So because I made you, that means I own you? The way Mrs. Woodcot used to own you?" Strix nodded. A chill went through Lizbet. "Then I'll just free you," she said quickly. "I'll do it again."

Strix shook her head. "You can't be freed from the one who made you. Not until you're unmade."

But . . . "Didn't you make me too?" Lizbet said. "You made my legs. And even more than that." She tapped a fingernail on her chest. The metal plates clinked. "So I belong to you, as well. We both own each other."

Strix's face was blank with surprise. "I guess we do," she said at last. "But I've never heard of such a thing."

"Since I've been with you," Lizbet said, "it's been one thing after another that I'd never heard of." She took both Strix's hands in hers. "We're in each other's power. We're each other's thrall. The only way it's going to work is if we're both good to each other. If each of us trusts the other. If we both treat each other as we'd want to be treated. Because if we fight, it's all over. We'll destroy each other."

At last, Strix nodded. "Is this friendship? I've been trying to figure out what friendship is. Maybe this is it."

Lizbet had always thought she wanted a friend. If this was friendship, it was more than she had bargained for.

But if it was Strix, it was okay. Whatever was to come, whatever Earth and Heaven and Hell had in store, Lizbet was ready, as long as Strix was there.

Acknowledgments

Endless thanks to the Nameless critique group: Judith Berman, Ann Tonsor Zeddies, Steve Berman, Vickie McManus, Ef Deal, Rikardou Sturgis, for their patient help with this novel, in many ways large and small. Special thanks to Steve, whose unflagging belief in this work inspired and sustained me during dark days and wrong ways. Without Steve industriously kicking my butt, *Half-Witch* might not have seen publication.

Thanks to my editors, Kelly Link and Gavin J. Grant, for their fine-tuning of the manuscript to make it run like a well-oiled mechanical bat with India rubber wings and patented steel springs; and to my agent, Sally Harding, for all her help, wisdom, and attention to detail in helping to make the publication of *Half-Witch* a reality.

Many thanks to my teachers at Clarion: Suzy McKee Charnas, Nina Kiriki Hoffman, Nancy Kress, Kelly Link, Gavin J. Grant, Jeffrey Ford, Andy Duncan, and Gordon Van Gelder, for their wise teaching and insights into the nature of fiction writing. Thanks to Tim Powers and K. D. Wentworth, teachers at Writers of the Future. Special thanks to Nina, who was there for both, and was an early supporter of my fiction. Encouraging words and deeds early in a career have positive effects well beyond what one might expect.

About the Author

John Schoffstall has published short fiction in *Asimov's,* the *Magazine of Fantasy & Science Fiction, Interzone, Strange Horizons,* and other venues, and was a Grand Prize winner of the Writers of the Future award. He is a physician, and once practiced Emergency Medicine. Now he follows Candide's advice and tends his own garden. He lives in the Philadelphia area. He has a website at johnschoffstall.com.